Forsaking All Others

Forsaking All Others

Victoria Petrie Hay

MICHAEL JOSEPH
London

MICHAEL JOSEPH LTD

Published by the Penguin Group
27 Wrights Lane, London W8 5TZ, England
Viking Penguin Inc., 40 West 23rd Street, New York, New York 10010, USA
Penguin Books Australia Ltd, Ringwood, Victoria, Australia
Penguin Books Canada Ltd, 2801 John Street, Markham, Ontario, Canada L3R 1B4
Penguin Books (NZ) Ltd, 182–190 Wairau Road, Auckland 10, New Zealand

Penguin Books Ltd, Registered Offices: Harmondsworth, Middlesex, England

First published 1990

Copyright © Victoria Petrie Hay 1990

Printed and bound in Great Britain by
Richard Clay Ltd, Bungay, Suffolk

Set in Linotron Sabon 11 on 13pt by
Cambrian Typesetters, Frimley, Surrey

A CIP catalogue record for this book is available from the British Library

ISBN 0 7181 3215 7

0868053856608

for my mother and father

Acknowledgements

Grateful thanks to Anne and Peter Francis; to Cliff Griggs and Major David Cameron; to Dennis O'Leary; to Judy and Graeme Moore; and to Jeff and – most particularly – Liz Moore who must have got bored listening but never said so.

Any mistakes, however, are entirely my own.

VPH
Bodiam, 1989

PART ONE

Chapter 1

Arthur dreams: a hot, white lane, the scent of honeysuckle on the air, the hedgerows abuzz with the sound of insects. The horse plods on, pulling the caravan down a steep, winding hill and out across the marshlands beyond, Da at its head murmuring in its ear. A foal shoots by him, kicking its long new legs and is called home by an urgent wicker from its mother, tethered among the other horses to the back of the caravan.

Gerry, leaning against Arthur, stirs in his sleep, wakes and cries, and Da takes hold of him and swings him on to the back of the horse pulling the van. Only five years old and he sits there like a king, one hand resting on the horse's collar, turning, his tears gone, to grin back at his brothers and his dozing mother.

Surely the boy will come to grief!

'Hold on wi' both hands, Gerry,' Arthur calls. 'You'll fall else.'

'Not him,' says Da. 'He's a natural.'

'I'm a natural, Arthur. Da says so.' And Gerry takes his hand from the horse's collar and waves both arms at the sky and the grazing sheep, at the rollicking foal and the shimmering sea in the distance, and he never falls from the rolling back of the horse.

Arthur awoke and shook the sleep from his head. The train was coming into Rye. One more stop.

They were Romany through and through, but Da said they were done with travelling and turned them into fishermen. Romany fishermen – what a thing! Arthur and Eric went to sea and Gerry

3

went to school. He had polio when he was seven and he lay in the hospital bed and screamed, 'I hurt! I hurt . . . Ma, Arthur, take it *away*!' They thought he would surely die but he made a remarkable recovery, the doctors said, and was only left with a very slight limp. He went back to school and he taught his brothers to read and write, he did, and got a scholarship to the grammar school. Da couldn't read, but he could count and figure and deal. One boat turned into a fleet of four, six, eight, sailing out of Rye Harbour, and they had a little cottage instead of the caravan, and then a bigger one and then a small brick house with all modern conveniences.

And there were the ponies. Da bought them or bred them and Gerry rode them at local gymkhanas and hunter trials and Da sold them to the nobs for their children to ride, because Gerry got them going so well. And Arthur stopped going to sea and him and Ma ran their fish shop and they sold Dover sole and lobsters to the nobs, too. They grazed the horses and ponies on the land Da somehow seemed to own – a field here, another there – and Gerry and Arthur would watch them stretch their legs and buck and grow, and they would dream. There was nothing Gerry couldn't do with a horse, provided he could get his legs around it. Nothing Gerry couldn't do.

And then the war came and Arthur and Eric went off to fight. Not Gerry, thank God, he was too young and too precious. Eric was gone, lost in the Atlantic, but Arthur had had a good war, ending up a corporal. They told him he'd get his sergeant's stripes if he signed up for another two years, and so he did and shipped with his regiment for India – posting a letter only the day before. Not that Da's raving could have any effect on the mighty British army, but somehow Arthur could never be quite sure. Da's letter – dictated to Gerry – caught up with him in Bombay. He could imagine the old man dancing with rage and brandishing his stick as Gerry, his dark curly head bent over the paper, struggled to keep up with the torrent of fury. Arthur was to get back here *at once*, and enough jaunting about. Too late, of course.

They said he'd have a good career in the army if he stayed on and he would have liked to have done, but his brief rebellion, his taste of the exotic, was over. Over when – no, in all truth long

4

before – he received the letter from Gerry when his two years was nearly up. He took the letter from out of the inside pocket of his demob suit, unfolded it and read it for perhaps the fiftieth time since it had reached him in distant Bombay. It still amazed him. Gerry had got a 'place', he called it, at Cambridge University. The Rector had tutored him and written to people and Gerry was going to Trinity College.

Cambridge! That's where the officers in India had talked about, that and Oxford and Sandhurst and such places. Because of it they wore flash uniforms and ran up bills they couldn't pay in the mess. And because they had been to such places he, Arthur Beviss, had to call them 'sir'.

So! Gerry would go to Cambridge and Arthur would go back behind the counter of the fish shop and not mind, and he would make sure Gerry had everything he needed. People would call his little brother 'sir' one day.

The train slowed. Arthur stood up, pulled his bag from the luggage rack, opened the door and leapt down on to the platform before the train had come to a halt. He showed his pass at the barrier and strode on out into the little yard, swinging his bag.

Home. The sun came out for a moment, shafting from between great dark clouds. Arthur stopped and looked and breathed deep. Behind him was the marsh and the hills of the Weald, and he could smell the sea.

'Arthur? Hey – Art!'

A young man had climbed out of a black baby Austin and was running towards him.

'Gerry!' Arthur dropped his bag and the brothers hugged each other. 'Gerry . . .' They stood back. 'How did you know I'd be on this train?'

'I've been meeting them all.'

'No, have you?' Arthur laughed delightedly. 'Oh lad, but it's good to see you. Eh, but you've grown.'

'I would have, wouldn't I?' said Gerry, his man's voice speaking in an accent so unlike Arthur's own. 'Four years is a long time.'

'It's that all right.'

Gerry stood before him, grinning, his dark eyes alight with

excitement. He was taller than Arthur by an inch or more and he held himself with all the confidence of a handsome nineteen-year-old with the world at his feet. He picked up Arthur's bag.

'Come on, let's go. We've moved again. You'll never guess where.'

'I won't. Tell me.'

'Ridge Farm.'

'The Marlings' place? Never!'

'Yup.' Gerry opened the door of the Austin and slung the bag on to the back seat. 'I don't know how Da does it. He came home a month or so ago and said he'd bought it. Just the house and a few fields, but I reckon he'll have the rest of the land before long. Dennis Marling got himself into a sight of trouble. They're living in Hastings, somewhere at the back of the net sheds.'

Arthur grunted. 'I wonder if I'd be considered good enough for Julie Marling now.'

Gerry started the motor. 'She's all right. She married a GI and has gone to live in America.' He looked at his brother. 'You don't mind, do you?'

'Nah!' Arthur punched his brother playfully on the arm. 'Stuck up bitch . . . Look, can you drive this thing or are we going to sit here for ever?'

Gerry engaged the gear and they drove out of the yard and back across the railway line.

'It's not just Ridge Farm, Arthur. Da's got twelve boats now, and he's taken old Thomas's yard in Rye. We've got land all over the place.'

Arthur laughed admiringly. 'The old bugger. Is he playing the black market?'

'That and everything else. There's a block who comes to see the fish weighed and allocates the catch to shops around the area. Da ranted on that the fish his boats bring in is his and has a good bit taken ashore off Winchelsea by dinghy, so even the fish is making a fortune. You wouldn't believe there's rationing, Art. We never go short of anything, except Da's still tight with the cash, of course.'

Arthur leaned back, loving the sound of his brother's voice, gazing with a great peaceful joy at the cosy green fields and the

6

whirling seagulls, and amazed that they were going 'home' to a big farmhouse in Ryehurst with the four oasts in the yard surrounded by the stretches of pasture on marsh and Weald that raised the best sheep in the land.

Ma was feeding the chickens, a peacock among the dull brown birds, for she had never abandoned the brightly coloured gypsy skirts. She saw Arthur getting out of the car and gave a great squawk that sent her chickens running in shame and brought her husband hurrying into the yard.

'Arthur, my boy! Oh my boy!' she cried over and over again. 'We got your telegram but I daren't believe you're safe home.'

'There, Ma, there.' Arthur held his mother strongly, wondering how such a tiny woman had borne three hulking sons. Then he remembered there were only two of them left, and it was as though the news of Eric's death had come anew. It was the first time that the family had been together without Eric and the four of them stood there, holding each other in silence.

'Look at that!' exclaimed Joe Beviss. 'Just look at the lep that horse has in him!'

He and Arthur watched Gerry take the big bay over the next fence, a parallel. It stood off and cleared it by six inches.

'He'll jump a ten-foot hedge, that one.'

'Where did you get him?' Arthur asked.

'From a bloke I met,' Joe said vaguely. 'We call him Florin.' He chuckled. 'I'll get a sight more'n that for him, I tell you.'

Florin threw his head in the air, fought Gerry briefly and then hopped cleverly over a brush fence.

'Don't sell him, Da,' Arthur said suddenly. 'Let Gerry take him to Cambridge.'

'Do *what*?' His father stared at him in astonishment. 'What'd he want wi' a horse there? He's going to study an' get a bit o' paper an' letters after his name. So Rector said.' He sniffed. 'Though what bachelors of arts an' things has got to do wi' the price o' fish he didn't say.'

'Let Gerry take Florin to Cambridge,' Arthur repeated. 'That horse'll help him get on.'

His father's eyes narrowed. Gerry and Florin powered over a triple bar.

'What'll he do wi' him there?' Joe asked.

'Hunt,' said Arthur, not having a clue. 'Race, maybe.'

'It'll cost money. *More* money.'

'It will, Da.' Of that Arthur was sure.

'So,' Joe said finally, 'what you're trying to say is that you reckon Florin there could make a splash at this Cambridge place and give Gerry a good soaking at the same time.'

'It's possible, Da. The nobs are simple folk. You know how they rate a chap by his horse and how he rides.'

Gerry was walking Florin around the far end of the paddock, letting him cool down and relax on a long rein.

'That's true 'nough. Or was before the war.' Joe Beviss swiped the heads off a clump of nettles with his walking stick and then looked up at his elder son.

'I'm an ambitious man, Arthur. You should know that. I gave us up travelling because I wanted us to be something, and it's hard to stop what's in the blood.' He laughed. 'Reckon that's why we move houses so often. Where next, Arthur lad? The manor? I ain't sold any o' the other places, you know. I'm a man o' property an' that's a fact.' He tapped Arthur's chest with the head of his stick. 'But I done it for you. My sons. There's no denyin' that Gerry's the likely one and it'ud please me dearly if he made his mark on the world . . . So if you say taking Florin off to this Cambridge wi' him'll help him do that, well, so it'ud best be.'

He waved his stick in an arc, taking in the Weald, the marshland below and the grey strip of the Channel in the distance.

'Not bad for a gypsy, Arthur, true Romanies though we be . . . Out there's our boats bringing fine fish back on the tide, we got a good bit o' land around hereabouts and down in that fancy house yer Ma's sitting like a lady.' He turned back to Arthur. 'You happy to be a fishmonger?' he asked.

'No, Da, not particularly,' Arthur said steadily. 'I was doing well in the army.'

Joe snorted. 'Army! What you want wi' that? No – you belong here wi' your family, and since our Gerry's off to this Cambridge place and poor Eric's gone, your place is here. I need you here.'

8

'In the fish shop.'

'For a year an' more. We won't be stopping there, though.'

'Where'll we be going, Da?'

'I'm thinkin' on it,' Joe growled. 'An' now I got to be off. Boats'll be coming in.'

He gave a final slash to the nettles and stumped away down to his car in the yard. Arthur stared after him until a warm breath on his neck caused him to turn. Florin's handsome, intelligent face met his gaze.

'I didn't want to interrupt,' Gerry said, jumping from the saddle to the ground. 'What were you two talking about?'

'I was persuading Da that Florin should go to Cambridge with you.'

'Arthur! Oh you're the absolute tops! A bleeding genius!'

In his excitement he let go of the bridle and Florin began to move away. Arthur grabbed the reins.

'Aren't I just? Now stop capering. Run the stirrups up and loosen the girths. And *don't* say "bleeding" – the word is "bloody".'

'*So* sorry, old chap,' Gerry said, 'but you are a bloody genius, don't you know?'

They began walking down the track to the yard, Florin's head bobbing between them.

'How about a drink at the Anchor tonight?' Gerry asked.

'What's the matter with the Rose?'

'Nothing. But the barmaid at the Anchor's a real corker.'

'Oh yeah?' said Arthur, still trying to reconcile this virile young man with the fifteen-year-old boy he had seen last.

'And Annie's one too,' cried Gerry, as a girl groom appeared in the yard and stood waiting for them.

'What one too?' she asked, taking Florin's bridle.

'Wouldn't you like to know?' Gerry said, putting an arm around her shoulder and planting a kiss on her cheek.

She was a pretty girl with long blond hair worn in a plait which hung down her back. Florin, impatient for his stable, began to nibble at it.

'Annie's folk moved here just after the war,' Gerry explained. 'Her Da's skipper of one of our boats, but Annie prefers horses to fish, don't you, love?'

Annie nodded and pushed Florin's head away.

But Gerry to both of them, Arthur thought.

They had the house and the fishing boats and the pockets of land between Winchelsea and Rye, but it wasn't enough for Joe Beviss. In the long summer evenings he would go up to the top paddock and gaze over the land that rightly belonged to Ridge Farm.

Desperation had made Dennis Marling sell the house, but he hoped to recoup his fortune from the wool and meat of the sheep that grazed on his green acres. Joe knew he couldn't do that: he'd lost too many ewes in the freeze last winter and couldn't afford to replace them with good young stock; not enough lambs would be born next spring to buy Nancy Marling a new pair of shoes, let alone the outfits she had paraded around Rye in the old days. Joe would take the land bit by bit, offering Marling just enough money to tide him over his immediate difficulties but never enough to allow him to buy the new stock he needed.

Joe Beviss was not really a hard man: he was on an upward spiral and Dennis Marling on a downward one, and that was that.

In the meantime, all the money Joe made through his various enterprises (and only he knew how much that was and how various they were) went towards his goal. The lads had to earn their keep, he said. So while Arthur weighed out mackerel and cod and joked with the women who came to buy, Gerry and Annie schooled the horses, taught them to jump and how to behave themselves, and went off in the horsebox to shows and returned with red rosettes and silver cups, Annie's face glowing, often, with a happiness that was not altogether to do with the success of the horses.

Arthur, weighing up cod and mackerel, weighed up other things too. He took his brother off to the Anchor, sat him firmly down at a table away from the bar and Molly's inviting eyes, and went to get their drinks.

'Two things,' he said, returning with two pint jars and putting one in front of Gerry. 'Number one: stop Florin winning. Da's getting offers he won't resist for ever. He's sold the young chestnut, you know.'

'Has he?' Gerry's jaw set, and he said in the voice that Arthur loved to hear, 'It would have been polite of him to tell me.'

'Maybe so, but he's no call to. It's his horse – and so is Florin.'

Gerry picked up his pint and drained half of it in one go.

'All right. What's number two?'

'Annie.'

Gerry stiffened.

'Leave her be, Gerry. She's stuck on you and you know it and take advantage. Leave her be,' he repeated. 'You get her into trouble and you'll be married to her quickerer'n you can count to five, and it's goodbye to Cambridge. You'll be in my place in the fish shop, never mind you can't fillet a sole. You'll soon learn and Da'ud have it no other way.'

Gerry's open face showed that he was examining this vision of the future and not liking it.

'But what'll I do?' he asked. 'If I can't jump Florin to win and Da sells the others as soon as they get any good. And no Annie . . . You can't blame me for wanting a bit of fun.'

'Have your fun, then,' Arthur told him angrily. 'And then, if you're a bit bored, come into the shop along of me and get some practice, or go out in the boats and haul on ropes till your hands bleed.'

Gerry reached out and grasped Arthur's forearm.

'I'm sorry, Art. Really. You're right.'

Arthur's anger evaporated. 'Oh, come on, lad. All you have to do is behave yourself for another couple of months . . . No, by heaven, you don't even have to do that. Look, there's Molly making eyes at you, *and* half the other easy ones in the area. Stay away from them as would drag you to church, that's all. I wish I had half your problem.'

Gerry laughed. 'You could, you know. They're for ever asking after my big brother. The strong silent type, they call you.'

Arthur paused in the act of draining his glass. 'Nah – you're kidding me,' he said. '*Do* they? Which ones?'

So Florin went off form and people said the horse was a flash in the pan and put their money back in their pockets. Gerry and Annie went off in the horsebox and came back with rosettes, but not red ones and no silver cups, and the glow in Annie's face died. After the day's work Gerry would go into the house to bathe and change and return to find Arthur and Annie rubbing the horses down and settling them for the night.

'Hey, Arthur,' he'd say, 'lend us ten bob. Or a pound'ud do', he'd add, as though it wasn't the third time that week he'd asked the same thing, as though he hadn't already persuaded his mother to open her purse. But Arthur would hand over the two brown notes, which Gerry would take and go to the Austin tossing a casual good night over his shoulder.

Arthur would hand over the two brown notes and ignore the pain and disappointment in Annie's blue eyes as she watched the Austin disappear in the direction of Hastings or Rye or wherever it was that Gerry was kicking up a lark that night.

Until one day, when the nights were closing in and there was a chill in the air that presaged autumn, Arthur found Annie crying as she unplaited the mane of a little bay horse. She'd got up before dawn to put the plaits in, all for the glory of Gerry so the horses he rode would look beautiful under him.

'Here, now,' Arthur said awkwardly, 'no need for tears.'

She flung herself on his broad chest.

'What did I do? Oh Arthur, what did I *do*?'

He found he had put his arms around her. 'Nothing, Annie love,' he said. 'Nothing. Gerry's going off to Cambridge and that's a thing we can do nothing about ... Tell you what,' he said, pushing her away from him and looking into her tear-stained face, 'why don't you and me go to the pictures tonight? And then we'll have a meal somewhere.'

They got on very well together. After all, they both loved the same man.

Gerry rolled off Molly and winced as pebbles ground into his back from under the thin rug. He gazed up at black sky.

'That was great, Moll. You're a treat.'

He heard her sigh above the sound of the waves breaking just a few yards away. High tide.

'You've always been the best of them, Gerry. I'll miss you.'

'I'll be back at Christmas,' he said, throwing aside the horse blanket that covered them both and groping for his clothes. 'It'll be too cold for it here then, though. It's bad enough now.'

He stood up, pulled on his trousers, found his jacket and felt in the pockets.

'Want a fag?' He took one from the packet, squatted down and held it out. 'Here . . . and put your clothes on.' He touched her blanket-covered shoulder. 'You're shivering.'

She was silent. He shrugged, sat down beside her, put the cigarette in his mouth and lit it. Molly's muffled voice came out of the darkness.

'I'm not shivering, you daft bloody pillock. I'm crying.' She sniffed and tried to laugh. 'Me! Over a silly boy scarce dry behind the ears.' She sat up and pulled the blanket around her. 'I'll have that fag now.'

He gave her one and lit it. His lighter revealed a glimpse of her naked breasts as she stretched her hand out to shelter the flame. She saw the look on his face and her hand stroked his jaw.

'One more last time?' she said softly.

'Oh Moll,' he groaned.

Gerry parked in the gateway of one of Dennis Marling's fields and walked the rest of the way home. He didn't want the house woken by the sound of the engine labouring up the hill and questions asked about where he had been until two o'clock in the morning. He cursed, therefore, when he saw a light on in the kitchen of Ridge Farm. He vaulted over the gate into the yard and made his way to the back door. It opened and a strip of yellow lighted his way.

'Gerry? That you?'

'Arthur?' Gerry went past his brother into the kitchen. 'What the hell are you doing up? Aren't you starting off at dawn?'

Arthur was going with Florin by train to Cambridge, taking two days, and was to settle him in the livery stables recommended by a friend of a friend of the Rector's. Gerry was leaving a day later in the Austin.

'I wanted to talk to you and fell asleep in front of the range.' Arthur ran his hand over his face and through his already rumpled hair. 'What time is it?'

'Late,' Gerry said.

Arthur grinned at him. 'Been saying your goodbyes to Molly, have you?'

Gerry grinned back. 'Yeah – well.' He dropped into one of the comfortable chairs by the range and stretched luxuriously. 'Hey, Arthur, Da's got some brandy hidden in the top cupboard. At the back. How 'bout it?'

Arthur opened the cupboard and found the bottle and some glasses.

'Da'ud kill us if he knew,' he remarked.

'We're big boys now,' said Gerry in the voice Arthur loved. 'No need to be frightened of *daddy* any more. Or pater as the Rector would say.'

He took the bottle and poured each of them a generous measure. Solemnly, they clinked their glasses together.

'To you, then, Gerry,' Arthur said, and they both drank.

'Well, *old chap*, what was it you wanted to say to me?' Gerry asked.

Arthur looked down at his glass, turning it round and round in his large red hands.

'Come on, Art. Spit it out.'

Arthur shifted his feet. 'Well,' he began, 'it's just that I'd like to see your billet – your room,' he corrected himself carefully, 'an' all at this Trinity College—'

'Of course you can, you great lug,' said Gerry. 'What a fuss about nothing.'

'But I can't be there as your brother . . . no I can't,' he said, as Gerry made to protest. 'I can't and that's that. So I've had an idea. Your Da – your father, that is – has sent his batman to put you right, see?'

'He's done *what*?'

'Hey, Gerry, it'll be a lark! I can be a bloody fine servant when I'm not selling fish.'

Gerry took another sip of brandy and contemplated this brother of his who was ready to pretend to be his servant. They had the same nose and eyes, the same curly dark hair and the same general build, but Gerry knew that in Arthur the mix was somehow distorted and in him, Gerry, it had come out right. Arthur had

14

plodding good looks and charm, like an honest working horse whose job it was to pull a milk cart, while in Gerry it had resulted in a sleek thoroughbred.

Arthur's voice came back to him, coaxing, full of the suffocating love Gerry could not quite return.

'What d'you say, lad? It'll be a lark,' he repeated.

' 'Course, Art, if that's what you want. I'll meet you at the stables, then. Leave me the directions.' He stood up, yawning. 'I'm for bed.'

'Me too.' Arthur retrieved the brandy bottle and put it back in its hiding place, and then rinsed out their glasses at the sink. He dried his hands and threw the cloth aside, and then went up to his brother.

'Well, so long, lad.' He put both arms around Gerry's shoulders and hugged him. 'See you in Cambridge.'

Gerry was horrified to hear the thickness in Arthur's voice and feel his brother's tears on his cheek.

Before he got into bed, Gerry went to the window, stepping around the suitcases his mother had been packing for him, and stared out.

He thought of Molly and their coupling on the beach; he thought of Florin in his stable, unaware of his long journey tomorrow; he thought of Annie asleep in her parents' cottage and of the soulful glances that had so tested his resolve throughout the summer. He thought of Arthur. He thought about Cambridge and the challenges awaiting him there. Enough hanging around: only two more days and he would be facing them. He stretched his arms above his head until he felt the muscles in his shoulders crack. People would like him there, be nice to him, probably spoil him . . . they always did, he thought easily, men and women alike.

He got into his bed and fell asleep, and he did not dream at all.

Chapter 2

Arthur and Gerry stood before the huge tower that was the Great
Gate of Trinity College, Cambridge.

'It's like a bleeding castle,' breathed Arthur.

'Watch your language, my man,' said Gerry. 'We don't say
"bleeding" here – remember? . . . Hey, Art, what's your name?'

Arthur stared at him.

'What do I call you?'

'Oh.' Arthur cast his mind around. 'How about Lockett? I once
knew a chap called Lockett. Decent bloke.'

'Okay, Lockett, let's be going.'

Gerry strode through the archway beneath the tower and
Arthur, wearing his demob suit, a bowler hat and his best military
bearing, walked after him carrying Gerry's two suitcases.

Gerry's rooms were in New Court; a porter began giving
directions but Gerry stopped him.

'I know where it is.'

'Very good, sir.'

There it was, then. Better than Arthur had ever thought. He
picked up the suitcases again and followed Gerry on.

Great Court, Trinity. Arthur gasped and Gerry paused, overwhelmed for a moment by the thought that for the next three years
this place was his: the tower behind him and this vast court, the
chapel to the right bigger than most village churches and the whole
pervaded by a solid, timeless dignity and a sense of quiet so that,
even from this distance and over the sound of voices all about, you
heard – or thought you could hear – the tiny tinkle of water in the
fountain.

Gerry pointed to the far left corner. 'We go through there,' he said. 'And we don't walk on the grass.'

'Why're they then?' Arthur nodded at two men, their heads close together, strolling across one of the closely shaven lawns.

'Must be dons.'

'Oh,' Arthur said, mystified.

They set off along a paved path flanked by cobblestones towards the fountain and then turned left.

'What's this?' Arthur asked, noticing the stained glass in the windows of the building to the right. 'Is it another chapel?'

'No, it's Hall.'

'For assembly and that,' Arthur said, remembering what Gerry had told him of the routine at Rye Grammar School.

'No, it's where we eat.'

'Bloody hell.'

They went through a narrow entrance, down to the right and under another archway.

'This is New Court.'

'How do you know?'

'The Rector showed me around when we came for my interview.'

It wasn't nearly as classy as Great Court or as the court they could glimpse through colonnades as they searched for Gerry's staircase but, Arthur thought, it would do.

They found the staircase, and there was Gerry's name painted white on black. Arthur gazed at it.

'You're here then, aren't you? Your name and all.'

'I am. Let me take one of those,' Gerry said, reaching for a suitcase.

'Nah, it'ud spoil the image. Up you go, sir,' Arthur added in a loud voice as a smartly dressed woman accompanied by a tall, fair-haired young man approached. A man in chauffeur's uniform was behind them with a trolley piled high with luggage. Arthur winked at him at him as he heaved Gerry's cases through the door and up the narrow stone stairs.

Two flights. Gerry opened a door to his left.

'Well, isn't this something!' he exclaimed.

It was a pleasant room, a bedroom off it with a view of the

17

river, and Gerry's trunk, sent on ahead, was sitting in the middle of it as another indelible mark of ownership. It wasn't that much smaller than the whole downstairs of the first cottage they had lived in, Arthur reflected, and a fat sight bigger than the caravan before that.

A clear, aristocratic voice accompanied by some bumping arose from the ground floor of the staircase.

'Can you manage the trunk, Mallet? Oh, I suppose you can't. Shouldn't there be someone to help? Now what are we to do?'

Arthur dropped Gerry's suitcases and ran back down the stairs. 'Can I help, ma'am?'

The woman looked at him from under the veil of her hat and her son lowered the end of the trunk he was carrying and turned to face him.

'It's kind of you, but we can manage.'

'Oh no, sir,' Arthur said firmly. 'Allow me.' He stepped forward and the young man moved aside.

'Very good of you.' The woman started up the stairs and her son, with a faintly apologetic glance at Arthur, followed.

'All right?' Arthur said to the chauffeur. 'I'll go first, shall I?' and they manoeuvred the trunk up the stairs and into the room opposite Gerry's.

The woman opened her handbag. '*Very* good,' she repeated, and held out her hand, fist closed.

'No thank you, ma'am,' said Arthur, staring straight ahead. 'Pleased to have been of assistance. Is there anything else you require?' He'd read that in a book somewhere. It sounded good.

'No,' said the woman. 'Mallet can manage the rest, can't you, Mallet?'

'Yes, my lady.'

Gerry's voice sounded, right on cue: 'Art— *Lockett*! Where are you?'

'Coming, sir.' Arthur tipped the brim of his bowler hat and went across the landing to his brother's room. Gerry was fiddling with the hasps of the trunk.

'I can't open this. It's locked.'

'I have the keys, sir.'

'Don't you think you're overdoing the "sir" bit?'

'Ssh.' Arthur closed the door as Mallet went down the stairs to collect the rest of his young master's luggage. 'The bloke opposite's mother is a lady,' he said.

'Wonderful! Half an hour in Cambridge and my brother discovers the facts of life.'

'No, honest. Their driver chappie called her "my lady". She offered me a tip.'

'Did she?' Gerry asked with interest. 'How much?'

'Dunno. Didn't take it.'

There was a knock on the door and Arthur opened it. A small man, in his mid-forties, Arthur judged, stood there. His gaze slid past Arthur and fixed on Gerry.

'Crystal, sir. I'm your gyp. Sorry I wasn't here to see you in.'

'That's all right, Crystal.' Gerry turned towards the window and felt in the inside pocket of his jacket. He then went over to Crystal and there was a rustle as a note – or notes? – changed hands.

'Thank you very much, sir. Is there anything I can do for you now, sir?'

'I'm well looked after at the moment, thank you,' Gerry said.

'Very good, sir.' Crystal bowed neatly and went to the room opposite.

'How did you know what to give him?' Arthur asked, impressed by Gerry's coolness.

'The Rector told me . . . Hey, listen!'

The door had swung open. The woman – or lady as Arthur would have her – was complaining and Crystal was agreeing that it was shocking no one had been there to help with the luggage. Mallet was standing to attention on the tiny landing, his cap under his arm. Behind the woman stood her son, fidgeting awkwardly, his fair face rapidly turning pink. He caught Gerry's eye and raised his own to heaven.

'Now, sir,' Arthur said loudly, when the cool, clear voice stopped at last, 'shall we get this lot unpacked?'

Gerry stood in the middle of his sitting room, a jar of raspberry jam in one hand and a chocolate cake on a plate in the other. The town and University of Cambridge were out there and he was stuck here

19

wondering what to do with the hamper of homemade delicacies his mother had sent – with Arthur and Florin, because she had known he would refuse to take it himself. Arthur had slipped it into Gerry's car when they had gone to Florin's stables before Gerry had driven Arthur to the station, saying there was no way he was going to take it home having lugged it all the way here. And anyway, Gerry would be pleased enough for it after a few days on rationed food.

Gerry stood in his room in New Court, Trinity College, Cambridge, a jar of raspberry jam in one hand and a chocolate cake in the other, and remembered the old Irishman who was now in charge of Florin sweeping a brush down the horse's shoulder and saying, 'What a grand crittur', and Florin, who was always embarrassed by compliments, giving him a friendly nip. And old Tomás – he had written it down in scraggly old handwriting so they wouldn't get it wrong – had pulled Florin's ears and whispered in one of them, and Gerry, now gazing out of the window, seeing but not seeing the tree in the middle of New Court and the scurrying figures, some in flapping black gowns, wondered if Florin would understand the Irish in his ear having, as he did, Romany as his first language.

A knock. Gerry put the jam jar down and went to open the door. The fair-haired man from the room opposite lounged against the doorjamb.

'Hello.' He held out his hand and Gerry, shifting the cake from his right to his left hand, gripped it. 'I'm James Flimwell.'

'Gerald Beviss.' Away with Gerry. A silly name for a grown man.

James Flimwell walked into the room and sat himself down in Gerry's armchair.

'Mothers!' he exclaimed. 'Yours didn't come, I notice.'

Gerry tried to imagine his mother in her gypsy colours at Trinity College and failed utterly.

'Just sent the servant,' James Flimwell was saying. 'And a damned good thing too. Mallet and I would have managed famously. I say . . .' He peered at Gerry. 'Is that a chocolate cake you've got there?'

'Yes,' Gerry replied. 'Mothers, as you say.' He gestured at the hamper. 'I was just wondering what to do with all this.'

20

'Really? My dear chap, if you want to dispose of that cake, don't hesitate a moment longer.'

'Would you like some?'

'Homemade chocolate cake? I'd say I would!' He reached out a long arm, picked a few crumbs from the edge of the plate and put them in his mouth. '*Real* chocolate! Your mother's a wizard.'

'I suppose,' Gerry said, improvising wildly, 'she saved up the ration.' James Flimwell's father – who, if Arthur was right, was a sir or a lord or something – hadn't been operating on the black market. Of that Gerry was sure.

'Well, if you don't mind broaching it, I'll ask that rogue for some plates, shall I?' James stood up and opened the door. 'Crystal?' A cool, authoritative voice, like his mother's.

'Sir?'

'A brace of plates and a knife to Mr Beviss's rooms. Hurry along, now.'

'Yes, sir!'

James finished his third slice of chocolate cake and leaned back in the chair, stretching his legs out in front of him.

'Delicious,' he pronounced. 'No . . . no more,' as Gerry pointed the knife enquiringly at the plate and the much depleted cake. 'I've got to watch my weight.'

Gerry looked at his guest's long, stringy body. 'Why, for heaven's sake?' he asked.

James raised his head and gazed down at himself. 'I look thin, but I've got heavy bones . . . I ride,' he explained. 'Point-to-points and that.'

'But the season doesn't begin for months.'

'Got to keep on top of it,' James said seriously. 'I say, you a racing man, then?'

'No. Show jumping and hunter trials. That sort of thing.'

'Got a horse?'

'Yeah – he's a right corker!' In his enthusiasm, Gerry let his accent slip but James – who had sat up and with much waving about of his hands was extolling the finer points of his own horse – didn't seem to notice.

'Tell you what,' he said, after describing in detail how he and his

21

horse Castor had won their last two races, 'we ought to get in touch with the drag-hunting people here. Shall we toddle along to the Pitt Club for a drink? There are bound to be chaps from school there who will put us up. Where were you, by the way?'

Where was I what? Gerry wondered frantically. What is drag-hunting and why do we need 'putting up' when we have perfectly good beds here? The Rector had said it was good to join clubs and had mentioned a few, but not the Pitt Club. Ignorance was closing in on him, drowning him.

He was saved by Crystal, who came to collect the plates and to remind the young gentlemen that Hall began in five minutes and they were not to forget to wear their gowns. James, notwithstanding the chocolate cake and the worries about his weight, greeted this news with enthusiasm and went to his room to collect his gown. Gerry found his, put it on and met James on the landing. James stared at him, a faintly horrified look on his face.

'You're a scholar!' he exclaimed accusingly.

Gerry looked at James's short gown and at his own long one. 'Well, yes,' he said.

James seemed highly disconcerted. 'Good grief . . . ! Did they push you like anything at school?' he asked. 'They did that to a friend of mine, yattering on about a first before the poor chap was out of short trousers. Was it like that with you?'

'It wasn't at school. I had a tutor . . . the Rector . . .'

'What! You weren't sent away, then?'

'No,' replied Gerry, the waters closing over him again. 'This is the first time I've ever left home.'

They went to the Pitt Club after Hall. As they walked into the foyer, James was hailed by a man standing among a group of raucous friends.

'Foggy!' he cried. 'Foggy Flimwell by all that's holy! How did you manage it? Your old man must have pulled anchor cables to get you here.'

James laughed, not a bit put out.

'Nick, old fellow, good to see you. Here—' He pulled Gerry forward. 'This is Gerald Beviss, at Trinity like me. He's a scholar,' he added proudly, indicating Gerry's gown.

22

'Foggy Flimwell and a scholar,' said Nick O'Rourke. 'Now I've seen everything.'

'Nick, will you sign us in and put us up and that?'

'*Do* we want these reprobates in our club?' enquired Nick at large.

'Sign them in, put them up and let's get a drink, for God's sake,' someone said.

And Gerald Beviss, son of Romany gypsies and the brother of a fishmonger, found himself nominated a member of Cambridge's exclusive club for young gentlemen.

He wrote a hurried note to his brother two evenings later.

Dear Art,

Everything is the tops here. Florin is looking nearly as well as when Annie was in charge. Tell her. We're going drag-hunting next week. Ever heard of it? The hounds hunt a smelly sock dragged on a string by some hearty running type over a special course. We follow on horses and go, the chaps say, like the blazes.

Listen, Art, will you talk to Da? The allowance isn't nearly enough. I've had to order a dinner jacket and trousers and I'll need a tail coat for balls and things.

I'll write properly soon.

Gerry.

He'd addressed it to the fish shop so, cunning little monkey, his parents wouldn't see it and demand to know its contents, and Arthur was left to do the dirty work. Da had grumbled enough about the allowance as it was, and he was paying for Florin's keep . . . Well, Arthur had a good bit tucked away from the army and Gerry could have some of that for his dinner jacket and his tail coat.

Tails! *Balls and things!* . . . What next?

All that day the customers buying fish noticed that Arthur seemed a bit distracted, often chuckling to himself for no reason at all.

'Get a bustle on, will you?'

'I can't decide whether to wear a tie or a cravat,' James said.

Mark Colley-Smythe sighed. 'We're only going out to tea, for God's sake. What's all the fuss?'

'Nick said there'd be girls there.'

'Real live ones?' asked Gerry from the doorway. 'Real live ones with all the bits attached? I don't think I've seen or spoken to a girl since I arrived here.'

'From the women's colleges, Nick said.' James selected a tie, put it on and the three of them clattered down the staircase.

'Anyone remember where Nick's rooms are in John's?' James asked as they reached Great Court.

'We'll ask at the Porters' Lodge. . . . Gerald, did you go to Framlingham's lecture this morning?'

'I did.'

'Can I borrow your notes?'

'And where were you, young sir?'

Mark flexed the muscles in his arms.

'On the river. If I train really hard I reckon I'll get into Magdalene's first boat this year – maybe even Goldie – and then I could get my Blue next year.'

'If you skip lectures, you won't be here next year,' Gerry pointed out.

'Ah, shut up,' Mark said amiably. 'Whoever was sent down from Magdalene for rowing too much? I say, James, I'm a bit worried about Gerald. He seems to take work a trifle too seriously.'

'Useful for you, though,' James said. 'You can crib all his notes.'

'Very true,' Mark said. 'Gerald, I take all criticism back. Every word of it.'

'You're forgiven, and you may have my notes,' Gerry said as they went through Great Gate.

'Hey!' James whispered. 'Do you think those two are going to tea at Nick's?'

Two beautiful girls, both tall, one with raging red hair and the other with a short dark crop, were walking down Trinity Street.

'Let's tell them they're going in the wrong direction,' Mark said.

Just then the dark girl stepped foward, her eyes fixed on Gerry.

'Gerry?' she said. 'Gerry Beviss?'

Chapter 3

He obviously didn't recognise her, couldn't remember her name. Why should he? It was a long time ago, before the war when they were both children, that they had competed against each other at the gymkhanas held around the borders of Kent and Sussex. The Beviss horsebox (no one else owned a horsebox, which made it worse) would turn up, out would come a string of ponies and the local people would sigh, knowing they didn't have a chance. Often she and her pony had been beaten by the dark, curly-haired little mite who enchanted those members of the crowd who didn't have a child riding in the class, but infuriated her and her friends because he was two years younger than them all. She wouldn't have recognised him now, except she had seen him compete at the Kent County Show during the summer. He had grown up into a startlingly handsome young man.

She realised now, standing in Trinity Street, that an awkward silence had descended upon the group.

'I'm Kate Earith,' she said. 'We—'

She was about to explain, but his brow cleared and he smiled in belated recognition.

'The doctor's daughter! You used to ride Benjy.'

Kate laughed. 'How clever of you to remember his name.'

Gerry introduced his companions: James, tall and fair-haired, and Mark, broad and stocky with nondescript brown hair and a somewhat ugly face – until he smiled, when it was transformed. He was staring with frank interest at Kate's companion, whom Kate hastened to introduce in her turn.

25

'Vanessa Hardgreaves . . . We're both at Girton.'

'Teeth,' James murmured.

Mark flashed him an angry glance.

'We're off to have tea with a friend in St John's,' he said. 'Why don't you join us? Oh, come on – do!'

'But we haven't been asked,' Vanessa said.

'Nick won't mind. He'll be delighted to see you, won't he, James?'

'We're going to have tea at the Whim and then hear Evensong at King's,' Kate said firmly.

'How very virtuous!' Mark exclaimed. 'I know . . . why don't you both come and have tea with me at Magdalene tomorrow?'

'Shall we?' Vanessa asked Kate.

'Why not?' Kate said absently. She was looking at Gerry, who was staring at her with anxious intensity in his rather beautiful dark brown eyes.

'Wonderful!' Mark took out his pocketbook, scribbled in it, tore out a sheet and handed it to Vanessa. 'Tomorrow at four, then. I've written down my name, college and staircase so you have absolutely no excuse.'

Kate took the paper which Vanessa was already beginning to crumple.

'If you want to see us tomorrow, I'd better have this. Vanessa loses things,' she explained.

They parted. Mark watched the two girls cross Trinity Street and disappear in the direction of the tea shop, then turned back to the others. They all walked on.

'You two weren't much help,' he grumbled. 'I've a good mind not to invite you tomorrow.'

'It's your style,' James told him. 'It's unbeatable. We couldn't have interrupted the flow. It would have been criminal, wouldn't it, Gerald?'

'What?' said Gerry. 'Oh – yes, it would.'

Mark nudged James. 'He's miles away. He's fallen in love with the beautiful Kate . . . At least I hope he has, and not with the beautiful Vanessa because I'm definitely in love with her. Which did you fall for, James?'

'Oh, both I think. I'll have to fight the two of you.'

26

'Pistols at dawn, then,' Mark said.

Gerry hadn't fallen in love with Kate, but she was very much on his mind. She knew about him, knew his father was a gypsy made good, knew he hadn't gone to some posh public school but to Rye Grammar.

He hadn't meant to lie, in fact he *hadn't* lied – not at first. He hadn't understood, that was all. How could he be expected to? His blood ran cold when he remembered, that first night in the Pitt Club, overhearing someone saying in an aristocratic drawl, 'I damned well don't care about the post-war melting pot. The Pitt Club is not going to be overrun by little blighters from grammar schools.' It was already too late: Gerry's name had been put forward, James had told Nick about how he hadn't gone to school and Gerry couldn't just turn round and say, 'Sorry, I'm a grammar school blighter and not fit to be here.' And why, he thought viciously, should he?

And then he *had* started to lie. When he was asked – and everyone was for ever asking, as though it mattered when the only thing that really mattered, surely, was that they were all here at Cambridge – where he had gone to school, he invented a lengthy childhood illness that had kept him at home. It wasn't even all invention – he'd had polio, after all – but if they found out about him now, they would think he'd got himself made a member of the Pitt Club under false pretences and shun him. And James – what would he do? Would he ever talk to him again? They had to live opposite each other until June, for heaven's sake!

He had to go to Girton before four o'clock tomorrow – no, tonight – find Kate and . . . do what? Beg her not to give him away? Would she think he was living under false pretences? Arthur's ploy and his yes sirs and no sirs had worked too bloody well, he reflected as he followed James and Mark through the gates of St John's College. James had assumed, from the presence of an apparent servant in his rooms, that Gerry was from a great family . . . Where *was* Girton, anyway? Did they allow men to go visiting there in the evenings?

'Wake up, man. We're here.' Gerry looked round to find the others had stopped a few yards back.

'He's got it bad,' said Mark. 'And did you notice she called him "Gerry"? I never really thought of him as a Gerald, you know.'

They gazed at him appraisingly. 'Definitely Gerry,' Mark said. 'Come on, Gerry! Shake a leg, old thing.'

Gerry grinned reluctantly and joined them. He would enjoy himself for as long as he could.

In the end it was easy. There were three girls at Nick's tea party and ten men: quite a decent ratio, everyone agreed, considering there were two women's colleges in Cambridge and nearly twenty men's. Two of the girls were from Newnham, but the third – a Miss Eileen McLennan – was from Girton. She complained that her bicycle had a puncture and James and two others volunteered to mend it.

'Thank you so much,' she said, taking a bun from the plate Nick was offering her and sitting back in her chair. 'It's at the Bridge Street gate . . . the only woman's bicycle with a puncture. You can't miss it.'

They went out looking rather sheepish and Gerry sat on the floor beside Miss McLennan's chair and offered to take her and her bicycle back to Girton in his car.

'Oh my, you have a car, do you?' She finished her bun, accepted a cigarette from him and then a light. 'How did you wangle that?'

'Special circumstances.'

Undergraduates were not allowed to bring cars to Cambridge as a matter of course, but the Proctor's office had agreed that Gerry needed one so he could visit his horse – something Gerry found rather beguiling as, after all, it was not so long ago that horses had been the principal mode of transport.

Miss McLennan was distinctly unimpressed by this explanation, merely remarking that surely one could bicycle to see a horse just as easily as drive. Gerry was wondering what on earth he was going to say next when James returned and announced that the puncture had been diagnosed as a ruptured inner tube.

'The chap at Girton will see to it,' Miss McLennan said. 'Thank you for trying, though.' Her cool gaze wandered to Gerry. 'And so I accept your offer.'

'My pleasure,' said Gerry and nobly yielded his place to James who had, he noticed, stained his shirt cuff in the service of Miss McLennan. He went to talk to Mark, who was standing by the fireplace, where, in a very short time, James joined them.

'That's one of your ones with teeth, Mark,' he said, making a pantomime of loosening his tie and wiping sweat from his brow.

'What is all this about teeth?' asked Gerry.

'Mark thinks bluestockings must have big teeth to match their brains. Only I couldn't catch a glimpse of that one's teeth because she never smiled. What,' he demanded of Gerry, 'possessed you to offer her a lift back to the witches' cauldron?'

'I was trying to be helpful.'

Mark stared and pointed accusingly. 'He's stealing a bloody march on us!' he exclaimed. 'He's going to see the glorious Kate Earith and the oh-so-divine Vanessa Hardgreaves.'

'I thought I might,' Gerry confessed, 'since I'm passing.'

'Well, don't get bitten on the way,' James said.

Miss McLennan directed him to Girton College, a great dark red brick building sprawling away on each side of the drive for ever, it seemed, into the dark. She seemed amused when, after untying the various ropes that secured her wounded bicycle in the boot of Gerry's car, he asked her if she could direct him to Kate Earith's room, but she went to the Portress's Lodge, discovered the room number and set him in the right direction.

It was all so different from Trinity. They had, Miss McLennan explained, corridors and not staircases and courts here, and the corridor he was walking along seemed to go on for miles. And the other difference was, of course, that it was full of girls. Bluestockings, every one of them. Would Mark ever dare set foot in here? he wondered.

At last he found Kate's room – next to the divine Vanessa's, he noticed – and knocked on the door. She opened it.

'Gerry!' She seemed startled but not displeased to see him. 'Well, come in.' She stood aside.

'I just brought someone back here. Her bicycle had a puncture. I thought you might like to go out for a drink somewhere . . . or something.' Gerry paused and shuffled his feet. 'Since I'm here and we're old friends, sort of.'

She smiled suddenly.

'Yes – I'd like that. Hang on, I'll get my coat.'

They found a pub in Madingley. Gerry brought his pint of beer and Kate's gin and tonic to a table by the fire.

'This is lovely,' she said. 'Cambridge is wonderful but it's nice to be among – well – real people for a change. People living ordinary lives. Because whatever else Cambridge is, it isn't ordinary, is it?'

'No,' said Gerry, making a puddle of the overspill of his beer and sliding his glass around in it. 'No, it's not.'

'You want to say something to me,' she said gently. 'What is it?'

He waited for a moment and then said, 'What did you tell Vanessa – Miss Hardgreaves – about me?'

'Why, that you were a little boy who was a whiz on ponies and that now you are even more of a whiz on horses. Vanessa didn't,' she went on reflectively, 'know the difference . . . between horses and ponies, I mean.'

'You didn't say where I went to school or anything?'

'Why ever should I do that?' she asked in astonishment.

He took a sip of his beer and put the glass down.

'Those people you saw me with today . . . Kate,' he burst out, 'James's father's a lord and they went to bloody Eton. They think . . . I've been made a member of the Pitt Club!'

He stared at her as though he was admitting to murder.

'I'm sure,' she began carefully, 'that's very admirable, but I'm afraid I don't know what the Pitt Club is.'

'It's the gentlemen's club of Cambridge, that's what it is,' Gerry muttered. 'And, as you know, I'm no gent.'

Kate looked at him. His handsome face was creased in misery as he gazed down at the film of wet he had made on the table.

'Ah,' she said. 'You're afraid I'll tell everyone I meet that your father is a fisherman and that you didn't go to Eton or any other fancy public school.'

'Well – would you?'

'I might have done, not realising it was something you wanted to hide, but now you've warned me of course I won't.'

His face cleared and for the first time he met her gaze directly. She had dark blue eyes, and they were full of sympathy.

30

'I didn't mean it,' he said. 'It was all a mistake . . .' And he told her everything. She listened in silence.

'Well,' she said when he had finished, 'it sounds as though you're having terrific fun—' She was tempted to add, 'though perhaps not working as hard as you should be' but didn't because she had no desire to be regarded in any kind of authoritative or, curse the word, motherly light by Gerry Beviss, who had been moved to cast her in the role of confessor. 'And you like these people and obviously they like you, so what are you worrying about?'

'You,' he said.

'Giving you away? I told you, I won't.'

'You don't think I'm being dishonest?'

She hesitated. 'In their view, if they found out, I suppose you are. I really don't understand it all,' she went on. 'I mean, no one at Girton ever asks where you went to school, or if they do it's only for something to say. It's not considered important.' She shrugged her shoulders. 'Aren't men odd? Anyway,' she told him, 'you *sound* as though you went to Eton.'

He laughed. 'I've always done it – speak like whoever I'm with. I used to get teased at school because I sounded like a fisherman and teased by the lads because I sounded like a nob. So I blended in.'

'Protective camouflage.'

'That's it.' He grinned at her, his worries gone. 'How about another drink?'

And eventually they discovered they had both missed Hall and so drove into Cambridge, ate in a restaurant and then Gerry returned Kate to Girton.

'Can you get in?' he asked, surveying the dark building.

'Yes. Safe until eleven-fifteen.'

'After which you turn into a pumpkin and bounce through the windows.'

'That's a mixed metaphor,' she said severely, 'or something of the sort. Thank you for supper, Gerry. Will I see you tomorrow at Mark's tea party?'

'You certainly will. Good night, Kate.' He would have liked to have kissed her but she was already out of the car and away.

He drove back to Cambridge, whistling happily to himself. He

31

parked the car along the Backs and, feeling too keyed up to go to his room and face the essay he should have written yesterday, he decided to walk back to Trinity the long way round. He wandered up Queen's Road and Silver Street, pausing as he crossed the river to admire the Mathematical Bridge, and then went on, thinking of Kate. She was older than him, but that didn't matter – and oh, she was beautiful and she looked at him with such a look in those navy-blue eyes, so astonishing under the dark brows and the short black hair. He hadn't got from her what he'd got from Molly, but he'd enjoyed this evening with Kate more. He stopped and thought about this for a moment and decided, to his great amazement, that it was true. He laughed softly to himself and strolled on, his hands in his pockets, along King's Parade. King's College Chapel came into view, incomparable against an autumn moon. He laughed again. Life wasn't just good, it was the absolute tops.

In his exuberance, he turned a backward somersault – a trick he'd learned years ago – and then another, a series of them. He tumbled down King's Parade – four, five, six . . . and fetched up, panting, in front of two bowler-hatted figures.

'Having fun, are we, sir?' one enquired.

A proctor appeared, his white bands glimmering in the dark, and waved his two bulldogs away. They circled Gerry warily, as though expecting him to make a bolt for it.

'Are you a member of this University?' asked the proctor.

'I am,' Gerry said, trying to sound suitably deferential but unable to keep the exhilaration out of his voice.

He was fined six shillings and eightpence for not wearing his gown after dark and for conducting himself in a manner unbecoming in a member of his University and College.

Kate, the next morning, found her attention wandering from Professor Simmonds's lecture on anatomy.

Gerry was younger than she was but that didn't matter, did it? Once he had been assured that his dark secret was safe, he had been a delightful companion: amusing, charming and oh so handsome with that curly hair and those wonderful deep brown eyes. She would have liked him to kiss her but had found herself out of the car and away before giving him a chance.

She shook her head and concentrated on the lecture. Well-brought-up girls did not wish to be kissed by young men they had only just met, especially not girls who were the third generation of their family to attend Girton College, Cambridge, and who, like their father, intended to be a doctor. And who, in any case, had just rid herself of one determined suitor. . . . Gerry Beviss's face, wearing its slightly wicked grin, appeared in her mind in place of Lieutenant Simon Bray's rather heavy one, scowling in furious disappointment when she said she did not want to marry him. All that fuss because he was frightened people would find out he hadn't been to public school!

The lecture ended and Kate guiltily closed her notebook on a woefully empty page, went to find her bicycle and rode, panting and cursing the wind, the two miles back to Girton thinking that she could get in a bit of work before lunch to make up for the morning's lapse. But there was a letter from Simon in her pigeonhole, which had to be read although she was tempted to throw it straight into the wastepaper basket. This was her last chance, he told her. He was being posted to Singapore. Life on the naval base would be the most enormous fun for her, and was she sure she wouldn't change her mind? She sat at her desk and wrote to him, a friendly, firm and final no, and had at last begun to concentrate on her pathology when Vanessa knocked on her door and came in, her red hair flying.

'Kate!' she wailed. 'The Bagwigs – look!'

She handed over a sheet of paper which Kate took, smoothed out the creases made by Vanessa in her panic, and read no more than a polite request for Miss Hardgreaves to visit Miss Bailey at three o'clock that afternoon.

Miss Bailey, known as the Bagwigs, was their tutor. Vanessa, who seemed to identify her with the most fearsome of the mistresses at the school she had so recently left, went in living dread of her, but Kate liked her. She had been at Girton with Kate's grandmother and had been tutor to both her mother and her aunt during their time at the college. It was a link Kate valued, for her aunt was now her only living relative. Girton had first offered Kate a place in 1946 immediately after she had come out of the Wrens and, in the person of Miss Bailey, had been patient and supportive as she blundered around for a year wondering what to do. As long as there was a war on she had felt she was avenging her family's death, and peace had seemed to take the purpose out of her life. She was twenty-one now, and content that she had made the right decision to come to Cambridge and read medicine, as she had always intended to do.

She handed Vanessa back the note. 'What have you done this time?' she asked. Vanessa's life was a constant eruption of molehills and Kate, since her room was next to Vanessa's, was all too often called upon to deal with them.

'I don't *know*!' Vanessa absent-mindedly stuck a lock of hair in her mouth and chewed on it. 'Kate, what am I going to do?'

'You're going to leave me alone until lunch and at three you are going to see the Bagwigs. You can't do anything else,' Kate pointed out.

'I suppose not,' Vanessa said, taking the hair out of her mouth, staring at it and tossing it back over her shoulder.

'And at four, we are going to tea at Magdalene,' Kate reminded her, hoping her voice did not sound too eager.

A library book taken out in Vanessa's name had been found in the JCR. This would not normally entail a summons from a tutor, but it was the fourth time something similar had happened and the term was scarcely three weeks old.

'She was quite decent about it, though,' Vanessa said as they cycled to Cambridge for their tea party. 'She said it showed I was working, but I should take more care of College property. . . . I swear,' she panted, leaning on the bicycle pedals, 'that this road goes uphill both ways.'

'And the wind changes direction, too, have you noticed?' Kate said. 'It's against you both ways. Our foundress chose the site of her college with great care. The pleasures of Cambridge only to be sampled at great personal cost . . . huge muscular thighs and calves, chilblains and wind-roughened cheeks.'

They arrived at Magdalene, parked their bikes and walked through the main gate, the wild red head and the neat dark one together, and neither girl with anything approaching the physical defects they had so direly been predicting. Any number of undergraduates in the college were willing – positively eager – to direct them to Mark's staircase and to escort them there. These offers they laughingly rejected, found Mark's rooms without trouble and knocked on the door.

After a brief discussion, Mark, Gerry and James had decided not to ask anyone else to the tea party. The room, they told each other – utterly mendaciously – wasn't big enough, and neither was the tea. As Mark opened the door to his visitors, he caught the eye of his neighbour opposite. He had obviously been to a tutorial for he was wearing his gown and was carrying some books; he looked at Vanessa and Kate, and then at Mark with burning resentment. Mark ushered the girls in and callously shut the door.

'Come and sit by the fire,' he said, as he helped Vanessa off with her coat and James divested Kate of hers. 'We have such a tea for you, you've no idea . . . cake and wonderful biscuits and things . . . courtesy of Gerry,' he added conscientiously.

'My father,' Gerry said boldly, 'has contacts in the black market, I'm afraid.'

'Cake!' Vanessa exclaimed. 'Don't be apologetic for heaven's sake!' And Kate looked at Gerry with such understanding that he suddenly felt the need to sit down. He was furious that he hadn't known to go forward and take the girls' coats: all the women he'd ever known would have thought him some kind of pansy if he'd offered.

Mark went out to organise the tea and the other four sat down.

'Kate's reading medicine,' Gerry told James, wanting to establish an intimacy – any kind of one – with her.

James looked impressed. 'Really?' He paused. 'Does that mean you'll be a doctor?'

Everyone laughed, including James.

'It does – in six years' time, if I pass all my exams,' Kate said.

'Six years! I say!' James gazed at her with more admiration than Gerry thought necessary. 'Did you hear that?' he said to Mark as he came back into the room and sat beside Vanessa. 'Kate's going to be a doctor.'

'In this National Health thingy the Socialists are setting up?' Mark asked knowledgeably.

'I expect so.'

Mark turned to Vanessa. 'What are you reading?'

'Eng Lit,' she said, and they had that conversation which is as automatic as introductions among undergraduates who are meeting each other for the first time. Gerry and Mark were both reading history and James economics. Even on their short acquaintance with James, Kate and Vanessa were surprised by this though were too polite to show it, but James was quick to dispel any wrong impression.

'Only for a year. Couldn't manage any more. After that I change to land economy.'

'That sounds just as complicated,' Kate said.

'Oh it's not, I promise you,' James said. 'So long as you actually turn up for the exams they'll pass you.'

'I don't believe it,' Kate said firmly. But then perhaps she did: a nice soft subject for the sons of the landed gentry who thought they had a right to go to one of the great universities. There had even once been a name for it, she now remembered: the Poll degree. While women had to fight so hard for their places at their two colleges and got no degree at all. . . .

'Now there's one thing you can tell me,' Mark said, picking up Kate's thoughts although he did not know it. 'It's got me well and truly puzzled. Why don't women at Cambridge wear gowns? There's us going around like a horde of black bats and you looking perfectly normal. How come?'

Vanessa's soft brown eyes stared at him.

'Don't you know?'

'Haven't a clue.'

Vanessa exchanged a glance with Kate, and they both shrugged their shoulders.

'You really don't know that women aren't members of this University?'

'Aren't they?' Mark exclaimed. 'Why not?'

'The University won't admit us.'

'Well, I'm blowed,' Mark said. 'I didn't know that. Did you?' The other two men shook their heads.

'We don't get degrees,' Kate said. 'Only titular ones, a certificate saying what class we would have got if we had a degree. Lots of women have been classed first, but it doesn't really count.'

Vanessa tossed her wild hair. 'It's going to change, though. A Grace is coming up later this term.'

'Will it be passed?' Gerry asked.

'I should jolly well hope so,' Kate said. 'Twenty-seven years after Oxford admitted women. It's a disgrace.'

'I'll say it is! This is 1947, for God's sake.' Mark seemed genuinely put out. Gerry smiled at Kate.

'And then you'll wear gowns?'

'I suppose we will,' she said.

'I'm sure you'll look lovely in them.'

They set about Mrs Beviss's tea and the conversation turned to more general matters which meant, as far as James and Gerry were concerned, telling Kate all about their horses and the activities of the University Drag Hounds, and Mark trying to explain to Vanessa the finer points of rowing.

When, later, the girls said it was time for them to leave, Gerry grabbed Kate's coat, helped her on with it, opened the door and followed her out, thus gaining a start on the other three. She paused at the bottom of the staircase, but he hurried her on towards the gates.

'When can I see you again? How about a drink tomorrow night?'

'You don't hang around, do you?'

'Not when there's a girl like you surrounded by thousands of undergraduates starved of female company I don't,' he said.

Great heavens! Did she want this hard on the heels of Simon? But Gerry was so handsome and had such mischievous promise in his dark eyes. And he was sharp as a scalpel, too, watching, listening, learning . . . Where would it, all of it, end? He stood before her now, at Magdalene's gate.

'Say yes,' he pleaded.

She laughed. 'Well – yes.'

'I'll come for you at six.' He was going to kiss her then, just a little peck on the cheek, but the others came up and he didn't quite dare.

The three men escorted their guests to their bikes and watched them go off towards Castle Hill and distant Girton and then went back to Mark's rooms.

'I've got some sherry somewhere,' Mark said. 'Ah!' He produced a bottle and some glasses and poured them all a drink. 'Lovely girls,' he commented. 'I wish . . .' He paused. 'James, I got a note from Sophie today. She's coming to the ball at the Pitt Club with me.'

'Who's Sophie?' Gerry asked.

'My sister!' James exclaimed bitterly. 'And I'd as soon take a boa constrictor to a dance. Or a wasp. She's a – a . . .' Words failed him and he took a gulp of his sherry instead.

'Who are you bringing, Gerry?' Mark asked.

Gerry stared at him. 'But it isn't for – what? – four or five weeks.'

'Book 'em early,' Mark advised.

Gerry turned to James. 'Have you invited a girl to this ball?'

James nodded. 'Back in September. Alice Camphrey. Nice girl, Alice . . . If I hadn't, though, I tell you I'd ask Kate Earith. Like a shot I would.'

'And I'd ask Vanessa,' Mark said.

James handed him his glass for a refill. 'But now you're stuck with my witch of a sister, aren't you?'

'I thought you were supposed to be watching your weight,' Gerry said irritably.

'I am, dear boy, I am. It's your mother's cakes. I can't resist 'em. She sends him one a week,' James said to Kate. '*Objets d'art*, I assure you. Each a perfect poem.'

'Haven't you some work to do?' Gerry enquired hopefully. 'An essay to write, lecture notes to ponder over – anything like that?'

'Yes,' said James, helping himself to another slice of Mrs Beviss's ginger cake, 'all of those things.'

Gerry sighed. He didn't mind James eating the cake but he wanted time alone with Kate. Whenever he invited her to tea, James would lounge in, sit himself down and generally settle in for the duration. It was even worse when Gerry went to see Kate at Girton – half the population of the college seemed to knock on her door wanting something or other, and often he had to give a lift to Mark so he could moon over Vanessa and the thing turned into a foursome. He and Kate would go to the friendly pub at Madingley, to a dance at Dot's or out to supper somewhere, but that could hardly be classed as being alone either. He just wanted to have all her attention, to know that she was thinking of him and only him. He hadn't even kissed her yet, not properly, and at least, he told himself fretfully, a chap should be able to kiss his girl occasionally. That's all he wanted. (He could hear the lads at home saying, 'Go on, Gerry, pull the other one,' but it was true.) He thought he was probably in love with her, but he never seemed to have a chance to find out.

She looked at him and gave him a gorgeous smile. He felt his heart lurch and a lump formed in his throat.

'Kate, didn't you use to ride?' James was saying now.

'*Used* to,' she murmured.

'You don't forget how. It's like riding a bike. Why don't you come out with the Drag one day? The hired horses aren't bad and it's terrific fun, isn't it, Gerry?'

'Yes,' Gerry said.

'I don't have the gear.'

'Send home for it, then.'

'Yes,' Gerry said. 'Why don't you come out for a day? You'd enjoy it.' He'd like to show Florin off to her.

'No.' She seemed, uncharacteristically, flustered. 'I don't have the gear,' she repeated.

'Get your people to send it,' James persisted.

She began to collect her things. 'I don't have any people, James,' she said. 'My parents, my brother, my grandmother *and* my pony all died when a bomb hit my parents' house. My riding gear was somewhere in there too. . . . And now I must go.'

'I'm terribly sorry,' whispered James, and Gerry sat in his chair staring straight ahead, looking as though he had been pole-axed.

'You weren't to know,' she said. 'It was a long time ago – over three years – but little things still get to me unexpectedly. Like thinking of my riding boots under a heap of rubble.' She laughed shakily. 'It's silly, but I can't help it.'

Gerry, his face frozen in shock, got to his feet.

'I'll see you to your bike,' he muttered and opened the door for her.

When they were outside in New Court, he took her arm and hustled her through the gate that led to Trinity Bridge and down to one of the willow trees that grew on the riverbank. He stood over her, his hands on the tree trunk on either side of her head.

'Oh Kate, I'm sorry,' he said after a moment.

'It doesn't matter, Gerry, really—'

'It *does* matter. Of course it does.' She had never heard him sound like that before and looked up, trying to see his face in the feeble light that came from the buildings behind him. 'It matters because your family is dead and it matters because I didn't know. I never asked you about yourself, just went on about me all the time, even telling you about my brother Eric so you'd feel sorry for me, and he died much longer ago . . . Kate, I'm a selfish pig.' His hands dropped to her shoulders. 'Will you forgive me?'

He sounded grown up. That was the difference. She moved forward and he put his arms around her.

'Gerry, of course I forgive you. I should have told you anyway.'

'Why didn't you?'

'I try to forget about it, I suppose.'

Her cheek was on the lapel of his tweed jacket. She felt his warm lips nuzzling her ear and turned her face upward. It was a long kiss, gentle, exploratory, totally unlike Simon's workmanlike no-nonsense ones.

'Ah Kate,' Gerry said, 'why did I take so long to do that?' And then, because it was so very lovely and he felt so tender, he did it again.

'You're trembling,' he said, and held her very close.

'So are you.' They both laughed.

'It's a bit much,' he said a little later, 'when the only place I can get my girl alone is on a frozen riverbank in the pitch dark.'

'Am I your girl?' she asked shyly.

'I hope so, Kate. Lord, I wish I could see you. Are you looking at me with those wonderful eyes?'

She chuckled. 'Well, since I'm looking in your general direction, I suppose I must be.'

'I think,' he said, 'I'll tell my mother to stop sending those cakes and things. James might leave us alone then.'

'Poor James. Will you apologise to him and tell him it wasn't his fault?'

'All right.'

'And now, Gerry, I must go.'

'I'll drive you.'

'No.'

'Please.'

'No.'

'Kiss me again, then.'

'*Yes!*'

Gerry arrived back at his rooms feeling – what was it the Americans said? – like a million dollars, to find Mark and James sitting in an atmosphere of the deepest gloom. Mark was wearing a dinner jacket, and Gerry remembered that they were all going to a dinner at St Catharine's to celebrate Andrew Coleridge's twenty-first birthday. A celebration – just what Gerry felt like.

'Cheer up, you two,' he said. 'You look as jolly as a brace of undertakers.'

'Gerry!' Mark said reprovingly. 'James has told me – he's frightfully upset, absolutely wallowing in remorse. I had to give him a slug of your whisky.'

James raised a face full of misery. 'How is Kate?'

'She's . . . she's fantastic! James, old thing, she says she's sorry for making a scene and it wasn't your fault. You're not to think about it again.'

James brightened. 'Really?'

'Really, honestly and truly.'

'Thank God for that! Well, I'd better go and change.' He poured himself another whisky from Gerry's bottle and disappeared, taking the glass with him.

Mark settled himself on Gerry's sofa and picked up his own glass.

'Had to keep him company,' he explained. 'You don't mind, do you?'

'Help yourself.'

'Thanks,' Mark said. 'Well, get a bustle on,' he added as Gerry hovered in the doorway of his bedroom. 'You look as though you're about to explode.'

'Isn't Kate beautiful? Isn't she the absolute bloody tops?'

41

Mark smiled. 'You're a lucky man, Gerry.'

The next morning Kate received a letter from her Aunt Beattie, with whom – and her Uncle Charles – she now lived.

You mentioned Gerald Beviss in one of your letters and, funnily enough, his name came up at a dinner at John and Elizabeth Holland's last night. A woman who lives near Rye is staying with them and when Elizabeth asked after you, naturally I mentioned Cambridge. The woman (I can't remember her name, not that it matters) said it was the talk of the area how young Gerald won a scholarship to Trinity. The Rector even preached a sermon about him and work getting its just reward. His brother is a fishmonger and so proud of Gerald, the woman says, that it almost makes one weep. His fish, apparently, is excellent. She also said he – Gerald – is a bit of a one for the girls but annoyingly couldn't give chapter and verse. So you, my darling, had better watch out. . . .

Kate laughed out loud. Too late, Beattie dearest. Too damned late.

Chapter 4

Florin rose at a hedge, stretched in mid-air to clear the ditch on the landing side and galloped across the next field.

' 'Ware hounds!' James cried away to his right and they both took a pull to prevent their horses running down the slowest hounds that made up the Cambridge University Drag Hounds pack. The rest of the field came to a halt behind them and a loose horse careered past. The Master and his two whippers-in veered across the field in front of them as the hounds scrambled through a five-barred gate.

'The hedge must be wired,' Gerry said, and they moved their horses over and waited for the hunt officials to go.

Suddenly it was like a scene from a silent film. The Master took the gate first, his horse hit the top and he was pitched off it into a ditch on the right. The first whipper-in, Andrew Coleridge – whose birthday they had celebrated two weeks ago – realising that the hounds were now in his charge, rode wildly at the gate, rose bravely and, for no particular reason that Gerry could see, horse and rider landed in different places. The second whipper-in's horse frankly refused to consider jumping the gate at all.

James whooped. 'It's up to you and me, Gerry boy! That show jumper of yours can give us a lead.'

Gerry collected Florin and set him at the gate: one, two, three ... hup! Copybook, as though he was schooling in the paddock at home. He approached the two loose horses slowly, not wanting to frighten them off, but they were caught easily enough and Gerry cantered back with them to Stephen White, the Master.

Stephen grabbed the reins, flung one lot at a rather dazed-looking Andrew, jammed his hat back on his head and swore bitterly as water poured down his face and neck. James had jumped the gate safely and was trying to tell Stephen something.

'Get after the bloody hounds!' Stephen shouted, trying to remount his horse, which wouldn't stand still.

Gerry wheeled Florin. 'Any wire?' He wasn't going to risk his horse for any number of hounds.

'Take the far gate, then it's clear. *Go*, damn you!'

They jumped the next gate carefully. The hounds were in full cry three fields away.

'Now we can go!' James yelled. 'Tally ho!' and they set their horses at a line of black cut-and-laid hedges reaching to the horizon. Florin and Castor, fired by their riders, began to race each other, the bay head stretching out next to the brown one. Gerry had never ridden Florin flat out before, never known how fast he was, never jumped a fence pushing on from a full gallop. Florin took off for each hedge upsides Castor, flattened over it and galloped on without checking. . . . Nothing but Gerry and a powerful horse and a line of hedges. James's shouts came on the wind, seeming from a great distance.

'Whoa, whoa! We're here.'

The mad gallop was over and they slowed their horses and brought them to a steaming halt. The hounds had reached the end of the line and were milling around grinning and panting. Gerry and James herded them into order and presented them to Stephen White when he and Andrew Coleridge arrived with the rest of the field a few minutes later. Of the second whipper-in there was no sign.

The owner of the land over which the line had been laid was heaving with laughter.

'By heaven!' he exclaimed. 'I haven't had so much fun in years. The Master and whipper-in coming to grief at my gate and then getting back on to the wrong horses . . . Oh my Lord.' He drew a large handkerchief from the pocket of his pink cutaway coat and blew his nose loudly. 'Oh, come on, boy,' he said to Stephen White, who was sitting – on the right horse – staring rigidly ahead, 'we all take a tumble now and again . . . though to be sure most of us recognise our own horse.' Laughter threatened to engulf him again. 'Come on!' he roared. 'Everyone to the manor for tea. All welcome!'

They made for the gate of the field and the horse boxes which were parked in the lane running alongside. Gerry's car was there, driven by Kate, and Mark – who had come along because he had heard about Raphael Rayner's legendary hospitality – was in James's MG.

Gerry dismounted and Tomás ran up the stirrups, loosened the girths and threw a rug over Florin's back.

'You were the absolute tops,' Gerry told his horse, and Florin grabbed the sleeve of his hunting coat between his teeth. 'Nah, come on, you silly beast . . . let go.'

'He's splendid, Gerry. No wonder you're so proud of him.'

Kate was beside him. She patted Florin's sweaty neck and pulled his ears.

'Did you have a good time?' Gerry asked her.

'Oh, yes! We could see it all from the road. Lots of people fell off and then there was all that fun at the gate, and then you and James galloped in the way they brought the good news from Ghent to Aix. I think the other whipper-in is still trying to find gates to open. His horse refused to contemplate jumping another thing . . . Oh I *did* enjoy myself, but my feet are cold.' She stamped them. They were encased in a pair of sensible brogues and she was wearing a blue tweed coat. Her cheeks were pink beneath a dark blue woollen hat that matched her eyes. She looked lovely.

'And my car is still in one piece, is it?' he teased, hoping to provoke one of those direct gazes from her which made him go weak at the knees. His ploy worked.

'I was a Wren driver!' she said, outraged. 'And you've got mud on your face.'

He laughed and put his arm around her as they walked towards his car.

'Well, you can Wren drive me to this manor place, then,' he said.

Those with dirty hunting boots and coats left them in a back kitchen, and everyone was directed to various bathrooms where

45

they could wash the worst of the mud off themselves. They then went into the huge dining room, the table laid for twenty or more, and were offered everything from boiled eggs and fruit cake to venison or steak and kidney pie and apple crumble. Raphael Rayner evidently didn't believe in post-war austerity or rationing. Mrs Rayner and a maiden aunt poured endless cups of tea and plied them with more and more food until even James had to admit himself bested. Raphael Rayner, having bathed and changed, came in half an hour after the rest of them had sat down and took his place at the head of the table. His wife poured him a cup of tea, which was conveyed to him by the butler. He peered at it, apparently revolted by the sight.

'Clipper!' he bellowed. 'Oh . . . there you are. Take away this nonsense and bring some whisky.'

Clipper bowed and went away, returning a few minutes later with three bottles which he put on the table, one at each end and the other in the middle, while his underlings removed unwanted teacups and replaced them with glasses. Even Stephen White – in his third year at Mark's college, Magdalene – began to mellow under the onslaught and joined in the ribald greeting of John Winter, the second whipper-in, who arrived a full hour late.

'Well, at least I didn't fall off,' he said, staring significantly at Stephen's mud-spattered waistcoat and Andrew's cut forehead and nicely ripening black eye.

'Even you couldn't fall off a horse that doesn't actually break out of a trot,' James said.

John ignored all further remarks and began to eat his way steadily through the dishes that were presented to him.

Raphael proposed a toast to the Cambridge University Drag Hounds and all who sailed in her, and Stephen made a graceful speech thanking Mr Rayner for his more than generous hospitality (shouts of 'Hear, hear!') and the members of the Fitzwilliam Hunt for their support. One of these, an elegant-looking man with silver hair, then proposed a toast to the noble sport of hunting and went on to say he looked forward to a rematch between James's and Gerry's horses at the University point-to-point.

'And I don't know which I'd put my money on,' he said. 'Damn me, I don't know,' and he sat down rather heavily.

46

'I'd go for the brown horse,' someone said.

'No, I think I'd have to go for the bay,' the silver-haired man said.

'We'll take bets!' Raphael bawled. 'Clipper, bring us some paper!'

Mrs Rayner rose to her feet. 'I think perhaps the ladies might care to retire,' she suggested delicately.

'Not bloody likely!' Raphael's slightly bloodshot eyes turned on Kate, who was sitting on his left. 'What?'

'*I* certainly won't retire, Margery,' the woman on his other side said calmly. 'I'm having much too much fun.' She was about forty and, Kate remembered, had ridden side-saddle and looked most graceful. She caught Kate's eye and smiled.

'See?' Raphael said to his wife. 'We don't want to lose you, my dear.'

Then the maiden aunt spoke for the first time.

'I've been watching that young man for some while, and he's gone quite white. I do believe he's going to faint.'

And Andrew Coleridge's eyes turned up in his head and he fell sideways off his chair and on to the floor.

Gerry drove into the courtyard at Girton and stopped the car.

'It's not late,' he said. 'Are you sure you don't want to go out and eat?'

'*Food!*' she exclaimed. '*More food?* No – and I must do some work, and so should you, I'm sure.'

'Probably.'

'I did enjoy my day out,' she said. 'Are the meets of the Drag Hounds always so full of incident?'

He laughed. 'Something odd usually happens, but today was special.'

'I'm glad Andrew is all right.'

The Cambridge contingent had expected Kate to do something about Andrew's prone body, but the silver-haired man had turned out to be a doctor. He had sobered miraculously and had, charmingly, invited Kate to confirm his diagnosis of a mild concussion exacerbated by alcohol.

Gerry put his arm around Kate, drew her to him and kissed her.

47

'Are you really sending me away?'

'I am. Let me go, Gerry.'

'Shall I tell you something?'

'What is that?'

'I think I'm in love with you.'

She was silent.

'Well – what do you make of that?'

'You're . . . you're too young to be saying such things.'

'Young in years, perhaps,' he whispered, 'but old in experience.'

'Oh be off with you,' she said crossly and got out of the car.

She was walking down the corridor to her room, her feet feeling as if they were not quite touching the ground, when she saw someone coming towards her – someone small and plump and very much loved. Kate stopped for a moment and stared, thinking the food and the drink and what Gerry had just said had produced hallucinations. Her aunt? Beattie – planting her little fat feet upon the polished wooden floors of Girton as she had done twenty-five years ago?

Kate rushed forward.

'What are you doing here?' she cried. 'Nothing's the matter, is it? Charles—'

'Nothing at all is the matter,' Beattie replied. 'Your uncle is as fit as a flea, though rather grumpy when I spoke to him on the phone at being deserted. Old Sally Cresset died, you see. I went to the funeral in Colchester, and when I arrived at the station to go home the train for Cambridge was being announced, and, well' – Beattie paused, apparently alarmed at her own impulsiveness – 'well, I remembered the Grace to admit women was coming before the Regent House tomorrow and I thought it would be such fun to be here. You don't mind, do you?'

'Mind? Of course not! I'm just sorry I was out.'

Beattie allowed herself to be turned around and propelled back towards Kate's room.

'I've had the most splendid time,' she said. 'When you weren't here I went to see the Bagwigs and was invited to dinner. I sat at High Table, which was most exciting, though the food was awful (oh, you poor darlings!). If you weren't back, I was to have taken

48

cocoa with the bursar, and I have been given a key to a guest room. How perfectly thrilling,' she went on placidly, 'to spend another night under Girton's roof. . . . But where have you been, my darling? Not that I wish to pry, of course, but a delightful girl, who from your letters must be Vanessa, told me you were with the *drag*, which sounds most odd.'

Flushing slightly, Kate told her about Gerry and the events of the day, and Beattie listened and said, when she had finished:

'Well, you have been having a splendid time too, and this Gerry sounds much more entertaining than Simon.'

'Oh he is, he is!' Kate said.

And Beattie had to agree when, the next day, they were in Cambridge and heard that the Grace admitting women to the University had been passed without a single dissenting voice, and they met Gerry in King's Parade. He seemed as thrilled about the news as they were, but was put out that they were on their way to the Copper Kettle to have tea.

'But shouldn't you be at Girton to celebrate?' he said. 'Surely you should be there!' He turned to Kate, his handsome face all sweet concern. 'I've got some things left over from Ma – my mother's – last parcel. Why not take them?'

Kate looked at Beattie. 'He's right. We *should* be at Girton. Great heavens, we might be first with the news . . . especially if,' she said, her eyes sliding up at Gerry, 'we were given a lift and could beat the buses and bicycles.'

'Of course I'll give you a lift,' he said. 'My Kate, of course I will.'

They rushed to New Court, Beattie panting to keep up, and Gerry drove them to Girton, helped them out of the car and thrust the package of his mother's black-market delicacies at them.

'But you must join us,' Beattie said. 'We can't accept these unless you do.'

'Yes you can – easily.' He flashed a grin that utterly devastated her. 'Anyway, it's definitely an all-girl affair.'

Beattie was enchanted and would not let him go until he agreed to have dinner with her and Kate at the University Arms that evening.

'He is delightful,' she told Charles when she arrived home after her errant forty-eight hours. 'Charles, my darling, he is delightful. I have quite fallen in love with him.'

James erupted into Mark's rooms.

'Disaster!' he announced.

Mark was changing out of his rowing things. 'What sort of disaster?'

'A treble whisky disaster, that's what.'

'Isn't it a little early in the day for that? Anyway, I haven't got any whisky.'

'Send your gyp out for some.'

Mark took off his shorts and pulled on trousers and a shirt. 'What's happened?'

'Chickenpox!' James held up the letter he was holding in his hand. 'This is from Alice's mother. Alice has chickenpox and can't come on Friday. . . . Chickenpox!' he exclaimed disgustedly. 'At her age! Who am I going to ask to the ball at two days' notice?'

Mark sat down to put on his shoes and socks.

'You could ask Vanessa,' he said. 'I wish *I* could. Sophie was jolly unfriendly at Priscilla Gwyn-Jones's cocktail party last week.'

'It's when she's friendly you have to worry,' James told him.

Mark had gone to the party in London in the hope that Sophie Flimwell would tell him that she preferred to go to the ball with one of her other many admirers. She had ignored him until she was leaving to go on to a nightclub with a crowd of friends, when she had asked him casually if he had booked her into a hotel in Cambridge.

'She's a devil,' James said of his sister. 'I warned you.'

Mark picked up his gown from the back of a chair and put it on. 'Look, old chap, I've got a lecture at eleven, and I must dash.'

'Fat lot of help you've been,' James grumbled as he followed Mark down the stairs.

'Ask Vanessa,' Mark said. 'The worst she can do is say no. Why not talk to Kate about it if you're worried?' They crossed the road and went into the bicycle shed. 'Where the hell's my bike?'

He found it, shoved his lecture notes into the basket, and they rode across Magdalene Bridge.

'I tell you one thing,' said Mark. 'Gerry's the lucky one. He's actually going with the woman he wants to be with.'

'Yes,' said James. 'He's going with Kate.'

'Of course she won't mind being asked at forty-eight hours' notice,' Kate said to James. 'Great heavens, she has trouble remembering what she's supposed to be doing from one second to the next.'

So James asked Vanessa, who accepted. She had an evening dress; she even had shoes and a bag to match.

'They are my mother's. She made me bring them just in case,' she said to Kate. 'Will I look all right?'

'You'll look lovely,' Kate said.

Chapter 5

Kate opened the door to Gerry's knock and they stood there a little self-consciously, unaccustomed to seeing each other in formal clothes.

'Am I allowed to touch you?' Gerry said at last. He took one of her gloved hands, leaned forward and kissed her gently on the cheek. 'You look . . . you look the absolute tops!'

She laughed, and the tiny constraint between them vanished.

'That's what you say to your horse.'

'It's what I say when words fail me.'

'Then *you* look the absolute tops, too.'

Men were not supposed to be called beautiful, but Kate could not think of another adjective to describe Gerry tonight. He was wearing the dark green tail coat with the white collar and lapels and brass buttons that was the formal evening livery of members of the Cambridge University Drag Hounds. His stiff shirt and white tie glowed beneath his vibrant dark face and curly black hair.

'Is Vanessa ready?' he asked.

'She's all dressed but she's writing an essay.'

'She's doing *what*?'

'Well, I've been studying Pinocchio,' Kate said, indicating her skeleton.

She fetched her wrap and he put it around her shoulders and then helped her on with her coat.

'I like that lipstick,' he said, 'but does it mean I can't kiss you properly?'

'It does.'

He pulled her towards him and stooped his head.

'Really?' he murmured.

'Now see what you've done,' she said a little later. 'You're covered in the beastly stuff.'

'It was worth it.'

'Don't talk.'

She wiped his lips and retouched her own, then they collected Vanessa who was, indeed, sitting at her desk wearing her green evening gown and writing furiously. She had been to a hairdresser's that afternoon and her hair was piled on the top of her head in coils of shining red.

'It's all done with lacquer,' she said to Gerry when he admired it. 'Knock it and it'll come to pieces, I promise you.'

'I'll do no such thing,' he said, and offered the girls an arm each. 'Shall we go?'

'Oh I say,' said James gallantly, 'don't you two look something?' He kissed Vanessa and Kate, took their coats and began opening a bottle of champagne.

'Where are the others?' Gerry asked.

James shrugged. 'Mark came for the car to collect Sophie ages ago. She usually takes about twenty-four hours to get ready so with a bit of luck we won't see her at all. Ready with the glasses, Gerry?'

He poured out the champagne and handed it around.

'A toast,' he said, and they all raised their glasses.

The door flew open just then and a blonde girl followed by Mark came in. The four people in the room, still with their glasses raised, turned. It was as though they were in a tableau, frozen in position, toasting the girl as she paused in the doorway, her eyes sweeping past her brother, past Kate and Vanessa (a flicker of interest there: danger? No, none) and alighting on Gerry. She slipped off her cloak and tossed it in Mark's general direction.

'Well,' she said. 'Who is this? Introduce us, James.'

'Gerry,' James mumbled. 'Gerry Beviss . . . my sister Sophie.' He introduced her to Kate and Vanessa but she paid no attention.

'Gerry!' she said. 'I've never seen you at any of the parties. Aren't you on the lists?'

'He's got better things to do than chase around your silly affairs,' said James.

She hunched a bare shoulder at him. 'You don't like them, but Gerry might. Wouldn't you like to come to some of our parties? I'm sure you'd be very popular.' She smiled at him and took the glass of champagne he was holding. 'Is this for me?'

She was very beautiful, and her dress was cut so low he could see the edge of her nipples. But it was not that which was holding his attention. It was something else. She reminded him of someone. Not the way she looked or sounded: that couldn't be more different . . . She reminded him of Molly. He felt a surge of desire . . . it had been so long. No, no, he thought desperately, and went over to Kate.

'You haven't got a drink,' she pointed out.

'No. It got swiped.' He glanced at Sophie and she raised her glass – his glass – to him. To show her who he belonged to, he took a sip of Kate's champagne before going off to find some of his own.

Twelve of them had clubbed together and taken one of the private dining rooms for their pre-ball dinner. Vanessa and Kate were the only girls from Cambridge there, for all day the London trains had been disgorging chattering flocks of society maidens. Several of them were here now, calling each other 'darling' and flinging their arms around each other's necks and loudly kissing the air as though they had not seen one another the previous night and probably the night before that as well. Kate felt dull in comparison, the red dress she had thought so smart seemed dowdy, and she was out of place among these girls whose lives were given over to the pursuit of pleasure and suitable husbands. The feeling was compounded every time she was introduced to them.

'Oh *Girton*,' they would say, and look at her as though she came from another planet.

And there was Sophie. She had seated herself determinedly on Gerry's other side and she and her outrageous dress were doing all they could to attract Gerry's attention, though so far without success.

So far.

It was snowing when they left for the Pitt Club. Great Court was already turning white and the maidens squealed about the hems of their dresses and damage to their shoes and hair. Sophie attempted to commandeer Gerry's free arm, saying she was sure she would fall over if she was not supported on both sides. Gerry shook her off, pointing out that there wasn't room for four abreast unless she wanted to walk on the cobbles, and she laughed and said that *for now* she would have to rely on Mark. They crossed Trinity Street and went into Whewell's Court opposite. The little courtyards were filling up with snow. Yellow light came from the windows where sensible undergraduates were working or playing records or talking among friends. Kate suddenly wished she was there with them, or back in her cosy room at Girton – anywhere but walking through the snow towards the Pitt Club, which would be full of smart girls calling each other 'darling'. . . .

And Sophie. And Sophie . . . The two words went in rhythm with her footsteps and she went down Jesus Lane with them thudding in her ears.

They arrived at the Pitt. Kate followed the others into the ladies' cloakroom – or the place that had been set aside for them that night, because, of course, usually women weren't allowed into the Pitt Club at all.

She checked her make-up and re-applied her lipstick. Vanessa's face appeared in the mirror beside hers.

'How extraordinary,' she said, 'my hair is still in one piece. Ready?' She closed her bag and took Kate's arm. 'Come along. Let's show them that the girls of Girton can go with the best of them.'

Out in the foyer, Sophie had hold of Gerry's hand and was trying to pull him towards the dancing. He saw Kate, and, laughing, he freed his hand.

'I'm going to dance with my girl,' he said, and came over to her. 'Aren't I?' he said, touching her cheek.

They disappeared in the direction of the music, followed by Vanessa and James. Mark looked at Sophie.

'So,' he said grimly, 'you're left with me.'

She gazed back at him speculatively.

'Yes,' she said, 'but you're in love with Vanessa and James has fallen for Kate. So I'd be doing you both a good turn by getting Gerry out of the way, wouldn't I?'

'You little minx!' he exclaimed. 'Come on.' He took her hand, resolving not to let her out of his sight for the rest of the night.

Gerry loved dancing with Kate, loved the way she smiled up at him, loved her eyes gazing into his. He loved *her*, didn't he? Then why was he so conscious of the other pair of eyes — bright blue ones, not a beautiful navy like Kate's — on him the whole time? What did he want with her, for God's sake? He was the lucky one, he reminded himself: there was Mark wanting to be with Vanessa; there was James with Vanessa but wanting to be with Alice who was covered with chickenpox; and here was he with Kate, his girl. He was the happiest man in the place.

So there wasn't much danger, was there, in having just one dance with Sophie when Kate went to the ladies' cloakroom some time later. Sophie put her arms around his neck and pushed her body against his, her breasts scarcely held in by the top of her dress against his stiff white shirt. He couldn't help looking down and she couldn't help noticing. She laughed softly and they danced on, very close. The music stopped and he took her arm to lead her off the floor. 'One more,' she said, and he waited, transfixed by her, a rabbit in front of a ferret, until the music started once more and she wrapped her arms around his neck and ground her body against him.

Kate came back and found Mark alone. He handed her a drink.

'I got this for Sophie, but you can have it.'

'Where is Gerry?'

'Dancing,' he said shortly.

'Oh.'

'Only one, he said.'

But the music stopped and started again; and again. And then again. She lost count. Mark invited her to dance but she didn't want to see what she might see if she went in there. James and Vanessa appeared and Mark, having punctiliously asked James's permission, took Vanessa away for a dance, his face at last showing its charming smile.

'What is happening, James?' Kate asked.

He shook his head miserably and she knew the answer, but her face was calm and she looked as she always did – very peaceful and lovely. She smiled and chatted when friends came up and showed no sign of the anguish and humiliation she must be feeling. James wanted to ask her to dance so he could put his arms around her and comfort her, but he couldn't take her into the room where she would see, in a corner, the dark head and the blonde one so close together. He felt furious with Gerry: how could he go off and leave Kate in this way?

Vanessa came up, Mark, no longer smiling, trailing behind her.

'Kate, do you realise what the time is? We must go.'

'Yes,' said Kate, immeasurably relieved. 'Let's go.'

When they got outside, they found that the snow had stopped but it was lying deep on the road. James suggested they wait inside while he fetched the car, but Kate didn't feel she could stay anywhere near the Pitt Club for another second. Instead, she and Vanessa hitched up their skirts and, like the page in the Christmas carol, trod in the footprints left by the men. They reached Trinity, their feet numb with cold, and the porter resolutely refused to allow them to take a short cut through the college to the Backs, where James's car was parked.

'Oh, come on, Mr McGibbons,' James pleaded.

'The back gates are closed, Mr Flimwell,' the man said, 'and I'm not opening them, not for no one and any amount of snow. You know that! I'll be closing this one in fifteen minutes so you'd better get a move on.'

He consented to allow Vanessa and Kate to sit in his lodge while James and Mark went to collect the car, and he contributed two ancient pairs of wellington boots.

'What a night,' Mark said as they tramped down Trinity Lane.

'Yes. Stephen's cancelled the Drag tomorrow.'

'I wasn't referring to the weather.'

James sighed. 'I know . . . Mark, did Vanessa see them?'

'Who?'

'You know who.'

'Yes.'

'Why didn't you keep her back towards them? I did.'

'I tried. Anyway, what difference does it make?'

'I don't want Kate to know, that's all.'

Mark kicked at the snow on Garret Hostel Bridge.

'Of course she bloody knows. Gerry dumped her, for God's sake. Dumped her in front of everyone for that trollop of a sister of yours. And don't,' he added wearily, 'say I told you so again. Anyway, Sophie dumped *me*, don't forget.'

'Yes, but you're not hurt, are you? I could murder the pair of them,' James said, 'for what they did to Kate.'

They reached the car and swept the snow from it, and then they had to push it to get the engine started. They arrived, slithering, back at Trinity's Porters' Lodge to find Kate and Vanessa, pink-cheeked and warm, mugs of cocoa in their hands, being regaled by Mr McGibbons with tales of the exploits of past undergraduates.

'This lot, misses,' he said, jerking his thumb at Mark and James, 'have nothing on them pre-war bunch of young gentlemen. No imagination, understand? And how,' he added, eyeing James fiercely, 'are you planning to get back into College tonight since I'm locking up now and late already?'

'Mr McGibbons,' James said sweetly, 'I haven't a clue.'

The two-mile drive back to Girton took over half an hour as the MG slid around in the snow, and twice Kate had to clamber into the driver's seat so James and Mark could push. When they finally arrived James was instructed to turn the car down the road that led to Girton village.

'Now what?' he asked.

'We climb in,' Kate said. 'We would have had to anyway. We didn't get late passes.'

That had been Gerry's idea. They didn't want a mad dash to get back by midnight, he said. Would this night ever end, though?

They all got out of the car, walked to the main gates and ducked under the trees flanking the driveway.

'Which direction?' James whispered.

'To the left,' Vanessa said.

The four of them crept up to the left wing of the college and edged along it.

'What are we supposed to be doing?' Mark asked James in an undertone.

'Looking for open windows, I suppose.'

'But there are millions of them, and who'd leave one open on a night like this?' Mark's voice had risen as the enormity of the task facing them registered and three dark figures, their feet buried in snow, turned on him, fingers to their lips.

'Ssh!'

'Sorry.'

'Look – tracks,' James whispered a few moments later. He pointed.

Kate peered at them. 'Are they human?'

'I think so.'

'Let's follow them. Felicity Myers's room is along here. She's half expecting us, but I can't remember which window it is.'

They tiptoed on until an extraordinary noise coming from Mark – sounding like a combination between a cough and a burp – caused the other three to turn on him again.

'I'm sorry,' he said. 'Really I'm trying not to laugh, but—'

'Ssh,' they told him.

'But James bent double like a truffle hound, his tails hanging out from under his coat and those old boots and . . . and you two following him like a pair of anxious dog handlers . . . I'm sorry, but it's very funny.' He put his hand to his mouth to try and prevent the noise escaping.

Then the others did see the funny side to it and the strain of the whole dreadful evening was released by all of them in hysterical suppressed laughter. Mark stepped forward, tripped over something hidden in the snow and fell flat on his face. Vanessa went to help him up, tripped over the same thing he had and landed on top of him. And Mark, his laughter notwithstanding, with great presence of mind put his arms around her and kissed her purposefully. James groped his way to Kate, who leaned against him weakly, tears running down her cheeks, her breath ragged from the effort of keeping the laughter in.

'Have you got a handkerchief?' she gasped.

He fished in the pocket of his coat, produced one and she took it and blew her nose.

'Ssh!' they all said.

'Help – sorry,' she said, and James took the handkerchief from her and wiped the tears away and then bent and kissed her.

'Just to comfort you,' he said, and did it again. There were tears on her cheeks again, but not of laughter this time. He pulled her against him and held her.

A window grated open. Vanessa and Mark scrambled to their feet, both of them covered in snow, and all four of them froze in horror.

'For heaven's sake,' said a disgruntled voice, 'do you want to come in or not?'

'Do you know what Sophie said to me?' Mark said when he and James were back in the car and making their cautious way to Cambridge.

'I didn't realise she'd spoken to you at all.'

'No – seriously.'

'What – *seriously*?'

'She said she'd be doing us both a good turn by getting Gerry out of the way.'

James was silent.

'And damn it all,' Mark went on, 'she was right. I mean, it didn't turn out so badly after all, did it?'

Gerry awoke and groaned as hideous white light assaulted his eyes. He looked at his watch. Eleven o'clock. He groaned again, turned over on to his stomach and hid his face in the pillow. *What had he done?* The only good thing coming out of the events of last night was that he had woken up in his own bed. That, at least, he had refused her.

He had wanted to get back to Kate after the second dance, but Sophie had wrapped her arms around him and held on and the music had started again. Then – when? – the lights had been dimmed and she had fastened her lips on to his – she was only eighteen, for God's sake: where had she learned all those tricks? – and every time he tried to pull away (though you couldn't have tried very hard, could you? he asked himself savagely) her arms

60

had tightened around the back of his neck and she had thrust her tongue further down his throat. Even so, he didn't think he had been away long when the lights were turned up and the last dance had been announced.

He had broken away from her then, freed himself from the grasping hands, and gone in search of Kate. She had left long since, of course, and Mark and Vanessa and James.

What had he done?

Cars had turned up outside the Pitt Club and Sophie had pushed him into the back of one and then clambered in and sat herself on his knee, and someone called Philip – he had been at Emmanuel before the war – had driven through the snow back to the Garden House Hotel where they were all staying. The night porter had tried to refuse to serve them drinks but Philip had tucked a five-pound note into his breast pocket and then another one and told him to bring along some bottles of champagne like a good chap, and they'd all sit quiet as mice in the lounge and drink them.

So they had sat there – not quiet as mice at all – and drunk champagne, though no amount of the stuff could lift the dreadful darkness that surrounded Gerry as he thought of Kate waiting and waiting for him. Then Sophie had whispered that he looked *tired*, sneaked him her door key and told him she'd distract the night porter and meet him upstairs.

He had hated her then. In front of everyone, he had handed back the door key, said, 'No, I shan't be needing this tonight, thank you,' and left.

He was proud of that line. Two things to be proud of, then.

He had climbed back into college over the high, spiked railings in Trinity Lane. He should have slipped and impaled himself. He would probably be feeling a lot better this morning if he had.

He got out of bed and gazed out of the window. The sun was shining on the snow. How dare it be such a beautiful day?

He washed, shaved and dressed, then opened his door. A cup of tea, very cold, put there by Crystal, stood on the floor of the landing. He stepped around it and went and knocked on James's door. James would understand, wouldn't he? He had called his sister a witch, he would understand how she had caught him in her spell. He knocked again. No answer.

61

As a penance, Gerry drank the tea and then he put on a coat and scarf and went to his car. It started eventually and he drove to Magdalene. Mark was out, too. Gerry sighed and turned the car towards Girton. He walked along the corridor and remembered that only last night he had come here, all dressed up in his new tails and white tie, and Kate was waiting for him wearing her red dress and looking beautiful . . . He had almost convinced himself that the clock had somehow gone backwards and that she'd open the door and smile and turn her face up for his kiss . . .

No answer. Silence.

He tried Vanessa's door. It, too, stayed uncompromisingly shut.

He drove back to the shining city, feeling utterly bereft. He had parked his car and was walking across the bridge to New Court when he remembered that, early on last night when it was obvious they wouldn't be hunting today, they had all arranged to have lunch at a pub on the other side of Cambridge. He turned and took a few paces back and then stopped. He couldn't go. He couldn't face Kate (if that was where she had gone) in front of all the people who had seen what he did last night. He stood and stared at the river, black between its white banks, and at St John's New Court, looking too perfect under its covering of snow. He shoved his hands in his pockets and wandered on.

Someone – a woman – was standing at the foot of his staircase. Her back was to him but she was wearing a tweed coat, its collar turned up to her ears, and some kind of woollen hat. He quickened his pace and the woman turned.

It was Sophie.

'Hello, Gerry.'

'Were you looking for James? He's out.'

'I know.'

He stood and scowled at her. 'What do you want, then.'

'You,' she said simply, and burst out laughing. 'Oh you should see yourself, Gerry. You look like a sulky schoolboy. I just came to say goodbye. Philip and Zelda are driving me back to London . . . I *did* enjoy last night, Gerry. Not quite all of it, of course. It was very naughty, what you did to me at the hotel, but I forgive you.' Her eyes widened as she stared innocently up at him. 'But then I

62

expect it was naughty of me too, wasn't it?' She stepped forward, stood on tiptoe and kissed him rapidly. 'Until next time, Gerry,' she whispered.

And she was gone.

There were eight of them at the table meant for four. James and Mark had been so proud of arriving early and bagging it, and too good-natured when others had asked to join them. Kate and Vanessa had shifted along until, they protested, they would be in the car park. Not that Kate minded. It meant she didn't have to talk the whole time and could gaze out into the snow and think. No one had said a word about Gerry and Sophie; their names hadn't been mentioned. It was as though they had disappeared overnight – which, come to think of it, they had. Looking around at the crowded pub, Kate thought that Gerry must be the only undergraduate who had been at the ball last night who had not brought his girl here for lunch. His girl: that was his expression.

Less than twenty-four hours ago, Kate had been his girl and the absolute tops. Beattie had said he had a reputation for being one for the girls . . . well, he had proved that all right. But then, Kate told herself, it was one of the things that had attracted her to him – the faintly rakish air about him, the experience . . . those and the laughter, the sudden seriousness, the caring. Where had *that* gone to last night? She felt her eyes fill with tears and shook her head determinedly. It would not do.

And now, it seemed, James was ready to take up where Gerry had left off. He was a bit like a golden retriever, all good nature, anxious eyes and wagging tail. He was sweet and kind (but then, so were golden retrievers) but . . . And that was the other thing about Gerry: he seemed much older, more mature than the others. Probably, she reflected, because he hadn't gone to one of the public schools he was always so worried about.

James nudged her gently and smiled at her. 'All right?'

'Very well,' she said, rallying. 'This food is delicious. I wonder how they manage it.'

'The chef is French,' Mark said from across the table. 'Resourceful fellows, the French.' Mark seemed almost handsome today, constantly turning to look at Vanessa as if he couldn't quite believe she was there, squashed satisfactorily between him and the window.

'Not so resourceful during the war,' said Nick O'Rourke.

'What about the Resistance?' James asked. 'Getting our chaps home and all that.'

'All what?' Nick demanded. 'All what, Foggy?'

'Oh shut up,' James mumbled.

'To turn to serious matters,' Nick said. 'How about tea in my rooms this afternoon?'

There were groans and protests about lunch only just being finished, which Nick overrode in masterful fashion.

'Liquid only. Liqueurs *followed* by tea. I've got some brandy.'

This seemed, to the men of the party at least, an excellent way to spend a snowy afternoon.

'You'll come, won't you?' Mark said to Vanessa.

Vanessa flung her now unlacquered hair back across her shoulders.

'No, I mustn't, honestly. I've got an essay to finish and I really ought to be getting on with it.'

'I know exactly how you feel,' Mark said earnestly. 'I really ought to be taking a scull out on the river, but I'll sacrifice that if you sacrifice your essay.'

Everyone laughed and, under the cover of it, James asked Kate if she too would come to Nick's tea party.

'I don't know, James.' She suddenly felt overwhelmed by his cloying attentiveness. She didn't particularly want to go to tea at St John's, but neither did the thought of her room at Girton appeal. 'I'll come if Vanessa does,' she added meanly.

'Good,' said Mark. 'That's settled then. You'll both come.'

'The Colley-Smythe technique prevails again,' said Nick. 'You ought to give lectures on it, old boy.'

Gerry had spent the most miserable day of all his nineteen and a half years. Nothing in his life had prepared him to face the fact that he was alone and unwanted, he who had always been the centre of attention and so loved. He went to Hall but there was nobody there he knew and Saturday lunch seemed the most depressing meal there could possibly be. He went back to his rooms, took out some books and stared at them for a bit and, as he did so, he convinced himself that Kate would be back again by now. She could have been anywhere this morning – visiting a friend, having a bath, working in the library – so he went to his car, drove to Girton, paced down the corridors to find both Kate's and Vanessa's doors as comprehensively silent and closed as before. He returned to his books, and after a while he realised he should have left a note. At least she would know he was trying to contact her. So he drove back to Girton, reflecting that, at this rate, he would use up all his petrol on the now depressingly familiar journey through the snow and have to buy more at exorbitant rates on the black market. He went to Kate's room just in case she was there (she wasn't), borrowed some paper from the portress and wrote: 'I came to see you, but you were out. Love, Gerry.' He stared at it. He couldn't leave that in Kate's pigeonhole. He added, 'I'm sorry', but it came out looking like a postscript, which made it worse than ever. He didn't dare ask the portress for more paper – she had been so mean with the first piece, even tearing the sheet in half – so he crumpled the note up, put it in his pocket and went back to Trinity.

It grew dark. Gerry sat brooding, no longer even pretending to work. Eventually he heard footsteps on the stairs and the door to the room opposite opened and then closed. Gerry waited, hoping that James would, as he usually did, come lounging over and suggest they went out or help himself to Gerry's whisky, but there was silence. Gerry had never felt more alone. He didn't want to see James if James didn't want to see him, but at least it might mean that Kate was back at Girton.

For the fourth time that day, he stood outside her door. For a moment he thought this journey was going to be as fruitless as the other three, then the door opened and there she was. She looked pale and there were dark smudges under her eyes, but she was as lovely as ever. How could he have left her for Sophie and her greedy embraces?

'Can I come in?' he asked, and she stepped aside. She didn't invite him to sit down and they stood awkwardly. At last she spoke.

'You'd better say what you've come to say, Gerry, and then go.'

'Kate . . . I'm – I'm so sorry,' he stammered.

'All right.'

'I didn't realise the time, you see.'

'You were obviously enjoying yourself.'

'You're not making this easy, Kate,' he said.

'Why should I?'

There was a knock on her door and she opened it. A woman's voice: 'Are you coming to Hall, Kate?'

'In a minute.'

'Can we go out somewhere?' Gerry said. 'We can't talk here.'

'I don't see what there is to talk about,' she said flatly.

'I just want to explain—'

'How can you possibly explain?' she burst out. 'You went off to dance with Sophie. Over an hour later you were still dancing with her and the rest of us left. What can you add to that? How *could* you, Gerry?'

He gestured helplessly. 'I don't know, Kate. It's you I – here, have my handkerchief.'

'No.'

He tried to put his arms around her, but she shrugged him off.

'Go now, Gerry, please.'

He felt like crying himself. This was worse than he had imagined throughout this whole, awful day.

'I don't want to go.'

'Please.'

'Will I see you again?'

She sniffed. 'Oh, I expect so,' she said with a brave attempt at lightness. 'We have friends in common, after all. But I won't go to James's when term ends.'

He had forgotten that they were both invited to Flimwell Place. Sophie might be there. The prospect of being in the same house as her made him feel quite ill.

'I won't go either.'

'But Gerry, you must! You've been so looking forward to hunting with the Quorn.'

Her concern made him feel better, but her next words plunged him back into despair.

'And you'll be able to see lots of Sophie, won't you? And now, Gerry, you must leave. I'm going to Hall.'

She opened the door and he had no alternative but to walk out of it.

The last few days of term passed unmemorably. Gerry had an interview with his director of studies, who told him he was not working hard enough – something Gerry had figured out for himself – and he promised to do better next term. It would be easy enough if he wasn't seeing Kate. He had been up to Girton several times. Once she had said, simply, there was nothing to discuss and all the other times she had been out, which made Gerry furiously jealous. He slunk around Cambridge in a state of despair, his mood exacerbated by James who was in indecently high spirits. Stung by Mr McGibbons's remarks about the lack of fire among modern undergraduates, he and two other first years had crept out in the early hours of the morning and built a giant snowman in Great Court, dressing it in a bowler hat to give it the appearance of a college porter. Gerry had refused to join the party and watched with glum satisfaction later in the day when Mr McGibbons and a fellow porter advanced upon the snowman, shovels at the ready, and demolished it. And then all the snow turned a dirty used grey and disappeared.

Home, then, and Christmas with his family. He thought of Arthur wanting to hear every detail of his first term at Cambridge, every triumph, wanting to know that the money he had got Da to send had been well spent. Gerry's heart baulked at the prospect.

But first he was going to Leicestershire, to Flimwell Place, with Florin. When he had told James that he had, after all, decided against it, James had looked at him in disappointment.

'Oh do come, old thing,' he said, and added, 'Kate won't be there, you know,' as though her absence would appeal to Gerry.

'I don't want to see Sophie,' Gerry told him frankly. 'Not now or ever.'

'But I thought . . . Oh, well.'

'I know she's your sister, James, but she's ruined my life. Kate won't even talk to me. Look, James, couldn't you speak to her for me? Tell her!'

'Tell her what?' James turned away and fiddled with an invitation card on his mantelpiece.

'Tell her I'm sorry. Damn it all, you know what your sister is like.'

'If Sophie was an animal, I'd shoot her to put the rest of the world out of its misery,' James said. 'But do come for some hunting, Gerry. Sophie won't be at home. Mother will stay with her in London since Kate isn't coming. To chaperon her, you know.'

If Gerry hadn't been feeling so awful, he would have laughed.

Chapter 6

'Tell us,' said Joe Beviss, 'about this drag-huntin' caper. Arthur's been on about it but me an' yer Ma can't get a-hold.'

Gerry told them and his father stared at him.

'You chase after a smelly sock? Well, of all the things Rector said you'd get up to at Cambridge that weren't one of them. A sock! D'you rate that, Ma?'

Meg Beviss shook her head and served her younger son a third helping of mutton stew.

'Hey, steady along, Ma,' he said, but began to eat again nonetheless. Rationed food and college fare had given him a great appetite for his mother's cooking.

Arthur leaned back in his chair and watched his brother as he ate.

'And Florin? What of him?'

Gerry gestured with his fork. 'He's fast. Arthur, Da, you've no idea . . .' And he told them of the day he and James had galloped neck and neck to save the hounds. 'Florin kept up, see, and Castor's won point-to-points.'

'That's James Flimwell,' Arthur said, just to make sure. 'Lord Flimwell's son. Where you've been staying.'

Gerry nodded. 'Hey, and Ma, James thinks your cakes are perfect poems.'

She smiled. 'Does he?'

Joe cackled a laugh. 'Hear that, Ma? Some fancy toff rates your baking!'

Gerry pushed his empty plate away. His mother brought him a

69

clean one and cut him a huge slice of apple pie before serving her husband and Arthur.

'You glad to be home, Gerry?' she asked shyly.

Gerry looked at them: all of them hanging on his every exaggerated word, each of them loving him. So different from the last few days at Cambridge when he had felt so desolate, and from his stay at Flimwell Place where he had simply felt insignificant.

'Yeah,' he said, 'glad to be home.'

Arthur picked up his spoon. 'One at the Anchor later? The lads'll be pleased to see you – and Molly, too, I daresay.'

'Who's Molly?' Meg Beviss asked.

Gerry glared at his brother. 'Just the barmaid, Ma. Art's joking.'

And it was good to go into the pub and hear the greetings, the fishermen's voices in gruff Sussex welcoming him home. Molly winked at him as she pulled their pints and placed them on the bar.

'Well, Gerry-lad?'

' 'Llo, Molly. How're you keeping, then?'

'All the better for seeing you,' she answered primly. 'I reckoned you'd be too grand for us with all Arthur's talk of lords' sons and that.'

'Never too grand for you, Molly,' he said, although his heart wasn't in it.

'Still one with the words, then.' She leaned towards him. 'What about the action, though?'

'Put him down, Moll, and get us a drink!' bawled a man from the other end of the bar. Molly went off to serve him and Gerry, somewhat relieved at the interruption for he didn't want Molly that way, not now, followed Arthur to a corner table. They both sat down.

'What's the matter, though, Gerry?' Arthur said, after he had asked and Gerry had answered every possible question about Cambridge. 'Something's wrong, isn't it?'

Gerry didn't reply.

'Is it money? I've got a bit set by and it's yours if you want it.' He'd have to talk to Da, though, about the allowance. His savings wouldn't last for ever, and Gerry would need the money to keep up with these nobs he'd got himself among – just like Arthur had said he would if he played it cleverly. And Gerry was clever. No one was in any doubt about that.

'No, Art, it isn't money,' Gerry said.

'The girl, then,' Arthur prompted. 'You've not mentioned her. You wrote that she'd be staying at this Flimwell Place.'

'Yes . . .' And for the first time Gerry told someone else about the whole awful matter of the ball at the Pitt Club.

Arthur listened in silence, trying desperately not to laugh. Gerry had treated half the girls in the district twice as badly and most of them had come back for more, but this Kate wasn't allowing him a second chance and here was Gerry moaning about being in love and his life lying shattered at his feet. Arthur said nothing, of course, only remarking when Gerry had come to the end of his sorry tale, 'Well, fancy a lord's daughter behaving the way you said this Sophie did.'

'Kate won't even talk to me, Art. When I went to Girton she just closed the door in my face.'

'But she's not at Girton now, is she?'

'No, she's at her aunt's,' said Gerry impatiently.

'Who you say lives in Kent. Kent's not far off, Gerry. Tell you what . . . offer to drive her to this New Year party you're going to. I'll sort out the petrol, no worry about that. Hey listen,' Arthur said, wanting his brother to be happy, 'where in Kent?'

Gerry laughed and slapped him on the back.

'Sissingham? . . . Sissinghurst? Up Cranbrook way. I'll find it. You're a bleeding genius, Art. Let me buy you a drink.'

He came back with another beer for Arthur and a whisky for himself. Arthur raised an eyebrow.

'Can't take more'n a couple of pints these days,' Gerry explained. 'We don't drink so much of it at Cambridge.'

'Oh don't we?' Arthur grunted. 'Well, a pint'll do me, all night if it has to.'

'What news around here?' asked Gerry, feeling on top of the world now he had a course of action to follow and scarcely having noticed Molly as she served him the drinks and he paid for them. The journey to Hampshire would take – what? – three or four hours. Four hours with Kate there, and four hours back . . .

'Da's up to something,' Arthur said gloomily.

71

'Isn't he always?'

'Yeah, but this is big. I wish the old bugger'd tell me. All he says is stay in the shop, boy, won't be long now, an' off he goes up to London an' places. I don't mind the bloody shop but it's like he's opening the door a little bit an' then closing it again. He's got another fifty acres off Dennis Marling. Reckon he's broken him this time. Oh, and Annie's leaving,' he added.

'Where for?'

'Live-in job over at Pulborough with hunters and kids' ponies. It's been dull for her with us, I s'pose.'

'But what about you and her?'

'Nah. She's nearly ten years younger'n me. I'm an old man of twenty-seven, remember. Anyway, they're all in love with you.'

'Except Kate,' Gerry reminded him.

A grey-haired woman with a duster in her hand told him, over the hysterical barking of a black cocker spaniel, that Miss Kate was out.

'Where is she?' Gerry demanded, and the woman said she didn't know she was sure.

Beattie came into the hall. 'Who is it, Sadie? . . . Gerry!' she exclaimed with what he thought was real pleasure. She took his right hand in both her plump ones.

'I was just passing,' he said awkwardly, 'and was hoping that Kate—'

'She's gone to the village on an errand. She won't be long. Come in, Gerry, and have a cup of something. And be quiet, Flash,' she said to the spaniel. She started towards the kitchen at the rear of the house, but Gerry hung back.

'Mrs Poutney—'

'Beattie,' she said. 'We're old friends, I hope.'

'Beattie, has Kate told you?'

'She has.' Beattie gazed at him reproachfully. 'How could you, Gerry? I thought better of you.'

'I – I'm sorry.'

'I hope you show better manners to your new girlfriend,' she said. Anyway,' she went on before Gerry could correct her, 'I'm delighted to see you even if Kate won't be.'

72

Gerry sat at the scrubbed wooden table and Beattie filled the kettle and put it on to boil.

'Will Kate speak to me, do you think?'

'I really don't know, but here she is. You can find out for yourself.'

The door to the porch leading off the kitchen had opened and Kate's voice called, 'Beattie?'

'Here, darling.'

Her back was towards them as she took off her wellingtons and Flash jumped around her as though he hadn't seen her for years.

'Sorry to be so long, but Mrs Lewis *would* tell me all about her carbuncle. She thought I'd be interested because I'm a medical student . . . There!' She turned and came into the kitchen and stopped. 'Gerry!'

He stood up.

'What on earth are you doing here?'

'I was up this way seeing a horse,' he improvised, 'and I thought I'd drop in. I wondered . . .' He took a deep breath and rushed his fence. 'I wondered if you wanted a lift to Andrew's party. It seems silly for us not to go together since we live in the same area . . . doesn't it?'

Beattie poured them all a cup of coffee, took a cotton bag from a hook behind the kitchen door, sat down and drew out her knitting.

'No, I don't want a lift, thank you,' Kate said. 'I'm going to London and Vanessa and I will get to Hampshire from there.'

'Oh.' Gerry had heard about people's hearts plummeting into their boots, but he'd never actually experienced it before.

'I don't know if I'll go at all,' Kate said.

'If you don't it will be very rude,' Beattie commented, her needles clicking furiously. 'Mrs Whatsit has asked you to stay and you have accepted. You'll have a lonely time of it here if you don't go, because your uncle and I have been asked to gad at the Bowerings'.'

'Who's Mrs Whatsit?' Gerry said. 'I've been asked by a Mrs Lucas.'

'Anderson,' said Kate. She looked at Gerry, who was staring in a

73

depressed kind of fascination at Beattie's knitting – a red and yellow affair at least four feet long.

'It's a scarf,' she told him. 'My surprise Christmas present.'

He turned to her and she smiled suddenly.

'Isn't it lucky Christmas is only two days away? Another week and I'd be in danger of doing an Isadora Duncan in my bicycle spokes.'

'Please don't,' he said, undone by her smile. 'Kate – you will come to the party, won't you?'

'Oh I expect so,' she said, and with that and her smile he had to be content.

Gerry put on his green tail coat and checked his appearance in the mirror of Mr and Mrs Lucas's seventh spare bedroom. He supposed he would get used to this kind of life but it felt strange to someone born in a gypsy caravan. At least he hadn't made the awful blunder here that he had at Flimwell Place. Not realising that a man's pockets were not his own, he had not emptied his and a maid had done so, neatly laying on the dressing table, among other things, the note to Kate, uncrumpled, that he had written and discarded at Girton, a stolen apple which was meant for Florin, and a French letter which must have been in his jacket pocket since his last meeting with Molly back in October. He still went hot with embarrassment when he thought about it, and the maid had given him some fairly odd looks whenever he had encountered her after that. Whether of invitation or condemnation he did not know.

He pushed his face closer to the mirror and glared at it. 'Cheer up, damn you,' he said to his reflection, which bared its teeth in a parody of the charming Beviss grin.

He straightened his tie, went out of the room and walked down the stairs. He was shown into the library, where Mrs Lucas's house guests were assembling for cocktails before having dinner and going on to Andrew's party. At dinner, Gerry found himself sitting between a pretty girl called Rosamund who had, she told him – as though it was a stunningly original thing to do – done the Season, which was 'frightfully fun'; and none other than Miss

Eileen McLennan whom, along with her bicycle, Gerry had driven back to Girton and then taken Kate out for the first time.

'And how is your horse?' she greeted him.

'Very well. And how is your bike?'

'Likewise.'

And that appeared to be the end of the conversation. Rosamund said the plates were frightfully pretty, weren't they, and on learning that Gerry was at Cambridge that he must be frightfully clever. Gerry, now pinning his hopes on persuading Kate to dance with him, sat impatiently through the meal – served and presented with pre-war style but consisting of uncompromising post-war indeterminate soup and then rabbit stew – and made what he considered frightfully inventive small talk.

At last the meal was over and they drove in convoy to Andrew's party. They were late, thanks to the rabbit and the minute pieces of cheese that had followed it, and the party was well on its way when they arrived. A marquee, its poles festively decorated with holly and ivy, had been added as an extension to the house. There was a wooden dance floor in the middle of it and tables for sitting out on the matting around the sides. Gerry scanned the dancers. He saw James with Vanessa, and both smiled and waved at him, and there was Kate in the arms of a tall man he had never seen before. Gerry glowered at them.

'Good Christmas, Gerry?' He turned. Mark raised a glass at him. 'Happy New Year and all that.'

'Thanks. And the same to you.' Gerry looked back at the dance floor. 'Who's that with Kate?'

Mark peered. 'Michael Coleridge. Andrew's brother. Nice chap, Michael.'

It was extraordinary how they all knew each other, Gerry reflected, how they had all gone to the same school or were distant cousins or their families were friends. The band stopped playing and Gerry began shouldering his way through to Kate.

'Gerry!' a horribly familiar voice said. 'I'd hoped you'd be here.'

Sophie, in that same outrageous dress, attempted to cast herself upon him, but he gripped her wrists and held her away.

'What? No New Year kiss?'

'No New Year anything.'

She pouted. 'That's not very friendly. Aren't you going to ask me to dance?'

Gerry cast around wildly. Kate and her partner had disappeared but Miss Eileen McLennan was near by, gazing dispassionately at the gathering couples.

'I'm not free,' he said. He thrust Sophie off and marched up to Miss McLennan – he dared not think of her as Eileen – and demanded she dance with him.

She gazed at him.

'Do you think you're up to it?' she asked. 'It's an eightsome reel.'

'I can do it,' he said boldly, having very little idea of what it was.

She laughed suddenly, a surprisingly pleasant laugh.

'Come along, then. You look desperate enough for anything.'

Kate should have been enjoying herself. She was never without a partner and was vaguely flattered by this, considering the competition and she a bluestocking and so much older than them. Michael Coleridge was pleasant enough, but his conversation was uninspiring. James was in attendance, but now that Kate had identified him with a golden retriever she found she was inclined to treat him like an over-friendly dog: kindly, but firmly. And there was Gerry, of course. He had asked her for a dance and she had accepted, not wanting to appear childish by refusing. Fortunately, or unfortunately, depending which way you looked at it, the dance was the Dashing White Sergeant, which rendered any kind of conversation impossible, apart from yelled instructions to Gerry who did not number Scottish reels among his accomplishments. Undaunted, he had asked her for the next dance, too, but that was promised to Andrew Coleridge, whose twenty-first birthday the party was belatedly celebrating.

Kate could not understand why Gerry was not with Sophie. She had seen, earlier, Sophie go up and claim him and had turned quickly away and asked her partner if they could go and find a drink, but since then Gerry hadn't danced with Sophie at all as far as Kate could see. Perhaps they were beyond the dancing phase. Kate knew Sophie's type: she had seen them in the Wrens and, no matter what kind of background they came from, they were easily recognisable. The women who go to bed with men.

She danced with Stephen White an appropriately stately foxtrot, with Nick O'Rourke, with James again and then with Mark. She was fond of Mark and pleased his patient siege of Vanessa had at last been lifted. Vanessa kept saying she didn't have time to cope with boyfriends – as though they may get lost along with everything else Vanessa owned – but Mark had no intention of being mislaid and every intention of becoming indispensable.

'Don't you think I could?' he asked Kate now. 'I mean, she does need someone, doesn't she?'

'She certainly does,' Kate agreed, and was rewarded by Mark's lovely smile.

When the music stopped, they found themselves at the edge of the dance floor beside Sophie and her partner.

'Mark!' she cried. 'Let's dance . . . or, no.' She paused. 'Later, perhaps.'

Gerry was coming towards them and Sophie turned to him. Kate hurriedly excused herself, went out of the marquee, through the drawing room and upstairs to the ladies' cloakroom. It was a bedroom with a bathroom attached and both rooms were occupied. One girl was in the bathroom talking loudly and receiving appreciative exclamations from the other, who was seated at the dressing table powdering her nose.

'I promise you, darling. I was *there*! It was after the ball at Cambridge. This chap – handsome as you like but with a face like thunder – just sits there and she's whispering sweet nothings into his ear and getting no – but *no* – response until . . . you won't believe this—'

'Go on, *do!*'

'Until he hands her the key to her room – she'd slipped it to him, you see—'

'Arabella – *no!*'

'And he says, "I won't be needing this tonight, thank you very much." And he goes.'

The girl at the dressing table turned, lipstick in hand, and stared at the closed door in the direction of her friend's voice.

'Arabella, I don't *believe* it! What *did* Sophie do?'

The cistern flushed and Kate stood rooted to the spot as Arabella came out of the bathroom, glanced briefly at Kate (not one of us, her eyes said) and joined the other at the mirror. Kate shot into the bathroom, closed and locked the door and pressed her ear against it. They continued in lower voices, but she could still hear.

'Well, you could tell she was livid. And embarrassed.'

'Darling, she'd have to be. Even her. At that.'

'It's about time someone gave her a set-down. Mummy says Lady Flimwell is in despair over her.'

'Remember how Sophie went after Alistair Weekes and he broke off his engagement—'

The outer door slammed and the voices ceased.

Kate returned to the marquee. Vanessa and Mark were dancing and Gerry and Sophie were still on the edge of the dance floor. She was standing close to him, holding his hand and gazing up at him. As Kate watched, she stepped back and tried to draw him among the dancers. Determination warred with seduction in her face, making it almost ugly. Gerry didn't move, then he turned and caught Kate's eye. He looked like reluctance personified and Kate could not help laughing at him. Seeing this, he prised Sophie's hand from his and almost ran over to her.

'Dance with me, Kate, please.'

Eavesdroppers weren't supposed to hear good of themselves, but Kate thought what she had overheard was good for her. She felt absurdly relieved to know that Gerry hadn't betrayed her *that* far and could almost believe that the whole affair at the Pitt Club hadn't been his fault. What he had done had been unforgivable, of course, and how could she trust him after that? But it was New Year's Eve and pleasant to feel Gerry's arms around her as they danced to an old Glenn Miller tune, speaking little and letting the sentiment of the old wartime favourite wash over them.

They danced on until the music stopped and the Master of Ceremonies called for hush and stood, his watch in one hand, his other arm raised; he lowered his arm and the band began to play 'Auld Lang Syne'. Kate found Vanessa and they all linked hands and sang.

'Happy New Year, Kate,' Gerry said amid the noise afterwards. He kissed her on the cheek and then, as with some of his old impudence he pointed upward to a bunch of mistletoe, her lips. 'Peace and goodwill between us?' he asked.

'Peace and goodwill,' she said. She turned to wish Vanessa a happy New Year and found herself face to face with James, so she wished him one instead. He bent and kissed her and returned the greeting a little sadly.

Gerry put his arm around her shoulders.

'Listen.'

Everyone fell silent as the sound of pipes crept into the house, bringing with it cold air from outside and also, it seemed, some of the mist of Scotland as well. The sound grew louder until the piper appeared among his swirling tartan and circled the dance floor, his music filling every inch of the canvas of the marquee.

Chapter 7

After the first meet of the University Drag Hounds the following term, Stephen White appointed James and Gerry whippers-in. In front of a large and amused field of followers, both on foot and astride, he had taken the unprecedented step of sacking John Winter and Andrew Coleridge from their positions: Andrew had managed to fall off his horse at the meet itself, before a fence or any kind of hazard was anywhere in sight; and John had caused hilarity by walking his horse around a churchyard, in and out of the gravestones, shouting 'Cheerful!'

That this was the name of the hound he was trying to summon cut no ice with Stephen.

'It's not just that you made the whole show a roaring farce,' he told John brutally, 'it's the fact that your bloody horse won't jump anything higher than six inches.'

So James and Gerry were handed over the hunting coats of dark green and moved their horses into the stables at the kennels, which the Drag Hounds shared with the Trinity Foot Beagles. They exercised the hounds three mornings a week, learned their names and tried to make them mind them. Stephen White had returned from the Christmas vacation with another four hounds donated by his local hunt, so they now had a pack of sixteen.

'Eight couple,' James corrected him. 'Stephen will have your guts for garters if he hears you getting it wrong.'

Gerry played along, but he found it all rather silly. They were dogs with wagging tails, for heaven's sake: why the hell did you have to call them hounds with waving sterns or be cursed for an ignorant fool?

'I think it's daft,' he said to Kate as they sat by the fire in the pub at Madingley.

'You only say that because you're afraid you'll be caught out,' she told him. 'What would you call someone who claimed to know about horses if he referred to its hocks as its knees?'

He smiled wryly. 'An ignorant fool,' he replied. 'And a sham. Not that I claimed to be an expert on hunting but, well, everyone seems to expect me to be.'

'And you are managing very nicely, becoming a whipper-in and all that.' She looked at her watch. 'Isn't it time to go?'

'No!' he protested. 'Go where, anyway?'

'I must get back to college.'

'Why? It's Saturday night.'

'I must, that's all.'

'Please, Kate . . . can't we go out to dinner?'

Since term had started, Gerry had tried everything he knew to put their relationship back on its former footing, but although Kate consented to have a drink with him and treated him with perfect friendliness, she had, apparently, meant what she had said at Andrew Coleridge's New Year party: that there would be peace and goodwill between them and, it seemed, no more. At this rate, he reflected, he would have to wait until next Christmas, when he could steer her under a bunch of mistletoe, before he kissed her again.

Apart from anything else, she was such a refuge. The only person who knew about this extraordinary double life he was leading. There were times when he felt he was running across a tightrope at ever-increasing speed, unable to stop or turn back, and at any moment someone would cut the wire or reach out a hand and knock him into the chasm below with a flick of a casual finger. It would be a tiny thing, and there was no way he could recognise it when it came. If he knew what the obstacles were he could avoid them, but it was all so complicated! He had just asked Kate out to dinner: a few months ago he would have assumed that to be what he had quickly learned to call lunch; and tea here was little bits of toast and his mother's cake when, for the first nineteen years of his life, it had meant what he ate in the early evening, the substantial meal the fishermen came home to before going out to the pub. And the most absurd thing about it was that it all seemed to be of paramount importance. It was the code by which these people – they used to be called the Upper Ten Thousand, he had read – recognised each other and made sure lesser mortals didn't muscle in and infect the blood. Gerry hadn't exactly muscled in, but he knew what they would say if he was found out: 'Wormed his way in,' they'd say. 'Wormed his way in, the frightful little blighter.'

And their women were the same! He had been asked to a party in London and, because Mark and James were going, he had gone too. Their hostess (of course) knew Lord and Lady Flimwell and her son had (of course) been at Eton with James and Mark, so they were all right. She had scrutinised Gerry as he had been introduced and he had been relieved (and ashamed at himself for being so) that his dinner jacket had been made by Cambridge's best tailor, which might not be Savile Row but at least it was not – that horror of horrors – off the peg. He had been the focus of much attention at the party, though, thankfully, Sophie Flimwell had ignored him, and other invitations had followed. He hadn't accepted any of them because he thought the girls were silly and shallow and nowhere near as beautiful and interesting as Kate.

Who seemed to be the only woman he could not attract.

'Do let's go out to dinner,' he repeated and, to his immeasurable joy, she replied, although without much enthusiasm, 'Oh well, all right.'

She picked up her red and yellow scarf and wound it around her neck. He helped her on with her coat and opened the door for her.

'Where shall we go?' he asked.

'Not somewhere smart, Gerry. I'm not dressed for it.'

'You look lovely,' he said. 'Though the scarf is . . . well . . .'

'Colourful?' she supplied.

'Just a bit.'

They went outside. January in Cambridgeshire and the wind coming straight from Siberia with scarcely a hill to prevent its passing.

'More than a bit,' Kate said. 'It was meant to be therapy for Beattie, you see. She knitted for victory like mad during the war and Uncle Charles and I have been trying to wean her off khaki socks and blanket squares ever since.'

'You succeeded – admirably. Congratulations.'

She laughed, entirely without constraint, and he took her hand in his.

'She should knit you gloves to match,' he said, and then, as she waited for him to open the car door, he leaned forward and kissed her cheek.

'Shall we go to the Arts Theatre restaurant?'

This was a risk: it was where they had eaten that very first time after having their first drink together in this very pub.

'All right,' she said again. And then, 'Oh, Gerry,' and this time his lips met hers.

'If I promise,' he said, his arms around her, 'never, *never* again to behave as I did—'

'Never is a long word, Gerry.'

'Never,' he repeated firmly. 'Kate, can't it be like it was before?'

Silence, and then her voice came out of the dark.

'It can't be, can it? Not exactly like.'

'Nearly, then.'

She sighed, and he felt her shrug her shoulders. 'I'm weak and silly and I should say no, but—'

'You'll say yes!'

Her cold hands crept under his scarf and around the back of his neck. He yelped.

'It serves you right,' she told him.

'I've done my penance, Kate,' he said, laughter welling in him. 'Forty days in the wilderness . . . Well, forty-nine actually.'

'You've been counting?'

'Of course! Haven't you?'

'I'm afraid I haven't.'

But nothing could chasten him now. He could have stayed all night standing in a pub's car park with his arms around his girl, knowing all he had to do was bend his head and kiss her, but cold and hunger got the better of them both. They drove to Cambridge to find the restaurant packed with people and the only possibility a

83

shared table, which Gerry was not prepared to endure, and so, overriding Kate's protests about her clothes, they went to the Blue Boar Hotel. Gerry recklessly ordered a bottle of champagne, and when the waiter had opened it and gone away, he clinked his glass against Kate's.

'To new beginnings,' he said.

'New beginnings.'

'Kate, I—'

'And no mention of the past.'

Their food came, and as they ate Gerry told Kate all the details of his and James's elevation to whippers-in.

'But what,' she asked, 'was this hound – Cheerful – doing in the churchyard anyway?'

'That was the awful thing,' he said. 'She was digging.'

'Gerry, no!'

'True,' he assured her. 'And Andrew says he's going to enter the Members' race in the University point-to-point. They've opened a book on it at the Pitt. You'll never guess what odds they are taking.'

'Tell me.'

'Fifty to one against the horse getting round and a hundred to one against Andrew being on it if it does. But,' he continued, 'they forgot to stipulate how many falls he's allowed, and a time limit, so he's put five pounds on himself and is planning to break his record. . . .'

'Oh?' she said, weak with laughter. 'And what is that?'

'Four falls in one day.'

'Great heavens! I hope he doesn't break anything else.'

'Yeah, well, you'll be around to patch him up if he does, won't you?'

'If he sustains a very small cut I might just manage it,' she conceded. 'But who's been made favourite, you or James?'

'James. His horse has the form. . . . Kate—' He took her hand. 'There's a ball the night before the point-to-point—'

'I know. It's at the Pitt Club again. I've been invited to it.'

He stared at her, but she was looking down at her plate.

'Three times,' she said.

'Oh,' he said blankly. Then: 'By who?'

'Whom,' she corrected. 'I'm not telling you by whom, and I've not accepted any of them.'

'Kate!' He squeezed her hand and she raised her eyes to his.

'Honestly, I don't want to go.'

'All right,' he said, 'we won't.'

But he had lots of time to make her change her mind. And, of course, he would.

Much of the excitement about the betting on the point-to-point was dispelled ten days later when Castor jumped a post and rails, crumpled on landing, threw James over his head and got up unable to put one of his feet to the ground. James scrambled over to his horse and grabbed the reins, saying, as Castor – one front leg useless – attempted to go after the hounds and the other horses which were now galloping past, 'Steady, old thing, just steady. It's all right,' although he was sure it wasn't.

Gerry yelled to Stephen that the hounds were all his and turned Florin back.

'Get a gun, Gerry, for God's sake,' James said, tears running down his cheeks. 'He's broken his leg, I know he has.'

Gerry dismounted and handed Florin's reins to James. He ran up the stirrups and loosened Castor's girth, then he studied the way the horse was holding his leg and bent down and gently felt it.

'Maybe he hasn't,' he said, straightening up. 'I think it's his tendon.'

James looked at him bleary-eyed.

'That serious?'

'Yes, old chap, but not as serious as a break. Take off your stock,' he said, and began to remove his own. 'I'll bind the leg and then you stay here with him while I go for help.'

Gerry unwound the stock from his neck and, using that and James's, bound Castor's leg as tightly as he dared, considering there was no give in the starched white material, and fastened it with James's hunting pin. He took off his coat and put it over Castor's hindquarters. James stroked his horse's nose and gazed at Gerry.

'Are you sure it's the tendon?'

85

'No, James. I'm not a bloody vet.' He got back on Florin. 'I'll be as quick as I can. Don't let him move. All right?'

'Yes,' said James bleakly.

Gerry held Florin up for a moment.

'You weren't hurt, were you?'

'No.' He raised a pale, mournful face. 'You got a flask? I forgot mine.'

'In my coat pocket,' Gerry said, beginning to feel the cold cutting through his shirt and waistcoat.

He sent Florin in distant pursuit of the rest of the hunt, leaving James standing in a wide February-dull field at the head of his stricken horse. They jumped four hedges and a ditch, following the hoofprints of the hunt ahead of them, Gerry riding with exaggerated care because Castor's injury had unnerved him. You had a beautiful healthy horse one moment and the next a miserable creature in pain, saying to you out of its dark eyes, *Why?*

He was feeling lonely, helpless and – oh! – so cold out there in unfamiliar country with a mist rising and now heavy rain falling when he saw two horses cantering steadily towards him a couple of fields away. He rode on and then, when he realised that they were finding gates and opening them instead of jumping, he opened the gate of the field he was in and waited for them. Rain dripped down his bare neck, soaking the inside of his shirt.

It was Sybil, their groom, and a local man who had been out with the Drag that day.

'You must have felt abandoned,' the man said. 'We didn't know it was serious until you didn't turn up at the check, and then it seemed wise to come equipped. The name's Maddox. I'm a vet,' he explained. Gerry saw the bulge in the left pocket of Mr Maddox's pink hunting coat.

His gun. Gerry prayed it wouldn't be needed.

'How is Castor?' Sybil asked after Gerry had introduced himself and they all began cantering back the way he had come. She had Castor's rug slung over the front of the saddle of her borrowed horse and Gerry could see the tail of a horse bandage trailing from the pocket of her riding jacket. At least she was looking on the bright side.

'I – I don't know. I think it's the tendon,' he said. 'But I'm not sure.'

'Your horsebox is coming,' Mr Maddox said. 'I directed the driver around the lanes and he'll get as close as he can. I saw him fall, you see, but they both got up and, damn it, if you stopped every time someone took a tumble you'd never get a run, would you?'

They were silent then until they opened another gate and could see, among the mist and the rain, James standing at his horse's hanging head, the two of them looking like the ghost of hunting past. Castor pricked up his ears and looked dully at the approaching horses and James turned, his face white.

'It's a vet!' Gerry called, and James managed a smile.

They all got off their horses and Gerry took the reins of the vet's and Sybil's. Sybil removed the green hunting coat from Castor's back and covered the horse with his own rug. James watched anxiously as the vet knelt, undid the pin and unwrapped Gerry's makeshift bandage. He looked up.

'Not a bad job,' he said.

'Get on with it, *please*,' James pleaded.

'Can I have my coat?' Gerry was shivering so much he could hardly speak.

Sybil took James's place at Castor's head and James brought the coat over and held the reins of the other three horses while Gerry put it on over his soaking shirt and waistcoat. He felt in the inside pocket.

'Got my flask?'

James handed it over. 'Finished it. Sorry,' he said, still staring at the vet as he probed Castor's leg.

'Oh.' With numb fingers, Gerry buttoned the coat up and took the reins back.

At last the vet spoke.

'You were right. It's the tendon.'

'Thank God!' James whispered and turned away, his shoulders shaking.

'But listen, young man. It's gone – lock, stock and barrel.' Mr Maddox stood up and patted Castor's neck. 'He's a handsome horse but he won't be much good for this kind of business again.'

He felt in his left pocket, tugged out his gun and dropped it casually on the ground, then pulled out a handkerchief and blew his nose.

Sybil, grinning broadly, produced a bandage and some cotton wool. Mr Maddox looked at them admiringly.

'Now that's what I call sensible.' He nodded to the gun where it lay glinting on the wet grass. 'Me, I always expect the worst.' He winked at Gerry. 'What's your friend's name?'

'James. James Flimwell,' Gerry said, his teeth chattering.

'Hear this, young Flimwell,' the vet said to James's back. 'Your horse is in a bad way, no doubt about it. He'll have to be fired, of course, but you may be able to ride him around quietly in a year or so's time. Good enough for you?'

'Yes. Thank you,' James said and sniffed. 'I'm sorry.'

The vet unravelled the bandage Sybil handed to him and began rolling it up tightly.

'If you are going to have horses, you must put up with this sort of thing. It happens. Horses have ever made strong men weep. Them and women,' he added gloomily. 'Now, will you come and hold your horse's head, please, and you,' he said to Sybil as he came to the end of the bandage, 'hold this for me.' He reached into the right pocket of his coat, removed another bandage, tightly rolled, and tossed it to her. 'Two's got to be better than one as we've got to bandage both legs. We don't want him straining the other one, do we? And ' – he drew a roll of cotton wool from his inside pocket – 'since we want them on as tight as can be we'll need this as well. . . . And this. You look like you need it.' He threw his flask at Gerry's feet.

Gerry laughed as he bent to pick it up.

'You're like a magician, sir,' he said. 'Something out of every pocket.'

He had seemed so grim, riding towards Castor with his gun in one pocket and all the time with help and succour in the others.

Mr Maddox again knelt by Castor and, aided by Sybil, began to bandage his off fore.

'Left the rabbit at home,' he grunted.

After phone calls to Flimwell Place, it was decided that Castor would stay with David Maddox and be attended by his grooms until a horsebox from home could be sent to collect him and bring James another horse to ride on the same trip. James went into the cosy, straw-filled stable to say goodbye to his horse. Castor, his mouth full of hay, had that smug look of an animal that knows it is well looked after and has every chance of being spoiled.

James pulled his ears and gave him a carrot donated by Mr Maddox's housekeeper.

'Well, so long, old thing,' he said, and Castor nuzzled his pockets hoping for more treats. James put his arm around his neck and stood there for a minute before turning back to Gerry, who was waiting for him at the stable door.

'I wonder if I'll ever ride him again,' he said.

When, eventually, they got back to Cambridge, James declared he needed his friends around him that night and, while he bathed and changed, Gerry, still in his hunting clothes, went round to Magdalene to summon Mark and then to St Catharine's to find Andrew. He had refused to come drag-hunting since his sacking and was, he said, training his horse in secret for the point-to-point. He was distressed to hear about Castor and agreed that a jolly evening at the Pitt Club would buck James up no end.

'I won't come, though,' he warned, 'if that fellow White is there.'

'No chance of that,' Gerry said. Stephen had been furious at the commandeering of the hunt horsebox for Castor and he, his horse and the hounds – 'with a notable absence of whippers-in, and *no* groom,' he had said acidly – had been kept waiting, all of them in warmth and comfort (though that he did not mention) for an hour before they were collected.

'Well, I'll come then,' said Andrew. 'Hey, are you all right, Gerry? You look a bit done up.'

'Tired,' Gerry replied. 'That's all. I'll see you later.'

Then he remembered he was supposed to be going to see a film with Kate. How could he have forgotten that? So he went back through Trinity to get his car and, feeling he had been through almost as much as James today, drove to Girton. Kate opened the door immediately he knocked.

'I've been so worried!' she exclaimed. 'You're over an hour late.'

'Am I? I'm sorry,' he mumbled.

She took his hand. 'Gerry, you're freezing. Come and sit by the fire.'

'Can't stay,' he said, and told her what had happened.

'Of course you must be with James,' she said. 'Don't worry about me. We can see the film any time. But,' she added, 'by the look of you, Gerry, you should go back, have a bath and get straight to bed. You're shivering, for heaven's sake!'

'Just a bit tired.' It was lovely in Kate's room and he wanted more than anything to stay there and be looked after. Much nicer than looking after James, which is what he had to go and do now.

He turned at the door. 'I nearly forgot,' he said.

'What?'

'To kiss you hello . . . and goodbye.'

She put her arms around his waist, inside his jacket.

'Gerry, you're soaking wet! No wonder you're so cold. . . . *Promise* me you'll have a bath.'

He grinned. 'If you'll come and scrub my back.'

She kissed him. 'And wrap up warmly when you go out again.'

'Yes, doctor,' he said, and lurched off down the corridor.

He arrived at his rooms in New Court to find his sitting room occupied by several men, all with glasses in their hands. It was obviously going to be quite a party.

'There you are!' Mark said cheerfully. 'We thought you'd disappeared from the face of the earth. Well – bustle along, old chap,' he added as Gerry sat wearily at his desk, it being the only available chair.

'I'm having a bath. Doctor's orders.'

'Later, Gerry. We're nearly out of whisky. We've got to get James drunk and the minutes are ticking by.'

Gerry stood up. 'At least let me change, then. And you can bloody well pull off my boots. I don't think I've got the strength.'

James did, indeed, get very drunk that night, and very maudlin.

'I stood in that bloody field, rain pouring down, not a soul in sight, and I reminded Castor about the races we'd won and told him we'd win more. But oh Lord,' he said, his voice thickening, 'all the time I was thinking we were just waiting for the bullet. And I was going through what I'd do . . . I'd stand just where I was, in front of him, and the man with the gun would be to one side, I thought, so Castor would never know a thing.'

He shook his head, drained his glass and called for more wine.

'But he's all right,' Andrew said. 'He's alive—'

'Yes,' said James, 'he's alive. And thanks to Gerry! Gerry was splendid! A toast to Gerry!'

'To Gerry,' they all said solemnly, raising their glasses.

'He knew all about it. Took one look and said, "I'd bet on a tendon," and by God that's what the horse quack said . . . How did you do it, Gerry?'

Gerry, who longed for his bed, could actually visualise it, the white sheets turned back ready to welcome him, said feebly, 'Dunno. Just did.'

He was, he now realised, more than tired. It wasn't the drink – he hadn't had a great deal of it – but he was sweating and at the same time he felt dreadfully cold, and the others' voices were coming sometimes from a great distance and sometimes they seemed to be booming in his ears. His left leg, the one affected by polio when he was a child, was tingling.

How did I do it? Dunno? 'Course he bloody knew! Da'ud made sure of that. Gypsies could talk to horses, ask them what's the matter . . . A lot of bloody nonsense that was, but gypsies knew about their horses and didn't leave it up to the groom. Da always said you find out what's the matter wi' your beast an' then if you can't deal wi' it yourself – an' most times you can, Gerry-lad – you call the vet an' tell him what to do. But had Da ever had to diagnose a mightily sprained tendon in a freezing field with a nob crying and yelling at you, 'Get a gun'?

But – Christ alive! *Was he saying this aloud?*

He awoke in his bed in his rooms in New Court, Trinity College, Cambridge. Kate was leaning over him, feeling his forehead. He stared at her wildly.

'Polio! I haven't got it again, have I?'

She smiled at him. 'You can't get it twice.'

'I'm cold, Kate.' He groped for her hand and held it against his

91

cheek. 'What did I say last night? . . . May have given the whole show away. All gone,' he muttered, and closed his eyes.

Kate tried to pull her hand away, but he whispered 'No' and held it tighter.

'Let me go, Gerry,' she said firmly, and with a little whimper he obeyed.

She went across to James's rooms. Mark had arrived.

'How is Gerry?' he asked. 'He had us worried last night, didn't he, James? Raving about gypsies and then fainting clean away.'

'He needs a doctor.' She turned to James. 'Have you called one?'

'Crystal's seeing to it.'

'A doctor!' Mark said. 'Poor old Gerry. What's up with him?'

'I don't know, but he's got a high temperature. James, can you see if Crystal's back? Tell him to bring clean sheets – Gerry's are soaked with sweat. You'll have to help change them and put Gerry into his pyjamas.'

James nodded and went out.

'Poor old Gerry,' Mark repeated.

Kate sighed. These were young men who expected to go out into the world and run other people's lives as well as their own, and they possessed not an ounce of common sense between them. They had carried Gerry back from the Pitt Club last night and tipped him into bed, having half undressed him (his jacket and trousers were on the floor of his bedroom) and gone off to their drunken slumbers. James had looked in this morning because Gerry had missed breakfast and James knew he had a nine o'clock lecture. He had realised something was wrong, but instead of calling a doctor straight away, or even Crystal who would have known to do so, he had run to his car, driven to Girton and caught Kate just as she was setting out for Cambridge – a first-year medical student, for heaven's sake!

James came back into the room.

'The doctor's coming, and so is Crystal. He's bringing the bedder. I wouldn't,' he said apologetically, 'be much good at changing sheets and things.'

'I don't suppose you would,' she said.

'I say, Kate, it's not serious, is it?' Mark asked.

'I expect it's only a chill, but he's got such a high fever. He was so cold and wet last night . . . He promised he'd have a bath before he went out.'

She felt a hundred years older than them and she knew she sounded like the nannies who had, no doubt, brought them up, but she couldn't help it when there was Gerry bathed in sweat saying, 'I'm cold.' And, indeed, Mark looked suitably admonished and a little shame-faced and James said, as though it excused everything: 'He put his coat on Castor, you see.'

Kate looked at them both. Would they turn their backs on Gerry if they found out who he really was? *Could* they?

'He's a good friend to you,' she said. 'Isn't he?'

'Oh he's the best,' they agreed easily.

Gerry was taken to the Infirmary, confined to bed for three days and was then allowed back to his own room with instructions to take things easy for another week. He began to enjoy himself. Kate told him that no one had paid much attention to his ramblings about gypsies, and he received a gratifying number of visitors as he sat before his gas fire, his books open but on the whole unstudied around him. Stephen White came and apologised for being so angry about the defection of his two whippers-in; Nick O'Rourke came and said he was honoured to be in the presence of a hero – because, it seemed, in every telling of the story James was further exaggerating Gerry's role and diminishing that of the vet; Vanessa came and spent half an hour attempting to make Gerry a cup of cocoa he did not want, until Mark appeared and they all had a whisky instead; even Eileen McLennan came, remarking in her cool voice that, you see, bicycles have a great advantage over horses: you don't threaten to shoot them when a wheel is damaged and you don't catch a chill when mending a puncture.

'How would you know? You get other people to mend your punctures,' he said, remembering.

She laughed her nice laugh. 'I try to.'

And, of course, Kate came. On the first afternoon, she brought her books and sat on the rug at his feet attempting to study. She didn't get much work done, for Gerry was constantly interrupting

93

her and then visitors would knock on the door and interrupt them both.

'Come again tomorrow,' he said as she prepared to leave.

'I mustn't, Gerry. You're so – so—'

'Attractive? Magnetic? Irresistible?'

'Distracting,' she said.

He kissed her. She felt his brow.

'What's the verdict, doctor?' he asked, running his hands up and down her back and then sneaking them forwards to try and feel her breasts. 'I'm sure my temperature's just gone up.'

She pushed him away. 'You're supposed to be ill,' she scolded.

He held his arms wide. 'Sorry, Kate, come back in.' She did and he hugged her, his arms innocent. 'Will you drive – *Wren*-drive – yourself back to Girton in my car?'

'No, I'll bicycle.'

'Please, Kate. It's horrible weather and I hate to think of you out there on your bike just because you've come to see me.' His illness had weakened him and he found that his voice was breaking. He thrust the car keys into her hand. 'Please, Kate' he said again.

He soon began to feel better and was fit enough to go to the ball on the Friday night (for of course he had persuaded Kate to go with him). He wasn't able to ride in the point-to-point but was allowed by his medical adviser to attend as a spectator.

'Yes, doctor,' he replied in answer to her query, 'I'm wearing a vest, a shirt, two sweaters, a jacket *and* an overcoat. . . . Now I want to know in as great a detail exactly what you're wearing.'

'Tell me if you get tired or cold and we'll leave,' she said, ignoring the last part of his remark. 'Promise you'll say.'

'I promise.'

He so loved being fussed over by her that it was almost worth being an invalid for life.

The Members' race was won by a man who had been at Jesus in the late twenties and, people said, his horse looked scarcely younger than he did. Andrew's horse pitched him off at the second fence. He failed to catch it and four fences on it jumped across Stephen White and his horse, bringing them both down, and then disappeared in the direction of Ely.

Gerry and James roared with laughter, and James's partner at the ball last night – the Alice who had caught chickenpox – turned questioningly to Kate. Kate explained the situation between Stephen and Andrew, and Alice who, amazingly, was not a society maiden but a secretary in a London publishing company laughed with the rest of them – once she had seen that both Stephen and his horse were safely on their feet and unhurt, for she was a kind girl and would suit James very well, Kate thought.

Summer in Cambridge, that loveliest of cities.

'Do you know what my mother once said to me?' Kate asked as she lay in the punt, her hand trailing over the side into the water.

'No.' Gerry shot the punt under the bridge at Clare and on towards King's.

'She said Venice has water and buildings but Cambridge has gardens and water and buildings.'

'I've never been to Venice,' Gerry said. 'Shall we go?'

She smiled lazily up at him. 'When? Tomorrow?'

He lifted the pole out of the water and considered for a moment.

'No,' he said and propelled the punt forwards again. 'Not tomorrow. We've got a picnic lunch, we're playing croquet in the afternoon and going to two cocktail parties in the evening.'

Kate yawned. 'Great heavens, so we are. Aren't we gadabouts?'

She turned on one side, stretched out her legs and then tucked the toe of one foot under the opposite knee. She was wearing a cotton dress of pale pink patterned with dark blue flowers which, apart from thin straps, left her shoulders bare, an old but very fetching straw hat and no stockings. Gerry, standing at the stern of their craft, wondered if punts had been specially designed so men could have such a splendid view of their best girls as they piloted them along the river while pretending to admire buildings and gardens.

He felt he deserved it as he hadn't seen much of Kate this term. She had been working hard for her exams and had only taken Saturday nights and Sundays off – and not even those recently. He hadn't tried to persuade her out more often after that once, when he had said, grumpily, that there were other things in life apart from work and she had rounded on him, eyes blazing, saying not for her, not for women in Cambridge there weren't, and would he please go? All the women seemed to drive themselves: the sense of urgency, only just this side of hysteria, was almost tangible in the corridors of Girton. Gerry supposed there were men who took their studies seriously, but he didn't know any. On the whole it was considered rather bad form. James, who, like Kate, had exams this year that would contribute to his degree, had been his usual self and the Pitt Club seemed normal enough, chaps going off to watch a spot of cricket at Fenner's or off to London or elsewhere for parties.

Gerry bent his legs, pushed the pole again and they glided under Silver Street and into the millpond. A punt full of noisy post-exam undergraduates lost its pole and one member of the party fell into the water. Gerry looked down at Kate, expecting her to be enjoying the fun, and found that she was asleep, her dark lashes closed under her hat, her lips slightly parted, her hand under her chin. Gerry steered the punt through the throng towards the weir and stepped out on to the ramp. He had to waken Kate, but she looked so beautifully peaceful he was reluctant to disturb her. He was still wondering what to do when a crowd of men came down the towpath.

'What's this then?' one said, staring into the punt and then, after an appropriate pause, added a reverent 'Cor!'

And Gerry, prey to a whole range of emotions from a feeling of intense protectiveness to raging desire – as he saw them look at the swell of Kate's breasts, exaggerated by her sideways position, and the bare knee showing from under the flowery dress – said helplessly, 'She's going to be a doctor, see? She's just finished some exams.'

'A doctor!' the man said. 'And us mere engineers.' He glanced briefly at Gerry's white flannels and striped blazer and then, after a low-voiced conference, the six of them lifted the punt, carried it up the ramp and tipped it carefully into the upper reach of the river. Kate shifted among her cushions but did not wake.

'Is she really going to be a doctor?' one of the men said, cutting short Gerry's thanks.

'She is.'

96

'Good luck to her,' he said softly and lounged off with his friends.

Gerry poled the punt towards Grantchester between buttercup-filled meadows where horses grazed and cows lay peacefully chewing the cud. Kate stirred and her dress rode up as she did so, revealing a generous portion of thigh. Gerry looked and laughed to himself. He felt like a prince in a fairy tale, on a boat on a river under a wide blue sky surrounded by yellow fields, conveying his lady love he knew not where.

She awoke at last while Gerry, as quietly as he could, was planting the pole in the river bottom to trap the punt against the bank. She muttered a little, sat up, took off her hat and gazed around in bewilderment.

'Have I been asleep? Where are we?' she asked.

'Yes, for ages, and I'm not sure,' he said. 'I was about to kiss my sleeping beauty awake.' He helped her ashore and kissed her anyway.

She stood, still drowsy, among the buttercups while Gerry handed her a rug to carry, took the picnic basket and cushions from the punt and led the way towards the middle of the field. She spread the rug out where he directed and sat on it, yawning again.

'I'm sorry. I don't seem to be very thrilling company today.'

'Yeah. I'll take you back and exchange you for a livelier model.'

'I wouldn't blame – Gerry!'

Out of the basket he had produced a bottle of champagne.

'Special tonic for medical students at the end of their exams,' he said. 'A late birthday present to celebrate your first.'

'Honestly!' She touched his cheek lightly. 'Are we going to drink it all?'

'No one else around to help, I'm afraid. ... Unhand me, woman,' he said, wishing she would touch more than his cheek, 'I'm unpacking our tea. I managed to hide one of Ma's parcels from James.'

He laid out the food and opened the champagne while she held the glasses. He put the bottle in the now empty basket and took a glass.

'To you, Dr Earith.'

'To you, Gerry.'

She sipped her champagne and bit into one of Mrs Beviss's biscuits.

'Heavenly! Could anything be more blissful? Now, Gerry, tell me what's been going on. How's your rowing?'

Gerry and Mark hadn't had important first-year exams and Gerry, with Florin at home and out to grass and Kate occupied, had taken up sculling under Mark's tutelage.

'I'm not very good at it,' he said. 'Still, it's quite fun . . . at least it is when my girl is in purdah in Girton.' He cut a piece of cake and offered it to her. 'But she's out of purdah now, isn't she?'

'She is.' Kate took the cake. 'And feeling she might even stay awake for another hour or so.'

'She's just as beautiful when she's asleep,' he said, and told her how she had been so tenderly conveyed up the ramp by the engineers.

'Six hulking men and every one in love with you. Well, seven including me. I am hulking, aren't I? Please say I am.'

'Gerry, how embarrassing!' she exclaimed. 'You should have woken me. Why didn't you?'

She was blushing. He could see it even in the shadow under her hat. He put the debris of their picnic into the basket, took her glass and put that in as well, tipped her hat off and pulled her down to lie beside him on the rug.

'Because I thought you needed the rest,' he said, and kissed her.

For a few blissful moments, his hand wandered over her body, feeling everything under the thin cotton dress. And he could feel her responding, too, her body straining to meet his roving hand. He felt the smooth skin of her calf, and then the thigh that had been exposed to his gaze as she lay sleeping in the punt. He stroked it, long, gentle sweeps, getting higher each time. His lips were on hers, his tongue in her mouth, her tongue meeting it, and his hand now at the top of her thighs . . . and even as, somewhere in his mind, a delighted voice was saying, This is it! It really is! her legs stiffened and closed and her arms, instead of holding him tightly to her, were pushing him away.

'No – no more, Gerry. Please.'

He stopped immediately, even though the throbbing in his groin was screaming at him to go on. He slid his hand back down her thigh and rested it there, but she was still rigid, still trying to push him away.

'It's all right,' he said softly. 'We won't do anything you don't want to.'

She relaxed then and smiled a little shyly at him. They kissed again, gently, Gerry using every ounce of self-control he possessed to keep it that way. He was in an absolute turmoil, his erection threatening to explode, his hands desperate to touch her all over, but she might get frightened again if he tried too hard too soon, might even insist on them leaving . . .

That was the secret: stop as soon as they tell you, because that way you don't lose any of the ground you've gained. His hand was on her thigh still, far higher than he'd ever managed to get it before. Patience, Gerry, he told himself and nearly groaned aloud. . . . For those dizzying moments had told him – surely they had! – that she wanted it as much as he did. All he had to do was to get her to acknowledge that fact. But there was time, there was lots of time and for now he'd gone far enough. Amazingly, his body obeyed his mind and he lay kissing his girl in a buttercup meadow under a wide Cambridgeshire sky, wanting no more.

And when their lips finally parted and she lay cradled in his left arm – his right hand *still* high on her thigh – he said, 'Oh Kate, I do love you!' and moved his hand to cover her breast, his thumb sneaking down to feel the soft flesh under her dress, she didn't draw away or move to stop him but gazed up at him out of her navy-blue eyes and said, 'Aren't we a lucky pair, then, Gerry? Because I love you too.' And then she did push his hand away and sat up.

'Have we finished the champagne?'

Feeling dazed, he picked up the bottle and the discarded glasses. 'You've never said that to me before.'

She stared out towards the river, its presence evident only by their punt pole standing straight against the sky and a boater sporting college colours gliding above the mass of buttercups.

'I've never said it to anyone before,' she said at last.

He laughed shakily. 'Well, what are we going to do about it then?'

99

She turned to him and smiled. 'Why, have some champagne to celebrate, I should think.'

He filled the glasses hurriedly.

'No, Kate, I meant—'

Her smile vanished. 'I know what you meant, Gerry, and the answer is no.'

'But if you love me . . . we love each other – Kate, it'll be safe. I know how to make it safe for you so you don't . . . you don't—'

'The answer is still no. Please, Gerry. Don't spoil our day.'

The expression on his face turned from eagerness to, momentarily, sulkiness, but then his devastating grin appeared and he reached out and tweaked her dark fringe.

'No. I won't spoil our day.'

'And we won't talk about it any more,' she said firmly.

There is time, Gerry told himself again, and for the next week, May Week, he thought he was the luckiest man alive as he escorted Kate to parties, proud to have on his arm a beautiful girl who, in spite of approaches from other men, some of them with titles and what not, had eyes for no one but him. They drank cocktails on the scented summer evenings in the fellows' gardens along the Backs, at King's and Queens' and Clare, at Trinity and St John's, sometimes going to three parties a night. They went to watch the Bumps where Vanessa caused hilarity by saying in a loud and concerned voice, 'Oh what a shame! Mark's boat hit the one in front,' and had to be told that bumping the boat ahead was the object of the thing. They went to two May Balls – Trinity's and Magdalene's – and danced all night then punted up to Grantchester at dawn, the women in their long dresses, stoles around their shoulders against the chill, the men in their tails and white ties, floating through the mist-hazed buttercup meadows where horses grazed and cows lay idly chewing the cud.

And term ended, the University year ended, trunks were packed up and put in store or taken home – some of them for good – and the shining city of Cambridge was left to dream the rest of the summer away, its colleges silent, the courts the preserve of tourists and the dons and fellows who called no other place home.

Chapter 8

Kate was given a first and rang Gerry to tell him. The phone was answered by a woman with such a strong accent that Kate had trouble understanding her but gathered that Gerry was off with the horses. She left a message, and he rang back that evening. He was as thrilled by her news as she was and said he would drive over to Sissinghurst straight away and take her out to celebrate. She put the phone back on the hook and went into the kitchen.

'I'm going out to supper, Beattie. Do you mind?'

Beattie put a pot in the oven, watched by an ever-hopeful Flash, and straightened up.

'Is Gerry coming then? I can give him his socks.'

Kate laughed and flung her arms around her aunt's well-padded shoulders.

'You're as much in love with him as I am. Admit it!'

'He's a very pretty young man.' Beattie pushed Kate back and looked up at her. Her niece's eyes were sparkling and her cheeks were pink, as they had been ever since the post had brought the news that morning.

'Kate, I can't tell you how happy I am to see you like this,' she said, weak tears starting in her eyes.

'I know they're only my first-year exams,' Kate said, 'and I was always going to study medicine, but I haven't been really sure if I was right. Whether it was just because Daddy was a doctor and Ricky said he'd be one too.'

Ricky, her brother, long gone. He'd be sixteen now.

'And now you *are* sure.'

'Yes!'

Charles came home, bringing a bottle of champgne. The three of them had just finished drinking it when Kate heard Gerry's car drive up. She flew out of the house and into his arms.

'Oh well done, my Kate,' he said. 'My sacrifice wasn't in vain, then. Mind you,' he added, 'I'd have personally assaulted the examiners if they hadn't given you *at least* a first.'

She clung to his arm. 'We've been drinking champagne,' she said.

He reached into the car and brought out another bottle.

'The pair to the one we had by the river,' he said. 'I've been saving it.'

She stood in front of him now. She couldn't keep still. He had never seen her like this before. She was electric.

'Oh, Gerry you . . . you're the absolute tops,' she said as they went into the house, where Gerry greeted Beattie and handed his bottle over to Charles to be opened.

'We shall get quite squiffy,' Beattie said. 'Charles and I aren't used to high living like you two are.'

'We used to be,' Charles said. 'Do you remember that May Ball?' He filled their glasses.

'I fell into the river,' Beattie confessed. 'Charles and Donald – your father, my darling – had to pull me out.' She saw the look on Gerry's face and added, 'I wasn't so fat then, you see. It wasn't too difficult for them.'

Gerry blushed, for that was exactly what he had been thinking, but then Beattie handed him a brown paper package.

'For you,' she said.

'For me? What is it?' Intrigued, he opened it. A pair of hand-knitted bottle-green socks. He was touched and – it was absurd but he couldn't help it – roused. It seemed so intimate to wear a pair of socks knitted by Kate's aunt.

'Thank you,' he stammered. 'Thank you very much.' And, boldly, he kissed Beattie on the cheek.

'Now that's made my day,' she said placidly. 'I thought you could wear them shooting, Gerry.'

'Yes,' he said. Nick O'Rourke's parents had taken a house in Scotland and he and Kate – along with other Cambridge friends –

had been invited to stay for a week in August. 'Except I can't shoot. The fishing bit's easy enough, though, isn't it? A worm on the hook and you're away.'

Charles spluttered into his champagne.

'It's the Spey, damn it, boy! The finest salmon fishing in the world. Didn't you tell me it's the Spey?' he asked Kate, honest shock on his face.

'Yes, but Gerry's only teasing you.' She turned her brilliant gaze on him. 'Aren't you?'

'No worms, I promise,' Gerry said, grinning. 'I'll just watch.'

Charles looked at him. 'No need to do that. I'll teach you to cast a fly line, and Kate too. We can start on the lawn here.'

'Come and join us for supper on Thursday, Gerry,' Beattie said. 'You can both have your first lesson then.'

'Well, thank you, Beattie . . . sir,' he said, clutching his glass of champagne and his socks, and feeling nicely overwhelmed.

Later, much later, Gerry parked the car in the gateway of a field near Charles and Beattie's house.

'Come on, let's go for a walk.'

It was a warm June night, moonlit, and they walked hand in hand between stooks of hay until Gerry drew her to him and they kissed.

'Wait here,' he whispered and ran back to the car, returning a few minutes later with a blanket. He pulled down some sheaves of hay and threw the blanket over them. 'Lie down, Kate. Please.'

'Gerry, I—'

'*Please!*'

Since that time by the river, Gerry's kisses had been undemanding and his hands had, on the whole, kept within bounds, but now he was nuzzling her neck and his hands were at her breasts and she couldn't help her body responding. And he felt it, the jolt that shot through her, and his lips were on hers, forcing them open, and she found herself on the blanket, the sheaves of hay soft under her back and Gerry on top of her, heavy for a moment. Then he lifted himself off her and to one side and she could feel him hard against her hip . . . and she was going to stop him then but he had undone the buttons of her dress and in the same instant had lifted her bra

103

to expose her breasts. His hand upon her naked breasts: intense pleasure followed shock as he touched one and then the other and then began stroking the right one, his thumb on the nipple, while he rocked to and fro, rubbing himself against her, his hand pulling and pinching now . . . And she freed her lips, saying, as he gasped and his whole body jerked, 'Gerry – no! No more now,' and immediately he was still, although he breathed as though he had been running, and so did she. They lay silent for a while, and then she spoke.

'Gerry, I meant what I said.'

'I know you did, Kate.' His voice was full of laughter. 'And so did I.'

'What did you say?' she asked suspiciously.

'That we wouldn't do anything you don't want to.'

She realised that his hand was still on her breast and tried to push it away.

'And,' he added virtuously, 'you said we weren't to talk about it. . . . It's all right . . .' His fingers stroked softly. 'It's nice, isn't it? You don't get babies this way, you know – and you with your first!'

He bent his head and kissed her other breast, his tongue lapping the nipple, and she lay there thinking there could be no harm in this: it felt good – so very good! – and she didn't know that her hands had reached out and were in his hair, pushing his head against her, and she was near to swooning with pleasure when he murmured, his lips against her breast, 'You like it, Kate. Say you like it.'

It brought her back to her senses and, because she couldn't admit that she did, she said, 'Enough, please,' and, very gently, he pulled her bra back down and buttoned up her dress.

She sat up, conscious of a feeling of anticlimax, disappointment even. He helped her to her feet and they righted the sheaves of hay they had been lying on. Gerry slung the blanket over his shoulder and took her hand as they walked back to the car. In silence they drove the short distance to Beattie and Charles's house.

'You're a first-class girl in every way,' Gerry whispered as he kissed her good night at the door. 'See you on Thursday.'

Kate wandered into the kitchen, shushed Flash – who was

inclined to bark once he saw it was a friend and not a foe in the house, the coward – and put some milk and water to heat up on the stove. She sat at the table and tried to still the tempest inside her. She felt hot with shame at what she had done – had allowed to be done to her – but at the same time her body tingled at the memory. And, yes, she had liked it, had wanted it to go on . . . Flash's cold nose pushed against her hand and she patted his head absently. He clambered on to her lap, the stupid dog, and frantically licked her ear.

Tongues. The world was full of them.

'I know what you want,' she said, pushing his head away. 'You want some of my cocoa, don't you?' Flash gazed at her with the mournful sympathy that only spaniels can achieve.

She hugged him and, his whole body wagging with his tail, he began licking her again . . . But it wasn't wrong, was it, what she had done tonight? As long as it went no further, and it wouldn't . . . A hayfield, moonlit, and Gerry stopping the moment she said no, his teasing voice reminding her of the limits she herself had set . . . A postcard from Cambridge with a casual '1' written in the blank left for the class.

She rose to her feet and Flash jumped to the floor, his ears cocked expectantly. She took the saucepan from the stove and stood there, aware, actually aware, that at this moment – out of all the hundreds of thousands of moments in her life – she was happy.

Gerry, driving home, laughed out loud. He had come in his trousers and it was sticky and uncomfortable there – but what timing! He had come just as she said 'no more', and could he have stopped himself earlier?

He pinned back his ears and prepared for a summer's hunting.

They had their fly-fishing lessons, standing solemnly on the lawn and learning how to cast the line so the fly would land on the water as delicately as the insect it pretended to be. And then, when they had the hang of it and the line didn't crack like a whip as they brought the rod forward but came down smoothly to lie on the grass near to where Charles had placed circles of string, Charles muttered, 'This is all very well, but we need some bloody water.' And he got on the telephone to a friend and organised a day's trout fishing on the River Test in Hampshire, and then, because, he said, they had to catch the morning and evening rise, he booked them all in for two nights at a hotel.

'Charles, really!' Beattie exclaimed when he explained the arrangements. 'This is most high-handed of you.'

Though what she really meant was that it was not proper for her and Charles to take Kate and Gerry to a hotel. It made assumptions about their relationship; it made Gerry look like a future nephew-in-law, which Beattie wouldn't have minded at all except it was all a bit precipitate.

'Bosh!' said Charles roundly.

'Perhaps Gerry is busy. Aren't you busy at the horse shows, Gerry?'

'No,' he replied.

He wasn't. Arthur and Joe had found another rider, a young woman called Grace Martin, to school the horses and ride them at the early shows while Gerry was still away. Under Grace's gimlet eye, Gerry had knocked poles down left, right and centre in the paddock at home and then, two Saturdays ago, had collected twenty-four faults riding one of their most promising young horses at an important show. Grace had won on the horse the previous week. Gerry protested he was out of practice, not having ridden since Easter, but Grace's shrug and her unconvinced grey gaze had made Gerry more nervous than ever and things had not improved. And then Grace had gone to Joe – behind Gerry's back to Joe! – and Joe had said it was best Grace rode the promising bay horse, and the chestnut, and the nice four-year-old that had been going so well for her. Gerry wasn't going to ride what was left, and Florin – who surely wouldn't let him down – was resting for the summer.

'No, I'm not busy,' he said.

'Oh well, all right,' Beattie sighed, and so Gerry spent his first night under the same roof as Kate sleeping in the next bed to a lightly snoring Charles.

Early the next morning, they stood on the riverbank as Charles, in a hushed voice, showed them pools where wily brown trout were likely to be lurking and told them not to stand between the sun and the river and to move quietly along the bank.

'Can they hear us, then, sir?' Gerry asked.

'Of course they can,' Charles whispered, and Gerry thought that'ud be a joke to tell the lads in the Anchor.

They didn't catch any fish but Gerry enjoyed the day. That evening, as they were eating supper, Charles remarked that it was a pity they weren't eating trout they had caught themselves and Gerry said that casting a fly where you wanted to put it without stirring a ripple on the water was just as satisfying, and if he wanted to catch fish he could go out in one of his father's boats and get tons of them.

Charles reached his right hand across the table and Gerry, bewildered, took it.

'Spoken like a true fisherman,' Charles said. 'That's exactly the point.'

For Kate – who had spent most of the day untangling her line from the trees and bushes on the riverbank and untying the knots the fine catgut seemed positively to revel in getting itself into – that time spent in Gerry's company was a wondrous relief. But afterwards, things went back to what had become the norm. He said he knew she wouldn't go all the way with him, but his hands wanted to be everywhere and, although he always stopped when she asked him to, he always tried again. He would park the car in the gateway to a field, get the horse blanket out of the boot (the first time she had thought it purely fortuitous he had it there, just as she thought it fortuitous that he always led her unerringly to the softest grass in the apple and cherry orchards or to meadows free of cowpats or sheep droppings: now she knew the blanket was kept in the car for this purpose and she was sure he reconnoitred the land he took her to) and they would lie on it and he would bare her breasts – she allowed him freedom above the waist; it seemed only fair – and then his hand would slide from her knee to her thigh and upwards. One night he had opened his trousers and guided her hand down there. She had felt the great warm hard thing and recoiled, and then he had rubbed it against her leg, moaning the while. When he had finished, he found that she was crying and had been horrified, had held her tenderly.

107

'Kate, don't. Please. I'm sorry,' he had said. 'I love you so much and I can't help wanting you.'

And she loved him and wanted him, too, but she wouldn't – *she couldn't* – cross that last bridge for him. It would be a betrayal of the way she was brought up . . . of her parents, of herself.

So after that, she tried to make their meetings more public. They went to Bodiam Castle, to the site of the Battle of Hastings, they looked round Sir Harold and Lady Nicolson's gardens at Sissinghurst Castle and had nice safe drinks at the pub in the village – safe because the Bull was within walking distance of Charles and Beattie's house and there were no dangerous fields on the way. As often as Charles could spare the car and petrol, Kate drove over to Ryehurst. Once she was asked to tea and was charmed by Mrs Beviss in her bright skirt as she shyly offered Kate food from a black-market-laden table. Joe asked astutely after her uncle's business and lost interest on hearing that Charles was a solicitor in Cranbrook; Arthur, Gerry's brother – his face such a strange distortion of Gerry's – gazed at her intently until Grace Martin arrived and he gazed at her instead.

After tea, they went to say hello to Florin, fat as a barrel in his green pasture.

'Do you realise that your brother is in love with Grace?' Kate said as Florin nibbled the cuff of her cardigan.

Gerry stared at her. 'D'you reckon?' He thought about it for a moment. 'Well, perhaps you're right. Rather him than me, though.'

They went down to the beach because Flash – whom Kate had brought along as an additional chaperon – wanted a walk. He ran about in circles, his ears flapping, madly chasing seagulls.

'Do you mind her riding the horses?' Kate asked.

'Nah, not really.' Gerry picked up a pebble and threw it for Flash to retrieve. 'The horses are going well for her, and' – he put his arm around her shoulders – 'there's the other thing, too.'

'What other thing?'

'You know . . . Smart people go to the big agricultural shows and someone may see me and – well – find out.'

'And report it to your Cambridge friends? For heaven's sake,

Gerry, will you ever stop fussing? You've survived a year at Cambridge. They like you because you're you.'

He wouldn't believe her, though, and they walked along the edge of the waves talking of other things until Gerry led her up the bank of shingle and put his jacket down for her to sit on. She hesitated and then sat primly, thinking that surely even he wouldn't want to try anything on these uncomfortable stones – just as he was thinking that it must have been around here that he and Molly had been last October . . . nine months since he'd done it! And Molly ready for him all the summer, and he refusing her unspoken invitations because he only wanted Kate . . . But as soon as he started to kiss her now, his hand only on her calf, she began to push him away.

'Kate!' He looked at her, all hurt innocence – innocence like hell! – in his dark eyes.

'It's just going to turn into the usual wrestling match, Gerry.'

The eyes danced. 'Two submissions and a fall and I'm all yours.'

'When will you realise that I *mean* no?'

He stroked her calf. 'Look, Kate, I'm not going to do anything wicked in broad daylight on an open beach, now am I?'

'I wouldn't put it past you,' she said.

He leaned forward and kissed her very gently, his hand not moving an inch.

'All right?' He smiled at her, but *still* she could see the confidence in his handsome face and knew this was only a temporary cessation of hostilities.

Hostilities! What a word to use in connection with the man you love. She looked at him as he lay with one hand propping up his head, the other – well, she knew where that was; the hair on his arms was thick, and very dark against the white rolled-up sleeves of his shirt; the top buttons were undone and black hair curled on his broad brown chest. She liked his chest – it was a lovely chest – but she didn't get into the state about it that he did about hers. His braces were a nice dark blue against his shirt and she thought there was something very vulnerable about a man in his braces.

He took his hand from her leg and used it to turn her face towards him.

109

'What are you thinking about?' he asked. 'My Kate staring at me so gravely.'

'Your braces,' she said, before she could stop herself, and he flopped on to his back and roared with laughter. 'I was!' she said, as he jumped up and pulled her to her feet in the same movement.

'Feel them,' he invited, hooking his thumbs in his braces and offering them to her. 'Go on – feel them *all over*!'

'Oh you idiot,' she said as, laughing with him, she fell into his arms while Flash, excited by the sudden action, began to bark.

'Hush, you,' Gerry told him. 'Your mistress is em*bracing* the new love of her life.'

In the middle of August, they went up to London, met Mark and Vanessa and travelled to Scotland by overnight train. As they got ready for bed in their cramped sleeper, Kate tried to discover whether Mark behaved like Gerry did. Vanessa was a bit confused.

'He kisses me,' she said, twisting her hair in a knot and climbing into the top bunk. 'What else should he do?'

Kate couldn't tell her. Knowing Vanessa, she would enquire innocently of Mark why he didn't do the same.

Charles had been a good teacher and Kate and Gerry acquitted themselves well on the banks of the Spey, the ghillie telling Gerry as he landed a nice four-pound salmon that he cast a right pretty fly. On the days they went shooting, Gerry strode about the moors in plus-fours and his bottle-green socks with a gun in the crook of his arm looking as though he had done this kind of thing all his life. He even fired the gun once or twice – safely in the air – but made a joke of being a poor shot and it was obvious everyone thought him a jolly good sport for doing so.

On their last evening, he entertained the large house party with the sad tale of how he had hooked and lost an enormous salmon that day, acting it all out: himself on the bank, the fish on the line, the rod bent, the huge fish leaping and then subdued; how he had picked up the landing net and waded into the river and how, just as he had the thing – so near and yet so far – one last wriggle and it was gone, his intense disappointment . . . how he had only wanted to catch it to be able to present it to his hostess – here he knelt before Mrs O'Rourke, the imaginary fish heavy in his outstretched arms – to thank her in a small way for giving them all such a splendid holiday.

Mrs O'Rourke who, like many others, was dabbing tears of laughter from her eyes as he came to the end of his act amid claps and cheers, said, 'Oh, away with you, you dreadful boy!' Then she kissed his cheek as he knelt in front of her and added, 'It's been a pleasure to have you here.'

Kate loved him so much at that moment that it hurt. He had been everything she could wish for during this week: loving yet undemanding (no roving hands), ignoring the interested glances of the other girls in the party, charming the older women – Mrs O'Rourke had fallen for him, just as Beattie had! – while their husbands murmured to each other that they liked the cut of that young man's jib.

'I didn't know old Gerry could act as well as do everything else,' James said, and Alice, smiling, added, 'He must be exhausting to be with, Kate. Doesn't he wear you out?'

In ways you don't dream of, Kate thought.

'Did you really hook a fish?' she asked Gerry later as the party broke up and people dispersed to bed.

'Kate' – his eyes widened – 'it was enormous!' His arms opened wide to show how big, she stepped forward and they closed around her briefly.

'Good night, my Kate,' he said.

Why couldn't he always be like this?

Then, in late September, when Gerry parked the car in the gateway of an apple orchard near Charles and Beattie's house and tried to persuade Kate to walk with him in the dew-filled moonlight, she refused.

'Just a walk,' he pleaded.

'But it won't be, Gerry,' she said wearily. 'Will it?'

He put one arm around her and the other hand on her knee, stroking it upwards towards her thigh.

'Gerry – no!'

He took both arms away and stared through the windscreen.

'Kate, you say you love me.'

'I do love you, but I won't give you what you want.'

'Why not, if you love me?'

'We've been over all this before . . . again and again we've been over it. Gerry, I – I can't. Please.'

'I don't understand why not. It would be safe, I promise you.'

'*No!*'

He thumped his hands on the steering wheel.

'Kate . . . I don't know if I can go on seeing you like this,' he muttered.

There was silence, and then she drew a sobbing breath.

'That's the oldest trick in the book, Gerry. And the most despicable. But,' she continued, her voice shaking, 'if that's how you feel, then all right. Perhaps it would be better for both of us. Please take me home now.'

He was aghast. He hadn't meant it, not really, though this had been the most frustrating four months of his life. . . . But he could go to Molly now – tonight – and the ache in his groin that had been a constant companion all summer would be gone. He could put his cock into Molly. They would do it on the beach somewhere and then perhaps it would all be all right with Kate. He wouldn't want her so much. He looked at his watch to see if he could get to the Anchor before closing time, but it was too dark to see.

'Take me home, please,' Kate said and, his mind entirely on his erection, he obeyed.

He stopped the car in front of the house and turned to her, not realising that he had been silent for the last ten minutes, had not responded in any way to what she had said.

'Good night, Kate.' Automatically he reached for her, but she was already out of the car.

He didn't remember the drive back, only that he had gone at breakneck speed and had rushed into the pub and stared wildly about him. Molly had turned away another man and had taken him back to her little flat – no censorious landlady now, no need for the beach – and he remembered, but only vaguely, undressing her and himself in frantic haste . . . and no voice saying 'enough'

112

as his hands travelled up and down a willing body, as legs had opened when he felt between them and his fingers and then his cock had sunk in there.

He shuddered and yelled and opened his eyes and looked down at Molly's painted face. For a moment he was startled, then her red lips stretched into an understanding smile.

'It's all right, lad. You done right. A man like you needs it, don't he?'

'Yes,' he whispered, 'he does.' He had come almost the moment he had entered her and still felt unsatisfied.

She pulled him down beside her. 'Moll'll always look after you, Gerry-lad. You know that. And now,' she said, her fingers working at him, 'that last one was for you. How 'bout one for me, eh?' She laughed as he rose against her hand. 'So quick when you used to be so nice and slow. They taught you nothing at this Cambridge place, then?'

He plunged into her again and again and would have stayed all night so he could have her in the morning but she turned him out, telling him to come back at four the next afternoon, which he did until she had to go for the evening session at the pub.

'I'll meet you after, then, shall I?' he said as he lay on the bed watching her dress and put on her make-up.

'No, lad.'

'Molly!'

'I've got a regular then.' She put her lipstick and powder compact in her bag and snapped it shut. 'How d'you think I pay rent on this place? Not the wages from the Anchor, I tell you. Get up now, lad. I got to go.'

He rose from the bed and began putting his clothes on.

'What about your girl, then?'

She offered him a cigarette and he took it. He hadn't had one since he'd been going with Kate, as she didn't smoke and he'd really only carried them around to be able to offer them to girls.

'Well – what?' Molly said as he stood, the cigarette between his lips, tucking his shirt into his trousers.

'Dunno.' He didn't want to discuss Kate with Molly. He didn't want to think about her at all just now. He might start feeling guilty and, in spite of last night and just now, his cock was wanting more. Molly was no good for tonight and already he planned to visit some of his old haunts in Hastings.

He took the cigarette from his mouth and stubbed it out. It tasted horrible and it made him feel funny.

'See you in the pub tomorrow night,' he said, and kissed her red lips. He went to the door and turned. 'Yes?'

'Yeah,' she said. 'See you, lad.'

Three days later he came down the stairs at Ridge Farm in high spirits. He'd met a corker of a girl last night and he reckoned she'd be his today. If not, there was always Molly, but he was a bit put off now he knew men paid her. He'd always thought she did it for fun.

There was a letter for him. Kate's writing. He'd scarcely thought about her except to wonder if he couldn't have someone like Molly, or this Sue he was seeing this afternoon, to keep him satisfied and Kate to love. He held the letter in his hand for a minute or two, not wanting to open it. It would call him back, he knew, and he wanted a few more days of freedom. Nearly a year's celibacy to make up for and he'd hardly started . . . He sighed and opened the letter.

Kate did not want to see him again. Their recent meetings had been painful and upsetting and a clean break now, while the memories were still good, would be best for both of them.

This decision was as final as that other one. He was not to attempt to make her change her mind. Please.

She was sorry. She loved him, but she could not do as he asked.

Chapter 9

You could avoid seeing people in Cambridge if you really tried. Kate worked diligently, went to and from lectures and refused invitations to tea parties where she thought Gerry might be. For the first weeks of term, she stayed away from her room as much as possible, settling with her books in the faculty or in the University Library, and in the evenings she worked, often, in the library at Girton. Gerry was hunting her again, she knew, convinced that, as ever, he could persuade her, that she would believe his promises this time. He had written to her, eloquent pleas and apologies, through the inter-college post and she knew he had been to see her at least once: someone had told her he had been knocking on her door and had described him with such accuracy that her traitor's heart had thudded and her eyes had filled with tears. She would see him again, she was bound to – but not yet.

She had told him in her letter that the memories were still good, and they were, but those would weaken her. So she concentrated instead on the bad ones: the endless circular arguments – '*if* you love me' – and the fact that he had not spoken to her, not a word had he spoken since he had said, in the car in the gateway to a field, that he didn't think he could go on seeing her like this. Not a word during the drive home, silence for three days until she had written the letter and then gone to stay with a round of Girton friends until the start of term . . . Oh he had telephoned when he received the letter. Beattie had told her so and, when she would not reveal where Kate was, he had rung Vanessa and heaven knows who else in search of her.

115

Had Beattie guessed the reason for her and Gerry's break-up? She and Charles had met in their first term at Cambridge, her mother had met her father here, and they had waited until they were married, she was sure. She couldn't ask Beattie, though. She wished her mother was alive. She wished it with an intensity she hadn't felt for a long time, since those first months after they had all died – her mother and father, and Ricky who had wanted to be a doctor, and her grandmother who, for heaven's sake, had come to Kent for a few days to escape the horrors of war-torn London. One of the last V2s of the war, a direct hit on the doctor's house as they had sat down to tea at four o'clock as they always did, it being after the day's calls and before evening surgery . . . She wanted them all alive, but most of all at this moment she wanted a mother. Someone who would say it was right to turn away the man you love rather than go to bed with him . . . Because it was, wasn't it?

She clasped her mug of cocoa in her hands and looked up at the photograph of her parents on the mantelpiece above the gas fire (too late for Gerry to visit; she was safe in her room). They smiled at her from a garden now overgrown, the house in the background a heap of rubble. She had never been back after the funerals, never answered the letters asking if she would 'entertain offers' for the site although Charles, when he discovered she was ignoring them, had done so with an elegant legal no in place of the hysterical one she would have given. Perhaps she would go back one day, perhaps be the village's doctor, but for the moment she wanted to know there was more of her there than the cold row of headstones in the churchyard.

. . . Gerry in a buttercup meadow opening a bottle of champagne to toast her first before she'd even got it; Gerry on the beach, laughing and jigging, holding out his braces begging her to feel them *all over* . . . the horse blanket beneath her as his hands were on her breasts, her knee, her thigh . . .

She looked at the photograph again. All the times she had overheard her mother and father talking about a fallen girl who had believed the promises of her boy and lain with him in the orchards and hop gardens on warm summer nights and ended up being sent away, to return, some months later, with such sadness in her eyes, her baby taken away from her and given up for adoption. And she was thought lucky, this girl, if someone took her into service, a kind and Christian woman who overlooked her past and allowed her to scrub and polish and dust and slave in her house for a pittance, while her boy married a respectable girl and the other lads of the village clustered around her like dogs around a bitch on heat because they knew she had done it before and was easy.

No. For every possible reason Kate would break her heart over Gerry Beviss. But, great heavens! why had God made it like this? The men always wanting and taking, losing nothing, and every one of them – the meanest as well as the highest in the land – able to walk away and do it again while the women lost everything.

She tried to cheer herself up, to rid herself of the awful weight she was carrying around inside her. Women had gained something in Cambridge, after all. She and Vanessa joined the crowds outside the Senate House to see the first woman who had ever been given a degree by this ancient and venerable University – and that woman was none other than the Queen! She came to Girton, took tea with the dons and afterwards walked among the undergraduates as they sat in groups at the tables in Hall. She chatted to them most charmingly and Vanessa, overwhelmed at being asked by Her Majesty what she was reading, went scarlet and finally stuttered, 'I can't remember.'

And now they had to wear gowns – to Hall, to lectures, after dark, when visiting tutors and other senior members of the University, when sitting exams. Kate put hers on for the first time, relishing the set of it across her shoulders, the satisfactory swirl of it as she turned a corner, aware that all through Girton and Newnham this night women were doing the same thing – donning this visible sign of the degree they would take away with them: at long last the right to put BA (Hons) Cantab after their names, if they so wished, for the rest of their lives. The corridors of Girton were transformed, filled with billowing gowns of grave and brave academic black, and every time Kate put hers on she felt she was wearing it for all the women who had aspired to it over the years, the women whose Tripos examinations had been marked alongside the men's since the 1870s, and who, like her own mother, had been

117

classed first but still went out into the world with a titular degree, which was not a degree at all.

They now came under the jurisdiction of the proctors, and six of them bicycled from Girton to Cambridge one night and roamed the streets without their lamps on just to hear the challenge, 'Are you a member of this University?' and to be able to answer a resounding 'Yes!' – all but eighty years after Miss Emily Davies, Girton's foundress, had established the College at a house in Hitchin and Henry Sidgwick and Miss Anne Clough had planted, as he called them, the 'garden of flowers' that became Newnham. The proctor and his bulldogs seemed rather bewildered by this first encounter with women, mainly because they had been so easily caught, and they went on their way, having issued stern warnings, hoping it would always be so.

The one disadvantage about the gowns was Vanessa. She constantly lost track of hers and every morning, without fail, a wail of despair arose from the next room – they had kept the rooms they had in their first year – as Vanessa attempted to gather her scattered belongings and get to a lecture on time. Then the gown went missing for three days, collecting Vanessa several fines and an interview with the Bagwigs, until Mark brought it back: he had not realised that there were two of them hanging on the back of his door.

Vanessa clutched the gown to her and stared at him.

'But Mark – that means you haven't been to a lecture for *three whole days!*'

She was so horrified that he actually felt guilty.

'It's the trials soon,' he explained defensively. 'I'm on for the Blue boat this year.'

'But why can't you row in the afternoons?'

'I do row in the afternoons but, damn it all,' he said, skewered by her intense brown gaze, 'a chap's got to have some time to himself.'

'For a good lunch at the Pitt Club, isn't that right, Mark?' Kate interpolated mischievously, and he turned to her in relief.

'That's right! – Oh, for heaven's sake!' he exclaimed as he realised he was being teased.

118

Even in this, Kate thought. Even in this men and women were opposed. Vanessa had been fined rather than miss a lecture and there was Mark skipping them for three days for the sake of his rowing and some boozy lunches.

'I've got James's car,' he was saying now. 'How about coming out for a drink? – both of you?'

Kate stood up. 'You take Vanessa. You don't want me along.'

'I most certainly do,' he said, and paused. 'I've got James as well, you see.'

'Oh? And who else?' Kate asked, standing still.

He smiled deprecatingly. 'Kate,' he said, 'give old Gerry a chance, do. He's as miserable as sin, sour as a bagful of lemons. He's making our lives a misery, I promise you.'

'I can't come,' she said, and almost ran out of Vanessa's room and into her own, where she sat trembling. She had almost been feeling all right until then, stopped thinking about Gerry more than a hundred times a day. She heard Vanessa's door close and their footsteps walk away down the corridor and was tempted to run after them ... But it would mean a few weeks of Gerry behaving himself and then it would all start again. And two years before they could get married, two more years under attack. Not that he had ever mentioned marriage as a solution – they weren't allowed to while they were undergraduates and the whole idea was absurd anyway: he had no intention of marrying her, and every intention of loving her and leaving her ... used.

This stiffened her resolve, and then, realising that it was quite likely that Gerry was on his way to her room now, since Mark's ruse hadn't worked and he knew she was in, she grabbed her books and went to the library. And then, having settled there, thought fearfully that this was the first place he would look for her, so she gathered everything up again and went to Felicity Myers's room where, as Felicity wrote an essay, Kate stared blindly into the gas fire.

Four days later, she received a summons from the Bagwigs. She examined her conscience and could find nothing amiss, so she put on her gown and went to her tutor's rooms in a lively state of curiosity.

The Bagwigs greeted her, tipped Herodotus, her marmalade cat, from a chair, invited Kate to sit down and offered her a cup of tea.

Now this was unusual. It had been planned – the tea tray with two cups and saucers was there ready – and as the tutor poured the tea Kate gazed at Herodotus (surely the only male resident of the college) and wondered what on earth was going on. Herodotus, who was now sitting on the hearthrug, gazed unblinkingly back. Oh yes, his look said, I know. I know what it's all about but I'm not going to tell you.

'Now, my dear,' the Bagwigs said as she handed Kate a cup, 'let's have our little chat.'

Half an hour later, Kate reeled into the corridor outside the Bagwigs's rooms after what was, surely, the most unusual and unlikely instruction ever issued by a tutor to an undergraduate in the centuries of the University's existence.

Kate, the Bagwigs had told her, was working too hard. She had lost weight this term and looked tired. A discussion with Kate's director of studies had confirmed her view that she was pushing herself to the possible detriment of her health.

Kate had been appalled. Work was her only escape: what was she to do in the long evenings without it?

Work, the Bagwigs said, was obviously important but it was also important to relax.

'You have not signed out of Hall once this term,' she had said. It may be that you are climbing into College every night but, my dear, I think you are not going out at all, and I do not believe it is because there are no opportunities.'

It was true, but Kate didn't see why it mattered. Why should she go out if she didn't want to?

'I daresay,' the Bagwigs had continued, 'I know the reason for this and it is none of my business, of course. But you are privileged to be in a wondrous place, Miss Earith, and you should take advantage of all it has to offer during your time here. Indeed, your extra-curricular activities are as much a part of your education as are your academic studies.'

Provided, presumably, Kate thought as she reached her room and took off her gown, those extra-curricular activities do not

120

include going to bed with handsome undergraduates from Trinity. Quite certainly they didn't.

She sat down and thought about what the tutor had said.

She wasn't going to get over Gerry by immersing herself in physiology and pharmacology night and day; Pinocchio had his fascinations but, now she could identify all his bones, his entertainment value was decidedly limited. Cambridge was full of men – stuffed to the brim with them – short of female company. She had been turning down invitations all term; now she would accept them, so long as the men didn't positively repel her, and see what happened.

She went to a concert with another medical student, who took her to a Chinese restaurant afterwards and, as they ate the speciality of the house, an omelette made from dried eggs, he either talked medical shop or kept saying that men – 'people' he corrected himself – who were going to be doctors should take an interest in matters cultural. Why, for heaven's sake? Kate wondered and crossed him and, most unfairly, all medical students off the list. But Kate had enjoyed the concert and had been introduced to a man who was a counter-tenor in King's College Choir. This was interesting for a couple of dates, but then she went to evensong, heard him sing and discovered what a counter-tenor was. She could not take seriously a man who sang like a woman and who took such obsessive care of his throat, but she kept him on the boil because he said he would get her a ticket for the Advent Carol Service. She went to the pictures several times. This was always satisfactory because she could see a film she wanted to and afterwards they could talk about it instead of floundering around trying to find other topics of conversation. She joined the Union and the President invited her out to dinner. In the hope of impressing her, he took her to the Blue Boar and ordered champagne, a combination that reminded her so much of Gerry that he, poor man, was crossed off the list too. She went to watch Cambridge University play rugby against the RAF with a giant of a man who said, proudly, he was in the front row of the Jesus fifteen, whatever that meant. It was the most stupid and coldest afternoon she had ever spent: enormous men, many of them

121

making her escort look like a midget, ran into each other, kicked and mauled each other, and the crowd appeared to find the spectacle delightful. As an RAF man doubled up after receiving a kick in the groin, one wit yelled, 'Don't rub 'em, count 'em!' which everyone but Kate seemed to find hilarious. She went to the Advent Carol Service in King's College Chapel where the congregation sat in darkness and in silence until the choir processed, singing, up the aisle, bringing candles and sweet music. More candles were lit as they passed: thus Christ's coming brings light into the world.

At a party in one of the choir members' rooms afterwards, Michael, the counter-tenor, greeted her warmly but distractedly, and a man who sang bass glared at her with overt hostility. Michael introduced her to Peter Broderick – 'my cousin' – and hurried to the bass's side.

Kate looked up at Peter Broderick and saw a kind face, slightly careworn, little lines at the corners of his grey eyes and more deeply etched around the mouth. His dark brown hair was uncompromisingly straight and he pushed it back off his forehead – a gesture she was to know well – and smiled at her.

'Kate Earith. A familiar name.'

'How is that?' she asked, surprised.

'You're the first woman Michael has shown any interest in. My aunt has high hopes, but they are soon to be dashed, I fear.'

'Oh,' she said, and looked at Michael, whose head was close to the other singer's, and understood. Ah well, the carol service had been memorable indeed.

'Will you have dinner with me?' Peter Broderick asked. 'I like the choir when they sing, but I find their conversation somewhat boring.'

She hesitated, calculating. This would be the thirteenth date since her interview with the Bagwigs. She had used up three late passes and had, four times, climbed into College after midnight. She didn't know if she was enjoying herself, but certainly Gerry Beviss was further from her mind.

'Is this your coat and gown?'

'Yes.'

Peter helped her on with them and ushered her out of the door.

*   *   *

He was at Corpus Christi reading law, in his second year. He was twenty-five years old and had been in the army during the war, had intended making it his career until a sniper's bullet in Palestine had put an end to that idea.

Kate exclaimed in concern.

'Smashed my right ankle,' he said. 'You must have noticed the limp.'

She had, but hadn't liked to say anything.

'So my old housemaster put a word in with the Master of Corpus,' he explained. 'And I came to Cambridge. You know how these things work.'

Oh, she knew. She knew.

After dinner (another dried-egg omelette at another Chinese restaurant) he was all for ringing for a taxi and escorting her to Girton, but she said she had her bike so he escorted her back to that.

'This doesn't seem right,' he said, standing on the cobbles outside the main gate of King's as she stowed her handbag in her bicycle basket and put on her gloves, scarf and hat – all now in matching electric yellow and red – and turned on the lights. 'Really. Let's get a taxi. We can put your bike in it.'

'We girls from Girton are a tough lot,' she said. 'We're used to this.'

He held on to the handlebars. 'Can I see you again?'

'Why not come to tea tomorrow?' she said, immediately astonished at herself and wanting to withdraw the invitation as soon as the words were out of her mouth, but:

'Thank you, I will. Safe home, Kate.'

He stood aside and watched her, she knew, although she did not look back, until she was out of sight.

He was a member of the Pitt Club, of course, but from what she could gather knew nothing of Gerry and his friends. The ex-servicemen tended to form a clique of their own into which she was drawn. She did not love Peter – nothing like it – but he was interesting, amusing in his dry way, and intelligent – a commodity in a man which seemed in remarkably short supply at this University of universities. And he was sensitive, too. On their

123

fourth meeting he said gently, 'There's someone else, isn't there? Who is it?' She had lowered her eyes and replied, 'It's over now . . . No one you know.' He had left it at that, and he had made no comment about her almost panicky refusal to accompany him to the ball at the Pitt Club.

The term ended soon after and she went home to Kent, talked of Peter endlessly and refused to answer any of Beattie's questions about Gerry, who — everything seeming like a carbon copy of the year before — turned up at the Poutneys' house wanting to see Kate, but this time was refused admission. Kate went to London to stay with Vanessa and, with Mark and Peter, they went to a show. At New Year, she went to a party with Peter rather than to the one she had been invited to in Warwickshire by David Smedley. She felt comfortable with Peter and stopped going out with other men.

But she could not avoid seeing Gerry for ever, and when it happened early in the following term she was totally unprepared for it. They were going to a tea party in Christ's and she was laughing over her shoulder at something Peter had said as she walked in. She turned to face the room and there was Gerry, his cheeks suddenly white, his eyes burning, starting towards her. What was he doing in Christ's College, for heaven's sake? His circuit was Trinity, John's, Magdalene . . . but here he was, the first time she had seen him since September, offering to get her a cup of tea, something to eat, anything. Peter, having hung up her coat, came forward and took her arm possessively, smiling and acknowledging Kate's stammered introductions, then bore her away to meet their host. She was fussed over, flirted with (there were only two other women there: really, Cambridge could turn your head and you might begin to believe you were the most beautiful creature on earth), was found a seat and then, as Peter was talking to someone else, Gerry was beside her.

'How have you been?' she asked, hoping her voice sounded normal.

'Sad,' he replied.

No. She would not listen.

'How is Florin and the hunting?'

'James and I are joint masters now . . . Kate—'

'That must be fun.'

124

'Nothing is fun.'

'Oh, don't be absurd, Gerry.' She looked at him directly. A mistake.

'See?' he said, grinning suddenly. 'You feel the same! You do!'

'No. No, I don't.' She got up quickly and went to Peter's side, and when she next looked round Gerry had gone.

And Peter, who saw everything, said later, as she was preparing for the ride back to Girton, 'That was him, wasn't it?'

Kate could only nod and Peter said, 'Well, he's one hell of a handsome chap. I wonder you go about with me.' And he waited for a denial, which Kate gave too late, then laughed and kissed her lips briefly – all he ever did; no worries about roving hands here – and said, 'Ah well, you seem to want to be with me rather than him, so what have I got to be worried about?'

She let her bicycle fall and flung her arms around his neck because he was so nice and kind and so impossibly under-standing . . . and found she was crying. Not so he'd notice it, she hoped: tears slipping quietly down her cheeks. He kissed her again in a prosaic way that reminded her of Simon, picked up her bike and said, as he always did, 'Safe home, Kate,' and, as he always did, checked the lamps were on and she bicycled away, wiping the tears from her cheeks with her glove, knowing that, as he always did, he would watch her until she was out of sight.

She would not, she *would not* even begin to think he was boring.

She began working in the library again, on the nights she was not going out with Peter. And Gerry found her there.

It would have been funny had it not been. She refused to move and so he was forced to say what he had come to say in a low whisper which still echoed around the high ceiling and caused the other women there to raise their heads and one to issue a demanding 'Ssh'.

'Just say you love me and I'll go away,' he whispered.

'Is that a promise?'

'Yes.'

'All right. I love you.'

'Kate—'

125

'You promised.'

She fixed her eyes on her book. She heard his slow footsteps go along the wooden floor of the library, pause at the door, heard them go down the stairs and on to the floor below; heard them long after it was possible she could do so.

She wrote to him: she had lied to get rid of him, she told him. He was not to come and pester her again. He was to forget he had ever known her.

He replied, once a week until the end of term, one line: 'You did not lie, Kate.'

Gerry had been at the tea party in Christ's because Patrick Morgan had rooms on the same staircase as Anthony Jones, who had given the party, and had invited Gerry along. He had met Patrick at the Pitt Club and they had got on well from that moment. Patrick was twenty-one and in his first year, having elected to do his National Service before going to university rather than after because, he said, the bookies were after him and so were the parents of a girl called Margaret.

'It was a pincer movement . . . brilliant strategy. Monty would look to his laurels if he'd seen it, I can tell you,' Patrick said, describing it with his hands – one usually with a glass in it, the other holding a copy of the *Sporting Life* – 'So I went to serve King and Country and gave up women and horses for the duration.'

He had hoped to go to Oxford but had been foolish enough to reveal his motives to the crusty dons who had interviewed him at Balliol.

'I told them. I said, "Balliol's the place for me, not too far from Newbury and Ascot, Kempton and Sandown within striking distance – what could be better?" . . . It's true,' he said as they all protested, laughing. 'I even said I was prepared to overlook the fact that they have Schools on Derby Day. They do, you know.' He shook his head and finished his brandy. 'Shocking,' he said. 'Absolutely shocking.'

When he heard that the only racing Gerry had ever witnessed was a couple of point-to-points, he gazed at him and then picked up his wrist and made a pantomime of feeling his pulse.

126

'You're healthy enough,' he said, 'and you seem quite sane.' And he bore him off to the races at Newmarket.

For Gerry, it was a revelation. So *this* was what horses were meant to do! Run as fast as they could, every ounce extracted from them, every muscle of the pampered beasts cosseted and gleaming, these beautiful thoroughbreds doing what over two centuries of breeding had intended: go, go *go*! What was show jumping compared to this? Titupping over coloured poles . . . absurd!

He ran to the paddock after each race so he could be at the rails, be near these fabulous creatures as they were led around by lesser mortals. While Patrick trailed yards of the *Sporting Life* and talked of form, weight, horses gone in the coat and put huge sums of money on – fifty pounds on a certainty which came fifth, twenty-five on a horse which won at 2–1 – Gerry simply fell in love. Patrick said he should bet, and so he did – in a race for two-year-olds on a colt so beautiful that it would be an insult if it were beaten. Three pounds he put on its velvet nose, all the money he had with him, and the glorious thing stuck out that velvet nose and won. It also won Gerry forty pounds.

Seductive money. But Gerry was not tempted by it. He saw Patrick's face when fifty pounds went, the ghastly relief when fifty pounds came back, the way he couldn't look at a race for the beauty of it but only for the result . . . No, not the betting. But he was hooked on this racing, and was devastated when the Flat season came to a close.

'See what I mean?' Patrick said. 'East Anglia's a bloody desert until spring. Let's go and see some jumpers at Ascot.'

It wasn't the same, though. The jumpers were big and coarse, a bit like Florin – though he tried not to think so of his wonderful horse, his head handsome and intelligent but too big, his legs too thick, the feathers around his fetlocks giving his plebeian origins away . . . He dreamed of those silken creatures cocooned in their boxes for the winter. He went to Newmarket in the early mornings – when he was not exercising the hounds – and watched them come in their strings from their yards and step out over the heath as though they had a divine right to be there: lines of them under a huge grey sky appearing from every direction and moving like gods, little pinched minions aboard them.

127

The jumpers had nothing on them and, apart from anything else, the Sport of Kings in winter left a great deal to be desired.

'Why,' he demanded of Patrick, when the wind was blowing fit to freeze the Arctic and he was hungry and thirsty and the tiny bars were full, 'why does it have to be such a bloody uncomfortable business?'

Patrick, looking drawn, tore up a betting slip and let the wind take the pieces away.

'I don't know, old boy,' he said. 'It's just the way it is.'

Gerry hated to see that look on Patrick's face and, in any case, he and James were busy with the Drag. As masters, they had to visit landowners, walk the lines, check wired fences were properly flagged. There wasn't time to go racing. Life was full.

Except that it had a great gaping hole in the middle of it, into which Kate had disappeared. Mark had told him how she was out with someone different every night – hearing it from Vanessa – and then, ominously, with one man only. One evening Mark and Gerry had drunk a great deal of whisky and Gerry had asked Mark about him and Vanessa. Mark had been shocked into sobriety at the idea of Vanessa saying yes, at the idea he would even ask her, that Gerry had asked Kate. He rose to his feet.

'I want to marry Vanessa,' he said. 'And I expect my bride to be a virgin on our wedding night.' Which sounded very noble until he added, 'And if she did it with me before then, she might do it with someone else, mightn't she?'

Gerry had got it wrong again. Sophie had been willing enough, after all, but apparently she was upper-class which meant she could do what she liked; Kate and Vanessa were middle-class and this meant they absolutely wouldn't. Where did all this leave Gerry? Among what the chaps at the Pitt Club called the Great Unwashed, it seemed. He began taking out a girl from Newnham. He had to have someone to take to balls and Penelope was nice. There was no pretence of love between them; he had never asked her, but he knew she wouldn't go to bed with him either – so where had it all got him?

Patrick went to prostitutes. Was perfectly open about it.

'I fancy a bit tonight,' he'd say. 'Coming?'

James always refused, but Gerry went a few times. It wasn't up to much and he told Patrick he didn't like paying for it. Patrick had looked at him and said, 'None of us does, dear boy, but how else are we to get it? You must admit it's awfully jolly.'

Not like that, it wasn't.

He thought he was cured until he saw Kate coming in, laughing, to the tea party in Christ's. He felt as though something had ripped his stomach out when he saw her turning to another man, but from the way she looked at him Gerry could tell she loved him still, no matter what she said. In a curious way he felt safe as long as she was going out with this man Peter. She didn't love him, that was certain, and she wouldn't give him what she hadn't given Gerry. So he bided his time, although for what he wasn't quite sure.

His hopes were raised briefly when, in March, he arrived at a party at a house in Chiswick for the University Boat Race. He saw Kate crossing the open-fronted marquee carrying two drinks and he went over and took one from her.

'That desperate, is it?'

'Hello, Gerry,' she said, and smiled at him. 'They're both for Vanessa, who *is* desperate. She's afraid Mark is going to drown.'

'If we don't win he'll probably wish he had. Can I get you a drink, Kate?'

'Well – yes. Thank you, Gerry.'

The chap Peter didn't seem to be around and Gerry stuck to her like a leech. They agreed this was not the time of year for garden parties and chatted until a roll of cheers came from downriver and two specks appeared, followed by a flotilla of motor boats. Gerry lent Vanessa his binoculars but her hands were shaking so much she was unable to see through them.

'We're ahead!' James cried, having run from the wireless set in the house. He grabbed the binoculars and raised them to his eyes.

'Just look at Mark! His face is red as a beetroot but he's going like a train.'

They all watched and yelled encouragement as the two gladiator boats, followed by their entourage, laboured over the grey-brown water and disappeared around the bend in the river, and a few minutes later the news came from the wireless that Cambridge had won.

Gerry put an arm each around Vanessa and Kate and gave them a congratulatory kiss, and then, since Kate didn't seem to mind, he kissed her again.

'You'll come out with us tonight and celebrate, won't you?' he asked. 'James and I are detailed to entertain Vanessa.'

'Oh yes?' she said. 'Who by?'

'By Mark, of course! Who else? He is obliged to get seriously drunk with the crews. . . . Come out tonight, Kate, please,' he pleaded.

She had to accept, because Vanessa had already done so and Kate had no alternative but to agree since she was staying in Vanessa's parents' flat. They went to a show, they ate and danced and they had a lovely time . . . but when term started again soon after, Kate disappeared back into the fastness of Girton, down among her books and the bones of Pinocchio, and would not go out with him again.

The Flat racehorses came out of their winter hibernation and into the spring sun, their gorgeous muscled bodies hurtling down Newmarket's Rowley Mile, their slender legs and tiny hooves creating thunder. Gerry went to the Two Thousand Guineas, the first colts' classic, in May – the best against the best – and was astonished at the rush of emotion he felt as the horses passed the post. He didn't even know which had won; it was so appalling that any of them, each so perfect, could go back to its stable an also ran, a failure.

'I just want one,' he whispered to Patrick.

'Ah,' said Patrick, 'wanting one is easy, getting one is easy – if you have the money. Getting one that wins . . . there's the difficulty. They promise you things, the foals and the yearlings, but the buggers don't keep their word.'

The normally easy-going Patrick sounded bitter, and Gerry understood why when he went to stay at Patrick's home after the summer term ended and they had been to the Royal meeting at Ascot where Gerry, sponsored by Lord Flimwell, had paraded in morning coat and top hat in the Royal Enclosure. Rede Park was a great sprawling house, obviously once beautiful but now in a terrible state of repair with tiles off the roof and windows broken and the gardens overgrown. Gerry, on Patrick's instructions, parked the car in a huge stableyard, empty of horses, the doors hanging off their hinges.

Patrick, like all other members of the Pitt Club, was always pleading poverty, always saying he hadn't got a bean, even though he bet heavily on the horses. But Gerry had been to their houses, seen their servants, their mothers' jewels, heard their fathers complain at the cost of their sisters' coming-out parties and then insist the best champagne was served. Gerry would die rather than admit he was short of money – and anyway, these days, his father gave him a pretty generous allowance – but James and Nick and Mark and the rest seemed to do it as a matter of form.

Not Patrick Morgan, apparently.

'This,' he said wryly as they got out of the car and walked across a weedy forecourt to the great porticoed front door, 'is my inheritance. It was requisitioned during the war and the Canadians made a fine mess of it but you can't blame them for the whole. It was in a pretty awful state before. Grandfather gambled the money away – what was left him by his father, but that's another story – and my old man tried to recoup the family fortunes by breeding racehorses.' He pushed the door open and Gerry walked into a massive hall, wood-panelled, with long windows looking out across a valley neatly crisscrossed with hedges and enclosed by folds of the chalk downs of Wiltshire.

'They didn't run fast enough,' Patrick said after a pause, and then smiled slightly. 'The same problem I have – as you have, no doubt, noticed.'

He went and gazed out over the sunlit valley, a house in the distance and a brick wall across the valley the only evidence of human habitation.

'Beautiful, isn't it? Queen Elizabeth slept here, you know. Will I be able to keep it, do you suppose? Or will the horses have it?'

There was love in his voice, and a great sadness.

It was the most extraordinary household Gerry had ever been in. Dogs lay all over the shabby furniture and cats marched up and down the dining-room table, stepping delicately around tarnished silver candlesticks and stealing the meagre and dreadfully cooked

131

food from the cracked Sèvres serving bowls. The only luxury was that four copies of the *Sporting Life* were delivered to Rede Park each morning, one each for Major and Mrs Morgan, one for Patrick when he was at home, and one for the ancient butler, O'Nions, who, having cleared the breakfast table, sat down with his employers and discussed the day's betting.

'But why do you do it?' Gerry asked, as they took some of the dogs for a walk one afternoon, leaving Major and Mrs Morgan, each with their own telephone, communicating with their book-makers. 'Seeing the mess it's got your parents into, why do you bet so heavily?'

'It's in the blood,' Patrick said cheerfully. 'Can't help it.'

'Of course you can. Just stop doing it.'

'It's in the blood,' Patrick repeated. 'Look . . . this is an old racecourse. Goes right round, do you see?' He indicated the oval-shaped valley. 'My great-grandfather made it. It was going to rival Epsom, Goodwood, the best. But he struck a bet: half the estate his colt would beat his brother's over ten furlongs at Salisbury. It didn't. So Great-great-uncle Cyril took half the land and built himself a house at the other end of the valley from Rede Park. Then there was a row about where the dividing line should be – partridges were shot a couple of feet to the bad or something – and so they built that wall, cutting the racecourse in two. The estate is joined now. My mother and father are cousins, you see . . . but there's no money.'

He stopped talking for a moment and stared out at the land that would be his. 'It would make a splendid racecourse,' he said at last. 'The turf is nearly a century old and has only ever been grazed on by sheep. No cattle in case the ground got poached and no thought of ploughing it up. No one, in all the years of the feud, ever dreamed of doing anything else. . . . Mad,' he stated, that bitterness in his voice again. 'Utterly insane, my family.'

Gerry, who had been thinking that they were walking across an unusually long field, could see it now: the strip of unbroken green around the edge of the valley, disappearing every so often behind trees or hedges, but the eye soon picked it up again. It was all there, a complete circuit, the top bend, the back straight, the home turn, bright-coated horses pounding around it into the home

132

stretch . . . the crowds standing and cheering in the grandstands – *there* on the hill, able to see every inch of the course! – watching the horses straining to the winning post, flowing past it, pulling up . . .

'Get the money from somewhere,' he said.

'Where, for God's sake?'

Gerry shrugged. 'Investors. Start a company. I don't know, but people do it all the time.'

Patrick shook his head and whistled to the dogs. 'Who'd invest in us?' he asked bleakly. 'We'd gamble it all away.'

Chapter 10

Arthur married Grace in August that year and Gerry went home and did his duty as best man, which included him and the lads getting Arthur so drunk the night before that he was white-faced and visibly shaking at the altar. Gerry was given a severe ticking off by his new sister-in-law at the reception.

'Oh come on, Grace,' he said, smiling down at the angry, determined figure so incongruously clothed in a long white dress and veil instead of the breeches, boots and riding hat she normally wore. 'We had to give Art a good send off.'

'You've made him ill!'

'He'll be all right on the night,' he told her, and she blushed, picked up her skirts and swirled away.

He stayed at home for a week to oversee the horses while Arthur and Grace spent their honeymoon in Devon, then went to Leicestershire for a fortnight, to Flimwell Place where he rode Castor carefully around the lanes and farm tracks while James showed off Canterlupe, the splendid thoroughbred his father had given him for his twenty-first birthday. Sophie was there, sporting a gigantic emerald engagement ring and a rich American fiancé, and everyone said that her departure to New York would do wonders for the export drive. To the Morgans again, and then back to Cambridge for his final year. Rooms in Nevile's Court, Gerry had, and an interview with his tutor. He had scraped a II:2 in his Part One last summer and could do better. He agreed and went off to lunch at the Pitt Club, resolving to work hard this year. II:2 was average and not good enough for a scholar. But there were the autumn race meetings at Newmarket to go to – he couldn't miss those, the last chance to see the Flat before the spring, when he really would be working – and the Drag Hounds to organise. Somewhere along the line he had stopped seeing Penelope and, at Patrick's urging, began going to the smart cocktail parties in London.

And at one of these, Patrick introduced him to Diana Dalton.

As soon as they arrived at the house in Little Venice, before they had greeted their host and hostess and the rather plain girl they were desperately trying to find a husband for, a shrill voice yelled, 'Patrick, *darling!*' And a vision began pushing her way across the crowded room towards them.

She had curly brown hair and was dressed in an extraordinary combination of 1920s England – a band around her head, dangling necklaces, a long cigarette holder held between her red-tipped fingers – and South American señorita – a black and red flounced dress, wide gold bangles on her long, black, handless gloves, very high-heeled shoes. By Carmen, she was, out of a flapper.

She reached Patrick and flung her arms around his neck.

'Patrick, how *are* you?' Then, without waiting for a reply, she turned a pair of vibrant brown eyes on Gerry and, letting her arms drop from Patrick, she blew a billow of smoke that wreathed around all their heads. 'Who is this?' she said.

Patrick told her.

'Why haven't I met him before?' she demanded.

'You've been in Rio,' Patrick said. 'Haven't you?'

'Only for four months.' Again she blew out smoke. 'Never mind. I've met him now.' And she took Gerry's arm and led him off.

Gerry looked over his shoulder at Patrick and made a mock-frightened face. Patrick grinned, raised his hand and disappeared in the opposite direction.

'Where are you taking me?' Gerry asked Diana.

'Somewhere we can survey the scene and discover if it's going to be exciting here.' She clamped her cigarette holder between her teeth, put her empty glass down on a tray carried by a passing waiter and in the same deft movement removed two full glasses and handed one to Gerry.

135

'Quite a trick, that,' he said, accepting the glass, 'picking up two drinks in one hand.'

'*That* impressed you?' She gazed up into his face. 'I do hope you're not going to be an utterly boring walkover. I'm looking for a challenge. . . . This'll do.'

They had reached the edge of the room. Diana let go of his arm and leaned against the wall, her eyes roaming over the chattering crowd.

'Shall I help you on to a chair,' Gerry said, 'so you can see better?'

'I don't need to. It's all the same. I can't think why I bothered to come back at all.' Her eyes came to rest on him once more, and she looked him up and down as though inspecting him for faults. He didn't think he liked it and was about to say something when she smiled radiantly. 'Still, things are looking up, aren't they?' she said. 'England seemed so frightfully dreary – grey skies, grey people and all this ghastly rationing, and *no*, but not *one* new man on the circuit. . . . Tell me,' she went on, 'don't you think débutantes are like policemen?'

'How, for heaven's sake?' he asked, intrigued.

'They get younger every year. I've done four seasons, you know. Four!'

'Well-seasoned then, are you? Do you, like wood and whisky, improve with age?'

'We'll have to wait and see, won't we? What do you think of me now?'

She struck a Carmen pose, one arm above her head, the other hand on an out-thrust hip. Gerry stroked his chin and surveyed her in the appraising way she had him.

'Well?' she asked.

'I think,' Gerry said, 'you have a number of interesting features. Closer inspection, of course, would tell me more.'

'You're flirting.'

'So are you.'

'I was utterly serious.' She fitted another cigarette into her holder and lit it with a gold lighter. 'Now, Gerry Beviss, I want to know all about you. Are you South American, by any chance? With that colouring, you could be.'

'No, I'm afraid not.'

She put out a hand and squeezed his forearm.

'Don't be afraid, darling,' she said. 'South Americans are beasts. Wicked things, you've no idea. They propose to one at the drop of a hat and all they want to do is shut one up in some utterly dreary hacienda, give one a baby to play with every year and carry on with their mistresses. Too ghastly.'

'What were you doing in South America? Apart from being proposed to, that is.'

'Mummy lives there . . . This is rather a boring party, isn't it? We'll go in a minute and find somewhere more exciting. . . . Oh look, there's poor little Johnnie Dalgliesh. He proposed to me when he was eighteen. His mother made him. It was too utterly funny in a pathetic kind of way.'

'How many proposals have you had?' Gerry asked.

'Thirteen. I got engaged once, but I didn't like it much. Perhaps it's time I settled down. Mummy says it is. I say, are you a fortune-hunter?'

'Yes,' he replied promptly.

But she wasn't listening. She dragged him over to a group of people, introduced him as 'this lovely new man I've found' and decided they should go off dancing 'somewhere exciting'. Gerry located Patrick, who equipped himself with a suitable girl, and they made for the West End, Patrick driving Gerry's car and Gerry joining Diana in her white Jaguar.

Diana Dalton was a flirt, no doubt about it, but she really wasn't very good at it. Gerry thought the thirteen proposals must be an exaggeration – or even pure imagination – as he watched her inviting other men to dance, casting him challenging glances as she did so, holding her partners closer than was quite done – and, in many cases, than they seemed to want. He realised that she expected him to sit at their table and brood, and was amused to see that she was disconcerted when he paid no attention and enjoyed himself dancing with other girls.

'Don't you like me?' she asked, when, eventually, she danced with him.

'Yes, I think I like you,' he answered after a pause.

'Only think?'

137

'Only think.'

'Oh,' she said.

'Are you used to every man falling for you when you decide he should?'

'Frankly, I am,' she said candidly.

He laughed then, and did like her.

He was amused by her agitation when, later, he and Patrick announced they had to drive back to Cambridge and he had made no suggestion of a further meeting. Amid the general goodbyes, she grabbed his arm.

'Well?' she said.

'Well?' he repeated, smiling at her.

'Gerry Beviss, for God's sake – am I going to see you again?'

'I'll ring you, shall I?'

He kissed her gently on the lips and left.

'Gerry, my dear fellow,' Patrick said, as they got into Gerry's car and made their way towards the A10, 'do you *know* who you were playing fast and loose with?'

'Diana Dalton. You introduced us.'

'I thought you *knew*. Everyone does. Sometimes I wonder where you've been all your life.'

'What about her? What should I know?'

'She is *rich*, old chap. Rich beyond anything. Her father was a millionaire – more. No one knows the amount of loot he had. He was killed in a car crash a few years ago and left a mansion in Esher and half his money to his wife, so long as she didn't marry again—'

'Selfish brute,' Gerry said idly.

'And half to his only child. Diana. And Elizabeth Dalton upped and married a Brazilian coffee grower eighteen months later, which means Diana comes into the whole bang lot when she is twenty-one.'

Gerry was silent.

'Except the mansion in Esher. Elizabeth sold that.'

'So,' said Gerry, 'she really has had all those proposals?'

'Absolutely. From every sensible man who could get near enough to her between here and Rio de Janeiro.'

138

'She'd suit you,' Gerry said. 'Sort out Rede Park with her pocket money.'

'Oh I tried,' Patrick said. 'Believe me I tried. Are you seeing her again?'

'I might. I said I'd ring her, but I didn't take her number.'

Patrick groaned. 'You're mad.'

'Money isn't everything,' Gerry said virtuously.

'True. It buys you everything, though.'

They did not speak again until they arrived in Cambridge. Two o'clock on a chill autumn morning.

'Too late for the bloody proctor, surely?' Patrick whispered as they parked the car on the Backs.

'Let's hope so.'

They crept through the empty streets and climbed into Trinity without being challenged. Patrick settled himself on Gerry's sofa, preferring this to the more hazardous climb into Christ's.

'I'll wake you at seven,' Gerry said. 'I have to be up to exercise the hounds.'

'You're too damned energetic,' Patrick complained. 'Diana Dalton could buy you ten packs of hounds and not notice. *And* men to exercise the blasted things.'

Gerry received a telegram the next day:

'Dinner Saturday 7 stop dress informal stop RSVP.' An address in Mayfair and a telephone number.

He waited a day and then replied, also by telegram: 'Yes.'

Diana Dalton had one aim in life: to have fun. She knew every drinking club, nightclub, jazz club and every other sort of club in London. She knew 'sweet little places' where you could find excitement beyond alcohol and to which, when Gerry discovered what the white powder to be had there was, he resolutely refused to go again.

Diana pouted at him and called him a boring old prude, and he said she could go there without him, and welcome, but he wasn't having anything to do with any of it.

'Don't you mind what I do when you're stuck in stuffy old Cambridge?' she asked.

'Not much.'

She stamped her high-heeled foot.

'*Why* can't I make you jealous?'

'Because you're so bad at it,' he said, laughing at her.

'Are you a fortune-hunter?' she asked him, time and time again.

'Yes,' he'd always reply.

'You don't have money?'

'Not that you'd recognise as money.'

'How can you afford to take me out, then?'

'I can't. You'll have to pay.'

He took her to cheap restaurants and ordered rough house wine. At first she found it 'fascinating', they were 'sweet little places', the waiters were 'divine'. But it soon became 'boring', and she took him to the Ritz, the Savoy, Ciro's, the Four Hundred, wherever she wanted, and she ordered champagne and she paid.

She refused to come to Cambridge for the ball. It would be boring, she said. Not exciting. Not *fun*.

'All right, don't,' he said.

'Will you go?'

'Of course.'

'Who with?'

He shrugged his shoulders, meaning it didn't particularly matter, but also (though Diana didn't know that) meaning he didn't have a clue.

She came to the ball.

She was furious when he said he was taking Florin to Flimwell Place when term ended.

'Can I come?'

'No.'

'Why not?'

'You haven't been asked, and, anyway, you'd be in the way.'

'I wouldn't!'

'You're not coming.'

She had obviously never heard the word 'no' before, had never been denied anything she wanted. Gerry hadn't set out to attract her, but the more he denied her – of anything, from his own presence to another glass of champagne when he thought she'd

140

had enough – the more fascinating she seemed to find him. His reticence about his background added to his mystique.

'Who *are* you?' she'd ask him.

'A fortune-hunter,' he would reply.

'Where are you going for Christmas?'

'Never you mind.'

'Mummy will be here. Will you come and meet her, Gerry?'

Doubt in her voice. He had her guessing. Presumably the droves of previous suitors had tripped over themselves in order to ingratiate themselves with Senhora Moitinho.

'Of course I will,' he said. '*After* I've been to Leicestershire.'

The Flimwells offered him the use of their London flat and he moved in there for a night after his stay at Flimwell Place. The phone rang before he'd had a chance to take his suitcase to the room occupied by James when he was in town.

'Gerry! At last! I've been phoning all day. Six o'clock this evening? Mummy's longing to see you.'

Gerry expected Senhora Moitinho to be a formidable matron whose every hackle would be rising in suspicion of this unknown man her daughter had found, but she was a charming, rather vague woman, with some of Diana's good looks and none of her style, determination and confidence. She introduced Gerry to her husband, Pedro, all tanned middle-aged muscle and teeth, smiled indulgently at Diana's effusive greeting of Gerry and invited him to sit on the sofa beside her. Gerry shook hands with Pedro Moitinho, nodded at Phyllis – Mrs Cunningham, a cousin of Diana's dead father who, along with Diana's old nanny, lived in the house in Mayfair and tried to keep track of the rich Miss Dalton's comings and goings – and sat, expecting polite but determined enquiries into his genealogy. Instead the senhora talked about how cold England was after Rio and how Harrods wasn't as it used to be.

'See?' Diana said, after they had all had dinner and she and Gerry were climbing into a taxi to take them to a new and 'frightfully divine' nightclub she had discovered in his absence. 'She was utterly charmed.'

'*Was* she?' Gerry asked. He rather thought the presence of an elephant at the dining table would have made less impression.

'Utterly,' Diana said. She snuggled up to him. 'Have you missed me, Gerry?'

'Too frightfully and utterly,' he said.

She sighed loudly. 'You're a complete beast, but I love you most frightfully much,' she said.

For Christmas she gave him a pair of gold cufflinks. He gave her a china dog which he had won at a fair they had been to and for which she had clamoured at the time. He drove home for Christmas, her protestations of undying love ringing in his ears. It was a joke, the whole thing. As Diana would have said, it was fun, too utterly exciting and not at all boring.

But at home he received news that put all thoughts of Diana out of his mind.

As usual, his mother had cooked something special for his first night home. Prawns they had, off the boats, in some kind of sauce, and then Dover sole. Grace and Arthur were there, and they and Ma and Da looked at him expectantly as he ate.

'Good, is it?' his father asked.

'Yes, Da. Thanks, Ma—' as she scraped the bones from his plate into the bucket kept for the chickens' food and put another sole before him. It *was* good, but his mother's cooking always was.

'Can't tell the difference?'

'Difference from what?'

Joe laughed delightedly and the others smiled.

'From the real thing, Gerry-lad. What you eatin' is Beviss and Sons Frozen Fish. Been frozen a month, that lot.'

Gerry hastily put down his knife and fork.

'Is it safe?'

' 'Course it is, lad. They been freezin' fish for years, but we're doin' it special. Deep freezes. That's the future. That's what that bloke said, dain't he, Arthur?'

'That's right, Da.'

'Restaurants'll have 'em. Hotels already have, some of 'em. Got to, see? No more chucking out what's not used. No visitin' fish markets every day, not if they don't want to.'

'Shops'll have them, too,' Arthur put in.

'Yeah, shops,' Joe confirmed. 'And nobs' houses like as not. Well, lad, what do you think?'

142

Gerry began eating again. There was a difference, now he was concentrating on taste and texture, but only someone used to sole straight out of the sea would notice it. Frozen fish! What would the old man think of next?

'Well?' Joe prompted.

'Sounds a good idea, Da, if what you say is true.'

'It's true all right, lad. We got to get rid o' this rationing rubbish yet, so I ain't talkin' about tomorrow, mark you, nor next year neither. Anyways, folks is slow to take to new ideas. And that's where you come in, lad.'

Gerry stared at him. 'Me?' he said. '*Me?*'

'Why yes, lad! What did that bloke say, Art? The one who's been to Americky and learned all about it?'

Grace spoke in place of her husband. 'Packaging and marketing, he said. That's what.'

Joe turned back to Gerry. 'Packagin' an' marketin'. That's your job. Arthur'll look after the fish an' you do this packagin' an' marketin' stuff. Right?'

Gerry was speechless.

'You know the sort o' things the nobs like,' Joe went on. ' 'Cause we ain't doin' cod an' that. Prawns, it'll be. Potted shrimps. Crab . . .'

'And smoked salmon, maybe,' Grace said, her eyes on Gerry's shocked face.

'Yeah,' Joe said. 'That freezes well, so this expert chappie says. You go an' talk to him, Gerry-lad. He knows all about it.'

'Da,' Gerry began, 'I – I can't . . . What about National Service, anyway? There's that to come. I've got to do that.'

Joe made an impatient gesture. 'Reckon your polio'll see you out of that.'

'You can't mean this, Da. Me? . . . And *fish?*'

'What else you goin' to do, lad?'

'A job, I suppose. In London.'

'This is a job,' Grace said. 'And London would be a good place to do it, I'd have thought.'

He looked at her and she met his eyes directly, which Arthur would not.

'You belong in your family business, Gerry,' she said.

143

'What the hell has it got to do with you?'

'Don't talk like that to Grace, son. She's got the right on it. Family business. We need those fancy friends you been making while you been spending all that money—'

Gerry stood up.

'You're calling in the loan. Is that it?'

'I ain't callin' anything in. I don't want money back from you, lad. Not as such.'

Gerry turned on Grace. 'It's your idea, isn't it?'

'Yes,' she said calmly.

'She suggested you for the job,' Joe said. 'But it's me as makes the decisions.'

'Well, find someone else for your job, then.'

'No. I told you we want your—'

'Connections,' Grace supplied.

'Connections. My money works for me, lad. I look for returns. You know that. If it don't I think of puttin' it elsewhere.'

'You're threatening me!' Gerry burst out. 'No. No, it's worse than that – you're bloody blackmailing me.' His voice rose as the horror hit him and he could hear his mother's voice saying, 'No, please, not on the first night home,' and Arthur's pleading, 'Gerry – Da—' and he put his fists on the table and leaned over his father. 'You're saying no more money unless I obey you. Use my connections! By God, what do you want me to do? Get Lady Flimwell to say "I couldn't be without Beviss and Sons' frozen fish three times a week"?'

'Could you do that, lad? It'ud surely help.'

'No, I bloody well couldn't. Beviss and Sons . . . oh no!' He sat down and put his face in his hands.

It served him right. He saw it all now. Pretending to be something he wasn't . . . he was always bound to be found out. He had never thought it would come from his own family, that was all. Well, he should have done. He should have suspected Grace from the time she took over the horses. And whenever had Joe Beviss given something and not expected it back, and with interest? Why should he, Gerry, be immune? Beviss and Sons . . . A vision sprang into his head: he was at some grand house wearing his dinner jacket – no: his boiled shirt and white tie – and his

144

hostess was saying, delicately, probingly, as she finished her potted shrimps, 'It's not a very usual name. Are you related?' . . . 'Oh yes, indeed, Lady So-and-So, I'm one of the sons on the bloody packet.' Senhora Moitinho fainted and Diana Dalton crowed, 'How utterly ghastly! The dreadful little man is a complete sham!' . . . Would Da stop his allowance if he refused? He needed money. He needed money for his two last terms at Cambridge, to keep it all up. Two more terms in the shining city and then bow out Gerry Beviss, gentleman, enter the rep from the frozen fish company. . . .

No and no, he would not do it.

Pretend. Easy.

So be it.

He took his hands from his face and was back in the kitchen at Ridge Farm, his mother at the sink weeping softly, his father still sitting calmly at the table, Arthur, his face suffused in misery, staring at his feet, Grace looking at him, a little smile on her lips.

He'd get even with her.

'All right, Da. I got no choice, have I?'

'I don't reckon you have, lad.'

'Tell you what, though,' Gerry said. 'I don't rate Beviss and Sons as a name for this caper. You – we . . .' He smiled sweetly at Grace, who now had a puzzled frown on her face. 'We need a name that says to the customer, "This is fresh fish, straight from the sea". And a symbol. A leaping fish and a name like . . .' Where was he getting this from? It was brilliant – 'like Blue Seas. No, Oceans . . . Blue Oceans. How about that?'

'I think Beviss and Sons has a good ring,' Grace said firmly.

Why did she hate him so? He'd never done anything to her. But Da was shushing her, flapping his hand to keep her quiet, the bitch, and was leaning forward, his sharp eyes on Gerry.

'Blue Oceans, eh? It's an idea, lad.'

'Something like that. What d'you think, Art?'

Grace opened her mouth to speak and Gerry said softly, 'Let him talk, Grace. He can, you know.'

'Blue Oceans is fine,' Arthur muttered, looking sideways at Grace. 'I like the leaping fish bit, too,' he added.

Gerry threw himself into it. He went to see the expert on frozen

145

food, who was the most crashing bore imaginable. Gerry agreed with him that when rationing stopped there was going to be a boom in the food business, he nodded in enthusiastic agreement as the man expounded his theories on the future of deep freezes and he tasted food that had been frozen one month, two months, three months. He went off to see deep freezes *in situ* in some of the big hotels, and admired photographs of them in American homes.

'What are you up to?' Diana asked him.

'Business.'

'What business?'

'None of yours.'

'What are we going to do for New Year's Eve? It's a special one – a new decade.'

'Anything you want.'

'Anything I want is boring . . . except you, Gerry.'

Gerry had no fewer than twelve leaping fishes drawn and Blue Oceans written in as many kinds of twiddly writing; he found little cardboard cartons for the potted shrimps, boxes for Dover soles and he stuck the twiddly writing and the leaping fish on them and he went down to Ridge Farm and laid them out on the kitchen table for the board of directors to consider.

'I still think Beviss and Sons is a more appropriate name,' Grace said.

'We don't need to decide yet awhile,' Joe said, contemplating Gerry's designs. 'But you done well, Gerry-lad. Very well.'

'What do you think, Ma? You're in on this.' Gerry put his arm around his mother's shoulders and drew her to the table.

'They're lovely, Gerry,' she said. She'd always stick up for him.

He drove back to London. One night only and then Cambridge. Was he safe? If they kept the name off the packet, he was safe. Grace's determined face appeared before him. She knew what he was up to – not all, but enough – and he wished he knew what her motives were. Why would she care what the bloody thing was called? She was poisoning Arthur. How had he come to be married to such a bitch?

That night a flashbulb went off as he and Diana walked into the

Four Hundred. Gerry pulled Diana on, as he had seen the film stars do in the newsreels, but she held back.

'He's Gerry Beviss,' she told the photographer and spelled out his name.

'Your new regular escort, Miss Dalton?'

Diana gave her tinkling laugh.

'As regular as I can make him. He's starting term at Cambridge tomorrow and will be studying for his finals. Trinity College,' she added.

'Diana, really!' Gerry said, when they were seated at a table adjacent to the dance floor.

'Really what?'

'You're outrageous.'

'I hope so. Anything else would be—'

'Boring,' he said, trying not to sigh.

She puffed on her cigarette and looked around the nightclub.

'Let's go somewhere else.'

'We've only just got here, for God's sake.'

'I want to go back to your flat.'

'It's not my flat.'

'I want to go there.'

'No. Let's dance.'

'I don't want to. I want sex.'

'You want *what?*'

'You heard.'

He was flabbergasted.

'How many men have you slept with?'

She shrugged her bare shoulders. 'A few.'

'Well, well.' He stared at the couples revolving on the dance floor, wondering why he didn't jump at her offer. This was what he wanted, wasn't it? He had lost Kate because of it.

Diana pointed her holder at him, the burning tip of the cigarette about an inch from his nose.

'See! You're jealous! Go on, admit it!'

He looked at her and what she saw in his eyes deflated her entirely.

'I was joking, Gerry darling. Honestly I was. I just wanted to shock you – and I did, didn't I?'

He returned to Cambridge the next day. How lovely it was, how peaceful Nevile's Court in grey January. He sat in front of his gas fire sipping a cup of tea, being *boring*, but who cared? The Christmas vacation, what with Diana and the frozen fish, had been enough to exhaust any man. Somehow the two things were connected in his mind, but he couldn't quite work out why.

Patrick came round and waved a copy of the *Daily Graphic* at him. 'Seen this?'

He shook his head.

'Turn to page seven.'

A photograph of him and Diana the night before, headlined 'Diana's swot suitor'. Then, in smaller letters: 'As regular as I can make him says millionairess Di'.

'Oh Lord,' Gerry groaned, throwing the paper to the floor. 'Patrick, save me from this.'

'Save you from all that money? Damn it all, Gerry, I'm your *friend*!'

Gerry had told Diana that he wouldn't be able to see much of her this term and this she had accepted with unexpected docility. She couldn't ring him either, but it didn't prevent her from leaving endless messages at the Porters' Lodge asking him to ring her, reversing the charges. And she sent telegrams as long as letters, and letters as long as novellas written in a great childish scrawl on distinctive dark blue paper with matching envelopes and saying how utterly boring London was without him. He was embarrassed by the bristling bunch of mail delivered to him day after day, while Mr McGibbons and his colleagues – *Graphic* readers to a man – would grin at him and comment on his good fortune.

This went on for two weeks. The next Saturday morning, there was a knock on his door and he opened it, and there was Diana, dressed in unaccustomed demure tweed with her mink coat over her shoulders and a matching hat hiding her curls.

'I utterly had to come, Gerry,' she said. 'You don't mind, darling, do you?'

She looked so pretty and, for once, not quite sure of herself that Gerry felt touched.

'Come in,' he said.

She did, looked around and took in his desk with papers and

books on it, the chair pushed back as he had stood up to open the door. By some miracle he had been writing an essay. She turned glowing brown eyes on him and smiled.

'You *have* been working then?'

'What else would I have been doing?' he asked, his voice with just enough hurt in it.

She flung herself at him and muttered something. He bent his head.

'I can't hear you.'

'Girls,' she said.

He laughed and put his arms around her.

'Everywhere, as you can see.'

'Kiss me, Gerry.'

As he did so, her mink coat slid to the floor.

'I love you,' she whispered, 'and you don't seem to care a bit for me.'

'A new experience for you,' he teased.

'Do you?' she persisted.

'Do I what?'

'Care for me, at least?'

'Yes,' he said. 'I care for you.'

'How much?'

'You're being boring,' he warned.

'I'm only in dull old England because of you. It'll be Carnival time in Rio soon and gloriously and utterly hot.'

'Why don't you go, then?'

'I told you. Because of you.'

He picked up her coat and helped her into it.

'Come on. I'll show you non-carnival Cambridge. You hardly saw it when you were up last term.'

She hesitated, and he thought she was going to say that seeing Cambridge wasn't *fun*, but, 'I'm not taking you from your work, am I?'

'Yes, you are, but I don't mind.'

Her untoward serious mood continued. Normally she had the attention span of a flea, stopping long enough to take one bite of whatever was on offer before hopping on again, but today she walked through the colleges and looked at what Gerry pointed out to her and murmured every so often, 'Too utterly divine.'

After an hour, he took pity on her.

'Do you want to see more?' he asked.

'*Is* there more? Oh. Yes, please!' But then she added in a small voice, 'Only I'm getting rather cold.'

'I'm sorry,' he said, concerned. 'What would you like to do?'

'Can we go for a drink somewhere? Have lunch?'

They ate in a restaurant crowded with scruffy undergraduates, and Diana said not a word of complaint. Afterwards they walked back to Trinity, where her Jaguar was parked on the cobbled forecourt outside Great Gate.

'How did you park here?' asked Gerry. 'They guard this space as though it was the Crown Jewels.'

'I gave a little man in a bowler hat a pound.'

'A pound!' Gerry gulped.

'Can I come to your room, Gerry?'

'What for?'

'Just so I can kiss you goodbye.'

He waved her off a little later, feeling quite fond of her. He did care for her, funny little article that she was . . . A pound! A pound just to park her car!

Diana Dalton drove her white Jaguar back towards London, smiling and feeling most pleased with herself. For once, silly old Phyllis had been right – apart from saying that if Gerry wanted to see her he would come to London and that it was no good her going to Cambridge, that is. She shouldn't throw herself at him, Phyllis had said; men don't like that. She should be more restrained.

And today she *had* been restrained. She'd trailed around all those boring colleges, eaten the most filthy meal, behaved like an utterly ghastly demure little débutante with no spark at all – and Gerry had been nicer to her than ever before! He'd smiled gently at her, been concerned when she said she was cold (as though she could be in her mink!) and had altogether been utterly divine.

So silly old Phyllis had been right about that. Now, what next? Should she go on being restrained? Stop sending him letters and telegrams, be out when he rang (if he rang, which he didn't often)? Would that work?

*　　*　　*

150

It was as though a tap had been turned off. Gerry was relieved to be free of the blue envelopes and the telegrams, and the college porters were more worried than he, hoping, presumably – and who could blame them? – for more visits from the white Jaguar at a pound a time. But then he began to wonder. Had Diana found someone else upon whom to lavish her capricious attention? Did he mind if she had? He'd never had a chance to think this out before: every single time they had met, he suddenly realised, was at her instigation.

Patrick was beside himself.

'You've let her slip!' he howled. 'By God, Gerry, how *could* you? You're mad. Mad! Isn't he mad?'

He turned in frustration to the other people in James's rooms: Richard Kellerway, who was one of the whippers-in to the Drag Hounds, and Mark and Vanessa.

'I wouldn't like Diana Dalton hanging around my neck,' James said. 'She is a bit much in every direction.'

'Think of the millions!'

'Isn't it only one?'

'Isn't one *enough*?'

Vanessa spoke for the first time. 'Perhaps money isn't important. Perhaps Gerry doesn't care about it.'

'If he doesn't he's a bloody great fool,' Patrick said.

Gerry did care about money. Money was freedom, and it was easy to say it wasn't important if you had enough of it. Gerry could have enough, but that meant the frozen fish . . . packaging and marketing frozen fish. . . .

He shook his head to get rid of the thoughts. Lots of things could happen. Maybe Da was wrong about him being turned down for National Service and he'd have another two years before he had to make a decision. Maybe someone else would offer him a job, though he didn't know how that would be. Everyone seemed to have a family firm to go to after their National Service was done – fathers, uncles, cousins all ready to welcome them and their old school ties. Gerry's school tie was from Rye Grammar and his family firm? . . . Ah, Blue Oceans!

Diana lasted a week – although Gerry didn't know this was what she was doing – the blue tide swelled once more and Mr

McGibbons slapped Gerry on the shoulder and said, 'Lovers' tiff, eh, Mr Beviss?'

He went to London to escort her to a Valentine's ball. Just before midnight, when she was dancing very close to him and had been silent for nearly two minutes – something of a record – she raised her head from his shoulder and looked into his face.

'I may as well do it myself,' she said.

'What?' he asked, not paying much attention.

'Propose. Gerry Beviss, will you marry me?'

For half a second his feet stopped moving, and then he danced her on.

'You've had thirteen proposals,' he said. 'How many times have you popped the question?'

'Just this once. It would be fun being married, Gerry. Think how utterly exciting it would be!'

He was amazed at how tempted he was. No frozen fish, the house in Mayfair. They could buy somewhere in the country – a farm, an estate! Holidays in the South of France . . . life would be one long holiday . . .

'Well?' she asked.

'No,' he said.

She wasn't much cast down.

'At least you hestitated,' she said.

He could not deny it.

Chapter 11

James and Canterlupe won the Members' race at the University point-to-point with Gerry and Florin coming a distant though creditable third. Diana congratulated James loudly and extravagantly, took them all to the bar and bought them drinks.

'Utterly marvellous,' she kept saying, as the farmers sitting over their beer at the little tin tables placed around the tent stared at her, a bird of paradise in Cambridgeshire. 'But why didn't *you* win, darling?'

'Canterlupe's a thoroughbred,' James explained. 'Even with me on board he goes faster than Florin.'

'But why isn't Florin a thoroughbred? Why don't you have a thoroughbred, Gerry?'

'For heaven's sake, shut up,' he said. 'I like Florin the way he is.'

Patrick held Gerry back as they all left the tent to watch the next race.

'Remember the million,' he said. 'A fleet of thoroughbreds, Gerry.'

They had the very last meet of the University Drag. The dark green hunting coats were cleaned and handed over to Richard Kellerway, who would be master next year, and the hounds were sent away to their summer quarters. Three seasons of the greatest fun Gerry could ever have imagined became memories, and nothing more.

Gerry remembered the million. He couldn't help it when he

arrived at Ridge Farm for the Easter vacation and found that Grace had prepared what she called a 'contract of employment' for him to sign.

'Just to sort things out,' she said, handing it to him. 'It's going to be called Blue Oceans, so you've won that round.'

'*Won?*' he repeated. 'Grace, you make it sound like a fight.' He scanned the document. 'Have you signed one of these?'

'I don't need to.'

'Then neither do I.'

'Your father wants you to. Isn't that right, Joe?'

'Yeah, it's right,' Joe muttered.

'You can't even bloody read it!' Gerry said, his voice rising.

'Sign it, Gerry. Don't row again,' his mother pleaded. '*Don't!*'

Gerry sighed. 'I'll read it through. I can't sign something I've not read, can I?'

'No, lad, you can't,' Joe said soothingly. 'Now come an' eat. Your Ma's begged lobsters off the boats to welcome you home. We used to say your first night, but that's as likely to be your last now, ain't it?'

'How long you staying, Gerry?' his mother asked.

'Just a few days, Ma.'

'You going to see the girl whose picture's in the papers?'

So they knew about that. Come to think of it, how could they not in a place this size?

'Yes, I am,' he said.

'Does she know about you?' Grace asked.

'Know what?'

'Who you really are.'

'I *really am* Gerry Beviss, and she knows that.'

'No need to be shirty,' Grace said, cracking lobster claws with awful efficiency. He knew she wished it was his balls she was cracking and, yet again, he wondered why she hated him so much.

He read her contract in bed that night. It declared that he would start working for Blue Oceans Ltd on the first of July 1950 and said, among all sorts of other things couched in legalese (so she'd paid money to have this thing drawn up?) that the agreement could only be terminated by six months' notice on either side. But he could find nothing in it that said what fate would befall him if

154

he signed it and then did not abide by its terms. It was daft. Grace gone mad.

He needed time, though, and he needed to know what his options were. The next day he went to see their family doctor.

'Off hand,' the man said in answer to his query, 'I should say you'll be one of the lucky ones. The services demand perfect physical specimens. . . . Mind you, you look pretty good. How is the leg?'

'Fine,' Gerry said. 'It tingles a bit sometimes, but that's all.'

'Even so, I expect they'll look at your medical record and reject you. Do you want me to check? I know someone who'd be able to tell me.'

'Could you, sir?'

'Wait outside, would you?'

He called him back a few minutes later and said, 'Well, young Beviss, my chap reckons there is no chance of you serving King and Country.'

'But I'll get the call-up papers, won't I?'

'Oh yes. Any day now, I imagine.'

The options were toppling.

'Where have you been?' Diana asked.

'Mind your own business.'

'Will you marry me?'

'No.'

'Why not?'

'You don't know anything about me. Perhaps I'm a fortune-hunter.'

'If you were, then you'd marry me. What are you going to give me for my twenty-first birthday?'

'A china cat.'

Before he went back to Cambridge, he told his father that he could not sign the bit of paper Grace had prepared, not until he knew for certain about his National Service.

'You'll be out o' that, I told you,' Joe growled.

'But you can't be sure. You wouldn't want me to sign something I couldn't honour, would you?'

'Honour! What use is that? Sign it, lad, an' be done.'

'I can't.'

Joe prowled up and down the parlour, his stick prodding the carpet. He turned and pointed it at Gerry.

'All right,' he said. 'All right. You take Grace's paper wi' you to Cambridge an' you bloody well sign it the moment you hear about your army doings. Can't say fairer than that, can I?'

It was the best he could hope for, and at least he'd get his allowance for his last term.

Joe left the room and Gerry turned to his mother, who had been hovering anxiously by the door.

'Why is he so set on all this?' he asked. 'He's never expected me to have anything to do with the fish before. It's Grace . . . Ma, why does she run this family now?'

'Dunno, Gerry. I just don't know.' Meg trailed into the kitchen and put the kettle on. Gerry followed. 'I reckon it's a'cos Grace always knows her mind an' speaks it an' Arthur don't, not always. An' your Da's got this frozen fish idea an' I reckon he's a little scared-like, seeing the idea is so new an' that, an' he don't read an' write so good . . . Oh, but what'm I saying? I dain't ought to be talkin' o' your Da this way. . . .'

She handed Gerry a cup of tea.

'I still don't see why I have to be part of it,' he said.

'Maybe you'll get to like it,' she said hopefully. 'You'll be good at it, Gerry, for sure. 'Twas a fine name you chose. Blue Oceans is a fine and clever name, an' you're my boy who's good at everything . . . Anyways, what's so bad about it?' she pleaded. 'I don't see what's so bad about working in Blue Oceans.'

'Honest, Ma, I don't think I can do it.'

She sighed a great, heaving sigh. 'I'm so proud o' you, Gerry, an' what you are. Such a grand boy, your picture in the papers an' all . . . such a grand boy. Not one of us any more.'

'Ma, that's not so!'

'It is, though,' she said sadly. 'You're just not one of us.'

And it was the awful truth. Gerry loved his family, loved the sanctuary of their love when things went badly for him, wanted their approval of everything he did – but in the end, yes, he was no longer one of them.

That evening, he drove down to the little brick house at Winchelsea Beach that they had all lived in before moving to Ridge Farm. Grace opened the door and looked as though she was about to slam it in his face until Arthur's voice came from the parlour.

'Who's there, Grace love?'

'It's Gerry,' she said flatly.

Arthur came into the hallway.

'Eh, Gerry, it's not often you come and see us . . . A drink for Gerry, Grace love,' he said, and, putting his arm around his brother's shoulders, he drew him into the parlour.

Grace brought them both a beer. 'Why've you come?' she asked Gerry.

'Art's my brother, Grace. I'm allowed to come and see my brother, aren't I?'

' 'Course he is,' said Arthur. 'Now, what can I do for you, lad?'

'He wants money,' Grace said. 'As usual.'

'Let him say,' Arthur said mildly.

'Of course it's money. He doesn't want to be associated with you or your father. He won't sign the paper to join Blue Oceans, but he wants money. Isn't that right, Gerry?'

'No.'

'Well, why've you come?'

Gerry had had some idea of him and Arthur going out for a drink. He wanted to talk to Arthur, ask his advice, ask him if he couldn't persuade Grace and Joe that the frozen fish wasn't right for him. Arthur had wanted him to come away from Cambridge a gentleman, after all; Arthur wanted what was best for Gerry. But Grace's hostility was overwhelming.

'Why do you hate me so much?' he asked her. 'I've never done anything to you.'

'She don't hate you—' Arthur began.

'No, you've never done anything to me, but you have to Arthur,' she said, as though she had been rehearsing this speech for years. 'Him stuck behind the counter in the fish shop, giving up his career in the army, because all money went on you, you demanding more all the time—'

'Grace!' Arthur protested.

'So,' she went on, not losing track, 'so you could go to balls and

157

Ascot races and play at being the smart gentleman, forget where you come from . . . Arthur gave his savings for you, you know —'

'No! Art, I'll pay you back.'

'No, lad.'

'Say yes for once, Arthur.'

'No, I will not.'

'A bit at a time,' Gerry said. He got out his chequebook and started writing frantically. Twenty pounds – could he afford it? This was awful. He tore out the cheque and handed it to his brother. 'Take it, Art, please.'

'Take it, Arthur.' And Arthur, obeying Grace, did so.

'Prancing around Cambridge for three years,' Grace was saying, 'and now seeing all the best places with that rich girl. Begging money off Arthur and your Da so you could seem a great man and never ready to give anything back—'

'I got his cheque, Grace.'

'Money!' she exclaimed. 'It's not the point, not now it isn't. The point is your dead years in the fish shop. The point is he doesn't want anything to do with his family. He's got too bloody posh for the likes of us – *haven't you?*'

'An' if I have?' Gerry cried, his temper gone. 'An' if I have, whose fault is that, then? You don't know, but it was his—' He indicated Arthur. 'He started the whole bloody sham, ain't he told you that? He thought it'ud be a lark to pretend to be my servant . . . ain't that right, Art? It'ud be a lark, he thought, an' it all came from there. That's right!' he said, stopping for a moment striding up and down the little room and staring at Grace's shocked face.'That's right, Art, ain't it? Did I ever ask you to do it?'

Arthur shook his head miserably. 'No. No, he didn't, Grace.'

'An' now,' Gerry went on, 'it's got so I can't come – go – back. I can't an' that's a fact. And I don't wish to. That I admit. I don't wish to.'

There was silence.

'But I did ask Art for money – least through him I was asking Da,' Gerry said at last. 'I didn't know it was Arthur's savings. . . . I'm sorry, Art. I'll pay it back.'

Without another word, he left. He'd seen a film once, a bit of a newsreel. They'd put a rat in a maze and cheese or something at

158

the exit, and the creature had run around demented, going up blind alleys and turning and going up more, tormented, able to smell the cheese and not able to find it. Gerry knew now how that rat had felt . . . except it had found the cheese (and what the hell had that proved to anyone?) and had, presumably, been happy. But what was at the exit to the maze Gerry was in?

It came to him with dreadful clarity: Diana or Blue Oceans. Each was as impossible to contemplate as the other, but what else was there? Blue Oceans or Diana. The frozen fish was the old Gerry Beviss, the one gypsy born; Diana was the new man, the one Cambridge had made, the one he wanted to be . . . the one he *was*! He could not see anything in between, or how the two sides of him could amalgamate into one.

He stopped the car and found he was weeping: for his mother's sad face as she begged him to do as his father asked, knowing that he could not but hoping all the same; for Arthur, so defeated by his wife, for his father infected by Grace's venom; for himself, most of all for himself, and for the impossibly fractured person he had become.

'Will you really not be able to see me this term?'

'Hardly at all. I must work.'

'Oh well, it's the season. I'll be frightfully busy myself.'

'So I see,' Gerry said, examining the invitations on her mantelpiece. 'But I'm still not jealous.'

'Don't you love me even the teensiest bit?'

'Perhaps the smallest teensiest bit . . . Hey!' He fended her off and then kissed her. 'All right?'

'Utterly, Gerry. But no more than the teensiest?'

'Absolutely not.'

'Shall we not go out tonight? Shall we stay here? Phyllis is playing bridge and Suckers is visiting relatives. I didn't,' she added disingenuously, 'say you were coming.'

'Now, what is that supposed to mean?'

'It means, will you marry me?'

'No.'

* * *

'She's asked you to marry her and you've said no?'

'Several times.'

'Why?' Patrick asked. 'Gerry, why?'

'I don't love her.'

'Love,' said Patrick scornfully.

Gerry knew what love was, and it wasn't what he felt for Diana. Nothing like it. In a turmoil, he found himself in his car and driving towards Girton one evening in late April. He parked in the courtyard and paced the once-familiar corridors towards Kate's room. He had his hand up to knock when he saw the name on the door: Miss L. M. Martin.

Who the hell was she and what had she done with Kate? He had a moment of perfect panic. He had seen Kate at parties, though not recently, and they had exchanged greetings. Out of habit, never questioning his motives, Gerry had kept an eye on her escorts to make sure she was not going to fall in love with any of them – though that had not seemed so important in the last few months – and had imagined her working in her room in the evenings, her dark head bent over her books. Now this comfortable picture vanished and was replaced by a blank.

He ran back to the Portress's Lodge, breathlessly demanded Kate's whereabouts and was absurdly relieved when he was given a room number and directions.

She was in. She greeted him and smiled. She was about to go to Hall, she said, but would he like a quick sherry? She was wearing her gown. She looked amazing in it, untouchable.

How beautiful she was. No make-up, no affectation, no billowing smoke and too utterly divines. Her room, like her, was wondrously calm and was now filling with westering sun. It lit upon her skeleton in the corner. What had they nicknamed it? How dreadful that he could not remember, but, 'Pinocchio,' he said. It jerked like the cartoon character.

She laughed, such a lovely sound. 'Pinocchio. I know all his bones now.'

'You always did, I thought.'

She handed him a glass and he took it, his fingers brushing hers.

'Kate,' he said, 'will you marry me?'

'*What?*'

160

She put her glass down on the desk and turned to face him, her glorious navy-blue eyes staring.

'Will you marry me?' He put his own glass down, went to her and wrapped his arms around her. Her body, under her gown and her dress, was rigid. 'Marry me,' he whispered. 'I'll do something terrible if you don't. I know I will. Save me, please.'

'Is this a joke?' she asked, her voice high with shock.

'I don't think so. It may be, but I don't think it is. You haven't answered.'

She pushed him away gently, resting her hands on the lapels of his jacket and then running them through her short dark hair, her eyes still staring at him uncomprehendingly.

'Gerry, I – I—'

There was a knock on the door and a voice called, 'Coming, Kate?'

'In a minute,' she called back. 'I must go,' she said to Gerry. 'I suppose I must. To Hall. Gerry . . . I can't think. My finals are in a month – less. Do you mean it?'

He shook his head helplessly. 'I'm all muddled up, Kate. All in a muddle.'

'I can't think,' she repeated. 'How can you expect me to? My work and everything . . .'

'I'm sorry.'

'Sorry? Why apologise?' she asked, more confused than ever.

'I'd better go,' he said. 'Can I kiss you?'

She put her hands around his neck and drew his head towards hers. Their lips met, parted. Briefly his eyes closed, then, 'Goodbye, Kate,' he said, and left.

Kate stripped off her gown and threw it over a chair back. How was anyone supposed to eat, work or do anything after that?

'We'll announce our engagement at my party, shall we?' Diana asked.

'We're not engaged.'

'Don't be boring, Gerry.'

Summer in Cambridge, that loveliest of cities. Loveliest, but soon to be lost. Oh, he could come back, no doubt he would, but it would never be the same. Always an outsider from now on. Others would hail their friends across Great Court, run to lectures with their gowns pulling at their shoulders, take half an hour to walk down Trinity Street because there were so many people to greet. If only he had worked harder he could, perhaps, have become a don or a fellow and stayed here for ever. Stopped time. A fly trapped in amber.

Where had the time gone? This ancient place had stolen it away, sucked it into its river, absorbed it into its great stone walls, thieved it while he had taken too long over lunch at the Pitt Club, squandered days on the hunting field, at the races, nights at parties in London. And now there was no more time. Only May Week, and then it would all be gone.

He stood on the bridge at Silver Street. They had been drinking champagne at the Mill to celebrate the end of the exams, and he felt light-headed. Drunk, in fact – that and a sense of loss, an unbearable love for the place he had to leave. He crossed the road and went into the Fisher Court entrance of Queens' College, then across the Mathematical Bridge and into Cloister Court, which always made him catch his breath. Out of Queens' and into the back entrance of St Catharine's. Many a good evening he had spent here when Andrew Coleridge had been up. Andrew was doing his National Service now. He'd come back: in a hideous uniform, his hair shaven above his ears, full of horror stories about life in the army. At least Gerry was spared that. He had been rejected for the services, as he had been told he would be, because of his polio. . . . Spared for what, though?

He went out of Cat's, past the imprisoning railings, on to King's Parade and into King Henry's college itself, saluting the porter as he went past his lodge. The porter had been a bulldog when, once, the proctor had chased Gerry and James down Senate House Passage and Trinity Lane and caught them, drunkenly and laughing helplessly, trying to climb into Trinity. Gerry didn't bear the man a grudge for the fine he had been given; he only wished he'd have the chance to catch him again.

Into the glory of King's College Chapel, tourists being told all about it. 'Where light and shade repose,' Wordsworth had said of the building. Vanessa had told him that. Out and down to the river, crossing King's Bridge, along Queen's Road and back over Clare Bridge. Clare Fellows' Garden . . . he was going to a party there tomorrow evening. Out through Clare and into Trinity Hall and back over Garret Hostel Bridge. It was becoming absurd, but the champagne was telling him to cross every bridge over the Cam. The next one was Trinity Bridge. He stood on it and looked up towards St John's. Gardens, water and buildings.

A punt came around the corner from behind the Wren Library . . . There were many punts on the water this summer day, with exams just finished, but this one was different. Gerry seemed to be looking at it through distorted glass.

. . . Kate lying in the bows, a pale pink dress patterned with dark blue flowers, an old straw hat on her head . . . but not Gerry poling the punt; some man he did not know. She saw him looking down at her as the punt went under the bridge he was standing on. Her eyes met his and widened. He ran to the other side and she was sitting up when the punt reappeared and her hat was in her lap. The man stopped punting and let the pole trail in the water as he turned to see who or what Kate was looking at. Gerry gripped the parapet, his knuckles white, unprepared for, startled by, the emotion that flooded him: did the man have champagne in the tea basket, plan seduction in the buttercup meadows up near Grant-chester?

He could see Kate was talking. He should have been able to hear her since she was not that far away, but a buzzing noise was filling his ears. The man angrily steered the punt towards the bank, ramming the bows into it so Kate nearly lost her balance as she jumped out on to the grass. Still with the buzzing in his head, Gerry saw the punt bowl away up river, water curling from its sides, ducks bobbing in its wake. Kate was standing on the bank, her hat in her hands, staring at Gerry.

He walked slowly to her.

'You've heard.'

She nodded, and her eyes filled with tears.

'Why, Gerry?'

'Come with me.'

He took her hand and led her through New Court to his rooms

163

in Nevile's Court, and there he explained why he was marrying Diana Dalton.

'By this time next week I'd have had nothing – nothing to live on, nowhere to live. It was between her and the frozen fish, see? The frozen fish and all that money.'

'All that money,' she repeated.

'Kate, you don't blame me, do you? You can see how it is.'

'You asked me to marry you,' she said, her voice shaking. 'A month ago you asked me. Save me, you said.'

'You didn't though, did you? You didn't answer.'

'I didn't answer yes but I didn't say no either. How could I answer anything when you turned up after so long and asked me, and it was time for Hall and I was having to work so hard? How *could* I? It might be a joke, you said.'

She was crying now, tears flooding out of her eyes and dripping on to the front of her dress. She turned away and stared out of the window, gulping, her shoulders heaving. He found her a handkerchief. She dabbed at her face and blew her nose.

'You couldn't wait a month. One little month,' she said, 'and you couldn't wait.'

'But you sent me away, Kate,' he said. 'It was you who stopped it between us. I tried to get you back—'

'But you didn't want marriage then. All you wanted was sex! Why did you come and ask me to marry you, Gerry?' she sobbed. '*Why*? I might never have known. I could have gone on in peace, not knowing it had ever entered your head.'

He took her in his arms and she cried and cried against his shoulder.

'You would have said yes?' he asked at last.

'Of course I would! But there was no time and you were so odd, saying it might be a joke. . . . If you'd asked me properly and meant it, of course I would. I love you, Gerry.'

In one of the rooms below, someone put on a record of Beethoven's Fifth Symphony. He'd been playing it all term: po-po-po-*pom*.

'Dear God,' Gerry whispered. 'What are we going to do?'

Kate pulled herself out of his arms and blew her nose again.

'You're getting married,' she said drearily, 'and I'm starting my

164

clinical training at St Thomas's Hospital in London. I can't see that our paths will cross again.'

'Don't say that, Kate. Don't!' Tears were in his eyes now. 'I'll break off the engagement—'

'You can't. How can you? It's been in the papers and everything. I'm sorry, Gerry,' she said, rallying, 'for making a scene. I'll go now.'

'No. Stay, Kate. Please.'

He put his arms around her again and they stood there close together, very still.

'What are you doing tonight?' he asked, his voice muffled in her hair.

He felt her shrug.

'I was going out with Tom – the man in the punt.' She laughed a little. 'I expect that's off now.'

And the long, light evening stretched away before her. Girton empty: laughing groups on the lawns or in the orchard; not even any work to do.

'Let's have dinner,' Gerry said. 'Let's drive a long way from Cambridge and have dinner somewhere.'

He should not have asked, she should not have accepted, but somewhere a shadow lifted and was edged across to occupy the sky of another day.

They went to Girton and Gerry waited in the car while Kate changed, and then they drove on, foolishly having a drink in *their* pub in Madingley, another in a pub in the postcard village of Hemingford Grey; walking along the river in the seductive summer twilight until it was too much for Kate and they turned back; having dinner in the cosy market town of St Neots, though neither of them could eat much. Reluctantly back on the road to Cambridge, the gates of Girton coming too soon, the college closed and dark.

'I'll have to climb in.'

Gerry opened the car door. 'I'll come and see you safe.'

'No. We'll say goodbye here. Now. Good luck to you, Gerry, in everything you do. . . . Don't invite me to your wedding.'

She hesitated a second, then kissed him hard on the lips and was out and gone.

Through a window – lots open at this time of year – and up to her room. Not stopping even to change out of her smart dress, she started to dismantle the fabric of the past three years. Everything into neat piles ready to pack into her trunk when she got it out of store tomorrow. She picked up the stack of May Week invitations and dropped it into the wastepaper basket.

She would be gone from this place before the first party began.

'I've changed my mind. I don't want to marry you.'

'Bad luck, darling. It's utterly too late. Anyway I want to marry you, and that's all that matters.'

'But why?'

She blew smoke at him. They were in her room at the Garden House Hotel, where she had just arrived with enough luggage for a three-month stay.

'You're my fourteenth time lucky,' she said.

'I never proposed to you.'

She laughed. 'But it doesn't alter the fact that we're engaged.' She spread out the fingers of her left hand. An enormous diamond ring sparked white light. 'And there's the proof.'

'I didn't buy it.'

'There's no law to say you should have done.'

'I'm in love with someone else.'

'Bad luck,' she said again.

'But why do you want a husband who doesn't want you as a wife?'

'Everyone has wanted me. Me or my money, which amounts to the same thing. It's boring. You're exciting because you don't.'

'What if I refuse to go through with it?'

'I'll sue you for breach of promise.'

'What good would that do you? I haven't any money.'

'Your father has.'

Gerry, who had been pacing around the room, stopped.

'Not enough,' he said cautiously, 'to make any difference to you.'

Diana fitted another cigarette into her holder and lit it. She gazed at him speculatively through half-closed eyes.

'Maybe that's so . . . but then maybe he could give me lobsters – as many as I wanted. Lobsters for life,' she said. 'That would be worth something, wouldn't it?'

'You know,' he said.

'Of course I do, darling. I had you investigated. I didn't like you disappearing without telling me where you were.'

'Don't you mind? That I'm a gypsy and my father is a fisherman?'

'He's a bit more than that, Gerry. So my chap reported.' She laughed again that tinkling laugh. 'Do you know how my grandfather and father made their money? Linoleum, Gerry. Lobsters are utterly preferable, wouldn't you say? No, I don't mind.'

She stubbed out her cigarette, came over to him and wrapped herself around him. At about this time yesterday, Kate, shaking with grief, had been in his arms.

'No,' Diana repeated, 'I don't mind, but you do, darling, don't you? Quite frightfully.' She looked up into his face. 'And so would all your well-bred friends. Deceived them beautifully, haven't you? . . . I won't say a thing, though, I promise you. I'll be like a sweet little clam. Now stop sulking, darling. It's too terribly boring. When do the parties start?'

'Six o'clock,' he muttered.

'Pick me up at six, then,' she said. 'We'll make an entrance.'

He left. He needed a drink. He needed several.

He was admired. He was envied. No one seemed to think badly of him because he was marrying for money: people he scarcely knew came and slapped him on the back and congratulated him; his father had roared with laughter, said he was a clever young dog and that he'd never have reckoned Gerry'ud come back from Cambridge with a millionairess.

'A lot more use than the bit o' paper the Rector was on about, eh, lad?' he had crowed over the telephone. Money always impressed him, and there was, of course, no mention of joining Blue Oceans.

Which is what he wanted, didn't he? And he was fond of Diana. She amused him. He'd never pretended to love her and, in spite of

167

her protestations, he was fairly sure she didn't love him. Patrick, among others, had been amazed he had held her off for as long as he had and they didn't even know about the threat of the frozen fish. Gerry himself had often wondered why: Blue Oceans or any other job could not begin to weigh against marriage to someone who was pretty and fun and had as much money as Diana had. And yet he had hesitated. And now he knew why.

It was Kate. Why hadn't he seen that? He had always loved her. He had loved her from the time they had first gone to the pub in Madingley and he had never stopped since. He couldn't believe how stupid he had been, looking back at it. He'd done everything during that summer short of raping her; he had said he couldn't go on seeing her unless she gave into him – hadn't he? – something like that he'd said. And then, to get her back, he'd forced her – that time in the library – to admit she loved him. He had said, in his letters to her, that he was sorry and he wouldn't do it again, but he had said that often enough before and hadn't meant it; he certainly hadn't stuck by it. What he should have said, he realised now – too late, too late – was that he understood her feelings, that he was prepared to wait. If he had done that, he and Kate could be celebrating their engagement along with Mark and Vanessa . . . And then he'd gone to Girton, hardly knowing what he was doing, and asked her to marry him – a mad, wild thing appearing after so long, interrupting her work on her finals. . . Except he hadn't been mad. It was his instinct knowing what was right. One little month.

He was stuck now. He had waited for Diana to arrive at the hotel convinced that she would release him from their engagement and that he could go and find Kate and ask her to marry him 'properly' and they and the frozen fish would live happily ever after. When would he ever grow up? Diana wanted him – God knew why, but she did – and she'd happily been photographed with him, had been delighted to have her intentions quoted: 'As regular as I can make him', 'He's my Valentine' . . . And he'd thought until an hour ago that she would let him go – not willingly, perhaps, but see the inevitability of it. How could she possibly? It would be the most awful, and the most public, humiliation. And he had planned to announce his engagement to someone else immediately afterwards, and had more or less told her so. And she had more or less told him that if he tried anything on she would reveal his secret to the world, sue him for breach of promise. Hell hath no fury . . . and Diana scorned would leave hell somewhere far distant in her wake. He might end up with Kate, but surely they would be rocking desperately on some raft in the middle of nowhere. Would Blue Oceans – let alone anyone else – want him after that?

He had to go through with it. He remembered something Kate had said yesterday: 'I could have gone on in peace, not knowing . . .' If he hadn't been standing on that bridge, if she hadn't been on a punt going beneath it, he would never have known so certainly that he loved her, that she loved him. If he could just imagine himself back to the day before when he didn't know, and had been – as Patrick was constantly urging him to – vaguely looking forward to a life of ease and luxury with pretty, amusing Diana . . . He tried, but all he could think of was a voice saying, 'Good luck to you, Gerry, in everything you do,' and her last kiss and the dreadful emptiness of the car when, at last, he had managed to drive it back to Cambridge.

He went to Patrick's rooms. Patrick was in, getting into training with a jug of Pimm's and Anthony Jones, who had once given a tea party to which Kate had come. It was a conspiracy.

'Benedick the married man!' Patrick cried. 'Dear boy, you look like you've seen a herd of ghosts. The engagement's not off, is it?'

'No, it is not.'

'Well, bloody cheer up then.'

Patrick poured him a drink, other people turned up and all of them, if they were not already aware of it, were acquainted with Gerry's good fortune and gradually, under the onslaught of alcohol and envious comments, Gerry did cheer up and went to collect his fiancée from her hotel in reasonably good spirits.

'How do I look?' she asked him.

'Extraordinary,' he said, meaning it. She was wearing a tiny hat with enormous feathers stuck in it – heaven knew how – and a bright yellow dress slashed with great black flowers.

'Have you stopped being a grumpy old bore?'

'Yes,' he said. 'I've stopped being a grumpy old bore.'

* * *

And so, May Week. The parties on the scented summer evenings in the fellows' gardens along the Backs, at King's and Queens' and Clare, at Trinity and St John's.

Gerry saw Vanessa and kissed her, congratulated her and admired her engagement ring.

'Nothing like Diana's,' she said.

'How is Kate?'

'Gone, Gerry. Gone.'

Like everything else, then. He walked towards the river, full of May Week revellers, and he felt a heightened sense of Cambridge, as he had done the previous day when he had travelled the bridges of the Cam. All gone? Surely not.

A vision surrounded by smoke appeared beside him.

'Why are you looking so beastly glum?'

'You wouldn't understand.'

'Try me.'

'I don't want it to end.'

She didn't understand.

'Darling,' she said, 'it's not. It's just beginning.'

And term ended, the University year ended, trunks were packed up and sent home for ever. Friends said they would meet, they would come back, nothing would change; they would come back and it would all be the same. And they did meet and they did come back until the streets of Cambridge and the courts of its colleges seemed to be filled with impostors, or ghosts.

PART TWO

Chapter 12

They were photographed wherever they went: at Royal Ascot, at Henley, watching the polo at Smith's Lawn, at parties . . . 'He's My Winner' . . . 'Happy Diana Names the Day' . . . 'They're Sailing Down to Rio' . . .

Kate could not escape from it and was not sure she wanted to. Prodding the wound did not heal it, but it helped to form a scab. Always in the photographs Diana was smiling and looking at the camera, Gerry grim and trying to avoid it . . . or so Kate thought.

He had written to her. He had tried to get out of this marriage, he said, but was trapped. Diana knew all about him – *all* – and did not mind. He loved Kate, he said, and was more sorry than he could say. He had got everything wrong and wished he had a chance to go back to the beginning and put it right, but it seemed it was too late. He should ask her to forget him, he knew, but that he could not do: he would never forget her and she was to remember that. Would she forgive him? he asked. Please, would she forgive him? And, again, he loved her.

It was a precious letter, but of what use? And the feelings it gave rise to were even more unprofitable. She should feel sorry for Diana, that she was marrying someone who did not love her, but she could not; and neither could she, absurd though it was, stop herself hoping.

Then there was a photograph of Gerry looking happy. Some horrible photographer had caught his wicked grin, and Kate did not know there was such pain in the world. But she wanted him to

173

be happy, didn't she? If you loved someone, you wanted happiness for them. Didn't you?

She was not meaning to scan the newspapers in this way, but she was painting her grandmother's flat, preparing it to move into when she began her clinical training, and she needed newspapers to supplement the old sheets Beattie had supplied to stop paint getting on the furniture and the carpets. Beattie had said it was ridiculous for her to do it. Why not get a man in, and have a good rest? Rest! Kate felt she never would again. Obsessively she painted every wall in the charming two-bedroom flat in First Street white. The tenants who had lived here since her grandmother's death would not recognise it: their rose-patterned wallpaper was slowly vanishing under layer upon layer of white matt paint. Kate was not going to live surrounded by roses.

She went up to Cambridge to collect her degree. Her first. Once it had been the only thing she wanted, but now she could not find it in herself to be proud. A bit of paper, two letters after her name – you couldn't live with those, or love them.

Vanessa, who was going to be Kate's tenant until her marriage to Mark at Christmas, came and helped with the decorating. Unbelievably, she was good at it, much better than Kate who sprayed paint everywhere and, each evening, looked as though she had spent the day exploring the Antarctic. Mark built bookshelves, David Smedley arrived with a large pot plant and a bottle of champagne as house-warming presents, and the four of them went out to dinner. Mark was being drafted into the RAF and had not stopped complaining about it since he had heard the news.

'Typical, abso-bloody-lutely typical!' he exclaimed over and over again. 'I have a rowing Blue and they expect me to take to the air.'

'What were you wanting to do?' David asked mildly. 'Row a naval frigate?'

'Lots of chaps long for the RAF. Why pick on me?'

'We've all got to do our bit. I don't see what difference it makes which service we join.'

David Smedley would be in the army and both of them were to begin their basic training in September, when Vanessa would start teaching at St Paul's Girls' School.

'Mind you,' David said, 'Gerry's got the best of it. No National Service and a millionairess – ouch!'

Evidently Vanessa had given his shins a kick, but David had no reason to know why Gerry's name should not be mentioned. Why should he? It had been over between Kate and Gerry for ages. Past history.

Vanessa knew, though. She had seen the photograph of Gerry, the one of him smiling, and had bent to look at it. Kate had thought she had put the sheet of newspaper that side down, but there was Gerry grinning up at them, unaccountably not covered in paint.

'Do you think he is doing the right thing?' Vanessa had asked, studying the photograph. 'I always thought you two would get together again in the end.'

Kate sloshed paint determinedly. 'Why?'

'You just seemed so right,' Vanessa said vaguely.

'Don't say that!' Kate threw down the roller she had been using and, her back to Vanessa, pulled out her handkerchief.

Little was required to put Vanessa in a panic and the sight of Kate in helpless tears – calm, complete Kate, who was never ruffled by anything – had her in a flat spin. Resorting, as Englishwomen always do in times of crisis, to the solace of tea, she put the kettle on the gas without filling it with water and poured half the precious caddy of tea into a cold pot.

'Oh Vanessa!' Kate said, drying her tears and half laughing between her sobs. She had taken the kettle off the stove, found half a bottle of Girton sherry in a cardboard box and then had, haltingly, told Vanessa what had happened between her and Gerry.

'He asked you to marry him and then got engaged to Diana Dalton?' Vanessa had said, shocked. 'Why, that's dreadful!'

'I didn't say I'd marry him,' Kate pointed out, still defending Gerry, though heaven knew why.

'But you would have done?'

'Yes. Yes, I would have done.'

There was silence, then, 'Why did you break up before? That's what I never understood.'

Kate shook her head wearily. 'A good reason. I don't want to talk about it.'

175

'Can I tell Mark what you've told me?'

'Must you?'

The story did not reflect well on Gerry, for one thing, and for another Kate had no wish to be regarded as an object of pity. She was glad she had told Vanessa, though, for it was a dreadful secret to hold alone; and you did not want the person who was to share your flat speculating, along with the whole of Fleet Street, it seemed, on the next move of Gerry Beviss and his bride-to-be. But neither could Vanessa go around kicking anyone who mentioned Gerry's name in Kate's presence, however touching the loyalty was. So, as David rubbed his shin, Kate said,

'One of the papers said they were marrying in Rio de Janeiro. Is that true?' There was also the ghastly – ghoulish, almost – desire to know.

'Yes,' said David, still puzzled by the kick, 'though I'm sure Diana hankers after the Abbey or St Paul's. She'd like both, presumably.'

'She can't marry there, though,' Mark said. 'Don't you remember she's Catholic? She converted when her mother did to marry the Brazilian. I reckon she's decided the Brompton Oratory isn't at all her style.'

'I say, have you seen the car she's given him? The latest in Aston Martins – a DBII. A peach of a machine!'

'He took me for a ride in it,' Mark said. 'Beats anything else on the road absolutely. She wouldn't have got much change out of two thou for that, you know. . . .'

Just the conversation Kate wished with all her heart to avoid. It served her right. She was relieved when her clinical training at St Thomas's began and she flung herself into it with all the desperation that a drowning man grabs a lifebelt. And she only ever read *The Times*.

But she could not hope to escape entirely. The flat in First Street was always crowded on Saturday evenings. Friends from Cambridge – Gerry's old friends, and now Mark's and Vanessa's more than Kate's – on weekend leave from their bases all over the country would congregate there, bringing their girls and bottles of whatever they felt like drinking, and then they would all go out on

176

the town. Pinocchio the skeleton had been discovered in a cupboard and, amid much hilarity, had been brought out and hung in a corner of the sitting room. He now wore a corporal's cap bearing the badge of the Welch Fusiliers and a swagger stick, filched by David Smedley from an officer of the Royal Artillery, was stuck between his left radius and ulna. Andrew Coleridge was determined that he would end up fully equipped as one of His Majesty's soldiers and Mark, despite himself, declared that the honour of the RAF was at stake and bet five pounds that Pinocchio would be dressed as one of His Majesty's airmen within six months. Kate said she and Vanessa would be arrested and detained at His Majesty's pleasure if they did not stop bringing stolen property to the flat.

But tonight she could not join in the fun as some regimental tie was placed around Pinocchio's skeletal neck. John Winter had brought a copy of the *Tatler* and it had been passed around, folded open at the page headed 'The Dalton–Beviss Wedding'. It had happened. It had really happened. On the second of September 1950 in Rio de Janeiro.

Kate had carried on filling her guests' glasses, agreed that Pinocchio looked splendid in his new tie and tried to be normal, knowing that Vanessa's anxious eyes were on her. They all went out dancing and she smiled and danced cheek to cheek with David Smedley and showed she did not care a bit. Only now, in the early hours of Sunday morning and with Vanessa sensibly asleep, she did she arm herself with a brandy and examine the magazine.

She had known it was going to happen. Of course she had. But if so why the frozen shock, the feeling that she had been stabbed every bit as fresh as it had been that day in Girton when Felicity Myers had casually thrust a copy of the *Daily Graphic* at her and commented that Gerry Beviss had 'got himself engaged to that millionairess'.

It was even more silly to be so upset when it had happened – as she knew it had – nearly three months ago. But here was the proof: a page of glossy photographs of the bride and groom coming out of the Metropolitan Cathedral, of them cutting the cake, of them surrounded by bridesmaids and pages – the nephews and nieces, the caption informed her, of the bride's stepfather. The bride was smiling radiantly, the groom – what was the groom doing? Kate looked more closely – the groom didn't look too radiant, but then grooms weren't supposed to. He looked in good spirits though, and so he should with all that money. Pictures of the bride's mother and stepfather, various smart people with foreign names, Patrick Morgan, the best man – who *did* look radiant, if not a little drunk, as he might well after a free trip to Brazil – and that was it. The Dalton–Beviss wedding.

The next wedding was in three weeks' time and was Mark's and Vanessa's. Mr and Mrs Gerald Beviss had been asked – 'We had to,' Vanessa said, and Kate had agreed: Mark and Gerry were friends – but they had not replied. They were not expected back from their 'extended honeymoon in the United States' (the *Tatler*'s words) until some time in December. Perhaps they would extend their honeymoon indefinitely. That would be the best thing.

But they were at Mark's and Vanessa's wedding. Kate, coming back down the aisle on James's arm behind the bridal pair, not looking at anyone in particular although she knew most of the congregation, felt herself being stared at and looked and saw Gerry crushed into the end of a pew at the back of the church, his wife beside him. They had obviously arrived late. He smiled slightly, but not with his eyes. They held that anxious intensity they had when, in that other time, in Trinity Street, they had all first met: James and Gerry and Mark, Vanessa and Kate. Then he had wanted to talk to her, to confide, to beg her silence. What did he want now?

He came up to her at the reception after she had been released from the endless photographs and had found herself a glass of champagne.

'How are you?' he asked.

'Well, thank you.' Very formal. 'And you?'

'As you see. Pampered.'

He was right: he was tanned and he had, she thought, put on a little weight. He would have looked sleek were it not for his curly black hair, worn a bit long – especially in comparison with the ruthless haircuts of the servicemen – and the fact that he was

178

fidgeting, shifting nervously from foot to foot, draining his glass and looking around for more champagne. Presumably he lived on the stuff these days.

'Kate, have you forgiven me?' he asked. 'You didn't answer my letter—'

'What could I have said?'

'That you had forgiven me! Have you? Please say you have.'

'Yes,' she said. 'All right. I have forgiven you.' And she meant it, she really did.

'Thank you. Thank you,' he said, and added rapidly: 'You look lovely in that dress, Kate. It matches your eyes.'

Then James was at her elbow saying something about more photographs and his best man's speech, and she was taken away. Gerry and Diana left before the cake was cut and she did not talk to him again.

She found, though, that their brief exchange had done her an enormous amount of good. She felt much better about everything. A door had closed and locked behind her, and this was the proof: Gerry escorting his wife to a wedding; though, great heavens! what more proof did she need? She enjoyed the rest of the reception, she caught Vanessa's bouquet, and she agreed with James that the bridesmaid and the best man should go out and celebrate that night.

She let him kiss her, several times. She kissed him back. She had once likened him to a golden retriever: he certainly was not now. He was much more assured and no longer blushed, was not so eager to please. Perhaps the change was wrought by the army, which was, he said, teaching him to drive tanks around Salisbury Plain, but it was more likely achieved by good, honest time. She had not, after all, seen a great deal of him for the past two years. He had spent the summer at home in Leicestershire, he said, and had not been in London much since. His stubble grazed her cheek. She had thought of him as a boy, but he was a grown man. He shaved – and not often enough!

In the taxi taking her home, he held her hand and played with the signet ring she wore.

'I'm on leave at Christmas . . . Would you like to come home and stay?' he asked. 'There's a New Year do and we're having a house party . . . But you could come a few days early. Get the soft south out of you. Would you like that?'

'James, I'd love it,' she said, and she really meant that too.

She had arranged, at Beattie's insistence, to take ten days' holiday and on Christmas Eve went home and allowed herself to be cosseted and cared for and be presented with a floppy sweater knitted in all colours of the rainbow, and a few that were not, and she slept and slept and slept. Beattie's plump face lost the worried frown it had worn since Kate had come down so suddenly from Cambridge, before May Week, looking haunted and bereft and she set about feeding up her niece, who, in her opinion, was far too thin.

'I never thought I'd relax again,' Kate said one evening. Charles was out. Beattie's needles clicked peacefully. Flash, illegally and he knew it, was lying next to Kate on the sofa, his head in her lap.

'Didn't you, my darling?' Beattie said.

'I'll always love Gerry, I think. I can't imagine ever not, but seeing him with his . . . wife—' Still, Kate gulped on the word. 'Seeing him, I realised that I can live with it. It's part of me, and everything else will just have to accommodate it. I've stopped imagining I said yes to him. It makes it so much easier.'

Beattie's needles stilled. It was a tiny sound, but without it the room was hugely quiet.

'He asked you to marry him?'

And so Kate told her – everything. Not the curtailed version she had given Vanessa. Everything.

'I was right – wasn't I? – not to give in.'

'Of course you were, my darling.'

'And it's a pity I didn't say yes straight away when he asked me. A pity, that's all.' Kate was scratching Flash's ears and reducing him to wriggling ecstasy. 'But I can't blame him. He was under pressure from all sides.'

Beattie said nothing, her needles flying again, her mouth compressed.

'Wasn't he?' Kate said, as Flash licked her hand, rolled over and invited her to tickle his stomach.

180

'Yes, he was,' Beattie agreed, but she was thinking of the things she would say to Gerry Beviss should she ever meet him again.

Five days Beattie had to restore her niece before Kate went off to Leicestershire via London. Vanessa and Mark were at the flat in First Street preparing to remove Vanessa's possessions to the flat they had rented in Bryanston Square. Mark was doing a course in air-traffic control at Shrewsbury and could come to London every weekend.

They'd had a wonderful honeymoon, they told her, and a wonderful Christmas.

'We're not disturbing you, are we?' Vanessa asked. 'We won't be long.'

'No. I've just come to pick up some things.'

'Where are you off to?'

'Flimwell Place,' she said and, ignoring their questioning glances, she went to her bedroom to pack suitable clothes for a sojourn in a large country house. She didn't have any clothes, she decided. She hadn't bought any for heaven knew how long – since they had stopped being rationed, in fact – and she had an irresistible desire to rectify this immediately. She swept into Harrods and acquired for herself a very smart tweed suit, a dress which would cope with everything from morning drinks to an informal dinner – the sort that her mother always used to pronounce 'useful' and which, therefore, Kate as a teenager had regarded with deep suspicion; and then, having thought her bridesmaid's dress would do for the New Year's Eve party, she fell for a silk concoction, figure-hugging and cut daringly low, which was totally unlike any dress she had ever owned but which she knew looked well on her. She could not go wrong now. She was buzzing. She felt alive for the first time in months – years, perhaps. She bought a hat which matched the suit, evening shoes and a bag to go with the silk dress.

What else? Her chequebook was itching. She was sure she could not afford all this, but she would repent later. A cream blouse and a full skirt in daring scarlet. Another hat which took her fancy, a pair of gloves.

She caught a taxi the short distance back to the flat, checked the shop assistants had removed all the price labels, packed everything but the tweed suit, into which she changed, then realised, not at all surprised, that the cream blouse would look stunning with it, unpacked that and exchanged it for the navy-blue one she was wearing, placed one of the new hats on her head, picked up her coat and was ready to go to the station and catch the train James had told her to be on. It was less than an hour and a half since she had first walked into the flat.

She went into the kitchen, where Mark and Vanessa were resting from their labours over tea. Mark spluttered into his cup and leapt to his feet, and Vanessa turned, a biscuit halfway to her mouth, and said, 'Oh – Kate!'

'I'm off,' she said.

'Shall I find you a taxi?'

'Would you? Thank you, Mark.'

He picked up her suitcase from the hall and went down the stairs. Vanessa, still staring at her, said wonderingly, 'What's happened? You look – well – incredible.'

'Nothing's happened.' She bent to kiss Vanessa's cheek. 'Happy New Year, Mrs Colley-Smythe.'

Vanessa grabbed her hand. 'Kate, it's not James, is it?'

Mark's voice called from downstairs and Kate released Vanessa's hold on her.

'No, it's not James.'

She strode down the stairs and out of the front door to the waiting taxi. Mark smiled his lovely smile and kissed her.

'Have a good time, Kate. James is a lucky man.'

The lucky man met her at the station at Melton Mowbray, said, 'Kate, you look more stunning than ever,' and enfolded her in his greatcoat. 'I've been wondering if it really happened,' he said, when he had let her go. 'Thinking all the champagne at the wedding had caused hallucinations.'

'I don't believe I'm a hallucination,' she said.

'No, you're not. You're here, aren't you? Come along.'

A porter picked up Kate's suitcase and followed them out of the station to where James's MG was parked. The case was stowed in the boot, Kate in the passenger seat and James drove out of the

182

town and along a little road that undulated through the country. Kate looked out of the window.

'It's all grass,' she said. 'All grass and hedges.'

'What do you have where you come from?'

'Hops and orchards and sheep. A few cows.'

'We need the grass. This is hunting country,' James said. 'The best in the world.'

'Only that?' she asked, laughing at him.

'God's own county, Leicestershire.'

'That's what they say of Kent.'

He stopped the car. The road ahead sloped away, and below the grass fields, bisected by black hedges, spread off to the right and left in the December dusk.

'The Belvoir Vale,' James said. 'God's own spot of God's own county, and I'll fight the woman who tells me otherwise . . . Hey, you—' He put an arm around her, pulled her to him and kissed her again. 'I'm glad you're here. Are you glad you've come?'

'So far,' Kate said, 'so good.'

James chuckled, restarted the car and drove on. After a few miles, they turned between lodge gates and wound up a long drive – Kate could not see beyond the headlights now – and came to a halt under a portico. Her door was opened, a hand was placed under her elbow to help her out of the low seat of the MG and then promptly removed. Another pair of hands took her suitcase and a man appeared out of the dark, slid into the driver's seat of the MG and took it away.

Kate was conducted into a warmly lit hall. At the far end of it rose a staircase which divided at the half-landing and the carved banisters continued to form a gallery on the first floor. At the foot of the staircase, and to one side of it, was a Christmas tree, the star at the top reaching into the dark of the upper floor. To the right of the hall was a fireplace in which burned logs measuring two feet in diameter.

Kate was introduced to the butler, Beamish, who removed her coat, and to Mrs Caper, the housekeeper, who bade her welcome and invited Kate to follow her. In a daze, she did so until she was on the third step of the staircase, when she turned back to James. He was standing by the fire, still wearing his greatcoat, although Beamish was hovering, obviously longing to have it off him.

183

He smiled at her. 'Come down as soon as you've powdered your nose,' he said. 'I'll wait for you here. Then we'll have tea.'

That was all right, then. She had, in her confusion, been wondering if she should change for dinner. She had stayed in what she had thought were grand houses before, but nothing like this. The housekeeper led her into a pleasant chintzy bedroom. A coal fire burned in the grate and a maid was already unpacking Kate's suitcase but, on seeing them enter, she bobbed a curtsey and left the room.

Mrs Caper opened another door.

'Your bathroom, miss. I hope you'll be comfortable.'

'I'm sure I shall,' Kate said.

'Will you be able to find your way back to Master James?'

'Yes, thank you.' It was a big house, but not complicated and Kate had been paying attention.

'Very good, miss.' Mrs Caper nodded her head, eyed the half-unpacked suitcase – thank goodness, Kate thought, for her new clothes – and then she, too, left.

Kate sat down on the bed. A bathroom all to herself! Not just a grand house, but warm and comfortable as well – a combination that Kate knew seldom went together. She had supposed this kind of thing had gone with the war. All the servants . . . it was amazing. What had Gerry made of it? He had stayed here often . . . Not in this bedroom, though. Surely not. It was too feminine. She would not think of him. The mood that had taken hold of her in Harrods was still upon her and she did not want to lose it. She washed her hands, powdered her nose as James had instructed, found her way to the head of the stairs and ran down to where James was waiting.

He took her hands. 'But you're gorgeous!' he exclaimed. 'Just gorgeous.' He tucked her hand in his arm. 'Come and meet the parents. I want to show you off.'

Lord and Lady Flimwell were in the library, a cosy room – if any room in that great house could aspire to the word – with book-lined walls and dark green velvet curtains drawn across huge high windows. A pair of cocker spaniels asleep in front of the fire awoke as the door opened and leapt around James and Kate. Their front paws battered Kate's new skirt, and she should have minded

184

but didn't because they reminded her of Flash – same breed, different colour, just as undisciplined – and made her feel at home. She bent down and patted them, telling them they were good dogs, and then, laughing, stood up.

She had absolutely no idea how lovely she looked. She had been told she was, often, but had never paid much attention. All her adult life she had lived, quite unintentionally, in places where women were in short supply: the Wrens, where the whole Navy thought (or hoped) you were fair game, at Cambridge, and now she was at St Thomas's Hospital where, even though there were the nurses and a city full of girls, she was the only female medical student in her year, having been given a place to honour her father, who had been there, as much as her first. Under these circumstances, men tended to think one beautiful if one had the required number of limbs and a halfway decent pair of breasts.

That she was unconscious of her beauty enhanced it, and now, as she faced James's parents with all this and the vibrance that had so startled James – and Vanessa and Mark – which was born of life rediscovered, there was a slight pause, action ceased for a moment before Lady Flimwell came forward to greet her and Lord Flimwell said fiercely, 'Down, Lily! Down, Cleo!' and Beamish and a maid brought in the tea.

Only after she had shaken her host and hostess's hand did it occur to Kate how very particular it was, her coming as James's guest in advance of the rest of the house party – and one in which, anyway, she had not originally been included. James had asked her and she had accepted, not realising what interpretation might be put on it, and suddenly she was embarrassed and felt a little shy. Lord Flimwell settled her in a chair, Lady Flimwell busied herself with the teapot, the spaniels settled once more in front of the fire – though keeping an ear cocked each for when food might appear – and Lord Flimwell said, 'James says you're going to be a doctor. Tell us about it.'

Kate did not know what to say: being a doctor might sound glamorous – well, if not that, the local doctor was the height of respectability and a pillar of the community – but the day-to-day process of learning to be one was anything but. Should she say how she was something of an expert on taking blood from patients

185

and was rather proud of it? That she had gained a curt nod (the height of praise from that very sticky consultant) when she had diagnosed correctly an enlarged liver? Neither would they want to know of the ribaldry in which medical students indulged, which might appear heartless and callous but which was the only way they coped with encountering disease, injury and death in all its various and usually horrible forms . . . So Kate smiled and said she loved the work, that it would be a long time yet before she was a doctor and she wanted to go into general practice as her father had done.

'A woman doctor!' Lady Flimwell exclaimed, handing James a cup of tea to take to Kate. 'What a splendid thing. *Much* nicer than the male variety who *never* understand how one feels. How could they, after all?'

'Do you do operations?' Lord Flimwell asked.

'Jimmy, you're not going to offer her your ingrown toenail, are you? The poor child will pack her bags and leave, thinking us quite mad.'

'I was not,' said her husband. 'I just want to know. I find it interesting.'

'No,' Kate told him. 'I don't do operations, not yet. I watch them, though.'

'Do you now? Better than any play, I bet.'

'That,' said James, 'is why it's called a theatre.'

Everyone laughed.

'Well, isn't it?' James persisted.

'I don't know,' Kate said, still laughing. 'It never occurred to me. Perhaps it is. The dialogue isn't up to much, though.'

She felt herself relaxing and that wonderful mood was upon her again. She didn't care how particular it looked. She was enjoying being in this splendid house. Lord and Lady Flimwell were welcoming and friendly, James was attentive without being cloying, and the two spaniels, having identified her as a sucker, were pinioning her with their four bright eyes. She gave them each a few crumbs from her plate. A lick and a gulp and the vigil was resumed.

'Don't let them pester you,' said Lady Flimwell. 'They shouldn't be here at all. I can't think why they're not out with the others in the kennels.'

'They prefer it in the house,' said Lord Flimwell mildly.

'So might the horses, but they don't get the choice.' Lady Flimwell turned to Kate. 'Do you ride, Miss Earith?'

'I used to. Not for ages, though. And please call me Kate,' she added.

'Thank you, Kate. I will.' She rose to her feet and her husband and son – followed quickly by Kate – stood also. 'I'm going to change . . . Jimmy, have you remembered people are coming to dinner? Which means Lily and Cleo *must* be put outside.'

'I'll take them now.' Lord Flimwell, calling the dogs to him, left the room with his wife.

'You know one of the people coming tonight,' James said as the door closed.

'*Do* I?'

'Alice. Remember her?'

'Yes,' she said. Alice had been one of James's girlfriends. Perhaps she still was?

'She's married some author chappie,' James said. 'Nice fellow. He's coming too.'

'Oh,' Kate said, and was conscious of the faintest feeling of relief as she went off to luxuriate in her warm bedroom, soak in her bath and change into one of her new outfits.

The next morning, Kate donned her woollen hat, scarf and gloves and, in a pair of borrowed wellingtons, was walked around the Flimwell Place estate by James. It was a brilliant cold day, blue-skyed, the world rimed with frost. Kate admired the outside of the house: it was, James told her, of classic Georgian design and the man who had built it had bankrupted himself in his search for perfection. James's great-grandfather had bought it from his son, had contented himself with giving it his own name and had never been tempted to embellish it with the neo-Gothic additions so beloved of the Victorians. It was a beautiful house, not seeming as big from outside as it did from within. Something to do with the size of the windows, perhaps, which let in so much light during the day and promised it – as Kate had seen in the library the previous evening – from their great curtained heights when it was dark.

James dismissed the gardens as being of no account, especially

187

at this time of year, and took her to what he called the Home Farm. Kate had rather imagined that this would somehow reflect its name and be – well – homely, but everything was formidably clean and ordered. The dairy, all stainless steel and mechanised, looked as though a cow had never set foot in it; the pigs were pink and sterilised in their straw-filled sties; the fat cattle stood in their great barn dreaming, or so it seemed, of the steak pies they would become. Not a muzzle, a snout or a nose out of place – except for those of Lily and Cleo who, released from overnight imprisonment in the kennels, terrorised the pigs by barking at them through the metal gates of the sties and charged around the heels of the cattle, much to the distress of the stockman.

James talked enthusiastically, saying this was the future of farming, that soon everyone would be rearing animals intensively in this way, and explaining the theories of concentrated feeding. Kate began to find it depressing: it was an animal factory, she felt, and although the beasts seemed perfectly content they had about as much soul as a packet of tea.

They left the farm and walked back in a circuit towards the house and the stables – 'the best until last', James said – and they passed a mud-churned paddock which would have looked normal on any other farm at this time of year but here seemed almost shocking.

'Bonny!' James called. 'Bonny – here, girl!'

Out of a rough wooden shelter came a mud-caked, very woolly and ancient pony followed by an equally ancient sway-backed carthorse.

'She was my first pony,' James said as the odd pair came towards them, their hooves breaking the ice in the pock-marks of the field. 'She was a complete devil. I can't remember the number of times she had me off. She's a terrible old brute, even now. Her friend is called Donald. Which do you think is boss?'

The two horses were at the paddock railings. Bonny, by craning her neck, was just able to get her head over the top rail. Donald towered peacefully above.

'Watch this.' James took a quartered apple from his pocket and, before he had even offered it to either of the horses, Bonny had flattened her little ears on to her stumpy neck, swung her head threateningly and Donald had lumbered away. She was tiny compared to him, could walk under his belly if she wanted to, but she had him completely cowed.

Kate laughed at the sight: you were tempted to feel sorry for poor Donald, gazing at them longingly from under his matted forelock, but it was utterly ridiculous.

James gave her two of the quarters. 'Here. You occupy her and I'll give the old boy his share.'

Bonny gobbled up the apple, her ears flickering in Donald's direction.

'He's henpecked entirely,' James said, as the old pony quested suspiciously around Donald's great feathered legs, 'but happy as anything.'

He whistled to Lily and Cleo, who were scouting for rabbits in the hedge, and they walked on.

'Do you keep all the farm horses on in their old age?' Kate asked.

'We try to find them an odd corner. It seems a bit much to shoot them because they're no longer of use. The tractors have taken over, anyway. The horses are nearly all gone.'

Not an animal factory, then.

'Will you be a farmer, James?'

'Absolutely!' he said. 'I'll finish with the army, sow a few wild oats in London and then settle down here for ever.' He stopped walking. 'Settle down for ever with one beautiful tame oat,' he said. 'Kiss me quickly. There's no one about.'

It happened before she could protest, and she didn't really want to anyway. Very quickly it happened, then he pulled off her woollen hat, ruffled her hair and put the hat back on.

'But there's no hurry, is there? No hurry at all . . . Hey, shall we go for a ride?'

'Ride? On a horse?' she asked, bewildered by the sudden change of subject, by the suggestion and by James's previous remark, which had been very particular indeed.

'On two horses, I'd thought. One each, you know.'

They arrived at the stables. The smell of horses, hay, straw, manure and leather took her back: to her child and girlhood and her pony Benjy, on whom she used to compete against and lose to

189

a little boy called Gerry Beviss. Was she ever going to escape him? No, for here was Castor, whose injured leg Gerry had tended; Gerry had used his jacket to keep Castor warm and had caught a chill as a result; Kate had ticked off James because he had been so hopeless about getting Gerry help ... except had she actually ticked him off? She could not remember, only that she had felt like it.

'His leg looks pretty dreadful,' James was saying. Kate put her head over the loosebox door. Castor nuzzled her shoulder. 'But he's sound enough. How about riding him?'

Kate looked at the horse's off fore. It was ridged and scarred between the fetlock and the knee, but the hair looked shining and healthy. Then James's words sank in and she turned to look at him, leaning against the stable door.

'Ride Castor?' she said. '*Me* ride Castor?'

'Why not? He's as quiet as a mouse, I assure you.'

Kate opened her mouth to protest but then thought, Why not? Why on earth not? It wasn't quite the New Year yet, but her resolutions had been made, and one of them was to accept new challenges and another was to do her damnedest to fall in love — the only cure, she was sure. Two here, in one.

'But I don't have the clothes,' she said, and felt disappointment.

'Mother has, and there are some around of Sophie's.'

Kate looked back at Castor. He was much bigger than any horse she had ever ridden before and, now she was studying him, wasn't there a rather nasty glint in his eye?

'Isn't it too frosty?' she asked, hopefully, cravenly.

'No. It's hardly in the ground. You'll be fine. I'll get Niall to take him out for a bit and get the springs off him.'

'Springs? You didn't say he'd have those.'

But her trepidation vanished when, in her borrowed gear, she was helped into Castor's saddle. Everything came back to her and, by the time the groom had tightened the girths, made sure the stirrups were the right length and she and Castor had taken a turn around the yard, she felt she had never been away. She was outraged to see that James was buckling a leading rein around Canterlupe's neck.

'All right, all right,' James said, backing down in the face of her fierce dark blue gaze. 'Here, for God's sake, Niall, give it to her. She can lead me.'

Niall took the leading rein and wondered what he should do, caught as he was most obviously and – as he and the rest of the staff at Flimwell Place thought – most romantically in the midst of a flirtation, but as he stood there Castor and Canterlupe clattered away out of the yard.

They rode through fields all belonging to Flimwell Place. Castor behaved like a lamb but Canterlupe jinked and shied at blackbirds in the hedgerows, thought pheasants getting up in the coverts were land mines and was definitely of the opinion that he ought to be jumping hedges instead of having to sidle up to gates so James could open them.

'Would you like us to do it?' Kate said, patting Castor's neck.

'No,' James replied, laughing and swearing cheerfully at his horse. 'I've got to impress you, Kate. Somehow.' He wrapped his long legs around Canterlupe, overcame his skitters and got him up to the gate and then to back away as James held it open.

'Thank you, kind sir,' Kate said as she and Castor walked through, Castor with his ears pricked demurely forward as though he would never dream of behaving the way that young varmint Canterlupe was.

'I'd doff my cap if I had another hand,' James said. 'But unfortunately the Almighty only gave us two.'

'I consider it doffed.'

She waited while James persuaded Canterlupe to close the gate and said, as he came alongside her, 'I *am* impressed. Really, I am.'

'Are you, Kate? Well, if that's all it takes . . .' He took his glove off his left hand, reached over and gently touched her cheek. 'So beautiful,' he said, 'with good Leicestershire air inside you and all the pallor of London gone . . . I say, shall we canter? Can you manage it?'

She could and, although she was horribly stiff, she rode the next day, too. That second afternoon the guests for the New Year party, which was to be held at a house some ten miles away, arrived, some by car, some brought from Melton Mowbray station by Mallet, the Flimwells' chauffeur. Tea was taken in the drawing room. Kate discovered herself to be an object of speculation and found the scarcely concealed probing rather amusing. 'How is James liking life in the army?' a woman asked her, a question which Kate had never thought to ask James, and her husband said, predictably, 'The best time of his life, no doubt about it. But what does he plan to do after that?'

As though she should know! But she said, wickedly, that he was going to sow a few wild oats, she gathered, and then retire to Leicestershire to be a farmer.

But later, as she lay in her bath, hoping the hot water would ease the pain in her unused riding muscles so she could dance with some grace that night, Kate considered it all.

Who was James's one tame oat to be? A lucky one, for sure. He was good company, not dangerous like Gerry or stolid like Peter, but somewhere in between. He wasn't devastatingly handsome but he was nice enough looking and, if his father was anything to go by, he would age in a distinguished fashion . . . not that, of course, looks mattered anyway. He'd been called 'Foggy Flimwell' at Eton, Kate remembered, and thought that was unfair. He wasn't brilliant academically (he had boasted at dinner last night about his Ordinary degree in a way that had been both charming and hilarious) but he wasn't lacking in know-how or common sense. His kisses didn't make her go weak at the knees, but how often did that happen? How often could you expect to meet a man who made you feel faint just by looking at you? Only once in your life, surely . . . And then, if you were interested in such things, James would in time become Lord Flimwell and own this great house and all its acres of Leicestershire. . . .

He had seemed different enough that night in London after Mark's and Vanessa's wedding, but here, surrounded by the people he had grown up among – the neighbours to whom they had gone for dinner last night, the people (including Alice) who had come to Flimwell Place on Kate's first evening here, the old family friends who had arrived to join the house party this afternoon; the servants and the farmworkers, even, all of whom greeted him with such genuine affection – he had become a whole person, one with good strong roots. . . . And he had, for every one of these reasons, and you could not separate one from the other: he had become glamorous.

Kate heaved herself, a trifle painfully, out of the bath, wrapped herself in a huge warm towel and went into her bedroom. There were some books in a glass-fronted cabinet, among them a copy of *Pride and Prejudice*. Kate picked it out and took it to the chair in front of the fire. She had little time to read novels, but this one she knew well, having been forced to read it for her school certificate. She turned to the back and flicked through the pages until she found what she was looking for.

'My dearest sister . . . Will you tell me how long you have loved him?'

'. . . I believe I must date it from my first seeing his beautiful grounds at Pemberley.'

Miss Elizabeth Bennet's dearest sister had entreated her to be serious, but Kate reckoned that she had been – at *least* – half serious. Money, comfort (Kate tucked the towel more cosily around her and felt the warmth of the fire blissfully on her toes) and the good things in life were greatly to be desired if you could get them. Why deny it? Look – although on the whole she would rather not – at Gerry. But then, what was it, all of it, without love? Miss Eliza Bennet had managed to achieve the mix, but then she had lived in a novel and not amid the trials and alarms of real life.

Kate wore her new dress to the party and she danced with James most of the evening, because she wanted to and because it was fun to be gossiped about, and because of the reason she had not admitted, even in the intimate discussion she had had with herself in the bath – for it was unfair on James and it was unworthy of herself, and it was all the vengeful things she didn't want to be – but she found she was hoping and hoping, and she fought against it for what possible use could it be? What could it do? Yet she could not stop herself hoping that somewhere in this gathering there was someone who would report to Gerry on what sparkling form Kate had been on this night.

Chapter 13

Kate's ebullient mood could not last, but at least she did not swing back to the brink of despair. She gained some kind of equilibrium and she worked hard – but without the fevered desperation of her first few months at St Thomas's – and she played hard as well, going out with just about whoever asked her but always with James in preference to anyone else. He managed to be in London quite often and felt he could not complain about the harshness of his National Service. David Smedley was in Korea fighting a real war; Nick O'Rourke was creeping around the Malayan jungle looking for communists and Jonathan Faulder, one of their contemporaries at Trinity, had also been posted there. James was very well off on Salisbury Plain hard by Stonehenge.

Kate knew he wanted to ask her not to go out with other men, and in a way she wanted it too, for she was by nature monogamous, but she was not ready for the commitment this might imply. She remembered the one tame oat. James never mentioned Gerry, no one ever did now; perhaps married couples were not of interest to the gossip columns? She did not know. But she liked this new, mature and thoughtful James and if he more than liked her he never said it. He made great efforts to please her, acquiring tickets for shows she expressed the most casual desire to see, bringing her flowers and being altogether charming, and the greatest good company ... No hurry he had said. A supplicant golden retriever? She had the feeling she was being pursued by an experienced and determined bloodhound, though one without the wrinkles and the lugubrious look on its face.

But Kate also went out with other men because she was now living alone. There were lots of people who would love to move into the flat in First Street and Kate had to make a decision soon, but found the prospect glum. She missed Vanessa dreadfully and felt no one else would suit her as well. Domestically they had dovetailed like Jack Spratt and his wife. Vanessa turned out to be a virtuoso cook, able to toss what the butcher had provided for their meat ration into a casserole together with whatever else was at hand – entirely at random, it seemed to Kate – and produce something delicious. She would put the concoction into the oven, murmur 'an hour and a half I think', and forget about it. Forget to turn the oven on as likely as not. Kate would tidy up the kitchen (invariably left in chaos), deal with the vegetables and take Vanessa's creation out of the oven at the right moment. When Kate tried throwing things into the casserole in the same spirit of careless rapture it tasted revolting.

But it wasn't just Vanessa's cooking Kate missed, of course; it was Vanessa herself and her constant loving friendship. Kate had to find another flatmate and kept putting the decision off – prophetically, it seemed, for Mark and Vanessa arrived one evening, he shocked, she utterly distraught.

Mark had received his posting. He was going to Canada in a month's time and there he would stay, unless the RAF changed its mind, for the next eighteen months. Vanessa said wildly that she would go to Winnipeg with him and teach there: they had schools in Winnipeg, didn't they? she asked.

'But the blighters would as like as not decide I have to do air-traffic control in bloody Rhodesia,' Mark said bitterly. 'With my luck it's certain.'

'Kate,' Vanessa asked hesitantly, 'can I move back? It seems so silly us each being on our own, doesn't it? Would you mind?'

Mind! Kate sympathised with them – to be parted so soon after their marriage seemed very cruel – but she couldn't help feeling a certain guilty joy. She hugged Vanessa.

'Of course I don't mind. I'd love to have you back. You know that.'

'It's not really so long,' Mark said.

'Eighteen months!'

'I'll get leave. At least the RAF has planes. I'll be able to get back for leaves. Maybe you can come over for the summer holidays.'

'Could I?'

'I'll see what's possible when I get there.'

Horribly soon Mark was gone. Vanessa tried to be brave about it and Saturday nights at the First Street flat were much as they used to be, but it was difficult for Vanessa: not only was she without Mark, but she was a married woman and her status was peculiar. Why, she argued, should chaps on precious leave partner her for an evening? It was much better if she stayed at home and marked some exercise books.

'Don't you dare,' James told her. 'Mark ordered me to look after you and make sure you got about a bit, and that's what you're bloody well going to do.'

'Oh, all right,' she said listlessly, and she dressed up and went out with the rest of them and looked as though she was enjoying herself.

Then, one evening, when a party of ten of them had gone out dancing, Kate and James arrived back at their table to find Vanessa sitting alone, her eyes wide, her red hair springing more wildly than ever from her head.

'Kate,' she said. 'Kate! What *am* I going to do?'

The words took Kate out of the nightclub in the heart of London, away from the pounding music and back to the long corridors of Girton during their first two years . . . the Bagwigs, my gown, my library book . . . Kate, what *am* I going to do?

And, as she had always responded then so she did now, saying a little wearily, 'Vanessa, what is it this time?'

Vanessa clutched her forearm. 'Kate, I've just this instant realised,' she whispered. 'It explains everything . . . I think I must be pregnant.'

Kate looked around at James, who quickly stood up, touched her lightly on the shoulder and went away.

'I must be,' Vanessa went on. 'I missed one after Mark left and didn't pay any attention – the upset and everything, you see – and I'm nearly two weeks late this time and I just realised. I'm never late! Kate, what do I do?'

'You can't do anything now, Vanessa. You'll have to wait until Monday and go and see a doctor.'

196

'But I see you all the time. You're a doctor, almost. What would a doctor do anyway?'

'Find out.'

'How?'

'You have to give a urine sample. The first of the day is best—'

'Kate!' Vanessa hissed.

The band was between numbers and Kate's voice, which had been raised to sound over its noise, was being heard with scandalised avidity by the people at the next table.

'Sorry,' she said, and went on more quietly. 'But you're feeling all right, aren't you? I know you've been depressed, but that's understandable. You haven't been sick in the mornings or anything?'

Vanessa shook her head.

'Any tenderness in the breasts?'

'No. Nothing. Does that mean it's all right?' she asked hopefully.

'Not necessarily,' Kate said.

'But I can't be pregnant!' Vanessa wailed, and once again heads were turned in their direction. 'We were only married for a few weeks before Mark went away.'

'A few weeks? Vanessa, it takes minutes . . . seconds,' Kate said, sure of the theory but not of the practice. 'But what's so dreadful? You and Mark want children, don't you?'

Vanessa chewed a lock of hair. 'I've never thought about it really,' she said. 'I suppose I do. I just wish Mark wasn't so dreadfully far away . . . Kate, another sixteen months! I'll have to stop teaching, won't I? And then how shall I fill the time?'

Kate understood that feeling well enough.

'Maybe you aren't pregnant,' she said helplessly.

'It looks likely, though, doesn't it?'

Kate sighed. 'I'm afraid I think it does.'

Vanessa tossed the lock of hair she had been chewing over her shoulder. 'Ah well, I'll just have to wait and see, won't I? . . . I'm not staying here, though. I'll go home now.'

'I'll come with you.' Kate looked around for James. He was dancing with Rosie Masefield, Andrew Coleridge's girlfriend, but he caught her glance and brought Rosie over to the table. He said immediately that of course he would escort 'his two women' home, made sure Rosie was not left sitting alone, put Kate's and Vanessa's wraps around their shoulders and asked the doorman to find a taxi.

He sat between them with an arm around each.

'This is the life,' he said. 'Hey, Vanessa, is it true what I overheard? Has the doctor pronounced?'

'She says I must have a test,' Vanessa said in tones of the deepest despair. 'But the chances are it's true.'

James clasped both girls to him.

'I can't wait to see old Mark's face. He'll be thrilled to bits.'

'Will he?' Vanessa asked.

'He'll put him down for Eton the moment he's born and have him rowing by the time he can walk.'

'It might be a girl,' Vanessa said, sounding slightly more cheerful.

'Then he'll fall in love with her, just like he did with you.' And he jollied her along until, when they arrived in First Street, Vanessa's wraps around their shoulders and asked the doorman to was a false alarm.

'Can I come up?' he asked.

'Of course you can,' said Kate. 'The least we can do is to offer you a drink from your own bottle.'

Vanessa went to bed and James sat with a brandy in the chair by the gas fire, Kate on the floor at his feet.

'You were marvellous, James,' she said. 'I couldn't cheer her up at all.' She looked sidelong up at him. 'What a very nice person you are, giving up your evening out to bring us back.'

'You gave up yours, too,' he said.

'Well — yes. But that's different.'

'I don't see why. I told old Mark I'd keep an eye on Vanessa and that was just part of the service. Anyway, who wants to go dancing? I've got you all to myself and that's worth any number of nights on the town. . . . I say, Kate,' he said, 'you wouldn't like to warm me up by sitting on my lap and giving me the odd cuddle, would you?'

'What would you do with your drink?'

'Now there's a point.' He reached out a long arm and drew a low coffee table towards him, put his brandy on it and held out both hands. She took them and he pulled her up on to his lap. He kissed her.

'*Much* better than a night on the town . . . Are you comfy? Sorry about the bony knees.'

'I'm comfy,' she said, and they were both silent for a long time, so long that Kate, her head resting on James's chest, began to feel drowsy.

'Kate,' James asked then, 'do you still think of Gerry?'

Immediately she was alert, her body stiffening.

'He's married,' she said, answering but not answering his question.

'Yes, he's married.'

Kate longed to ask if he ever saw Gerry, but he wrapped his arms around her and kissed her again.

'It doesn't matter. I shouldn't have asked, but it doesn't matter.' And, for the second time: 'There's no hurry.'

Kate smiled sweetly at a lab technician and persuaded him to do Vanessa's test. She was indeed pregnant. Kate went home that night, the underground trains full of men behind their evening papers, the headlines all about the Korean War. Would men ever stop fighting each other? she wondered. Hadn't there been enough of it? She felt it more because of the news she was bearing: one woman was going to have a baby and other women's sons were dying. She thought of her brother, Ricky. Next week he would have been nineteen and perhaps have been out there in Korea, killed by Chinese communists instead of German fascists . . . except that he was going to be a doctor and would surely have already started his training, either at university or at one of the teaching hospitals.

Nonsense. Stop thinking about it. And Kate looked up and realised she had said the words out loud and that the train was at South Kensington. She leapt out and walked briskly up the platform. Vanessa had convinced herself that she was pregnant and, thanks to James, was ready to receive confirmation of the fact with equanimity though no excitement. This was the first, but how

199

many times in Kate's life would she bring this news to women and in how many ways would it be received?

She was walking down Pelham Street when she stopped suddenly. This should be made into a celebration, lots of people around Vanessa telling her how wonderful it all was, completing the work James had begun. She should have rung up Mary and Felicity – others – and she could scarcely do it from the flat. Vanessa would, understandably, feel her emotional reactions were being manipulated. Kate needed a telephone box and somewhere that would sell her a bottle of champagne. She turned and started back towards South Kensington station and found James walking down Pelham Street towards her.

She stared at him, open-mouthed.

'It's really me,' he said, reaching her and kissing her. 'Well – what's the verdict? . . . On Vanessa and the latest Colley-Smythe? You said it would be today and I wangled an evening. Plus or minus, I thought I should be in on it. Come on, Kate, tell me!'

'It's yes, or plus as you'd say. . . . James, you're the answer to a prayer.'

'Good. I've always wanted to be one of those.'

'Is that,' Kate asked, 'a bottle of champagne you are carrying?'

'Two, actually.' He held up the bag.

'Are you a man or a miracle?'

'A miracle, I should think. But look, Kate, don't sound so bloody amazed. Mark and I go back a long way and I told you he asked me to keep an eye on Vanessa. It might suit me because it means I can see you, but I gave a chap my word. He didn't want Vanessa having to run to her mother every two seconds. I mean, it wouldn't look good – he having taken her off the parental hands with all that ceremony and an expensive reception only to chuck her back at them. Anyway, Vanessa wouldn't like that either, would she?'

'No,' said Kate. 'No, she wouldn't.'

'Am I still a miracle?'

'You are, dear James. You are.'

Four days later, at three o'clock in the morning, the doorbell rang long and insistently. Kate roused herself, put on her dressing gown and went downstairs. She opened the door on the chain, peered out, undid the chain and Mark walked in, red-eyed and unshaven. He dropped his kitbag and lifted her in a great hug.

'Isn't it tremendous news? Kate, isn't it *wonderful*? I'm going to be a bloody father!'

'How did you get here so quickly?' she asked dazedly.

'Got the telegram, grabbed some leave and hitched a lift on a Hastings. God knows where we've been. It's taken two days . . . Still, I tell you, it's the first time I've been pleased that the RAF has planes. Where's Vanessa?'

'Asleep.'

He picked up his kitbag and followed her up the stairs. Vanessa, awoken at last by the noise, was in the doorway of her bedroom, yawning, her hair like an aureole, her feet bare beneath her long white nightie. Mark rushed to her.

'My dearest love,' he said. 'Oh Vanessa, my darling . . .'

The door closed upon them and Kate was left in the hallway, feeling dreadfully alone.

'Are you sure,' Mark said, 'are you absolutely and positively sure that you want Vanessa here? – in her condition?' he added, a trifle proudly.

'Absolutely positive,' Kate said. 'And stop talking about her as though she's a piece of left luggage.'

'And you'll look after her? Both of you?'

'We'll look after her,' James said. 'Won't we, Kate?'

'We will. Now don't fuss, Mark.'

'I can't help it.'

'Mark, I'll be fine,' Vanessa said. 'Between my mother and your mother and James and Kate, I'll be fine.'

It was extraordinary: over the past five days Vanessa had become pregnant, looked it in some indefinable way. Kate wondered why there had ever been any doubt.

'And she's to drink lots of milk and things. And she's to eat fish. That's good, isn't it? And, Kate, you must make sure she does, and if she's not a hundred per cent you mustn't let her come to Canada in July. Is that clear?'

'As mud,' Kate said, giving him the scouts' salute.

201

'Come on, old boy,' James said, 'you'd better catch your train.'

'Oh Christ,' Mark groaned, 'I suppose I must. I'll miss the bloody plane otherwise. Now you—' He turned to Vanessa. 'You report to me if these two don't come up to scratch.'

'Roger,' Vanessa said. 'Over and out.'

James put an arm around Kate's shoulders. 'We'll all do our best and we can't do better than that, can we?'

Mark looked at them and his lovely smile dawned on his face.

'No, you can't. And I'm so pleased to see you two like this – Vanessa's best friend and mine. It's as it should be, isn't it?'

'If the world was ordered to benefit you,' Kate said, 'there could be no possible argument about it. . . . James, shall we go and find Mark a taxi and let them say their goodbyes in peace?'

'Good idea. And no tears, mind,' he said severely to Vanessa.

In fact, Vanessa seemed rather less depressed than Mark. She swanned through her pregnancy with not a moment's discomfort, finished the summer term teaching at St Paul's and shortly afterwards sailed on the *Queen Mary* for New York. There Mark would meet her and take her by train to Winnipeg, where he had booked her into a hotel (he was worried about the heat, he wrote: it was already terrific and would it harm the baby?) and where Vanessa would stay for two weeks. After that he would take her, again by train, down into the United States. A friend of a friend of a cousin had invited them to stay in a house on Martha's Vineyard and – provided World War Three was not declared and Mark's services were not required elsewhere – there they would both be for ten days before he returned her to the gangplank of the *Queen Mary* in New York and himself go back to Winnipeg. It sounded wonderful, Kate thought, if you liked trains.

Kate and James took Vanessa to Southampton and escorted her aboard the great liner. James sat with Vanessa and a bottle of champagne in one of the lounges while Kate went in search of the ship's doctor. She found his assistant, a young man not much older than herself, demanded his name and that of his teaching hospital, nodded in a condescending way when he admitted it was Bart's and told him that she was holding him personally responsible for the welfare of Mrs Colley-Smythe, who was five months pregnant.

She then sought out Vanessa's cabin stewardess and cowed her in a similar fashion, but this time with the sweetener of a pound note. She joined James and Vanessa and helped them finish the bottle of champagne – quickly, for the 'All visitors ashore' gong was already going. As they went to the head of the gangway, Kate spotted a couple, in their thirties Kate guessed, who were having a cheerful but firm discussion with their small son, who wanted to go and explore the ship but was not being allowed to. Kate liked the look of them and approved of the way they were dealing with their child. She marched up to them and introduced Vanessa. The woman – Angela Evans, she said, somewhat bewildered, she was called – having had Vanessa's circumstances explained to her said of *course* they would watch over Mrs Colley-Smythe, nothing would give them greater pleasure, and Francis Evans promised the would arrange it with the Purser's Office that they would all share a table in the dining room.

Vanessa, Mr and Mrs Evans on either side of her and Master Ian Evans squeezed between her growing bulk and the ship's rails, waved excitedly as the tugs butted importantly at the huge ship, nosing her out into the Solent towards the Channel and the distant Atlantic, and the band played.

'You're crying,' James said. 'Hey, don't do that.' Gently he wiped the tears away.

Kate could not say why she was crying, and she was not, of course, the only one, but people around her were saying goodbye to relatives – their faces now the size of pinpricks as the *Queen Mary* shook off the attentions of the tugs and steamed purposefully around the Isle of Wight – and she was only saying goodbye to Vanessa for a few weeks.

'You were like a mother hen. No, not that – a lioness, a splendid lioness. But Vanessa isn't your cub, you know.'

She could not explain it if he didn't feel it. It was something to do with the grandeur of the ship, the promise of adventure it held, the way it spoke a different language as it flew its flags and let out a blast of steam as, triumphantly and disdainfully, it bade England and dull Southampton goodbye and set off for the New World. She felt she was anchored in convention: six feet of predictability surrounded her . . . And it was taking Vanessa and what they

203

called 'the lump' away with it, and she'd loved the lump and nurtured it as though it was her own. . . .

'Are you still here?'

She came to. The steam from the *Queen Mary*'s funnels was a drift in the air. The crowds on the dockside had gone. A few men were doing things with ropes among the crêpe paper streamers, and the bunting above the deserted bandstand fluttered with ridiculous gaiety against the cloudy sky.

'Yes, I'm here,' she said, and they began to walk back towards James's car.

'What will I do now I have no excuse to visit you for the next six weeks?'

Kate stopped and stared at him. 'Excuse? Why should you possibly need that?'

His face, under what hair the army allowed him, was a little pink but his grey eyes were challenging.

'I never know, when I say goodbye to you, if I'm going to see you again.'

'Surely not. James, surely not!'

'True . . . You go out with other men—'

'Not any more,' she said.

They had started walking again, and now he stopped.

'Really?' Eagerness in his voice.

'Really,' she said. And it was true, though it might have been because of the lump and not James at all. But she didn't want to lose him. Not at all she didn't. She took his arm.

'You don't need any excuse to see me. I would miss you horribly if you didn't, so please do. James, *promise* me you will!'

He gave a great shout of laughter and took her in his arms. A tram went by them, on its way to the cargo ships in the distance. The men clinging to the footplate whistled and shouted encouragement.

'You have my love,' he said. 'No strings attached. I don't ask anything of you – nothing at all. I'm just terrified of making a nuisance of myself. I can't bear to think I might be boring you.'

She flung herself on his chest.

'You're not a nuisance, you're not! How could you think such a thing? And you don't bore me one bit, not a single little bit.'

He held her close. Another tram went by, going in the opposite direction.

'Am I,' he asked, hating his weakness. He had been so patient so far. 'Am I the only one, then?'

'You are! No one but you. I am so very fond of you. Please let's go on as we have been.'

'Of course we will, Kate. Of course we will.'

Only him and that declaration. It was enough.

Charles Henry Mark Colley-Smythe was born on the fifth of November 1951. His father arrived in England three days later and was instantly besotted; his mother, naturally, thought he was the best and most beautiful baby the world had ever known; both sets of grandparents – whose first grandchild he was – discovered resemblances to relations dating back to the reign of George IV; and his godmother, Kate Earith, also fell madly in love with him. In the face of all this, his godfather, James Flimwell, tried hard to find something interesting to say about the wrinkled little scrap who so fascinated everyone, but found it not easy. Charlie, as he was called, was in truth the most ugly baby imaginable. He had inherited his mother's red hair, already sticking in tufts on his pink scalp, and his father's rather plain, heavy features. No one else seemed to notice this, though, and if they did they would not say.

Vanessa sat in her bed in Queen Charlotte's Hospital, her son in her arms.

'Just think,' she said. 'Only *think* how clever he was to be born on Guy Fawkes day! We need never worry about his birthday party – he'll always have fireworks and a bonfire.' She gazed at him lovingly, as though she believed that the date of his birth had something to do with him.

And, furthermore, Mark seemed to agree with her.

Never was a baby's head more thoroughly and enthusiastically wetted, Mark declaring that Charlie's arrival was even better than getting his Blue and winning the University Boat Race twice.

'Now that means he really *is* pleased,' said James.

'Oh?' said Andrew Coleridge, turning to Rosie. 'I still think I need convincing, don't you? . . . No,' he added hastily as Mark was about to speak again, 'don't, *please*, tell us how Charlie grabbed your fingers in his perfectly formed little hand. We've heard it before . . . fathers!' he exclaimed. 'I say, James, do you think we'll be as bad?'

But James did not have to answer this for Mark was fussing once again about Kate's and Vanessa's ability to take suitable care of Charlie when Vanessa came out of hospital. The grandparents had muttered darkly about nannies and said it was time Mark set up a home for his wife and child, but the idea of leaving the First Street flat had so upset Vanessa that the vaguely formed scheme had been abandoned.

'I'm sure we'll manage,' Kate told Mark for the fiftieth time, 'and if we can't we'll call in the cavalry, I promise we will.'

'But it might be too late,' Mark said, the alcoholic euphoria suddenly deserting him. He was returning to Canada the following day; another nine months there, apart from these exhausting snatched leaves in London.

'The cavalry,' Kate said firmly, 'is *never* late. In fact, I think we'll have trouble keeping it away . . . And, for heaven's sake, late for what?'

'Something might happen—'

'Charlie will grow. He'll get bigger. Nothing else will happen. Isn't that so, James?'

James put down his glass and said, with admirable confidence, 'Absolutely, old chap. Listen to the doctor.'

Charlie did indeed grow. In due course he was christened, and James and Kate, and a cousin of Mark's who was the other godfather, renounced the devil and all his works on Charlie's behalf. He didn't cry and let the devil out. He was a most contented baby and Vanessa a most contented mother. The flat in First Street was no longer the place where people congregated on Saturday evenings. Many of the men had finished their National Service, many others had discovered new friends and new lives. The umbilical cord that had attached them to Cambridge gently weakened and then parted.

But even so there were always plenty of visitors, and foremost among them was James. Vanessa, prosecuting this match for all she was worth, would push them out of the flat and tell them to go somewhere *lively*, convinced that the air of domesticity she and Charlie provided was an antidote to romance.

James's refusal to attend débutante parties was, Kate gathered from overheard comments, causing 'the mothers' to tear their hair out in frustration that their daughters could not exhibit their charms to this great catch, but Lady Flimwell was not tearing her hair out. Kate had been back to Flimwell Place often and was always warmly welcomed. Once James's sister had been there with her American husband and the most adorable golden-headed baby girl. She was unrecognisable from the person who had attempted to cause havoc on a snowy night in Cambridge. She had been charming and friendly to Kate, saying, as she gathered up her daughter who, for the fourth time, had crawled up to Lily and Cleo and curled up among them in front of the fire, 'Mother wants lots of grandchildren, you know. Sometimes I'm glad I'm three thousand miles away from the nagging questions.' And Lord Flimwell always greeted Kate with unaffected delight, introducing her to the family friends who came for drinks or dinner as 'Dr Earith' even though she wasn't yet.

And Beattie, hearing of all this, her knitting needles clattering away, said to Charles with as much anxiety as she could inject into her voice, 'It's all most worrying. I don't think we're up to a society wedding. I mean, do you think our little church could cope?'

Mark's exile in Canada ended and he removed Vanessa to a house in Richmond from where he commuted to the City and did things in the Stock Exchange. Vanessa talked of returning to teaching, for Charlie now had a nanny, but within four months of Mark's return she was pregnant again.

'It doesn't matter,' she told Kate as she tasted the stew she was cooking for a Saturday lunch and added salt and pepper. 'Charlie should have a brother or sister and we may as well get it over with now . . . except Mark is talking about a full crew for a boat.'

'How many is that, for God's sake?'

'Eight. Plus the cox.'

'Eight children? Vanessa, you don't mean it.'

'No! I'm settling for a double scull.'

'Coo,' Kate said. 'I'm not half impressed by the jargon.'

'And what about you?' Vanessa asked, putting carrots on to boil. Automatically Kate checked to see if she had remembered the water. She had. Vanessa had become a wife, in such a short time her scattiness had been tamed to practicality. She was still vague, but there was an efficient edge to it now. Kate felt a little sad.

'Well?'

'Well what?'

'You and James.' Vanessa directed springing coils of her hair in the direction of the sitting room, where James and Mark were discussing their gins and tonic.

'He hasn't asked me,' Kate said after a while.

'He will, though. He has to really, after monopolising you for two years. What will you say?'

Kate picked up her drink and paced around the kitchen.

'And,' Vanessa went on, 'you have been monopolising *him* for two years. . . .'

Kate stopped her pacing and looked at her.

'Why are you suddenly going on about this?' she asked suspiciously. 'You never used to. Mark's put you up to it, hasn't he?'

Vanessa flushed slightly. 'What if he has? It's true, isn't it?'

It *was* true, but until the proposal came – which surely it must – Kate would not think about it. She had already taken her pathology finals and was just coming to the end of her obstetrics, which meant several late nights as she sat in the hospital waiting for calls to go out to attend women in labour. Her final exams were rushing towards her. Suddenly she felt she had forgotten everything she had learned over the past five years and started revising frantically. James accepted the restrictions she placed on seeing him with his usual good humour.

'Of course I understand, Kate,' he told her. 'Of course I do. It would be awful to fail now after all this time. Not that you will. You'll sail through the whole damn thing as you always do, and in no time at all we'll be celebrating like mad. . . . Lots of celebrating,

208

perhaps.' He tilted up her chin and kissed her. 'What do you think?'

She laughed and pretended not to understand, and wondered vaguely how the future Lady Flimwell could be a general practitioner, dealing with the estate's labourers' bronchitis and delivering their wives' babies. No, she'd have to be out of the immediate vicinity, in Melton Mowbray, perhaps. And there was another year in London first anyway, her houseman's year, but she would be a doctor then, a real doctor . . . She felt a great surge of optimism and kissed James goodbye with a fervour that astonished and pleased him, then turned back to her books. She would not get a new flatmate, she decided, having been wavering about it since Vanessa had left. She would work like mad, see James at weekends and perhaps once during the week. And when he asked her to marry him, as surely he must, she would say yes, provided he understood that she was going to practise medicine, because he was a lovely, charming man and she was lucky to have him.

But three months later, before her finals and before James had proposed to her, Gerry Beviss came to the flat in First Street.

Chapter 14

Gerry discovered many things about his wife in the first few months of their marriage. The first was that she was not a virgin, which scarcely surprised him in view of what she had said. It didn't particularly worry him for, after all, neither was he, but he couldn't help wondering who her former lovers had been. Not young men, surely: Diana liked sex in ways Gerry had not dreamed existed, ways Molly had not shown him – and he had always thought she knew the lot.

Their ship had steamed north from Rio to Miami, where they stayed for a week. Miami was hot, that's all he remembered. In Miami, Diana had wanted them both in the shower slippery with soap, she on her hands and knees, he pumping away at her like a dog, water pouring down on them. He had seen Miami: he must have done, for they had gone to parties and restaurants and met people, but he retained no sense of the place at all; although ever afterwards the scent of that soap would remind him that he had been there. And then Cuba, where Diana's stepfather, Pedro Moitinho, had friends and again they were entertained lavishly. Gerry remembered the hotel where they had stayed and the casinos where Diana had won and lost vast sums of money, but most of all he remembered that in Cuba Diana had wanted it standing up.

'Ah'm a slave girl cuttin' cane,' she would say, pulling up her dress and pulling down her pants, 'and you am de slave driver and you want to drive it in here . . . Oh honey . . .' in a parody of how she imagined a slave girl would have talked, 'put it in there right now.'

Cuba, then, Havana and the casinos and the crack of his arm muscles as he held her up, the ache as she linked her hands behind his neck and leaned backwards riding him. It was a wonder his cock didn't come off. When he had time to think – which was seldom – he reflected how he'd had two years of total celibacy (apart from Patrick's prostitutes, and he didn't count them; he had never been back to Molly) and that he was making up for it now, by night and by day. He rather thought that Diana had been celibate for a lot less than two years, but who was he to complain?

Ten days in Cuba and then aboard another ship, which took them through the Panama Canal. Diana had bought 'a sweet little thing' in a shop in Havana, and now produced it: Gerry threw it overboard and they nearly had their first quarrel, but she found enough to do with his own 'sweet little thing' to last them through the Canal, up to Acapulco and Los Angeles, where they left the ship.

By the time they arrived in Palm Springs, in a huge Cadillac followed by a pick-up carrying Diana's luggage, Gerry was longing for a good night's sleep. They were staying with another friend of Pedro Moitinho's, in a huge Spanish-style palace. There was a party on their first night there, and after dinner and dancing some of the young people swam in the neon-lit, kidney-shaped pool. There were swimming costumes provided in the changing rooms in the pool house, and Gerry dived into the blue water and swam a few lengths and thought, for the hundredth time since he had been married amid the panoply of a Roman Catholic nuptial mass in the Metropolitan Cathedral in Rio de Janeiro, that this could not possibly be him. Could not be Gerald Beviss, born in a gypsy caravan, here in California swimming in a pool which contained a girl who had just starred in a film opposite David Niven and another who talked of Walt Disney as though he were her favourite uncle . . . Gerald Beviss who had learned to swim in the cold grey waters of the English Channel here in a warm blue pool in Palm Springs.

The floodlights went out. There were screams and giggles and Diana was beside him, her hand in his swimming trunks pulling him towards the shallow end of the pool . . . pulling him by his cock! He yelped in pain and she put her free hand over his mouth, and then, when she could stand, she thrust the crutch of her swimsuit aside and tried to stuff him into her.

'No,' he said. 'Diana, *no*!'

'Yes – into me, into me!'

She rummaged around, her hand urgent, but there was nothing there. Fear of discovery as others frolicked near them in the dark, distaste at her wanting to do it here, virtually in public, general overuse, exhaustion and the shock of being treated in so peremptory a manner had defeated his cock. He took her arms and pushed her away.

'Diana, not now. For God's sake!'

He was shocked by her reaction.

'Shit!' she hissed. 'Shit! You're useless!' And she swam away, using his groin as a springboard to get her moving.

Gerry doubled over, water pouring into his mouth, and tenderly held his balls until the throbbing subsided. He coughed, wiped water from his face and, feeling angry, humiliated and – for no reason that he could precisely define – horribly alone, he pulled himself out of the pool, went to the men's changing room and got back into what he had learned to call his tux. He left the top button of the shirt undone, draped his tie around his neck and went and stood at the poolside. The floodlights were back on, but he could not see Diana in the pool. He assumed that she, too, was changing and waited, his balls still aching, thinking what he would say to her.

'Cigarette?'

Gerry turned. A tanned blond hulk of a man wearing swimming trunks, a towel about his shoulders, was standing beside him. He was holding out a packet of Camels.

'I don't, thanks,' Gerry said, and then, 'Oh well, maybe.'

He took a cigarette and the man lit both, and said: 'I'm Dave Packer. Good to meet you.'

'Gerry Beviss.'

They shook hands.

'You British?'

'Yes.'

They chatted, Dave asking Gerry what he thought of California, Gerry explaining that he'd only just arrived, Dave saying that he hoped to get to Europe one of these days. Then Dave stubbed out his cigarette and said he'd best be getting changed and Gerry turned to go back to the house, thinking that a drink would be nice. As he did so, he saw Diana in the pool amid a crowd of laughing girls. She smiled at him and raised her hand.

'That's my husband,' Gerry heard her say as he walked away. The other girls screamed. 'Oh no you don't,' Diana's voice cried above them. 'He's only got time for me.'

She was full of remorse when they finally got to bed, stroking his balls and saying she was sorry, she hadn't meant to kick him. He pushed her away and turned on to his side.

'Well, don't you bloody do it – or anything like it – again,' he said, still angry but also relieved that his cock was having a night off.

'Darling, I *said* I was sorry.'

'I'm going to sleep.'

Diana waited until he was breathing deeply, then slid out of bed and went to the bathroom. She turned her back to the mirror and craned her neck to look at the reflection. There was a red mark all the way down the spine and the skin was broken in one or two places. What would she say to Gerry if he asked about it? She'd think of something. The man – it had been so utterly thrilling because she didn't know who he was, what he looked like even, nothing about him – had pushed her up against a tree and simply belted away at her. It had been so lucky. As she had swum away from Gerry and his silly little limp thing, she had bumped into this man in the dark and her hand had accidently, absolutely and utterly accidentally, touched him and it had been enormous! He had taken her to the side of the pool and she had touched him again, not accidentally this time, and he had shoved a finger inside her and pushed her towards the steps and said, 'Out.' That was the only word he had spoken and she had said utterly nothing at all, but had followed him through some bushes until he had stopped, turned, stripped off her swimming costume, arranged her against the trunk of the tree, spreading her legs apart, and had thrust into her, almost lifting her off her feet. The floodlights had come on

213

again – she could see the bright blue of the pool over his humping shoulders – and after that she didn't remember much at all, only that it had been divine, until she had found herself alone. She had scrabbled around for the swimsuit and put it on, realised that she had to get back into the pool because she could not parade alongside it to where the changing rooms were, for the costume and her, surely, would give everything away, and had nipped into the water while Gerry was talking to a man at the poolside.

She peered at the reflection of her back again. That was it – she had slid on the steps going into the pool. Anyone might have done it. She just hoped it wouldn't leave a scar.

Gerry did not question the explanation (why should he?) and some two weeks later said only that she should not drink so much when she claimed to have cut her knee by tripping up a step. Diana did not know what had caused the cut . . . a shell, perhaps? A piece of broken, sea-washed glass? . . . But this time she did know who had pleasured her in the dark, on the beach away from the lights of the house where Gerry was sitting along with the man's wife: it was her host.

But this was not one of the things Gerry discovered about his wife straight away. Not for a long time, in fact. As they made their way slowly up the coast of California to San Francisco, an invitation, a wholehearted welcome and yet more lavish hospitality always extended from somewhere further north, Gerry simply assumed he had a wife who enjoyed sex, which was, after all, something that many men would envy – even if, during those first wild weeks, he had often thought he was no more than an erect cock with a person attached to it. But Diana seemed to have calmed down since Palm Springs, perhaps because of the orgy of spending in Los Angeles or the mad ten days in the casinos of Las Vegas, or, perhaps, Gerry thought fancifully, because as they went north and the year advanced the weather became cooler. Wasn't the cold supposed to dampen sexual ardour?

What he did discover, though, was that without sex – of which there was still a very great deal – there was nothing between him and Diana. Nothing at all. This fact was forced upon him when they were on the train bound for New York. Within a few hours of the beginning of the journey, she was bored. She looked over the

214

other passengers and pronounced them impossible. She took no interest in the spectacular scenery as they went through the Sierra Nevada and the Rockies. She fidgeted and complained, said they should have gone by plane even though flying made her ill. It was the first time in the two and a half months since they had been married that they had spent any time (apart from in bed) on their own, and she made it clear to him that his company was not adequate.

At ten-thirty in the morning, she ordered a whiskey sour from the steward and lit her fifth cigarette of the day.

'We'll fly from Chicago,' she said.

'We can't, Diana. No plane could leave the ground with the amount of luggage you have.'

'It can come on by train.'

Gerry shrugged. 'As you like. But will it be safe?'

'You stay with it, then.'

'I will not. I'm not your courier, Diana. I'm going to the observation car. Are you coming?'

'No. I'm staying here.'

'It might be interesting.'

'No it fucking well won't. You're like bloody Phyllis, Gerry. Always trying to see the good side of things. Christ, you're boring.'

Gerry went alone to the observation car. A young couple were also there and after a short time they introduced themselves: Mike and Mary Goldsworthy, they said they were. They were on their honeymoon and fulfilling a lifetime's dream of going to New York, courtesy of Mary's father. They held hands all the time and looked lovingly at each other, and Gerry found himself envying them. They asked Gerry about himself and he told them that he was on his honeymoon too; his wife, he said, was in their compartment 'not feeling well'. They exclaimed in concern and invited him to take lunch with them if she was not better.

But Diana was sparkling by lunchtime. She looked appraisingly at Mary Goldsworthy when she enquired about her health, said she was utterly divine, thank you, accepted their invitation to lunch and proceeded to flirt with Mike. Gerry was horribly embarrassed. Mike was impervious to Diana, but Diana could not see it, could not see how uncomfortable everyone was, how the

Goldsworthys were so polite, waiting until Diana had finished her brandy before calling for the bill although it was obvious they were longing to get away.

Afterwards, in their compartment, he remonstrated with her. She flung herself at him.

'Darling, I'm sorry. Really, I am. The train is so utterly boring. Say you forgive me, *please!*' Her expert hand was in his trousers and in spite of himself his cock was coming to attention. 'That's better, isn't it?' she said, her mouth on his.

He did not, of course, know that he was the second man she'd had that day. He put her change of mood down to the whiskey sours and didn't consider it might have anything to do with the steward. He was her first black man and she was elated.

She was a different person again when they arrived in New York. She knew the city well and it was her kind of place: thrusting, grabbing, eager, restless. What you want I've got, it said. And if you've got money, why, then I've got things you never *dreamed* you wanted! Gerry and Patrick had spent two nights here on their way to Rio and had thought that they had pinned the city down, but Gerry now looked back on those two English boys and laughed at them. They'd drunk in a few bars, gone to a sex show on 42nd Street – 'Your stag night, old boy,' Patrick had said – to the top of the Empire State Building, to Times Square, and considered that they had returned to their hotel dangerously late.

With Diana and her money it was as though they owned the city. She was on the phone as soon as they arrived in their suite at the Plaza, arranging meetings with all her friends and acquaintances.

'Darling!' she cried when at last she put the phone down. 'It's going to be utterly divine. We're going everywhere, starting tonight!'

Gerry looked out of the window. By pressing his face to the glass he could see Central Park.

'It's snowing,' he said. 'I'm going to need an overcoat.'

'Buy one tomorrow. I'm going to buy lots of clothes.' She stretched. '*Lots!*'

He turned from the window and smiled at her. 'We'll have to ring Cunard and tell them to clear half the hold of the *Queen Elizabeth*. How will you have time to wear them all?'

'You buy some too.'

He had a dollar chequebook. It had been given to him by Pedro Moitinho, who told him that Diana had an American bank account and a sample of Gerry's signature had been sent to the bank's headquarters here in New York. It was his to use as he liked.

'But how much money is there in it?' Gerry asked. 'Will there be enough?' They would be travelling huge distances and the prospect was unnerving.

Pedro Moitinho had roared with laughter. 'It's now a joint account. Diana asked and I arranged. There's enough money,' he said. 'Enough, no problems.'

Gerry had paid the hotel bills – though there had not been many of those – and their train fare over from the West Coast and had always been amazed that the cheques had been accepted. He had bought a few things in California using the travellers' cheques he had brought with him. Presents for his family, silly little things that Diana would laugh at and which he had hidden at the bottom of his suitcase. It was odd. He had married Diana to get away from Blue Oceans, the family firm, but he couldn't wait to see them all again, see his mother's face as he handed her the bead-fringed Indian shawl, see Arthur putting on the tooled leather belt and hear him saying, 'Eh, lad. From California? What a thing!' He'd even bought something for Grace.

He looked out of the window again, straining to see the street below. Cars streamed along it. Beyond, Central Park was a white glimmer.

'I'll buy an overcoat,' he said. 'I must. I'll freeze else.'

He enjoyed their time in New York. Diana sizzled as she always did when occupied by parties, people and shopping. She chose his coat for him, and a hat which she said made him look like Humphrey Bogart. Wherever they went she knew people and, although he was aware that it had all been arranged, he couldn't help being impressed. Money met money, it seemed, in the way iron filings met a magnet. Diana would greet her friends with cries of delight and Gerry would wait, smoking a cigarette, until he was dragged forward and presented as 'my lovely husband'. He was

217

doing this one evening at the Stork Club, thinking of other things, when he heard his name being spoken and he looked down into a pair of bright blue eyes.

'Gerry Beviss,' Sophie, once Flimwell, said. 'Congratulations on your marriage.'

'You know Diana?' Gerry asked. Stupid question.

'Of course I do. We were debs together.' She drew him down to sit beside her. 'We heard you were coming but we – Jack and I – have been out of town. In Maryland. Jack's mother has been ill. . . . Tell me, Gerry, how is my brother? How is dear old England?'

He heard the longing in her voice and responded to it. Forgetting what had happened that night in Cambridge – she had come between him and Kate, nearly forcing them apart; how trivial that seemed now, with Diana being laughingly called 'Mrs Beviss, *ma'am*' – they chatted away like old friends until he said, 'How about a dance?' and then added cheekily, 'For old times' sake.'

She laughed and stood up. 'For old times' sake, then.'

She was lovely to be with. Marriage had matured her and she obviously adored her husband, Jack van Rhoon. They hadn't been to England since their wedding, she said, but she hoped they would next year. She knew it was grey and cold and depressed, what with the rationing and everything, but—

'Well, it's home, isn't it? And I want to go there, if Jack's mother is better and if I'm all right . . . I'm having a baby, you see. Do you mind if we join Jack now? I feel fine, on top of the world, but he worries so.'

Gerry took her back to the table and sat talking to them both. Diana was dancing with various other men and he could see that Jack and Sophie thought it odd, but he suddenly felt optimistic: Sophie had been just like Diana when he had first met her and look at her now! Perhaps Diana would settle down and be like Sophie. Gerry was tempted to ask Jack how he had done it when Sophie went to the ladies' room, but that would have meant revealing that he knew how Sophie used to behave. Jack, however, seemed to understand. He saw how Gerry glanced over to where his wife was noisily laughing and fake-punched him on the jaw.

'Be firm, boy,' he drawled. 'Be real firm and get her pregnant. That'll do it.'

When he told Kate at Mark's and Vanessa's wedding reception, two days after they returned to England, that he was pampered, he meant it. At that moment it was true. Kate was beautiful and he couldn't resist telling her so; and he was desperate to clear his conscience, to know that she had forgiven him. They were gone from each other now, he and Kate, and he had to make a life with Diana. He held the example of Sophie van Rhoon before him and tried not to notice the bad side of Diana. She had walked out of the reception shortly after his brief conversation with Kate, leaving Gerry no option but to follow her, after saying in a loud voice it was boring and the champagne second rate. The truth was, of course, that another woman was the centre of attention. Diana refused to attend any weddings after that, saying she was Catholic and not allowed to go into other churches, and when Gerry pointed out, teasingly, that she never went into any of her own either she slapped his face.

Her self-centredness was ruthless, heartless. Diana's old nanny – known for some reason as Suckers – was housekeeper in the Mayfair house and much in evidence, but of Diana's other chaperon, the retiring Mrs Cunningham, there was no sign. Gerry asked about her.

'Phyllis?' Diana said. 'We don't want her here. I told her to get out.'

'Where's she gone?'

Diana shrugged. 'I've no idea. I told her to go and she went.'

'Where to?'

'For God's sake, Gerry, how the hell should I know?'

'Has she any money?'

'I doubt it. If she had she wouldn't have been so eager to come here in the first place . . . Who cares?' She threw a letter at him across the breakfast table. 'Can you deal with this? It's utterly, achingly boring.'

'She might be starving.'

'Phyllis?' Diana looked at him in absolute amazement. 'Why would she be starving?'

'People need money to live, Diana.'

'Well, I expect she's got a little,' Diana said carelessly. 'Gerry, will you go and see Bernard? He says things must happen now I'm married.'

Gerry looked at the letter. It was from one Bernard Rosenthal, principal trustee of the late Michael Anthony Dalton, and it asked Diana to come and see him and attend to details concerning the winding up of the trust.

'How can I do this?' Gerry asked. 'I can't sign these documents he talks about.'

'Bring them back and I will.' She stood up and paced around the room. 'What are we going to do for Christmas, Gerry?'

'Your mother and stepfather are coming.'

'Yes . . . let's have a Christmas tree and lots of decorations. And a party, Gerry, at New Year.' She came and sat on his lap. 'Shall we?'

'If you like.'

'It would be fun, wouldn't it? . . . No it wouldn't, everyone will already be going to parties.' She slid off his lap and began her pacing again. 'Must you go off today? I'll be bored.'

'I have to collect the Aston, and I want to see my family.'

'How utterly gruesome. You could just pick up the car and come straight back though, couldn't you?'

'They're expecting me for lunch.'

'Put them off, then.'

'I can't, Diana. And I don't want to.'

She lit a cigarette. 'So you'd rather sit around with your ghastly family and talk about fish. Is that it?'

'I said I'm going, and I'll go. Why don't you buy the Christmas decorations?'

She blew furious smoke at him. 'Christmas decorations? I'm supposed to spend the whole day buying a few fucking paper-chains?'

Gerry stood up. 'You're not *supposed* to do anything. I'll only be gone a few hours . . . Come on, Diana.' He went over to her, but she turned away. 'Come *on*,' he repeated, 'you're looking forward to seeing your mother and I'm looking forward to seeing mine. It's the same thing.'

'It's pansy for a grown man to want to see his mother,' she said. 'And it's not the same thing. Not at all. *My* mother isn't a gypsy.'

He left.

They knew he was coming but not on which train. He hitched a lift to the bottom of the lane and walked the mile or so to Ridge Farm, swinging the bag which contained the presents he had brought for everyone. The Weald and marsh were white with frost, the mud at the roadside hard as he kicked at it. He felt free under the cold blue sky and laughed at the ewes, fat with lamb, as they skittered away from their hay as he passed.

'I don't want your bloody hay, or you,' he told them, stopping and staring into their vacant yellow eyes. 'Honest, I don't.'

They huddled together and stared back, not believing him. He leaned on the gate.

'But,' he whispered, 'I wouldn't say no to a nice lamb chop if you have one to spare in a couple of months. Hey – how about it?'

They stamped their feet and eyed their hay, and then him again. He left them in peace and walked on. He would go for a ride this afternoon, him and Florin. The tide would be out. He couldn't see it, but he could feel its pull . . . He and Florin and a wide grey beach.

He arrived at Ridge Farm, jumped over the gate into the yard and yelled at his mother, who was hanging out washing. She threw one of Joe's shirts back into the basket and came running.

'My boy! My *boy!*' she cried. 'Oh, my Gerry!' He dropped the bag he was holding and picked her up, twirling her around. 'Are you well?' she said anxiously when he put her down. 'Everything's right wi' you?'

'It's right, Ma.'

She clung to his arm. 'They been taking care o' that car o' yours, Arthur and your Da have . . . not driving it, but starting it up an' that . . . I knew you'd come back for the car.'

'I came back to see you, Ma.'

'No – did you?' she said shyly. 'And . . . an' you're staying for dinner?'

'If I'm asked,' he teased.

'Oh Gerry, *course* you are! The others'ull be along soon. Now you come along inside and have a cup of tea to warm you.'

A cup of tea? A cup of tea! He bent to pick up the bag.

'Why are you laughing?' his mother asked. 'What's so funny?'

He put his arm around her narrow shoulders.

'Nothing's funny, Ma,' he said.

In fact, he was close to tears.

Chapter 15

Gerry went to see Bernard Rosenthal early in the New Year.

'So you're the lucky man,' Bernard said, smiling and reaching out his hand as Gerry was shown into his office on the second floor of a building in Threadneedle Street. Gerry took the hand and shook it, and Bernard introduced him to the two other men in the room. 'Andrew Gummer of the stockbrokers, Gummer, Lloyd and Selwyn, and Denis Cole of himself, accountant. . . . Would you like some coffee, Beviss?'

'Thank you, sir, I would.'

Coffee was brought. The accountant handed them folders and, taking out the first batch of papers, began explaining Diana's enormous assets to Gerry. He had to put his coffee cup down as he was suddenly afraid of spilling its contents over Bernard's smart carpet. Patrick had underestimated, was all he could think. And no wonder Pedro Moitinho had laughed when Gerry had asked if there was enough money in Diana's American bank account. Now Andrew Gummer was telling him smoothly that the late Mr Dalton had anticipated the war in Europe and had bought considerable assets in North America all at Depression prices . . . office blocks in Toronto and Vancouver, in Pittsburgh and Chicago, one in Manhattan itself, all yielding so much per annum in rent, a 'substantial annual income', and this money had been re-invested by Mr Gummer's New York colleagues 'quite profitably'. Diana's father had sold the factories which made the linoleum but had retained the trademark, and since the war there had been a massive demand for it as the working-class houses were rebuilt after the Blitz. And Diana was paid a royalty for every square foot of the stuff sold.

'I don't wish to influence you, of course,' Bernard Rosenthal said to Gerry as the accountant gathered up papers and put them in a briefcase, 'but I don't think you and your wife could do better than to continue having your affairs handled by Mr Gummer and Mr Cole. In my opinion, they could not have done a better job.'

'Yes,' Gerry said. 'Yes.' And then, although it seemed absurdly inadequate, 'Thank you very much.'

Bernard's lips twitched. 'You will want to talk it over with Diana, I am sure. I have the documents for her to sign. I'll explain them over lunch, shall I? . . . Now would you excuse me for a moment?' He escorted the other two men out of the door and their voices receded as they went down the corridor.

Gerry sat still, trying to work out what their stay at the Plaza Hotel in New York had cost. The bill had seemed huge when he had written the cheque, but it was about an hour's rent from the American properties, fifty minutes if you included the Canadian ones. And his new overcoat? Maybe five seconds. It was unreal.

Gerry stood up and wandered around Bernard's office. There were framed paintings of racehorses on the walls and, near the desk, a group of photographs. He was studying these when Bernard came back.

'Are you interested in racing?' he asked.

Gerry turned to him. 'Yes, sir, I am. . . . Wasn't this one at Newmarket? A horse called Frantic? I backed it.'

'The best I've ever owned. He's won eight races and I'm keeping him in training as a four-year-old. When you are lucky enough to have a horse like that you want to see it race.'

Gerry looked back at the photograph. The rather grave man in the room with him was leading Frantic into the winners' enclosure, his right hand on the rein, his left raised, his whole face laughing.

'I'd love to own a racehorse,' Gerry said. 'One like this, which gives you pleasure.'

Bernard chuckled. 'Hasn't this morning told you that you could own two dozen racehorses and still your bank manager wouldn't complain?'

'Yes – but just being able to buy them doesn't make them win,

224

does it? And buying a horse that has already won is cheating in a way.'

Bernard stared at him, interest dawning in his eyes.

'Cheating the challenge, you mean?'

'That,' Gerry said. 'And you shouldn't be able to buy luck. It's a kind of contradiction, isn't it?'

'I suppose it is,' Bernard Rosenthal said.

He had been wondering what kind of a man would marry Diana Dalton. He had been expecting someone as careless, callous and rapacious as Diana herself, someone only interested in knowing that the money would keep flowing. The sort of man who accepted an Aston Martin as an engagement present, in fact. He was surprised by this Gerald Beviss. He was polite, even deferential, to the older men; after the initial shock (Bernard had seen that: very little could be hidden from those sharp eyes) he had noted how young Beviss had taken in the enormous sums of money, had concentrated on the details which had been so pedantically spelled out to him instead of simply absorbing the bottom line with its six and seven figures – which would, after all, be understandable under the circumstances. And his remark about money not being able to buy luck . . . Had Gerald Beviss already learned that it also could not buy happiness? Bernard rather hoped he hadn't. He liked him. He was a surprising young man.

But even having determined this, Bernard nearly choked over the City Club's beef and onion pie when the surprising young man asked him if he would offer him a job. Bernard wiped his mouth with his napkin and said, 'Will you say that again? I'm not sure if I heard you.'

'Will you give me a job?' Gerry repeated. He'd had no idea he was going to say it until it came out, but now it had he knew this was what he wanted and needed. 'I've got to do something,' he went on, diagnosing it as he spoke. 'I can't loaf around doing nothing but spend Diana's money for the rest of my life, can I?'

Bernard gazed at him.

'I'd make you work, you know,' he said. 'Many firms in the City take chaps down from Oxford and Cambridge and some expect them to do little more than have lunch with other chaps down from Oxford and Cambridge. Not Rosenthal's.'

225

'I want to work.'

Bernard divided the remaining claret between their two glasses, and picked his up.

'All right then, Beviss,' he said slowly. 'I'll give you a try.'

'Thank you, sir,' Gerry said. 'Why – *thank* you.'

He grinned, and at last Bernard understood why Diana had married him, but was more than ever mystified as to why he had married her. He told his new employee that his salary per annum would be a lot less than Diana's income per month and fully expected a rapid change of mind, but Gerald Beviss thanked him again and they agreed he would start work at the beginning of February.

'You understand, don't you, that you will be a mere junior,' Bernard said as he called for the bill.

'What else should I be?' There was a pause, and then Gerry added, 'What exactly is it that you do? Could I read up about it or anything in the meantime?'

Bernard laughed until he had to bring out his handkerchief and wipe his eyes.

'I'm sorry,' he said, as Gerry watched him anxiously, smiling slightly but unable to see the joke. 'I'm a merchant banker,' he explained. 'Broadly speaking, I raise money and lend it out . . . There are no books about that, I'm afraid, although a study of economics and how the money and commodity markets work would be necessary, as well as learning accountancy procedures and Company Law.'

'Oh,' said Gerry. 'Well, it sounds challenging enough anyway.'

'Good,' replied Bernard.

Diana was furious.

'A *job*?' she said. 'What do you mean you've got a job?'

'Just that – I've got a job.'

She had bought a Siamese kitten in Harrods and had called him Rio. She was playing with him, throwing a ball of wool and watching as he chased it and patted it around the carpet, but for now Rio was ignored as she stared at Gerry, her eyes hard.

'I sent you to Bernard Rosenthal to sort out my trust, not to get a fucking job.'

226

'You didn't send me. You asked me to go and I went. I've got the papers for you to sign—'

'Fuck the papers.'

'Look, Diana,' he said reasonably, 'I've got to do something.'

'Why?'

'I need to . . . I need to – for my self-respect,' he said, at last understanding his impulsive request to Bernard Rosenthal.

'Don't be so bloody stupid!' She tapped her foot and sucked at her cigarette holder, smoke pouring from her nose and mouth. Rio, seeing the laces on her shoes swinging, found them irresistible and pounced. Diana looked down, saw the kitten, swung her foot back and kicked. Rio sailed through the air and landed some five feet away.

'Christ, Diana!'

Gerry rushed to pick the kitten up, Diana behind him.

'Darling Rio! I'm sorry! Let me have him, Gerry. Is he all right?'

'Don't touch him.' Gerry turned his back on her, the kitten against his chest. 'Give me time to see.'

He took each of the tiny legs and ran his finger and thumb down them, gently felt the cream-coloured body, then scratched with one fingernail under the little jaw. Rio's dark brown ears went back, his blue eyes closed to slits and he began to purr gigantically. Gerry could feel the vibrations through his waistcoat and shirt. He bent and put the kitten down on the carpet and rolled the ball of wool past his nose. Rio chased it, much less affected by the episode than the two humans in the room. Gerry found he was shaking and Diana was on the sofa sobbing that it had been an accident, that she hadn't meant it, though they both knew she had.

You love something, you kick it and you love it again. Gerry thought he and Rio had a lot in common.

She made no further fuss about his job, perhaps because doing so might remind her of a time when even she knew the meaning of shame. There are certain things decent people do not do and high on the list, just beneath abusing a child, is kicking an eight-week-old kitten. She did not even mention the job, though on the evening of his third day at work she announced that she was going ski-ing the following week.

'To Gstaad. With Mummy and Pedro.' She looked at him, trying to gauge his reaction.

'I thought they were on their way back to Rio, in time for the Carnival,' he said, wondering what she expected him to do: be angry? Jealous? Appear chastised or mortified because he was missing a treat? 'Ski-ing will be fun,' he said at last. 'What a shame I can't come.'

She came back after a week, saying snow was cold, ski-ing was boring and she much preferred to be with him.

He laughed and kissed her, said he was glad to hear it but that he was still going to work. Which he did, wearing a dark suit, a sober tie, a shirt with a discreet stripe in it which, he had been assured, was quite acceptable for a young merchant banker, a bowler hat, and – no matter the weather – an umbrella in one hand and a briefcase in the other. He enjoyed his work and Bernard Rosenthal seemed pleased with him. Rio grew, learned to interpret his mistress's moods, and ran when danger threatened; and, anyway, he became less popular as his kittenish charms faded and soon discovered that the kitchen held more promise altogether, where Suckers spoiled him in a much less spasmodic fashion than Diana did. Again Gerry thought he knew how Rio felt. Suckers spoiled him, too: Diana, invariably still asleep in bed, had no idea of the understanding Gerry and Suckers had or of the delicious food she cooked him for breakfast now that more and more things were coming off the ration. Whenever Gerry managed to get to Ryehurst, he would come back with fresh eggs from his mother's hens, kippers for himself and a bit of coley for Rio. On weekdays he deserted the dining room and ate breakfast in the kitchen, and he learned all about Suckers's old mother who lived with Suckers's sister in Ealing and how Suckers went off every afternoon to sit with the old lady to give her sister a bit of a break.

All this might have made Rio happy, but not so Gerry. He thought about it on his way to work one day. Their first anniversary passed and he realised that he had given up hope of seeing a Sophie-van-Rhoon-like transformation in Diana. She was as restless and dissatisfied as ever, complaining if they stayed in, always wanting to be somewhere else if they went out, which they did most nights – though never with Gerry's friends. The only one

228

of those she would tolerate was Patrick, and Gerry could not understand why. He had seen James a few times for lunch, had heard about Mark being in Canada, about Vanessa being pregnant.

Gerry thought he was firm with Diana, as Jack van Rhoon said he should be, but it made no difference. Nothing seemed to. There were evenings when she would dance with one man (not Gerry — never him) all night or attempt totally inappropriate flirtations as she had done that time on the train going to New York. She would swear at Gerry when he tried to tell her she was making a fool of herself or, which was worse, preen herself because she thought he was jealous. As for her getting pregnant, well, there was no sign of that and on the whole Gerry was relieved. He could not imagine what kind of a mother Diana would make.

He had never pretended to love her, and she certainly did not love him, but he had hoped for affection between them and was sad that even this did not seem possible. The fact was that marriage bored her. However could it have been otherwise, Diana being as she was? She liked the fuss when they were engaged, enjoyed being the star of the show at her wedding, had found the new faces and places encountered on their honeymoon stimulating, but the day-to-day realities of marriage did not suit her. She was furious that they were no longer of interest to the gossip columnists and was constantly plotting ways of attracting their attention, but, thank God, had so far not hit on anything too outrageous. That, to Diana, was marriage: not being in the papers.

He stood up as the train came into Bank station, and heard his name being called as he stepped on to the platform. He turned.

'Nick, by all that's holy!' he exclaimed.

'Gerry, you old icicle, how are you?' said Nick O'Rourke.

'I'm well.' They began walking down the platform towards the exit, two drops in a moving river of bowler hats. 'The army's released you, then?'

'It has,' Nick said. 'For this! It's one uniform for another, isn't it? I heard about your marriage, Gerry, even as I served King and Country in the steaming jungles of Malaya. Congratulations.'

'Thanks,' Gerry said.

They climbed the steps and came out into the open air.

'What are you doing now?' Gerry asked him.

'To be honest, old chap,' Nick said earnestly, 'I'm not perfectly sure. But I do it in that direction—' He pointed with his umbrella up Threadneedle Street and they began walking again. 'My father found me the job. It's in Throgmorton Street and it's broking of some sort. Insurance I think,' he added vaguely. 'I've only been at it for a week.'

They arranged to have lunch together the next day. Nick went up Bartholomew Lane and Gerry, the point of his umbrella striking the pavement purposefully with each stride, marched on up Threadneedle Street. He paused at a bomb site on the way. Rosenthal's had arranged for the loan for the building that would go up here, and Gerry had done all the preliminary work. Bernard had said his analysis was faultless and, even though he had gone on to find several faults, Gerry had been delighted. It was one of Bill Staple's sites, this. Lord, the man was clever! His rivals were forever saying he was overpaying for the sites that came up for sale and was altogether stretched beyond his means, but Gerry could see the overall strategy. Every penny Staple made was put back into the business. Not for him the Rolls Royce, the holidays on the Continent, the wife in an extravagant fur coat. Not now, not yet . . . but in a few years, if he so wished, Staple would be sipping cocktails on the terrace of some villa in the South of France while his rivals were still reaping heart attacks in the City of London. To be sure, his debts were huge, but his potential assets were beginning to make Diana's fortune look . . . well, if not puny then something near life size. Gerry liked and admired Bill Staple but he did not envy him. If there were no risks in this business of rebuilding London, then everyone would be doing it and everyone would be a millionaire, and Diana would complain even more about her favourite haunts being filled with 'utterly unsuitable people'. And what if Staple's contractors went broke, or there was a stoppage in any one of the factories on which he depended for supplies? A month's stoppage would soon knock the gilt off the top.

Gerry went on and through the door of the building that housed Rosenthal's. He ran up the two flights of stairs and greeted Mrs Stein, the receptionist and switchboard operator.

'You're to go to a conference,' she told him. 'Now.'

'A conference? Where?'

'Mr Rosenthal's office. . . . It's all right, Gerry, you're not late.'

Gerry went to his desk, nodded at young Daniel Borchardt, who was always in first, just as Gerry was always in second and Rupert last, dumped his briefcase and went down the corridor to the room where all this had started. On the wall now there was a photograph of Frantic winning the Rose of York. Gerry and Diana – and Patrick – had been there and it had been a thrilling day.

Bernard's secretary indicated that he should go in, so he knocked on the door and did so.

'Ah, Beviss,' Bernard said. 'We were just discussing Hamer's Gracechurch Street development . . . This is Paul Marling, Beviss, who will be overseeing all your work from now on. He's been in New York working with my cousin—'

'But *for* you, sir,' the man put in quickly.

'—though I'm sure you'll find he understands London well enough. This is Gerald Beviss, Paul. He's been with us for less than a year but is rapidly coming to understand the complexities of our business, and is something of an expert on construction. Isn't that so, Beviss?'

'Hardly that, sir, but I'm trying.'

Paul Marling looked sharply at Gerry, inclined his head and said nothing.

'You'll want to talk Hamer's proposal through,' Bernard said, 'so I'll let you go now.' He stretched his hand out to Paul Marling, and they both stood up. 'Thank you for the work you did in New York.'

'I'm your man, sir. You know that,' Paul Marling said.

Gerry collected his file on Giles Hamer and went to the room assigned to his new boss. Paul Marling spoke hardly at all as he read through the file, just asking two or three questions and nodding at Gerry's replies.

'I'll keep this if I may,' he said when he had finished, closing the file and pushing it to one side. He kept his hand on it as though Gerry might try and grab it from him.

'Of course, sir,' Gerry said, unnerved by the man's distant

manner and his cold blue eyes. 'But I'll need it later . . . Will we be working on it together?'

Marling did not speak for a moment. His long fingers tapped the file. 'Tell me,' he said at last, 'where did Mr Rosenthal find you?'

'Find me?' Gerry repeated blankly.

'How did he come to offer you a job?'

Gerry paused. He did not want to go into details.

'We were having lunch, and I asked him for one,' he said. 'We had some . . . business to discuss.'

'Business!'

Paul Marling considered this, frowning a little, and then something that might have been a smile stretched his lips.

'To answer your question, Beviss: yes, we will be working on this together and several other projects. As Mr Rosenthal said, I shall be supervising your work in future, and' – he consulted a piece of paper on his desk – 'that of Mr Rupert Stevenson. Would you be so kind as to ask him to come and see me?'

Gerry escaped, returned to the office he shared with Rupert and Daniel and told Rupert – who had only just arrived – to go on parade before their new sergeant major. Rupert picked up a file at random from his desk and went out. Half an hour later he came back, looking somewhat shell-shocked.

'You next, Daniel,' he said, and nineteen-year-old Daniel turned pale and fled. Rupert brought out the bottle of brandy he kept in his desk for emergencies and poured some into both his and Gerry's coffee cups.

'I don't like this, Gerry. I do not. This man Marling has plans. It's very worrying.'

'Plans to make you work, you mean?' said Gerry.

Rupert had been at Rosenthal's for five years, could easily have been a few rungs up the ladder by now and not sharing an office with the new boys like Daniel and Gerry. He was more than capable at his job – as Gerry was beginning to recognise – but he was idle and only ever did the minimum to get by.

'Very worrying indeed,' Rupert said again, as Daniel came back from his talk with Paul Marling. He waved the bottle. 'Want one?'

'No thanks,' said Daniel.

'How did you get on with the *Führer?*'

'He's not so bad. He knows what he's doing and wants to be sure that we do too. ... Here's your file on Hamer, Gerry. He asked me to give it back to you.'

Gerry took it, picked up his phone and asked Mrs Stein to get him a number. This Marling would not trouble him: he knew what he was doing and when he didn't he knew to ask. He worked hard, and if Bernard approved of him so, too, would the new man.

Nick O'Rourke was not the only one to emerge from exile in the armed forces and appear in the City of London in civilian uniform. Many of the men who had been a year ahead of Gerry at Cambridge came, and Patrick – who had already done his National Service – was occupying himself, not very strenuously, in a stockbroking firm. One day in November, Mark turned up at Coate's Wine Bar, homing in on it instinctively, it seemed, and bought them all champagne to celebrate the birth of his son. Lunchtimes were like the Pitt Club, or, rather, a combination between there and the Bullingdon at Oxford, with the atmosphere bracingly masculine and the laughter flowing with the booze. It was, for Gerry, a marvellous antidote to the petulance, hysteria, the protestations of love or of indifference (most people could not protest indifference: Diana could, and did it often) he encountered in the Mayfair house. Remembering Bernard's strictures on these lunches, Gerry kept his down to an hour and a half, but for the others three hours out of the office was regular. And the contacts were undoubtedly useful, for even other novice merchant bankers would offer a tip or two, or information, and soon Gerry had a network of contacts all connected by the old school tie he did not possess and knotted by his membership of the Pitt Club. Now, when he needed to know something, he would pick up the phone and say, 'Listen, old fellow, what do you know of So-and-so? What's the gen on the such-and-such?' And a call would come back saying, 'We hear he's sound and the site's all right, but talk to Bailey of Roche's. Know him? He's a nice chap. Tell him I said to call.' And Gerry would call Bailey of Roche's, they would have lunch or a drink together and the network would extend. And Gerry received the phone calls too.

But in spite of all this, things were not going well for Gerry at work. Paul Marling did not like him and Gerry was at a loss to explain why. On the whole, Marling left Rupert, lazy Rupert, alone and Daniel he positively beamed at, but nothing Gerry could do was right. At first it didn't particularly worry him because Bernard was there and always found time to see all his juniors and give them a word or two of encouragement and support. He amazed Gerry by the way he knew everything that was going on.

'You've got into the Oxbridge set, then,' he had said one day . . . 'No—' as Gerry opened his mouth to apologise or protest. 'No, an hour and a half is perfectly acceptable. I have no objection, only a word of warning: don't overlook the groundwork. Your friends don't know as much as either they or you think they do. You have an aptitude for this business, Beviss, an instinctive approach which is of incalculable value. Don't lose it.'

'Yes, sir, and thank you.'

'Oh, and Beviss—'

Gerry, about to leave, turned at the door.

'Back my horse at Newbury next week. He's a big colt who's taken all year to come to himself, but he's leaving them standing on the gallops now. We want to get a run into him before the end of the season . . .' He laughed in the way Patrick laughed when he was sure the horse he'd backed was going to run as he dreamed it should. 'He's a certainty. The trainer is talking about the Derby. Imagine that! . . . Ah well, someone has to provide the also-rans, don't they?'

But early in the New Year, Bernard went to Israel for three months, and left Paul Marling in charge. Marling never shouted. He would tell Gerry in his cold, clipped voice – within the hearing of the secretaries, if possible – that he had made mistakes, left calculations out, was guilty of misreading a situation, and would Mr Beviss kindly remember that it was errors of judgement like this that could lead to Mr Rosenthal losing his credibility in the City? Gerry, already having taken to heart Bernard's warning,

234

now began to treble-check everything he did, and this made him lose the intuitive sense that Bernard had so admired. And, in addition, because of his caution, he was reprimanded for being slow.

'It's not fair,' he said to Diana, so upset that he had forgotten for a moment that he did not have the kind of wife who would sympathise with his plight and soothe his worried brow. 'There's Rupert, sitting with his feet up reading the paper all morning, and I'm accused of being slow. It's not fair.'

He turned, his drink in his hand, and found his wife was staring at him in angry amazement.

'Of what possible interest could this be to me?' she asked. 'You and your fucking job. Either you *or* your fucking job? . . . I can't think why I'm here.' She stood up and handed her glass to him for a refill. 'I'm going to Rio for the Carnival, I've decided.'

'I thought we'd said we'd both go next year—'

'Next year! Twelve utterly boring months away!'

'I can't come now, Diana.'

Another furiously amazed look.

'Who the hell invited you to?'

'No one,' he said. 'No one.'

She sailed with her mother and stepfather the following week, and as he left the *Queen Elizabeth* to go ashore, she clung to him and kissed him and cried that she would miss him quite dreadfully.

He drove back towards London. He could not help a great bubble of freedom rising inside him and coming out of his mouth in a huge, stupid smile. He was free. Free for maybe two or three months, for Diana surely would not come straight back, and he could not feel guilty about it. Any guilt Diana had felt had been dispersed in those tears she had shed and Gerry had no doubt that she was, as he was thinking about this, already on her third elaborate cocktail in one of the liner's first-class bars.

He stopped the car. It was Friday and he wasn't expected back in the office. He had a whole weekend. He turned the Aston around and headed eastward along the A27. A weekend of his mother's cooking, a few jars with the lads in the Anchor tonight – not served by Molly, Molly wasn't there; she had married one of her regulars and was a respectable matron in Hastings now – he

235

could have a good chat with Arthur, long rides on Florin instead of the short, snatched ones he usually only had time for between arriving and leaving.

His respite lasted only for that weekend. On Monday Gerry was once more summoned to Paul Marling's office. The secretary, Linda Levy, who was taking dictation, rose and made to leave but Marling gestured to her to stay, and she sat back and reluctantly watched and heard Gerry, yet again, being ground up in Marling's mill. Gerry was recommending another loan to Bill Staple . . . Was he, Marling asked, quite mad? Did he know exactly how big Staple's debts were?

'Yes, sir, but I also know his asset strength,' Gerry said. 'He's never defaulted on his payments yet, and the building on Cheapside is finished four months ahead of schedule. He'll sell it or let it out—'

'Which?'

'I don't know, sir. Whichever is best.'

'Isn't it your business to know?'

'He will do what is best.'

'For him or for us?'

'What is good for him is good for us.'

'What if he does neither?'

Gerry stared blankly at his boss. Bill Staple allow a completed building to stand empty? He'd sell or let it next week!

'I said, what if he does neither?'

'He won't,' Gerry said, and then he added, his temper getting the better of him, 'You know he bloody won't!'

'I don't know any such thing,' Marling said, a look of satisfaction crossing his face. 'And I will thank you if you will not in future swear in my office. I do not care for your street habits here. You will say no to Mr Staple—' He tossed the file across the desk, and Linda Levy picked it up and handed it to Gerry. 'And' – Marling flicked over another file – 'yes to this man Smith.'

'Harold Smith?' Gerry said, aghast. 'But he's in trouble. All his work is at a standstill. He's only come to us to pay off his other creditors, not for the construction at all.'

'How do you know that?'

'It's common knowledge.'

'Did Mr Staple tell you?'

'Him – and others,' Gerry admitted.

'Ah,' said Paul Marling, 'so Staple is not only duping you about his own position, but about his rivals' as well . . . I said, you will deny Staple and accept Harold Smith. No more arguments. That will be all, Beviss.'

'It's crazy,' Gerry said, for the fifth time as he brought drinks from the bar to where Andrew Coleridge, Thomas Ewhurst, Patrick and Nick were sitting.

'Harold Smith has defaulted on us,' Thomas said. 'We'd love you to fund him because then we'd get our lolly back.'

'He came to us,' Andrew said, 'and we told him to run away.' He took a gulp of his gin and tonic and looked at his watch. 'You're right, Gerry, your Marling man is not making sense. Help, I must dash. I've got to meet Rosie and her parents for dinner so I better scuttle along and shave and things.'

He and Thomas left together. Nick looked at Gerry.

'I don't pretend to understand,' he said, 'but you've been told to refuse this Staple who everyone says is as solid as twenty tons of rock and take on Smith who is as safe as quicksand. Is this right?'

'Yes.'

'Who gets the blame if Smith defaults?' Patrick asked.

'Marling must, I suppose, but it wouldn't look good for me,' Gerry said. 'Not at all, it wouldn't.'

'Put lots of memos to Marling in the files,' Nick advised him. 'Cover yourself, that's the thing.'

'And I'd ask the bloke why he's got a down on you,' Patrick said. 'Ask him, man to man. If you don't like his answer you can always walk out. It's not as though you need the job, after all.'

'But I do need it.'

'Nonsense,' Patrick said, and then a thought struck him. 'Diana hasn't left you, has she? This trip to the Southern Hemisphere isn't a euphemism for the old divorce, is it?'

Gerry smiled faintly. He'd had a letter from Diana that morning, pages of it, reminiscent of those she'd sent him at Cambridge.

'No,' he said, his mind still on Paul Marling. 'No, she hasn't left me.' But his heart lurched as he spoke, and so rapidly did it happen that he could not identify it as either hope or fear.

Gerry sedulously researched Harold Smith, and discovered he owed money everywhere, not just to other merchant banks, but to his professional advisers, his builders and suppliers as well. And everything he had always known about Bill Staple proved to be true: the man was as solid, as Nick had said, as a rock. As Gerry had predicted, he had tenants ready to move into his new building as soon as the plasterers had moved out.

'There won't be trouble about the other site, will there?' he asked Gerry. 'The money from these new leases is going into some flats up Stepney way, and I can raise the readies for this other development anywhere.'

'I know that, Bill. There'll be no trouble,' Gerry assured him, hoping it was true.

'I like you, young Gerry, and I know you'll see me right – not, mind, that I need any favours.'

He didn't. He was as near to gold-plated as anyone could be, and he knew it and Gerry knew it, and why could or would not Paul Marling see it?

Gerry went to Paul Marling with the evidence against Harold Smith and laid it before him: Smith could be near bankruptcy, four other merchant banks had sent him away with an unequivocal refusal, the site he was proposing to develop with the money loaned through Rosenthal's had no obvious potential. It was not in the City, not in a residential area and was, in fact, a warehouse on the river somewhere near Wapping and it seemed that Gerry's original assessment – that he intended to do nothing with the site but use Rosenthal's to pay off debts and provide funding for his other half-completed projects – was absolutely correct.

'I thought I told you to put that loan through a week ago,' Marling said sharply, but the evidence was there before him and he could not insist now. His fingers drummed on the desk as he scanned Gerry's report and, for once, he seemed discomposed. Gerry stole his moment and slipped the assessment of Bill Staple's business across the desk under Paul Marling's steely blue eyes.

'All right,' Marling said, without looking up but with fury in his voice. 'Refuse Harold Smith.'

'And accept Staple?'

'Refuse him too.'

'But sir—'

'Refuse him.'

'Why?'

'Because I say so.'

Gerry took a deep breath. 'I was right about Harold Smith and I'm right about Staple. I want to know why you block everything I suggest and decide against my recommendations all the time. It doesn't seem reasonable.'

Marling steepled his fingers.

'Not reasonable?'

'No, sir.'

Paul Marling looked at him, and then said to Linda Levy, 'Please leave us,' which she did, with a quick, anxious glance at Gerry.

'Evidently,' Paul Marling said after a long moment, 'my name means nothing to you. But your name means a very great deal to me. It was the double *s* you spell it with. I noticed it at once. Unusual, I thought. But what, I asked myself, is a man with this name doing talking like a gentleman, looking like a gentleman and, by all accounts, acting like one too? Could this man, I asked myself, could this same man who has an address in Mayfair and met Bernard Rosenthal on a "business" matter be none other than the son of thieving gypsy Beviss?'

Gerry started forward and then stood very still. Marling waved a hand.

'Sit, Beviss.'

'I'd rather stand.'

'Sit, I say.'

Gerry sat on the edge of the seat Linda Levy had vacated. Marling nodded, satisfied.

'Gypsies are supposed to be wild, but this one, I see, is nicely tamed.'

Gerry half rose.

'Stay!'

Gerry sat again. Again Paul Marling nodded.

'Quite nicely tamed. It knows how to sit and stay. Now, where was I?' He tilted his chair back and gazed at the ceiling. 'So I made some enquiries,' he went on. 'It was very simple . . .' He looked hard at Gerry. 'All I had to do was go and see my parents in the shack they inhabit in Hastings . . . Ah! *Now* my name means something? Four generations of Marlings lived at Ridge Farm on the edge of the Sussex Weald before thieving gypsy Beviss took it away. . . . You don't speak, Beviss with a double *s*?'

He was Dennis Marling's son! Gerry knew there was a daughter – Arthur had gone out with her for a time – but he didn't remember a son. But then why should he? He'd been away, first, presumably, because of the war and then in New York. It didn't matter. There was a son and he was sitting opposite Gerry now.

'It doesn't seem inclined to speak. A pity. I had hoped it might come out with some gypo curse. Never mind. To continue my tale . . .' Marling swung his chair round and stared out of the window. 'The gentlemanly appearance of my little Beviss puzzled me, but a visit to the south coast soon cleared that up. Thieving gypsy Beviss had spawned three sons and one of them managed to scrabble its way to Trinity College, Cambridge, and it came back to the place it dares call home transformed. Not looking or sounding like a thieving gypo at all. Not at all . . .' Now Marling swung his chair back and faced Gerry again. He folded his hands on his desk and continued, almost conversationally. 'From this point I proceeded with my investigations most carefully, because I discovered an extraordinary thing. . . . Do you want to know what it is?'

'You're going to tell me,' Gerry said.

Marling laughed coldly. 'I am! The thing I discovered was that thieving gypsy Beviss junior had made all manner of smart friends at Cambridge, it had married a millionairess, who turns out to be no better than it deserves, it had acquired a respectable job in the City of London and was even regarded as being promising by its employer . . . and the extraordinary thing I discovered was that no one, *no one*, had any idea whatsoever that it was a thieving gypo under all the trappings! I found this interesting, as you can imagine. It was trying, this little gypo, to hide its background and

240

on the whole it was succeeding admirably. But it *minded* that it was a thieving gypo and didn't want its friends and acquaintances to find out. . . . What do you think of *that*, Beviss with a double *s?*'

Gerry could only think of yesterday lunch, and a crowd of them laughing as Nick O'Rourke described a man in his office, some poor bloke who had achieved officer status in the army during the war and who, apparently, thought this entitled him to be accounted a gentleman. Not as good as Gerry as it, he wasn't: he called his wife 'my lady wife' and, sin of sins, he wore a soft collar. 'My lady wife and Ai—' Nick had begun, and they'd all started talking like that, Gerry among them . . . Gerry had done the best imitation of all.

'Has it got a tongue?' Marling asked.

Gerry stood up and made for the door.

'I'll resign,' he said. He did not, after all, need the job, as Patrick had pointed out, even though he needed it in ways Patrick could not imagine. Paul Marling's voice, steel-clad in velvet, followed him.

'Oh no you will not.'

Gerry stopped.

'If you resign I will tell everyone what I know of you and your family. Such tales will I spread of you in the City that your fancy friends will wish they had never met you. . . . Stay and I will not reveal your secret. That I promise you.'

Gerry turned, a puppet on a string, hope springing. Not all gone, then? Not everything?

'Come back and sit down,' Paul Marling said gently.

Feeling utterly humiliated but unable to resist, Gerry did so.

'Good!' said Paul Marling. 'No, little gypo, I will not reveal your secret—'

'But there are conditions,' Gerry said wearily.

'Of course! Your father watched mine suffer as, acre by acre, he took his land away and now I'm going to have the pleasure of watching you suffer too.'

'How? How am I going to suffer, for God's sake?'

'Not to the same degree,' Paul Marling conceded, 'but one must work with the tools one has. My conditions are these: that you stay in this firm, that you do not reveal this conversation to a single soul, and you do not again question any orders I give you. If you run to the shelter of your wife's money or attempt to find another job, I shall tell the world that you are what you are – a thieving gypo. I think,' he went on reflectively, 'that I've judged you correctly. You don't need the salary this firm pays you, so you work for another reason . . . to get away from your wife, perhaps? You could be with her in Brazil now, after all, instead of here with me. Yes, my little gypo, I think I've got you worked out.'

'What satisfaction can it have for you?'

'Me? Oh, I'll make your life as difficult as I can without jeopardising my own position. I don't know about satisfaction, though it will feel good to know that thieving gypsy Beviss junior is under my heel, that's for sure. As I said, one must work with the tools one has.' He smiled at Gerry. 'Come, my little gypo, don't look so tragic. Being a heathen, you have probably never read the Bible, but it says there that the sins of the fathers are visited upon the sons. It's bad luck for you, isn't it?'

'Yes, sir. I'll go now, if I may.'

'By all means. Here—' He slid Gerry's two files over to him. 'Say yes to Staple. He is, as you say, a very sound investment.'

Somehow Gerry got through the rest of that day, accepting the offer of a nip from Rupert's emergency bottle, though refusing to say why he was in such dire need of it, ringing up Staple to tell him the good news, going to Coate's as usual for lunch. He went home that evening and sat in the drawing room, Rio on his knee, and drank whisky steadily. He hoped it would blur the memory of his interview with Marling, but instead it seemed to bring the details into sharper focus: Marling's cold voice calling him 'it' and 'my little gypo' and saying – and oh! how right he was – that he thought he had judged Gerry correctly. Gerry minded about his job and the position he had in the City, minded about them dreadfully. Kate always used to tell him that it didn't matter where he went to school, where he came from, and of course people would speak to him, they were his friends, weren't they? But it did matter, it did, it did! *They* did not like impostors and imitators, and all the war was supposed to have done to destroy the old order, and those few years of a socialist government, did not alter that fact. Look how cruel they had all been about that poor man in Nick's office! . . . They would be even worse about Gerry because they had accepted him and would feel cheated. They would turn their backs as he walked into Coate's and refuse to talk to him . . . It was too horrible to contemplate. He would do whatever Paul Marling said rather than have that happen to him. All he had that was his own was his job at Rosenthal's and the camaraderie of the Oxbridge set, as Bernard had called it. These things were his, and he'd do anything to keep them.

Chapter 16

It turned out that Gerry didn't, in fact, have to do a great deal. Since Diana was away and he was not going out every night, he took work back to the Mayfair house and ensured that there were no loopholes, not the tiniest pinprick through which Paul Marling could drive his withering wedge of criticism, and – remembering what Nick had said – he wrote interminable memos after every meeting with Marling, recording what had been said and decided, timed and dated them and had them filed. Marling would call him 'my little gypo' and insult him in every way he could think of but the man was not very imaginative and the repetition took the sting out of what he said. Gerry worried that he would become as bored with the whole thing as Gerry himself was and decide to take further action, so he always looked what he hoped was suitably chastised. And then Bernard came back and Marling had less time to torment his little gypsy.

In spite of everything, it was a peaceful time for Gerry. He and Suckers and Rio got on beautifully together. Suckers, at first shocked, then intrigued and finally challenged, was teaching Gerry to cook. He went to Ridge Farm most weekends and brought back fish – some of it frozen, to Suckers's scandalised exclamations – and said he wanted to learn how to make it taste delicious, and if Suckers wouldn't show him he'd give the lot to Rio. Suckers was flattered by the idea that she could, indeed, make it delicious for nannies, she told him, were not usually turned into cooks and housekeepers in their later years but, she conceded, she'd picked up a thing or two.

'At least ten things, I'd say, Suckers,' Gerry said.

'Well, perhaps I have. But if you and Mrs Beviss are going to do a lot of entertaining when she gets back, we'll have to employ a cook.'

'We could save the money if you teach me properly.'

'Oh you *silly* boy!' she said, consigning him to the nursery but heaving with laughter at the idea of anyone in this house having to consider money. She wanted to tell him that she had only been employed by the Daltons when Diana was nine years old and already hopelessly spoiled, that her authority had been constantly undermined by Mr and Mrs Dalton's indulgence. And much had to be forgiven a child who had lost a greatly loved father so suddenly and horribly when she was fifteen. Much, to be sure, but Diana pushed everything to the limits and beyond. Suckers knew what Gerry had to put up with and thought he was a saint to remain so sweet natured . . . But of these things, of course, neither of them could speak as they tasted sauces and Rio entwined himself around their legs, his purrs turning to young growls as he smelt the fish being cooked.

And most Friday evenings, Gerry went home to Ridge Farm and came back on Sunday ready to face Paul Marling on the Monday morning, not considering for a moment the irony of it. He was not ashamed of his family – he was *not* – but they were and always had been in a different world than the rest of his life. As a child he had moved from one world to the other by switching accents . . . too posh for the fisher lads, too rough for the boys at the grammar school. One man born and another one made by education and polished into a gentleman by Cambridge. He was used to travelling from one world to the other and hiding one from the other had become second nature, the little lies coming so easily that he no longer considered them lies at all. And now Paul Marling was threatening a collision between the two worlds and this would ruin him, he was sure. Ruin him and leave him floating in a limbo between them.

Patrick and Gerry were going to the Guineas meeting at Newmarket – 'Your last outing as a bachelor,' Patrick told him, for Diana was coming back a week later. They had booked rooms .

245

at the Blue Boar in Cambridge and would drive to Newmarket in the Aston Martin each day; the evenings would, they decided, be spent in the Pitt or around the colleges. They would pretend they were undergraduates again, but with all the advantage of seniority.

'We'll bustle up the proctors,' Patrick said. 'Give them hell and they won't be able to lay a finger on us.'

Gerry was looking forward to it. It meant he had to take two days off work and, as only he was required to do, he wrote a memorandum to Paul Marling saying which days he would be away and detailing how much holiday this left him. Rupert was forever not turning up and nothing was ever said to him, but Gerry was used to the unfairness. Even so, he was surprised to receive a summons from Paul Marling and shocked to be told that the days he wanted off were 'not convenient' and he could take them the next week instead.

'But it has to be that week,' Gerry said, wondering how on earth he would explain to Patrick that he would not be able to come, and the hotel rooms booked and everything.

'Dear me, why?' asked Paul Marling. 'Why is my little gypo so insistent? I thought I had it well trained.'

'I'm entitled to—'

'You are entitled to nothing, gypo. I wish you would remember that.'

'It must be that week,' Gerry repeated. 'I've given plenty of notice.'

Marling laughed. 'When will you learn, gypo, snivelling little whelp of a thief that you are, that between you and me normal rules do not apply? You want—'

He stopped, his face suddenly white. Gerry turned and saw Bernard Rosenthal standing in the doorway.

'Leave us, Beviss, please,' he said, his eyes on Paul Marling.

Half an hour later, Gerry was called to Bernard's office.

'Is it true?' Bernard asked.

'Is what true?'

'That you come from a gypsy family.'

'Yes, sir,' Gerry said, unable to lie before Bernard's steady gaze. 'But my father didn't steal the house from Mr Marling's father. He paid a fair price. He told me so.' Joe hated revealing anything about his dealings, but this much Gerry had squeezed out of him. Bernard was silent, and Gerry went on: 'He was in trouble, Dennis Marling was. His sheep were starving that winter of '47 in all the snow. The boys would go up and count the corpses . . . their idea of fun. Dennis Marling didn't have the money to feed them, you see.'

Bernard came over to him and put his hands on Gerry's shoulders.

'You a gypsy, me a Jew. We have a lot in common, do you know that?'

'No, sir,' Gerry said, feeling completely confused.

'You don't know that Adolf Hitler planned to rid the world of gypsies as well as Jews? Tribes of gypsies – your people, Gerry – vanished in Europe. No one will ever know how many went.'

'They're not my people,' Gerry said. 'I don't see what it's got to do with me.'

Bernard shook him gently.

'Face up to what you are.'

'I'm nothing. I was born in a gypsy caravan and my father is a fisherman.'

'My grandfather,' Bernard commented, 'was a Ukrainian peasant. I said we had a lot in common: the difference between us is that I never pretended to be anything other than what I am – Jewish. No enemy, real or imagined, could hold that over me.'

'It was all a mistake,' Gerry said. 'I didn't mean it to happen.' And he found himself telling Bernard everything – about the Rector, Arthur, the chain of events that got him elected to the Pitt Club. Everything. Bernard listened and said, when Gerry had come to a somewhat incoherent halt:

'You couldn't have hidden it for ever, you know. It's best it comes to an end now. You will lose some friends, I daresay, but you will know that they are not true friends and so not worth bothering about, and you will find, as I do, that some doors are closed to you. You will also find that Paul Marling cannot . . . torment you any more. A man who calls you a gypo may call me a yid and such a man I will not have in my firm.'

Gerry was horrified. 'You've sacked him?'

'I have invited him to leave my employment, yes.'

'But now he'll tell everyone about me. Everyone will know.'

'You haven't been listening to me, Gerry. Listen now: you are a fine, intelligent young man. You are not "nothing" and I wish never to hear you say that word about yourself again. Do you understand?'

'Yes, sir,' said Gerry distractedly.

'And remember: face up to what you are.'

After all that, they did not go to Newmarket. Patrick's father died of a heart attack two days before the meeting started, the phone to his bookmaker in one hand, a copy of the *Sporting Life* on his knee. And the bet he had just struck was another losing one.

Diana came back and for a while seemed happy to be with her husband. She burbled away about how wonderful Rio was, how divine the Carnival, what fun the endless parties had been, how an utterly sweet couple she had met were taking a villa near Cannes for July and August and had invited her – and Gerry, too, of course – to visit them there.

'Shall we go, Gerry?' she asked.

'Why not? We'll drive down.'

And so Diana, with another trip abroad to look forward to, was uncomplaining and, for her, undemanding, and Gerry could concentrate his mind elsewhere.

Paul Marling was spreading his poison. Gerry could see it in the curious glances he received from the men Marling knew, from the way heads leaned towards each other as they discussed something they did not want other people to hear (this is the way to spread gossip: whisper it. Shout it out loud and no one will listen); from the way, once, as Gerry went to the bar to order drinks, a group fell abruptly silent before beginning to talk, rather obviously, about the team just announced for the Test match. Gerry could only hope that the talk would die away in time – for, after all, what possible interest could he be to these senior City men?

But, relieved of his daily presence, Gerry underestimated Paul Marling. In spite of the fact that, with Bernard's influence and excellent references, he had quickly found another job, he blamed

Gerry for the humiliation of being sacked. As far as he was concerned, this was the second time a Beviss had ruined a Marling, and he would make sure Beviss's precious Oxbridge friends knew exactly who and what he was. Ridge Farm was lost for ever, but this thing he could gain.

They went to France, driving south in convoy with three other couples, Diana explaining blithely that they could swap travelling companions and this would make the journey 'less utterly tedious'. Gerry had stopped noticing how his wife avoided being in his company. Another woman in the house party at the villa near Cannes saw how it was and attempted a flirtation, but Gerry swam, sunbathed and drank cocktails and didn't have the energy to do anything else other than satisfy Diana every night which, for once, he seemed to be able to do and get a good night's sleep as well. He returned to London, fit and brown, and went back to work. He had almost forgotten about Marling, and was startled, when he walked into Coate's, to be greeted by Nick O'Rourke, a set look on his face, saying, 'Is it true?'

As he had said when asked that same question by Bernard Rosenthal, 'Is what true?' Gerry asked.

'They say you're some kind of gypsy . . . that you went to a grammar school' – he made the words sound like a curse – 'and your father catches – *fish*! Is it true?'

Gerry took a deep breath. He had never told a direct lie about it before. Lots of half and quarter truths which added up to a mountain of lies, but never a direct one.

Face up to what you are.

'Yes,' he said. 'Yes, it's true.' And then he added: 'I'm sorry.'

'Well . . . well, good God! A grammar school squirt . . . And to think,' Nick said, his voice high with indignation, 'and to think I bloody well put you up for the Pitt Club. You're a damned bounder, Beviss, a bounder and a worm. Excuse me.'

He put down his glass and walked out.

Gerry stood there, stunned. His drink was on the bar, but he didn't think he would be able to pick it up. This was as bad as his worst imaginings.

'The Anglo-Irish,' someone remarked finally, 'always were the most crashing snobs.'

'Is Nick Anglo-Irish?' someone else enquired.

'Must be with a name like that.'

'But the Anglo-Irish are Irish with English names, not the other way round, aren't they?'

The wrangle went on and another round of drinks was bought.

'Do you have a caravan, old boy? One of those ornate painted jobs with pots and pans hanging around it?'

Gerry turned. It was James Thorpe, an Oxford man who worked for another merchant bank. One of the network.

'No,' Gerry replied, smiling faintly. 'We don't. Not any more.'

'Where do you live then?'

Gerry lifted up his pint of beer, pleased to see his hand wasn't shaking.

'Actually,' he said, 'I live in Mayfair. Clarges Street, you know.'

Everyone laughed.

'So you're not a real gypsy at all.' James Thorpe sounded disappointed.

'Yes, I am,' Gerry said, feeling more confident. 'The only reason you can't tell straight away is because I don't wear my earring with my suit. It gets tangled in the collar of my shirt, you see.'

The conversation then became general and Gerry walked back to the office, still feeling shaken by Nick's reaction but thinking if that was the only one and as bad as ever it would be he would survive.

'Of course you'll survive,' Bernard told him. 'And I'd like my firm to survive, too, so perhaps now you could do some work?' But then he gripped Gerry's shoulder and added, 'Well done, Gerry. I understand the courage it takes, you know.'

Gerry thought that he probably loved the man, loved him as though he were another father.

There was whispering and gossip and, as Bernard had told him, he did lose some friends. Nick O'Rourke and some others simply did not speak to him, but no one else seemed to take violent exception. Would this have been the case if Gerry had told the whole truth about himself from the beginning? He was sure it wouldn't. He had no regrets.

'Your old man's a gypsy and a fisherman?' Patrick exclaimed. 'Come on, Gerry, that's pushing it.'

'Strange, maybe, but true. He has a fleet of fishing boats.'

'Well, it's a sight more than my father had, I can tell you.'

Patrick had given up his spasmodic job as a stockbroker and had been at Rede Park since his father's death. Gerry had seen little of him and was taken aback when he came to stay for a night in September. He was nervy, drawn and tired and there were lines about his eyes.

'I reckon it's all over,' he said. 'I can't tell you the debts the old man left. Two thousand to his bookmaker alone, and I can't begin to pay that, let alone the death duties. I'll have to sell.'

'Sell your house?' Diana said. 'How utterly dreadful.'

'Must you really?' Gerry asked.

'Gerry, the place is falling about my ears. The roof leaks and meets the rising damp somewhere on the first floor, and I'm sure there's every sort of rot known to man, fungus and insect in the woodwork.' He paused. 'I'll hate to see it go but there's no choice.'

They talked on until Gerry got to his feet and said he was going to see about supper.

'See what about it?' asked Patrick.

'He helps Suckers cook,' Diana said dismissively. 'God knows why.'

'I enjoy it, and I don't get much chance to practise on you. It's fun entertaining at home.'

'It's not.'

'Well, thanks,' Patrick said.

'Oh darling, I didn't mean you! Patrick, I didn't . . . You go away,' she said to Gerry. 'Go and do your stupid cooking. Patrick and I can manage here utterly, can't we, darling?'

Gerry left them, went downstairs and, supervised by Suckers, made a mornay sauce.

'Just don't tell her it's cod she's eating, that's all,' Suckers said. 'It's all the fishmonger had, and now you don't go to your folks so often I have to take what's there.'

'Why will she mind eating cod?'

'Just don't tell her.'

'All right. I'll say it's fillets of sole. . . . Taste this, Suckers.'

'Excellent,' she said, rolling it around on her tongue as though it were a fine wine. 'You get them to the table now. The pâté's there, and I'll bring up the toast.'

Gerry went back upstairs. As he opened the drawing room door, Diana launched herself at him.

'Darling!' she cried. 'We've had an utterly super idea. We're going to get Patrick's racecourse going, and then he won't have to sell his house. Isn't that exciting? A racecourse of our very own!'

Gerry, his wife's curly hair tickling his chin, looked at Patrick, who smiled and winked at him.

'Say it's a super idea, Gerry. *Say* it!'

'It is,' Gerry said, 'a super idea.'

Diana would not have noticed if it was cod or whale she was eating, so taken was she by the racecourse. She seemed to think that all they needed was the horses and then they'd be away, and when Gerry pointed out that they'd also need grandstands, car parks, a paddock, enclosures, stabling – the list went on – she shrugged her shoulders and said casually, 'We can build them.'

The look of outraged disbelief on both their faces when he said that she didn't have enough money was comical.

'I know about construction,' Gerry said. 'I can't tell you how much it would cost, but, Diana, I know it's more – a lot more – than you could comfortably afford. All in one go, anyway.'

Diana lit a cigarette and steamed.

'But you also know about raising money,' Patrick put in, quickly recovering his composure. 'You're forever loaning the stuff out: why not borrow it for a change?'

'We lend it for something that's going to be let or sold. This is different. It's total speculation . . . Still,' he went on, excited in spite of himself and in spite of his suspicions about Patrick, 'we could bring other people in, spread the risk – Bernard!' he exclaimed. 'Bernard's our man. He'll know if it's possible.'

'Gerry, that's bloody brilliant . . . No, Diana, it *is*,' Patrick said as Diana was about to protest that Bernard was boring. 'Gerry's right. We need an older head. Rosenthal's not a member of the Jockey Club, but he knows a lot of chaps who are, and we'll need them too. Ask him, Gerry. Ask him *tomorrow*.'

'Promise, Gerry. Promise, utterly.'

'I'll ask him.'

They went out to a nightclub, where they met up with a party of Diana's friends, and arrived back in the early hours of the morning. Diana went straight to bed and Gerry forced a nightcap on Patrick.

'To Rede Park Racecourse,' Patrick said, raising his glass.

'All right, but Patrick, how long have you been planning all this?'

Patrick laughed. 'Come on, drink the toast . . . Look here, old boy. If she wouldn't have me, you were the next best thing. You don't mind, do you? It'll keep her out of mischief for a while, I'll have my house and we'll all have a racecourse to play with. Think of it, Gerry: the turf great-grandfather laid down put to its rightful use at last. Think how exciting it is!'

So Patrick had had Diana's money in mind for Rede Park from the moment she had shown an interest in Gerry . . . well, so what? Gerry didn't mind. And he never thought to ask – or even think about – the mischief Patrick mentioned that Diana might get up to.

For it *was* exciting. Gerry would never forget how Bernard's all-seeing eyes swept over the oval-shaped bowl and began to sparkle as he said, 'Come on, let's walk!' How, leaving Diana and Bernard's wife, Rebecca, to the dubious comforts of Rede Park, they set off in a soft rain which cleared as they rounded what would be the home turn and the sun shot a beam of light between the clouds on to the hill where the grandstands would be. How Bernard stopped a little way up the straight and said, 'Something's missing,' and turned, laughed, and said to Patrick, 'Your great-grandfather was a wise and clever man. We have a course capable of staging any race here! . . . What? You've not noticed it before? *Look*, boy! Can't you see?' And he had to show them that the three fields they were looking at were, in fact, also part of the racecourse, extending it beyond the oval so there was a straight course for sprint races. Patrick and Gerry were sent into the hedges that made the fields as though they were a couple of terriers and they came out looking bedraggled and reported that there were no ditches. 'Of course there wouldn't be,' Bernard said with

253

satisfaction, accepting the handful of blackberries Gerry gave him. 'By God, Morgan, I wish I could have met your great-grandpapa! . . . What's up there?' He gestured to the hill where the sun was shining. 'Is there a road?' he asked Patrick impatiently.

'About a mile away. The road to Leighminster.'

'Perfect! Is it across your land?'

'Not all of it.'

'Not so perfect. Gerry, have you some paper and a pen? I've got a pen – here.' Gerry found a crumpled envelope in his pocket and was told to write 'access' on it.

They arrived at Great-great-uncle Cyril's wall, which Bernard studied carefully before they climbed over it, using rotting wooden steps. Gerry wrote down 'wall'. On down to the far turn, where Bernard stopped and stared back at Rede Park at the other end of the valley. 'Write "valley – flooding" ' he said to Gerry, and turned to look in the opposite direction. 'What's that?' he asked, peering through trees.

'It's the house Great-great-uncle Cyril built,' Patrick said.

Bernard tramped off through the undergrowth, came back. 'Cyril's house,' he said to Gerry and marched on, the two young men behind him feeling a little like Alice trying to keep up with the Red Queen. Halfway up the back straight, Bernard stopped again and stared for some time at the valley through a break in the trees and hedge, then he paced across the width of the whole course counting as he went.

'Impossible,' he muttered. 'Shame.'

Patrick looked anxiously at Gerry, who grinned at him and turned up his collar as the rain began to fall again.

'Write down local council,' Gerry was told, 'and the distance of the circuit, of course . . . and bloody wall again,' as they negotiated where it crossed this side of the track.

Bernard was silent then until they arrived back at Rede Park, removed their wet outer clothing and entered the library where the ancient dogs occupied the sofa and Diana and Rebecca sat on hard chairs.

'What's the news?' Diana cried as soon as they opened the door, interrupting Mrs Morgan's rambling explanation of how she decided to place the day's bets. She jumped up and ran to Patrick. 'What did he say?'

Patrick shrugged. 'All I heard him say was impossible and what a shame.'

'Bernard – no! Don't be such a spoilsport!'

Rebecca chuckled. 'He's not being a spoilsport. Not when he's looking like that, or I don't know my husband.'

'Why did he say impossible then? Bernard – why?'

'He was trying to fit a jumping track in,' Gerry said. 'And couldn't. That's what I think.'

Bernard smiled at him, his eyes still with that sparkle in them. 'All right, Beviss, since you can read my mind, what do you think I'm going to say?'

'A feasibility study,' Gerry said promptly. 'We have to know the approximate cost of all the work to be done before horses can race here. We need to know as well if a racecourse would be viable at all . . . what the local competition is, what the local council would think, if we could get a right of way for traffic. But I'm defeated by Cyril's house, and "valley flooding" I don't understand at all – surely you don't plan a jumping track there, do you?'

'Does the valley flood?' Bernard asked Patrick.

'Never!' said Mrs Morgan suddenly in a loud, firm voice. Everyone jumped. 'There's a stream. Patrick, tell them about the stream.'

'It gets in and out of the valley underground,' Patrick told Bernard.

'How extraordinary. And it provides drainage?'

'Yes. Then do you think it's possible?' Patrick asked him. 'Could we have a racecourse here?'

'My dear young man, you *have* a racecourse. You're halfway there . . . No, Diana!' he exclaimed as she squealed, wrapped her arms around his neck and kissed his cheek. 'There's a long way to go, much to be done. The cost of the necessary buildings will be enormous – how will that be recouped? Gerry, your report must include studies of other racecourses – which, if any, make money, and why and how.'

'Am I to do it then, sir?'

'If you would like to.'

'I would!'

Diana transferred herself to her husband. 'I'll help you, darling. It'll be utterly super, won't it?' The smoke from her cigarette seemed to dance around her head, taking on her mood.

Bernard stood up. 'I'll have a word with some chaps I know and find out what the Jockey Club would say to all this.' He laughed. 'A new racecourse! Well – why not? . . . And now I suggest we have lunch. Is there a hotel or a pub we could go to, Patrick?'

'The Rede Arms will do us a pie. But what of me?' Patrick said. 'What can I do?'

'You? Ah yes, there are jobs for you. Talk to your neighbour about an access road and find out what your local council would say to the whole scheme. If planning permission is going to be refused we can stop dreaming now, but if the reactions are positive, you can get rid of the wall and those two hedges. By hand, no machinery and no short cuts. Remove the roots with as little disturbance as you can, dig out the foundations of the wall and then leave everything alone. We'll have to get expert help on how best to fill it all in.'

'Right,' said Patrick.

Bernard put out his hand and helped his wife to her feet.

'It's greatly premature,' he said, 'but I think we should drink some champagne.'

Neither would Gerry ever forget those next six months when they all went about their appointed tasks. Patrick courted the old woman who owned the land across which they would need a right of way to the main road and he entertained, in uncharacteristically responsible and sober fashion, the mandarins of the local council. Gerry travelled to racecourses all over the country and examined every aspect of them, talked to the men in charge and made reams of notes. Not one seemed to be making any money and so many were contemplating closure that at times the idea of opening a new racecourse seemed sheer insanity, but the more Gerry saw that winter the more he became convinced it could be done. Bernard's idea of putting a golf course in the valley – that had been 'valley flooding' – and making Great-great-uncle Cyril's house a country club meant that the place would be working for its living most days of the year, not just the few they would have racing on, and this led Gerry to think more. He took architects to Rede Park and made them stand on the frosty or snow-covered hill where the grandstands would be while he explained what he wanted.

It was a time of optimism altogether. Although Diana quickly bored of coming to the racecourses – he couldn't blame her, it was winter and cold – at last they had something in common, something to talk about. For once he was doing something of which she completely approved and they lived in harmony.

Meanwhile, Bernard was doing his work in clubs, at parties and in restaurants, talking, persuading, convincing.

'It's going to happen,' he said to Rebecca. 'It really is!'

'Who is going to pay for it, though?'

'If there's one thing I've learned in my life it's how to raise money. Diana Beviss and I will put in working capital, and so will David Collins and Lionel Moreton. We don't want any others. It would spoil the fun.'

'Fun! Will we have a roof over our heads? I ask myself. You're a careful man, Bernard, or so I always thought. I've never known you plain mad before.'

He laughed, his eyes alight. 'A madcap adventure on a truly grand scale should be allowed every man in his lifetime. But it will work, Rebecca, believe me! Rede Park will rival Goodwood for sheer beauty. For the setting alone it will work.'

'But what if it doesn't?'

'Then Sam will inherit rather less money than he might otherwise have done, but how will he spend it anyway, on his kibbutz?'

Rebecca sighed. 'On wells, on machinery . . . Bernard, on things that make sense!'

'Rede Park Racecourse makes sense,' Bernard said firmly. 'And I have great faith in young Gerry Beviss.'

Patrick set about demolishing the wall, and one evening he rang Gerry and ordered him to Rede Park the following day.

'Bring Diana,' he said. 'You've both got to see this.'

257

When they arrived, he refused to say anything. He found Diana a pair of his mother's wellingtons to replace her high-heeled shoes and led them in the teeth of a brisk wind towards the wall.

'But there's nothing there,' Diana said, who had walked all this way miraculously uncomplainingly.

'That's just it,' Patrick said. 'Nothing but bare earth.'

Gerry clapped Patrick on the back and they both began to laugh.

'What is it? What's so funny?' Diana asked.

Patrick picked her up and hugged her.

'No foundations,' he told her. 'There could – should – have been a two-foot trench here and it wouldn't have been safe for horses to gallop over for God knows how long. It's the best possible news.'

He put Diana down and ran to the side of the course, retrieved the bottle of champagne he had hidden behind a pile of rubble, and they stood there in the biting wind and toasted those two mad, wonderful Victorians who, against all the precepts of their age, had built something definitely not meant to last. The wall would be the finishing line, they decided, and a short section of it left to put the winning post on. The first race run on the course would be called the Cyril and George Morgan Stakes.

'It'll be famous,' Gerry said. 'They'll call it the Cyril and George.'

'And Diana can present the prize,' said Patrick, ever assiduous about keeping the fickle millionairess's interest alight.

Bernard's faith in Gerry was strengthened a few days later when Gerry brought him a series of architects' drawings and plans.

'Look,' he said excitedly. 'The whole thing is designed to be built in three phases to spread the cost, and each phase can be slotted into the previous one. Our stands are going to be very special indeed.' He spread papers all over Bernard's desk. 'I've been going racing all winter, and it's so bloody uncomfortable it's untrue. The bars are tiny, the food – if there is any – is lousy, putting a bet on the Tote is murder . . . We're going to have big bars, and lots of them, and restaurants, too, good ones, so people will want to come to the races early and spend money there.

They'll be able to buy drinks easily, be able to walk from the bars straight out on to the grandstands and watch the racing in comfort, still holding their bloody drinks if they want to. Lots of doors out – see? . . . Now this is where the Tote windows will be, in this circular hall. Clean and spacious. It's got a marble floor—'

'Marble!' Bernard exclaimed. 'Very grand.'

Gerry grinned. 'Ha! The second difference. From the front, the racecourse side, it will look like a grandstand and not much else, but from the back, we want it to look more . . . intimate, if you like. Less functional.'

He drew across another sheet of paper and laid it before Bernard.

'Panels can be fitted from floor to ceiling to cover the Tote windows, even to change the size of the room, maybe, making it look as though the hall just has blank walls. The big plate glass windows on the other side face west, so in summer it won't feel closed in because it will get the evening sun. In winter we'll hang curtains so it all looks cosy.'

Bernard stared at the drawings and shook his head.

'You've lost me, Gerry. Explain.'

'We're not just going to have a country club,' Gerry said. 'It's going to be Rede Park Catering. It will manage the club, the racecourse restaurants and perhaps do outside catering as well. This room could be hired out for wedding receptions, dances, twenty-first birthday parties. Now rationing's just about done with, there's going to be a boom, I'm sure of it, and there'll be a demand for this sort of thing.'

Bernard studied the drawings and was silent for a long time.

'What do you think?' Gerry asked, beginning to feel deflated. 'Is this your idea?'

'Well – yes. I asked the architects if they thought it could be done and they came up with this. People can dance on marble floors, can't they? We don't think a wooden one would stand up to the racecourse crowds and the only other alternative is concrete.'

'People can dance on marble floors,' Bernard said slowly, and then: 'It's brilliant, Gerry. A brilliant idea. Every other racecourse in the land will envy it . . . and copy it, so keep it under your hat.

259

Rede Park Catering,' he went on, still examining the drawings. 'Where do you get it from, Gerry? You are quite in danger of wearing me out.'

Gerry looked at him boldly. 'Why, sir,' he said, 'I think it's in the blood.'

Bernard smiled at him. 'It must be. It surely must, for you didn't learn this at Cambridge, now did you?'

The Jockey Club implied that it had no specific objections and would await a formal application for a licence to hold races under its Rules at Rede Park; Patrick's neighbour said yes to the access road; the local council seemed not to oppose the scheme and the architects drew up blueprints to be submitted to the planning authorities. A company, Rede Park Racecourse Ltd, was formed, with six directors: Bernard Rosenthal, who was chairman and managing director, Patrick Morgan, Mr and Mrs Gerald Beviss, and two friends of Bernard's who, he told his excessively young board, were providing working capital and a bit of much-needed age and wisdom. The company was to buy from Patrick outright the racecourse, the valley it enclosed, the site of the grandstands and the car parks, Great-great-uncle Cyril's house and a hundred acres of, mainly, woodland surrounding it and, in addition, would lease from him Rede Park House itself for an initial period of fifteen years and undertake to put the place in order. Patrick would have sole and full use of the house: the arrangement was designed to compensate him for the fact that so much of the money he was paid for the land went on death duties and his father's debts.

At the first board meeting of Rede Park Racecourse Ltd, Diana complained how unfair it was that Bernard should have a controlling share in the company and she only fifteen per cent and Patrick twenty, especially since it was Patrick's racecourse and the whole thing had been her and Patrick's idea to begin with. Bernard said someone had to be boss and he rather thought he was the most experienced. He went on to propose to the board that the directors, for the time being at least, should be unpaid, with the exception of Gerry whose time in future would be divided between

260

Rosenthal's and Rede Park. Would the board, he asked, leave it up to the chairman to decide a suitable salary? The board said, impatiently, that yes it would, and went off to celebrate.

After that, all they could do was wait. Gerry returned to his old routine and found that during his absence many more friends had come to the City: James was there, and Mark – Mark, such a proud husband and father, dashing back to Richmond on the stroke of five every night, never joining the others in an end-of-day drink, saying, 'No, old chap, Charlie is waiting for his bedtime story,' with such devastating seriousness that no one dared tease him. Jonathan Faulder was back and David Smedley, too, unscathed from Korea.

Gerry assumed that everyone knew about his dark secret and imagined it was no longer worth talking about. In any event, they seemed more interested in hearing about the racecourse.

'When will it open?' Mark asked.

'The summer of 1957, we hope.'

'Four years away! Why not sooner?'

'Because everything has got to be perfect. Because we want to start big and make sure people come back for more, and because there are a few false bits of going on the track and the last thing we want is for a horse to put a foot in there and break a bloody leg.'

'Fair enough,' James said. 'But we'll get VIP badges and all on the opening day, won't we?'

'You will,' Gerry promised.

He and James arranged to have lunch the following week. It had been too long, they agreed, since they'd sat down and had a good natter.

Gerry was back in his old routine, and so was Diana. It would be four years before she could present the prizes at what she regarded as her own racecourse, and if she had known how long it would take she wouldn't have been nearly so interested. She would have gone to Rio, she said, and (as though she had personally overseen all the work) left them to get on with all the boring details on their own. *Now* what was she supposed to do?

'You could design the writing paper for the company,' Gerry said. He hated to see her like this. Her discontent seemed to spill over into unhappiness and it infected everyone. Suckers went around grim-faced, Rio hid, and Gerry was left to face the flak alone. 'It must be very smart,' he went on. 'Very classy.'

'Classy!' she snarled. 'What the hell would you know about that? Me design writing paper? What a fucking stupid idea. *Christ*, but you're stupid sometimes.'

Nothing he could do or say sweetened her mood. It was even more depressing because during the last six months Gerry had dared to hope that their marriage had some kind of solid foundation. Now he had to recognise the fact that she was like a child, a little baby: if she was happy she laughed, if she was unhappy she screamed, and, like a baby, she made no attempt at all to regulate her emotions. But a baby had an excuse; and for Diana there was none.

Two days after this conversation, he woke with a raging sore throat. Suckers fed him aspirin with his breakfast and said he shouldn't go to work. He said he was fine, but by lunchtime he was sneezing, every one of them setting his throat on fire and exploding in his ears. He went to Coate's at lunchtime and was asked – in the nicest possible way – to remove himself as the rest of them didn't want to catch the plague he was obviously incubating. He returned to the office, where Rupert gave him a nip of brandy before he and Daniel firmly escorted him downstairs and out into Threadneedle Street, found him a taxi and ordered him home. He arrived at the house in Mayfair. Suckers was, as usual, visiting her mother, and there was no sign of Diana. He walked up the stairs thinking that bed would be very nice indeed.

Then he heard Diana have an orgasm. He knew the sound well enough, and anyway it was unmistakable: a loud, trilling scream. He ran up the rest of the stairs and opened the door to their bedroom.

Diana was lying in bed, reaching to the bedside table for a cigarette. Slumped across her, his cheek resting against her left breast, was a fair-haired man. They were both, of course, naked.

Diana looked at him. 'Gerry, it's you,' she said lazily. She fitted the cigarette into her holder and lit it. The man lifted his head, gasped, said, 'Oh my God!', leapt out of bed and began frantically to dress.

262

'What's your name?' Gerry asked him, vaguely aware of being surprised that he was not surprised.

The man was pulling on his trousers. He paused, stared at Gerry and opened his mouth to speak.

'Don't tell him,' Diana said. 'If you do, it will mean the end of things between you and Arabella, I promise you.'

The man put on his shirt, rammed the tails of it into the waistband of his trousers without doing up the buttons and fell to his knees to look for his shoes and socks.

Gerry began to sneeze.

'Oh, Christ!' Diana said. She pulled the sheet up to cover herself and smoked her cigarette.

Gerry escorted the man downstairs.

'Look – I'm sorry,' the man said at the front door.

'How long has it been going on?' Gerry asked. He was trying to remember if he'd seen him before. He didn't think so.

'Between me and Diana? This is only my second time . . . But, well, you know—'

'What do I know?'

'She's a good sport. Gives a chap a nice time.'

'Who is Arabella?'

The man's face turned even pinker. 'She's a girl I know.'

'A respectable one?'

He seemed relieved Gerry understood. 'Yes, that's it.' He thrust a sock into his jacket pocket and said, 'Well, I'll be off then . . . Thanks very much.' And then, realising this was not at all – but then perhaps entirely – appropriate, he let out a strangled groan and shot out.

Gerry closed the front door and went up to the sitting room. He poured himself a large brandy and sat down. Now he *was* surprised. He was stunned. Diana wandered in, wearing her dressing gown, smoke trailing behind her.

'Can I have one?'

He gave her a brandy and they both sat.

'I want a divorce,' he said.

'No.'

'Why not?'

'You haven't grounds.'

263

'I haven't grounds?' he said, his voice rising. 'What more do I need, for God's sake?'

'You can't prove anything . . . nothing at all. And *stop* fucking well sneezing, Gerry.'

He blew his nose, and then said, 'How can we go on being married – after that?'

'Easily. I like being married.'

'So you can have other men. Is that it?'

'Yes.' She sipped her brandy.

A thought struck him. 'What if there had been a baby? What if you had got pregnant?'

'I did.'

Gerry's cold was filling his head. There seemed no room for anything else there.

'What happened?'

'I got rid of it. In Switzerland, when I said I went ski-ing. You fell for it, didn't you? As though Mummy and Pedro would go ski-ing! Can you imagine anything less likely?'

Knowing them, in retrospect, Gerry supposed he could not. He was trying to work it out.

'But that was just after we got back from our honeymoon.'

'It was.' She fitted another cigarette into her holder.

'Then – it must have been my baby, mustn't it?'

'Must it? I haven't the faintest idea.'

'Oh Lord!' Gerry buried his throbbing head in his hands. 'How can we go on being married? We can't!'

'I'm not giving you a divorce, and that's that.'

'But why not? Why the hell not? I'll give you grounds, go to Brighton and be found with a chambermaid or whatever . . . Why not?'

She smiled and blew smoke at him.

'It's against my religion. I'm Catholic, remember?'

He lurched to his feet. 'I'm ill. I've got to go to bed. I'll use a spare room.'

'So you should,' she said. 'With a cold like that. You might give it to me.'

He wasn't really ill, but he didn't want to be better. He had no

264

incentive to get out of bed and face things. Suckers looked after him and Rio lay on his feet and purred at him. Diana came to see him occasionally and, when he would not speak to her, she told him he was being a boring old grump. On the third day, which was Friday, he waited until both Suckers and Diana were out, and he got up, shaved, dressed himself, moved all his clothes from the small part of the wardrobe in Diana's bedroom he was allowed to the spare room he had taken to. Then, leaving a note for Suckers, he went to Ryehurst to be fussed over by his mother.

The sea air, the air on the Weald which smelled of spring and the world turning, the long rides on Florin, cleared the last of the cold from his head and he went back to London on Sunday evening sure that, now Diana had had a few days to think about it, she would agree a divorce was inevitable. How could they go on, she giving chaps 'a nice time' and he knowing that she did?

She changed tactics. She threw herself at him, sobbing that she loved him, that she was sorry and she'd never do it again. Her hand was at his groin, but he felt nothing, nothing at all. His cock would never talk to her again.

'I want a divorce,' he said.

'No. I'll deny it all.'

He went back to work the next day, amazed that nothing else seemed to have changed. Daniel was at the office before him, Rupert arrived an hour after him. There were things to do and he got on with them. He didn't feel sad, he realised. Far from it, in fact. He felt cleansed. He had tried to make the best of their loveless marriage and had failed, but failed with honour. He hadn't slept with – been near – other women, while she had gone with other men, and often. A baby had been conceived on their honeymoon and might not have been his . . . A clean break and that was the end of the whole sad affair. In time she would have to agree this was the best course.

Gerry wanted two things: a good lawyer and a good friend. He had friends, but there was no one he could talk to about finding his wife in bed with another man. Patrick was the only possible candidate, but Gerry had a feeling that Patrick knew all about Diana, and he did not want to discover how thoroughly he had been used. Before he arrived at the office, Gerry knew he would go to Bernard. Bernard was his boss, but he felt he was also his friend and minded what happened to him. He requested a meeting, which Bernard granted that very morning, and he listened to all that Gerry had to say, his face serious and sympathetic against the triumphant laughter of the photographs on the wall behind him. His also-ran in last year's Derby had won the August Stakes at Brighton, and it might have been the Derby Stakes at Epsom by the way Bernard was looking in the photograph.

But not here and now in Threadneedle Street. Here and now he was looking very grave.

'Gerry,' he said, 'I'm more sorry than I can say. Of course I can recommend a lawyer, but I don't think it's as easy as that. Let me go through it again. You found Diana in bed with another man. Do you know his name?'

'No, but I could find out. A private detective could, maybe.'

'And Diana says she will deny it?'

'Yes.'

'So it is your word against hers.'

'I suppose it is.'

Bernard was silent for a while.

'It will be a hideous divorce case, Gerry,' he said at last. 'You standing in the witness box saying what you saw, Diana weeping and saying you made it up. The papers will love it.'

'That should please Diana.'

'The judge would have to decide which of you to believe: the beautiful millionairess who can look as innocent as a lamb when it suits her or the man who, she would no doubt point out, married her for her money and who lied about his background. It will be very bloody and very vicious.'

It was Gerry's turn to be silent, until he said, 'I need proper proof, don't I? Photographs or something?'

'I rather think you do. And, of course, although this is not something that should necessarily weigh with you, it would also look fairly ghastly for our company – having two of the directors in this sort of scandal.'

'What should I do then?' Gerry said. 'I can't go on being married to her!'

'Could you contemplate waiting? Diana will divorce you

266

eventually, or she will if she can be convinced that you don't care one way or another. I don't wish to dictate to you how your wife's mind works, but it has always seemed to me that she wants precisely the opposite to what others want her to want. Is that not so?'

It was indeed. If Gerry had worked that out when he had first met her he would not be married to her now. It was his very indifference that made her want him.

'Well?' Bernard prompted gently.

'I'll wait then. I'll get the proof and go to court with a watertight case.'

'I'm sure it's the best solution,' Bernard said. 'For all of us.'

He tried once more. Diana changed tack again.

'You were ill,' she said. 'You were seeing things.'

'Seeing things! That man said you were a good sport.'

'How utterly sweet of him.'

'Would you really lie on oath? Lie having sworn on the Bible?'

'I don't know what you're talking about. I'm not divorcing you, Gerry, and you can't divorce me.'

On Friday he met James for lunch at Sweeting's. Too late he saw that the table at which James was sitting was next to one occupied by Paul Marling and another man. Gerry sat down, Marling saw him and called for the head waiter.

'You might not mind serving a thieving gypsy,' he said, 'but I do not care to sit next to one.'

Noisily, and with the maximum of fuss, Marling and his friend were moved. James stared at Gerry.

'What was that about?'

'The man doesn't like me.'

'I heard about you being a gypsy and that,' James said. 'Is it true?'

'Yes,' Gerry replied, wondering why he hadn't stayed in bed longer – preferably for ever. 'Yes, it's true. But I'm not a thief.'

'You should sue that bloke for libel or slander or something.' The waiter brought their drinks, and James picked up his glass. 'Anyway, it's good to see you, old boy, and here's to your racecourse and riddance to the bloody army. Cheers!'

Gerry drank, gratitude washing through him. James had more reason than Nick O'Rourke to revile him: it had been James upon

267

whom Gerry's first deceptions had been practised, and James didn't mind. The events of the last days had left Gerry feeling he had just gone ten rounds in the ring with a heavyweight boxer, and a rejection from James could have been the knock-out punch. Suddenly he felt strong again, ready to fight: things would be all right. Marling was an enemy with no weapons left. So what if Diana was at this moment in bed with another man? So bloody what? She would have to give him a divorce eventually, and, as Bernard had said, the less he showed he wanted it, the more likely it was to happen. She had crept into his bed in the spare room last night, thinking she could seduce him; he had hugged her and kissed her in a friendly way and gone to sleep. He really had, even while she was stroking his limp cock and doing everything she knew to get him going. David Smedley had offered him a room in his flat and he was moving there tomorrow.

His reflections came to a halt as what James was saying hit him.

'Kate?' Gerry said. 'Kate?'

'Yes – Kate. Kate Earith, you remember her?' James's voice was heavy with exaggerated emphasis. 'The girl you went out with for a time . . . the girl you stole from under our noses. Well, my nose anyway. Mark was always after Vanessa.'

'I know who you mean. What about her? Have you been taking her out?'

'For more than two years. I'm a bit of a grass widower at the moment because she's working like hell for her finals.'

Gerry remembered and smiled. 'She always worked hard.'

Kate.

Gerry could not speak.

Kate.

'I know she was a bit keen on you,' James went on, 'but I think it's my turn now. I'm hoping—' He flushed slightly. 'I'm sort of hoping that she'll say yes when I pop the old question when her finals are done with.'

James continued to talk and Gerry listened and made the right responses, while all the time there was a pounding in his head. So loud was it that Gerry thought James must hear it.

Not too late then, it said. Not too late, not too late.

Chapter 17

She could not think why he had come. She offered him a drink and he thanked her and sat down.

'I'm not disturbing you, am I?'

'No,' she said, although he was. Her heart was doing things which, as a doctor (or nearly one), she knew were medically impossible and she told it, severely, to behave itself. He was as handsome – more handsome – than ever but he looked, somehow, mangled. He lit a cigarette and she brought him an ashtray.

'You never used to smoke,' she said.

'No, I didn't, did I? I don't really now.' And he stubbed the cigarette out.

They talked about her work, his work, and she asked about the racecourse, which she had heard of from James. He was sober and serious and she missed his wicked grin. She was disastrously pleased to see him, far too disappointed when he refused a second whisky and said he knew he was disturbing her, in spite of what she had said, and must go.

He came back, though, often. Always when she was on her own in the flat and not going out with James, never staying for more than half or three-quarters of an hour, always just a little distant so she could not ask him what he thought he was up to. Once his grin reappeared, and she was quite, quite lost.

One evening he brought her some smoked salmon. Frozen. She could keep it in the freezer compartment of her fridge, he said, for up to a week, and then she could eat it and think of him.

'Gerry—' she began.

'It's all right. It's perfectly safe.'

'Gerry, I don't *have* a fridge.'

How could this prosaic piece of domestic intelligence have engendered what followed? She was in his arms, the frozen smoked salmon on the floor at their feet, and he was kissing her and murmuring as he nuzzled her neck, 'Don't marry James, Kate, *don't*! Marry me!'

She came to her senses then, and pulled away.

'But you're already married.'

'Could you take the evening off? From your work? I'll tell you everything.'

It was the second time he had appeared within a month of her finals with a proposal. She was not going to send him away this time, not after the way her body sang with his kiss.

'Stay,' she said.

He bent to pick up the smoked salmon.

'We could eat this for supper.'

'Yes – but there's no lemon,' she said. 'Help! And no bread either. Only stale.'

He gathered her into his arms again. 'My totally practical Kate, so hopeless,' he said, laughing. 'How lovely. How lovely you are altogether.' His lips were everywhere on her face. 'Have you got eggs? And hot water?'

'Yes,' she said when she was able. 'And there's masses to drink.'

'We're all right then.'

He put the salmon into a bowl of hot water, saying it would be thawed in an hour or so if they kept changing the water to keep it hot. And then he told her everything: that he had moved out of his wife's house and their marriage was over. He told her why. He said there would be a divorce but he could not say when. He had a detective following his wife but so far her behaviour appeared innocent and he couldn't prove anything against her. He told her about Bernard and how the truth about his background had come out. Then he went into Kate's kitchen and, his face gravely concentrated, he made them scrambled eggs, chopped up half the smoked salmon into thin slivers and stirred it in.

'Buy some brown bread and eat the rest tomorrow,' he said, handing her a plate with the delicious concoction on it.

He had been frightfully extravagant with her eggs, but she could not mind anything that he did. She tried to listen to what he was telling her.

'You do understand,' he said, when they had finished eating, and he took their plates and dumped them in the kitchen sink – and she was able to register, with a feeling almost of relief, that he was not, then, quite perfect, for a perfect man would have washed up as well as cooked. 'You do understand, don't you, that Diana doesn't want a divorce?' He took her hands and pulled her to her feet. 'I don't know why, but she doesn't. You understand that?'

She nodded.

'So now you know everything . . . Kate, I love you. Only you and ever you.' He bent his head and kissed her lips very gently. 'Do you still love me?'

She was helpless. 'I do, Gerry. I do.'

'You once said that if I asked you to marry me properly, and meant it, you would say yes. . . . Kate, this is as proper as I can make it under the circumstances, and God knows I mean it. Kate, I'm not free and won't be for some time, but it's only you and ever you. Will you marry me?'

'Yes,' her mouth said, while her mind screamed, Insane, insane! And what are you going to say to James?

She felt wonderful. She couldn't help it. She must have looked it, too, for two nights later James asked if her finals had been brought forward and she had qualified in secret. Something good must have happened to her, he said: what was it?

She had to tell him. She owed him a great deal, but most of all she owed him honesty. His knuckles whitened around his glass, but all he said was, 'I see.'

'James, I'm so sorry. I'm so dreadfully sorry,' she said. 'I can't help it.'

He smiled sadly at her. 'I know, Kate,' he said. 'Life would be easy if we could determine these things, wouldn't it? At this moment I wish I didn't love you, and there must have been times – and perhaps this is one of them – that you wished you didn't love Gerry.'

'Maybe, but I do love him,' she said, and again: 'I can't help it.'

'No, neither of us can.' James was silent for a while, and then he said, 'I knew I was always a compromise, but I'd thought – I'd rather hoped – I was a bloody good one.'

'You are, James, you are!' She found she was crying and this cheered James up. Girls didn't cry if they were really wanting to be rid of a chap, did they? He took her hands across the restaurant table.

'Come on, Kate, it's not so bad. We can still be friends. We can still see each other, can't we?'

'You mustn't, though.' She pulled her hands away and wiped her eyes.

'Mustn't what?'

'Waste your time on me. I've treated you so badly, James, and really I didn't mean to . . . And what will your mother and father say? They've always been so kind.'

'What on earth has that got to do with anything? I decide what to do with my time. No one else does, not even you. . . . And until it's all settled between you and Gerry—'

'It'll probably take years. *Years!*' she said, and added fiercely, 'But I don't mind waiting. I love him.'

'All right,' he said. 'But until then you might need me . . . You are fond of me, aren't you?'

'Yes – yes!' she said, her eyes overflowing again. 'I'm so very fond of you, James.'

'Well, that's all right then,' he said, once more comforted by her tears. 'Just remember, I'll always be here for you.'

He saw Gerry in Coate's Wine Bar the following day and confronted him.

'I'm not giving her up,' he said. 'Not without a fight I'm not. I'm sorry about your marriage and all that, Gerry, but I give you warning that I'm not going to walk away from Kate and leave you a clear field. Do you understand?'

'I understand,' Gerry said, somewhat taken aback, not by James's fighting talk so much as by the fact that he was so open and friendly, buying Gerry a drink and lifting his glass in a toast, saying, 'Well, cheers, old boy, and may the best man win. All's fair in love and war, they say.'

272

Gerry would have found it a dreadful blow if he had lost James's friendship because of Paul Marling's poisonous talk, but he had been entirely reconciled to the possibility of James shunning him because of Kate.

'May the best man win,' he echoed, although he was perfectly sure that the best man had already lost.

A new queen was soon to be crowned and the country was gripped by coronation fever. Kate didn't notice it as she sailed through her finals. In the written exams, the words jumped into her pen; in the vivas it was as though the patients whose illnesses she was invited to diagnose had placards three feet high above their heads saying what was wrong with them; she had to restrain herself, force herself to wait, when the examiners asked her questions for she seemed to know the answers almost before they had finished speaking and an over-hasty response, even if correct, would not give the right impression.

She qualified, of course. She was a doctor! She was a doctor!

She took three weeks' holiday, first spending a few days with Vanessa and Mark in Richmond, Vanessa as enormous as she had been with Charlie and finding this pregnancy as trouble-free as her previous one had been – which slightly disappointed Kate as she wouldn't have minded a minor crisis to deal with. Charlie was walking now, or, rather, tottering around like a drunken old man. He was convinced he could talk as well, and had long, one-sided conversations with his godmother while he did important things with his bucket and spade in the sand pit.

Kate told Vanessa about Gerry and all that had transpired. Vanessa was shocked that a marriage could be so brief but – faced with Kate's blazing blue gaze – hastily agreed that it wasn't Gerry's fault, and then said, horror rising in her, 'But James is coming to dinner tomorrow. Won't it be frightfully awkward?'

'Not at all,' Kate said. 'We're the best of friends.'

After that, Kate went home to Beattie and Charles. Very little could shock or surprise her aunt, but Kate's news caused a ripple of alarm to course through the ample flesh.

'Gerry Beviss!' she exclaimed. 'Him again! But he's married, Kate.'

'He's getting a divorce – eventually. Look, Beattie. Look at the ring he gave me.'

'A sapphire,' he had told her, 'but there's not one mined that would match your eyes.' She wore it on the fourth finger of her right hand, for on her left hand it could invite difficult questions about her fiance's status.

Beattie looked at it. 'But my darling,' she said doubtfully, 'it's a bigamous engagement ring.'

Kate burst out laughing and hugged her. 'Maybe it is, but I'm happy with it. And you will be nice to him, won't you, when he comes here? Because he's going to be staying at his parents' house.'

'But where's his wife?' Beattie asked.

'On the Continent for the summer. We're hoping she'll meet someone and fall in love and want to give Gerry a divorce. She won't at the moment, you see.'

'No, I don't see,' Beattie said, with more worry and upset in her voice than Kate had ever heard before. She rose from the garden bench they were sitting on and paced to and fro on the lawn. 'When will he be divorced then? Not that I approve of such a thing – great heavens, Kate, he's been married less than three years! – but when will he be free?'

Kate stood up and went to her. 'I don't mind waiting, Beattie dearest.'

'When?'

'We – we don't know . . . Don't cry, Beattie, please don't. I'm happy. I'm happier than I've been for – oh, for ages.'

Beattie mopped her eyes and gazed at her. 'Yes,' she said, 'you are, aren't you?'

'And promise you'll be nice to him?'

Beattie sighed. 'I promise,' she said, although she thought she'd give him a good talking to first.

But when he arrived, driving a very smart motor car, Beattie had not the heart to admonish him in any way. She had expected the old Gerry, confident and grinning, and, if not thoughtless about having wrecked Kate's chances of a safe and comfortable marriage to James, then at least casual about it, and about his own disastrous marriage. He was none of those things. He greeted

274

Kate, kissed her with great propriety and smiled at her, and then turned to Beattie. His handsome face was very serious and he looked – how could she describe it? – world weary; and Beattie thought, how dreadful. What a dreadful way for a young man of twenty-five to look. He held his hand out to her and said, 'I'm sorry, Mrs Poutney, so very sorry for all the trouble I've caused,' and she found herself taking his hand in both hers and saying, 'But, Gerry, you always used to call me Beattie . . . Charles will be home soon. Would you like to stay to lunch?'

They spent every day together during the next two weeks. They rode – Kate a little grey horse called Sprite, Gerry on Florin who was now a venerable thirteen years old – on the beach or round the lanes; they went for drives, for walks, for picnics, out to dinner in the evenings or Gerry would be invited by Beattie for supper. One day when they came back from a ride, Meg Beviss, catapulted from her shyness by the outrage done to her son (for Gerry had told them all about Diana: only the truth made a divorce acceptable to his family), boldly asked Kate to eat with them, saying, 'We got lobsters. Good fat 'uns they are.' And when Kate said, 'Lobsters! Try to keep me from them!' Meg turned away, muttering, 'You're the maid for him. You're the one. He's that damaged it's right terrible to see.'

Meg packed them a picnic basket which would have fed a troop of hungry boy scouts when they set off early one morning for Rede Park. Kate wanted to see it, but when they arrived Gerry would not go to the main house and instead drove the Aston up an overgrown drive and stopped it outside the house that had been built by Great-great-uncle Cyril.

'Patrick is away,' he said, 'and we don't want to disturb his mother.'

Patrick was on the Riviera, in the same house party as Diana in fact, but even if he had been here Gerry would have avoided him. He did not want Patrick to meet Kate. Gerry's detective had, hopefully, asked if he should follow his quarry to France, but Gerry had said no. He knew all the men of the party and there would be no chance of taking incriminating photographs there – not without the risk of getting arrested for breaking and entering.

The detective, anyway, was costing Gerry a great deal of money and he had obtained no evidence that would help Gerry at all.

They got out of the car. At first, because of the absence of the sound of the engine, it seemed as though there was a profound silence, as though the birds had held their breath while the intruders came. Then a cuckoo called, and a blackbird whistled and a wood pigeon whirred away among the trees, and the air was full of the songs of birds.

Gerry led the way through to the racecourse, and Kate caught her breath. The valley, clothed in its summer dressing of every shade of fresh green, looked most beautiful, and at the far end Rede Park House stood basking peacefully, smugly almost, as though it was in some way aware that it was pampered and being treated as it should be once again. They walked along the track itself, which, to Kate's untutored eye, seemed fit for thoroughbreds to race on at this very moment.

'It's cut, harrowed and rolled constantly,' Gerry told her. 'It will be the best turf in the country when we finally have racing here.' And he went on to describe how the grandstands would look in phases one, two and three, where the paddock would be, and the car parks, and Kate admired it all and made the right noises but secretly she wished that the place could be left in peace. A golf course on the valley floor, she thought, would spoil the place utterly, though Gerry assured her that it wouldn't. They walked right round the circuit of the track and back to Great-great-uncle Cyril's house, soon, apparently, to be a country club.

'How could they have allowed it to get into such a state?' Kate asked as they went inside.

'No money,' Gerry said.

'Yes – but to leave this furniture here! And, Gerry, look!' she went on as they walked into what used to be the kitchen. 'It's like the *Marie Celeste*. When they finished scouring and scrubbing these pots and pans and hung them up, do you think they knew they were doing it for the last time?'

'We could ask Patrick's mother if you really want to know. She lived here until she married his father.'

'No. Don't let's. It's much nicer to be able to imagine it, isn't it?' She turned the handle of the back door and, when it failed to open, he went over and put his shoulder to it. It fell away, dangling on one rusty hinge, to reveal an expanse of cow parsley.

'We could picnic here,' Gerry said. 'Are you hungry?'

'Very.'

'Do you love me?'

'Even more, Gerry, if that's possible.'

'You've got a cobweb in your hair.'

'Have I?' she asked. 'With or without spiders?'

He removed it. 'Without, I think. . . . I'll go and get the picnic basket, shall I? Don't run away.'

But when he came back, she was gone. He could see her tracks through the cow parsley and followed them, the basket in one hand and a rug over the other arm. He caught up with her a couple of hundred yards through the woods.

'There's a path,' she said. 'Do you see? We must follow it, but there's a patch of nettles and I can't get through.'

He put down the basket. 'So I've got to be the brave, strong man, have I?'

'Only brave because you're wearing trousers and I'm not, but a bit strong because you'll have to carry me. We must see where this leads.'

'All right,' he said, enchanted by her determination and unable to refuse her anything. He handed her the rug, picked her up and, trampling down the nettles, he put her down on the other side and returned to collect the basket.

They went on, the path winding through the trees, for half a mile, more perhaps, until they came to a clearing full of sunlight and the noise of birds. A derelict stone cottage overlooked it.

'It must have been the gamekeeper's cottage,' Gerry said.

'Yes, but there are two front doors and two chimneys. Two of everything.'

'Two gamekeepers' cottages then.'

In spite of the dereliction, the building looked friendly and peaceful as it sat in its clearing in the woods, the warm stone lapping up the sun.

'Shall we explore?' Gerry asked. 'Or are you too hungry?'

'Let's explore.'

Each cottage had two rooms – a kitchen and another room –

downstairs and two small bedrooms upstairs, all of them smelling musty, many of the floorboards rotting, but the cottages faced the light and were filled by it. Gerry put his head out of one of the bedroom windows. All he could see was trees and sky, all he could hear was the birds. He turned back to Kate and found her standing in a dust-filled beam of sunlight.

'I'm going to live here, aren't I?' he said. 'And, eventually, you too.'

'Yes . . . Gerry, it's so simple! You make one of the back bedrooms a bathroom, knock down the wall between the two rooms below to make a sitting room and one of the kitchens becomes a dining room—'

'Do you want a dining room? Why not a nice, big, warm kitchen?'

'Much better! And French windows instead of one of the front doors, and a patio where we can eat in summer . . . Oh Gerry, will it happen?'

'I don't see why not,' he said. 'I'm fairly sure this is part of the estate the company bought from Patrick. I'll ask Bernard. . . . Hey, but listen, woman: why do you want me here when you're going to be in London?'

'Only for the next year. After that I can work anywhere, can't I?'

They went downstairs and outside and made heroic inroads into the picnic Meg Beviss had prepared for them. Afterwards they lay on the rug in the sun, Kate's head in the crook of Gerry's arm. He kissed her, pulled her closer to him and she slept there, her head now on his shoulder, his free hand loosely holding hers.

If only, he thought. If only he could have been happy like this that summer five years ago. He had no great desire for her in that way now. Here she was, so close to him and so vulnerably asleep against his shoulder, and all he was worried about was that she might get sunburned. The last two weeks had given her a tan, but the sun today was very hot. Carefully, so as not to disturb her, he pulled her dress further down over her knees and calves, and he remembered that time he had punted her up the River Cam and had been delighted to see the amount of thigh she had exposed in her sleep then . . . How horrible he had been that summer, what a

278

miracle it was that she was here, sleeping peacefully, trustingly beside him . . . And he realised, at long last and too late (but not entirely too late for he had been given – or, rather, had grabbed, wrestled from James, which he should feel guilty about but could not – a second chance) that there was a great chasm between love and sex, that the two things were quite different. It was as though you were weighing a pound of gold against a pound of coal. He had love here, asleep beside him, and it was enough. And sex? His two and a half years with Diana had cured him of it, for the time being at least. His cock, like the rest of him, felt weary and betrayed. He would have sex freely given, and given with love, or not at all.

Kate opened her eyes, eyes bluer than the ring she wore.

'Is your arm all right?' she murmured. 'It's not gone numb or anything?'

'No, it's not numb.'

'Good,' she said drowsily, and they both slept then, in the sunny glade with the stone cottages overlooking it, surrounded by the sounds of birds.

PART THREE

Chapter 18

Early on a morning in May: two racehorses, their exercise sheets fluttering, spun past the winning post and on to the Club turn; two more walked out on to the racecourse, and stared about them, their ears pricked. Gerry hoped they liked what they saw, for indeed it was most beautiful.

'Lord, I hope we've thought of everything,' he said.

'Too damn late now, what?' said Captain Nicholas Beech. 'You know, I've seen it hundreds of times before – a racecourse coming alive like this, the circus arriving, don't you know – and it's always exciting, but today's a special thrill. I cried when they closed my last place down and damn me if I won't cry to see this one open.'

'What do we do now?' Gerry asked him.

'I'm going to put my feet up in the office and wait for something to go wrong. Nothing else we *can* do,' Captain Beech said, and strolled away. Gerry, his stomach in knots of tension, watched him go. Surely he couldn't be as calm as he seemed. The enormity of what they had taken on had only come to Gerry two weeks ago when they had had their first dress rehearsal and all the theory had become practice. So many things to think about, so much detail, everything dependent upon so many people carrying out their orders to the letter and at the right minute; and everything terrifyingly complicated at this racecourse because, even though the officials were all experienced and many had come to the second dress rehearsal, they and the trainers and the lads, the vet, the farrier, the medics and everyone else whose presence was required before racing could take place (as well as the general public) did not know their way around. One of the regiments stationed in Leighminster had provided soldiers and, although it made the place look as if it was under military occupation, at least there would be easily identifiable people to ask. The regiment had offered its band as well.

Gerry walked off the members' lawn and into the clerk of the course's office. Jennifer Cody, their secretary, was there with her checklist and charts. It looked like the preparation for the invasion of Europe.

'So far so good,' she said in response to his query, and handed him a cup of coffee. 'Everything's going like clockwork.'

Gerry and Captain Beech sat down and again tried to think if they had forgotten anything, then Gerry, finding it impossible to be still, went up to one of the restaurants in the grandstands. The tables were already being laid and the waiters and waitresses bustled back and forth carrying cutlery and vases of flowers. Elizabeth James, the catering manager, was behind the bar on the telephone.

'Is everything all right?' Gerry asked her when she had put the phone down.

She smiled at him. 'As right as any normal day at the Club,' she said. 'We could have five people or fifty. We're used to it. Stop fussing and have a brandy.' She poured him one. He drank it and felt better, then another and felt very much better, and went back down the stairs and out into the Tattersall's enclosure. Captain Beech was right. It *was* a circus. The band had arrived and was setting itself up, bookmakers were putting up their boards and umbrellas – even though it was the most beautiful May morning God had ever created – and shouting greetings at each other as if they'd been coming to Rede Park Racecourse all their lives, though Gerry heard one say, 'Quite a place, in't it? Almost beats Goodwood.'

Almost! Gerry thought. We'll bloody show them. He walked around the end of the grandstand, through the winners' enclosure and out towards the main entrance. A coach had pulled up and out of it were climbing lots of little old ladies. They swirled about him, chattering among themselves, looking like everyone's granny or maiden aunt, and Gerry was sure they should be at home baking cakes for the village fête or telling bedtime stories and not be here at a racecourse at all.

'Who are you?' he asked one of them.

'We run the Tote,' she said. She peered past him into the betting hall that had already played host to several dances and today for the first time would be put to its proper use. 'Mabel!' she called. 'Mabel, come and look. It's palatial!'

The Blue Oceans Seafood Bar was situated near the paddock. It had been Grace's idea, but the original thought – that Blue Oceans should sponsor a race – had been Gerry's, after he had read how Whitbread were sponsoring a race at Sandown. Grace had done her homework and had persuaded Joe to part with five thousand pounds, which would make the Blue Oceans Handicap one of the richest in the country.

'We have the product,' she had told Gerry. 'The thing is to let people know it is here, and to persuade them it's good. The bar will be a real chance to push the product at the general public, and the race will ensure the name sticks in their memory.'

'Yes, Grace,' Gerry had said. Let her have her bar and her product. He had a race which had attracted the Two Thousand Guineas runner-up and twenty-one other good horses. He was stunned, though, at the amount she had got out of Joe, but then she'd always got what she wanted out of him.

The Blue Oceans van was parked beside the bar now, being unloaded, and Elizabeth James's staff, who were running the bar, were directing the men where to put things. Grace and Arthur were there and turned to him, their faces beaming. Grace even greeted him with a kiss.

'Have you seen the papers? Gerry – look!'

They had them all spread over the front seat of the van, opened at the racing pages. 'Quorum to win the Blue Oceans' . . . 'Weight will sink Quorum in Blue Oceans' the headlines screamed and when Blue Oceans wasn't mentioned there it featured prominently in the text. Of course it would. Gerry hadn't thought.

'It's worth the five grand already, isn't it, Gerry-lad?' said Arthur.

'Yes,' Gerry murmured. He was reading the papers. 'The most comfortable modern stands' . . . 'excellent facilities' . . .

285

'picturesque' . . . 'revolutionary, a day out for all the family' . . .

And so it was, and so it was! Gerry knew it, but here it was, in black and white. They had invited the racing Press down for lunch several times and filled them to the gills with champagne and good food and this was the result. Gerry walked on in a daze up towards the racecourse stables, now revelling in the atmosphere. A Rolls Royce drove into the owners' and trainers' car park and halted beside a Daimler. People were coming, making journeys to be here . . . But then, even so – what if *only* owners and trainers, who after all had to come, turned up? Them and the members of Rede Park Country Club who had been offered special rates for entry to the members' enclosure since their club would be closed on race days? Army chaps would come, there were plenty of them in the area, and there was the large party Gerry assumed Diana was bringing and all those invited by Patrick, so many that Gerry, taking a lead from Bernard, had decided to abandon the directors' box and take one of the others for the two days of this meeting. Mark and Vanessa would be in Gerry's box, and Andrew and Rosie Coleridge and other Cambridge friends; and Kate, of course, who was being picked up from her flat in Leighminster by James, who seemed delighted to provide this service and be Kate's escort for the day, though surely by now he had given up hope? So maybe altogether enough people would come and it wouldn't look embarrassingly empty. . . .

Two men were coming towards Gerry, talking intently: one was fresh-faced and thin, the other older, taller and trilby-hatted. Gerry felt like turning somersaults as he had done that night down King's Parade after the first evening he and Kate had spent together. He recognised the two men: the trainer and jockey of Crepello and other top-class horses, the trainer and jockey every race-goer talked of and revered – Noel Murless and Lester Piggott . . . here. *Here!*

'Excuse me, sir,' a polite voice said, 'but you can't come through here.' Gerry came out of the clouds to find his way into the stables barred by a large man in a bowler hat.

'But I'm – my name's Beviss,' Gerry began.

'I know, sir' – Captain Beech and Gerry had engaged him, after all – 'but only trainers are allowed in here.'

286

Gerry was about to argue and then burst out laughing and turned away. His baby had grown up and was leaving him, and had given him a nasty little nip as it went. He went to the clerk of the course's office and told Captain Beech what had happened.

'Didn't you know you weren't allowed in?'

'No, I thought I could go anywhere.'

'You might have been intent on nobbling Quorum.'

'I might have been at that.' Gerry took a badge from his desk and threaded the string through the buttonhole in his lapel. Not everyone would recognise him and he did not want the embarrassment of being refused admittance to the members' enclosure. 'Is all quiet?'

'As the grave.' Captain Beech stood up and paced around. 'Something's got to go wrong,' he said. 'I just wish it would show its damned face.'

Gerry went back out into the grandstands. The horses were back in their boxes now, and owners, trainers and jockeys were walking the course. Little knots of people were strung right round the circuit. Gerry spotted George, the odd-job man around the Club and golf course, summoned him, gave him some money and told him to go into Leighminster and buy fifteen copies of all the national papers.

'Why?' George asked, as he always did when given an order he didn't much want to carry out, and Gerry tried to explain that they wanted more sponsors and how impressed they'd be by Blue Oceans' showing. 'Then maybe I'd as well get twenty-five,' George said.

'Are the horses in?'

'Yessir, like you said.'

Florin had jumped out of his field once when the hunt had come through, and Sprite had followed. Gerry wouldn't put it past the old boy not to attempt to show these pansy thoroughbreds a thing or two when he heard their hoofbeats so close. For that reason he had not dared offer him as the starter's hack.

Having sent George on his way, Gerry wandered on. Like Captain Beech he found himself wishing something would go wrong so he could occupy himself. He had been here since six o'clock and it was now only twelve. He went to the box he had hired and admired it, but there was nothing wrong there, or in the stewards' room; just Elizabeth James's staff waiting patiently to provide every possible service. Only five out of the twelve boxes, apart from the ones he and Bernard had hired, had been taken for this meeting, which annoyed Gerry as he had tried hard to interest local people and had offered special rates. Bernard told him not to expect too much too soon, and Gerry agreed, but it was frustrating when you knew everything was so comfortable and perfect and you weren't believed.

He went back down the stairs and a familiar figure detached itself from a knot of people standing outside the directors' box.

'Darling! Isn't it too utterly exciting?' Diana cried. 'We had to come early. We utterly couldn't wait, and Patrick said our champers would be ready on ice for us.' She kissed him on both cheeks, and said vaguely, 'Darling, how are you?'

He hadn't seen her for six months – more, and then only briefly. She spent the winters in Rio de Janeiro or the West Indies, and the summers in the South of France or somewhere else fashionable in Europe, and only brief periods in England. He hadn't mentioned divorce to her for four years in the hope that, as Bernard said, she would think he didn't care one way or the other, but was determined to do so after tomorrow. His lawyers thought his grounds against her were somewhat circumstantial but said, primly, that the fact that they had not lived together as man and wife for so long might possibly persuade a judge in Gerry's favour.

He pushed his wife away from him in as friendly a manner as he could manage and said, 'I'm well, Diana, thank you. Your box is here and so is your champagne, or will be if Patrick has ordered it.'

Diana looked around. 'Where is darling Patrick?' she asked.

'With the bookies,' someone said. 'Where else?'

They all crowded into the directors' box and, for something to do, Gerry had a glass of champagne with them. Diana borrowed a racecard from one of her companions, a man in his late thirties, Gerry thought, and with that slightly orangey tan that comes to people who follow the sun. Diana had it too, and it was beginning to coarsen and harden her features. She opened the racecard and begged a pen from the same man.

'Now darling,' she said to Gerry. 'Which races am I presenting the prizes for? I must get it utterly right. The first one I know.' She ticked the top of the racecard and turned the page. 'And the second?'

'The Lady Mayoress of Leighminster,' Gerry said.

'How frantically boring. And the third?'

'You, Diana.'

She ticked the card again. 'And the fourth?'

This was what she was after. The Blue Oceans Handicap, the richest prize of the day, not just at Rede Park but in the country; the race which the newspapers would be interested in.

'Rebecca Rosenthal,' Gerry said.

Diana frowned, the pen poised. 'Darling, are you quite sure? Are you perfectly sure it's the right thing? – for the racecourse, I mean.'

'Perfectly,' he said.

Grace didn't want to present the prize and neither did Arthur, both of them recoiling at putting themselves forward in that way; Joe and Meg wouldn't dream of it for the same reason, and, in fact, were not even here today. Rebecca Rosenthal was the wife of the chairman of Rede Park Racecourse and was the best choice in every way.

Diana looked at Gerry, opened her mouth, closed it and said, 'Oh, all right then, if you must. And I'm doing the fifth and sixth, aren't I?'

'You are,' Gerry said.

'Four out of the six, Di,' the tanned man said admiringly. 'You'd better not drink too much or we'll have to carry you to the dais.'

This they all found hilarious and Gerry escaped and met Patrick in the foyer.

'Sorted out the bookies?' Gerry asked him.

'By God, I hope so,' Patrick said cheerfully, although Gerry noticed there were lines of worry around his eyes. 'It's what I've always dreamed of, you know, having a whole bunch of them more or less in the back garden. Mama and O'Nions are almost beside themselves with excitement too. It's all down to you, old boy,' he added. 'It couldn't have happened without you.'

'Without me marrying Diana, you mean? . . . No, I'm sorry,

don't answer—' It was something they had never discussed: how Patrick had encouraged Gerry to marry Diana knowing all the time that she would open her legs for any man as willingly, and frequently, as she drank a glass of champagne. Patrick had, presumably, been happy to overlook this little foible for the sake of Diana's money, but it was unforgivable that he had not told Gerry about it so at least he'd have had the chance to see if he'd make the same decision. Unforgivable. They still spoke to each other but were not really friends any more and, in fact, Gerry saw little of him. He did not encourage casual visitors to his house in the woods and Patrick was more often than not away from Rede Park. He was not a part of the close-knit team which had been working to make this day happen: Captain Beech, Elizabeth James and her pleasant husband Andrew, who had been injured in the war and was now confined to a wheelchair and kept the accounts in immaculate order; Jennifer Cody and, watching over them all, Bernard Rosenthal.

'I'll buy you a drink,' Patrick was saying now, as though that would make up for it all. 'We'll crack a bottle in the Cyril and George Bar, shall we?'

'How about your guests?'

'They're Diana's mostly, and from the sound of it they're doing fine.'

'All right, then,' Gerry said. 'I'll just go and make sure everything is all right in the office and join you up there, shall I?'

Patrick went up to the bar at the top of the stand, overlooking the winning post, which was marked by a short section of the wall Great-great-uncle Cyril had built. He scarcely noticed (as Gerry did, his heart leaping) the crowds – *crowds*! – now flocking through the main gates, the cars driving in a steady stream into the car parks; he did vaguely notice, however, that the bar named after his ancestors seemed rather busy for this early on a race day as he ordered a bottle of champagne.

. . . If Alchemist won he was in the clear. If he was placed, he'd make significant inroads into his debt. Not that his creditor was pressing him for the money: the two of them had been the best of friends since they had met in a bar at Kempton after a particularly bleak day and had commiserated with each other on the incompetence of jockeys and trainers and the general bloody-mindedness of horses. Paul had a system of betting which was in turn terrifying and exhilarating, but if you stuck with it, if you had the guts, Paul said, it couldn't fail in the long term. So confident was he about it that he had lent Patrick money to play it, because Patrick, when he had first met Paul, hadn't been doing any really serious betting as he was determined to use the money he had been paid for Rede Park – that not taken by death duties – to get the farm on its feet and to make the whole place profitable.

Paul's system was simple: you backed your fancy for the first three races, doubling your stake every time you lost, and then, in the last three races, still doubling your stake, you backed one of the three market leaders, either each way or on the nose, depending how courageous you felt. On the first two days, betting with Paul's money, Patrick had won spectacular amounts; the next six days he had lost and the amount to an initial forty-pound stake (anything less, Paul said, was kids' stuff) was a staggering £2520 a day. Patrick had given up the crazy system then and gone back to his usual method of taking each race as it came. He hadn't been doing too badly, but he owed a huge amount to Paul. All his money was tied up in the farm, and he really would give up gambling if Alchemist won today. He had put on huge amounts of money with various bookmakers, for what was the point of betting piddling little amounts when you wanted really big ones back? . . . And why hadn't Paul come here today? Was it really because he had been called abroad on business, or was it because he didn't care to see Patrick and remind him that he owed him so many thousands of pounds?

Patrick did not know, of course, that Paul Marling was lying low in his bedsitting room in London, nor that he had never bet more than sixpence on a horse race in his life. He did not want the eight thousand pounds back, not in cash and not just now he didn't. It was an investment, and he had been saving up for this ever since thieving gypsy Beviss had stolen Ridge Farm from his parents; and he had been even more assiduous in putting every penny by since he had learned that a compulsive gambler owned twenty per cent

291

of Rede Park Racecourse . . . No, Paul Marling did not want the money back. He wanted the shares Patrick owned.

Gerry fidgeted around Captain Beech in the clerk of the course's office until Bernard came in and Captain Beech said, 'For Pete's sake, Rosenthal, tell him to go away. He's making me nervous, don't you know.' And Bernard smiled and said, 'Be off, Gerry. Go and see your racecourse at work.'

Gerry stood up. 'Well, sir, if you're sure you can manage.'

Captain Beech said, gravely, that if he couldn't he would call for Gerry over the public address system.

'I'll go, then,' Gerry said.

Bernard caught his arm as he went by. 'Go to the stewards' room, Gerry, and welcome them. Remind them who you are.'

'All right,' Gerry said, blenching a little at the prospect of facing these personages.

'I've just come from there. They are enjoying their lunch and are very friendly, I promise.'

So Gerry went to the stewards' room and found that indeed they were enjoying their lunch. They barked all sorts of compliments about it and the racecourse. Gerry left them as they called for brandy, and wondered if they would be able to see the races at all, let alone discover and make judgement upon any misdemeanour. He then made his way to the box with 'Mr G. Beviss' on the door. His guests were in great high spirits and Elizabeth James's waiter provided him with a drink and a plate and indicated that he should fill the latter from the buffet. He thought he was starving, but after a few mouthfuls he discovered he wasn't hungry at all.

'Pack it in, old thing,' Mark told him. 'Wouldn't that be the doctor's advice?'

He turned to Kate and she said, very impersonally, as though they didn't love each other at all, 'Yes, it would be – is. Eat, Gerry. You look quite done in.'

'Nerves,' James said knowledgeably. 'Hey, but Gerry, isn't this a show? Aren't we all frightfully glad to be up here in luxury and not among the heaving crowds below?'

Gerry, his plate in his hand, joined James, along with Andrew and Rosie Coleridge, on the balcony and looked down. Heaving? Perhaps not, but crowds certainly. Wafts of laughter and lively conversation drifted upwards.

'They're enjoying themselves,' Gerry said. 'They bloody are, aren't they?'

Kate was beside him then. 'We all are. Gerry, it's going splendidly. Now *eat*.'

He was hungry again and cleared his plate. And then everyone began behaving as if this was a proper racecourse and studied their racecards and discussed which horses they might put their money on and drifted away to the paddock to view the runners for the Cyril and George Morgan Stakes, a sprint over the straight six furlongs.

Gerry accompanied James and Kate to the paddock, and little Charlie Colley-Smythe, abandoning Vanessa and Mark in favour of his godparents, came too. He had been given sixpence to bet with, and Gerry gave him another one, as did James. Charlie thanked them both politely and looked hopefully at Kate, offering her a miniature version of Mark's lovely smile. Kate gave out an exaggerated sigh and opened her purse.

'Not more than threepence a race, James,' she said. 'You'll have to take his bets ... Great heavens! We're setting him a dreadful example.'

She handed Charlie a sixpenny bit and he put it carefully into his shorts pocket.

Gerry felt a spasm of jealousy at the intimate way they were talking about their godchild, but it vanished as Kate exclaimed, 'My darl – Gerry! Just look! You're going to need stands, specially for the paddock.' She smiled at Gerry very beautifully and then turned to Charlie. 'Charlie, you lead the way and keep saying "Excuse me, please" in your best voice. They'll always let a child through, and we'll follow pretending you've run away.'

'A wheeze?' Charlie asked, dancing around them. 'Is that what's called a wheeze?'

'It is,' Gerry told him. 'Your godmother has no shame.'

Kate pointed. 'There's a promising gap. Go for it, Charlie – but, sweetheart, for heaven's sake don't lose us for real, will you?'

'You'll be behind me?'

'Yes, but keep looking back . . . No, better still, take my hand and don't pretend you're running away after all. Just drag me along, and I'll have to keep apologising to everyone.'

Charlie frowned. 'I know. I pretend I'm a spoiled brat and you pretend you're my mother and father and can't control me.'

'Where does he get it from?' James wondered, and Kate bent down and hugged her godson, planting a swift kiss on his cheek before he could pull away, for already he found kisses embarrassing.

'Exactly!' she said.

'Okay.' Charlie took her hand determinedly and the three of them vanished.

Gerry stood there for a moment, his mind, amazingly, not on the spectacle of an overcrowded paddock area. He was imagining Kate as a real mother, not just a godparent, and thinking what a lovely one she would make. His heart gave a little thump as it told him how much it would like to be the father of Kate's children. He would talk to Diana soon. It was time their ridiculous marriage was put painlessly, humanely, to sleep.

The racecourse reclaimed him. Arthur was pulling at his arm, his good, honest face red with excitement.

'Gerry-lad, I need a phone. I must ring Da. We've had to send the van back acos we haven't enough to see us through tomorrow, the way it's going today. . . . Gerry, they're asking for our little cartons of potted shrimps and prawns to take *home* with them. I must call Da.'

Gerry took him to the clerk of the course's office and let him use a phone there. Captain Beech, after a quick look round, produced a hefty silver flask from his pocket, which he drank from and then handed to Gerry. It was Glenmorangie malt whisky, Captain Beech's favourite tipple, and he and Gerry had drunk quite a lot of it these last three years. Nicholas Beech had been a clerk of the course since leaving the army in 1918, apart from during the last war, and he had been generous with his knowledge and experience as he and Gerry – and the Glenmorangie – had paced around the place in all weathers, trying to pre-empt every criticism and consideration anyone might have.

'The paddock is too crowded,' Gerry told him, handing the flask back. 'We should have a viewing stand.'

294

Captain Beech's red-rimmed eyes widened. 'Too crowded? Is it, by God? Well, a little wooden stand there won't break the bank, not after what's been spent here already. But mind you,' he went on, trying to sound judicious and logical, 'we can't make judgements after today, or even the two days, you know. People are coming just for the novelty. And the weather has been kind to us, of course.'

'Yes,' Gerry said. 'Yes, of course.'

He stood at the door, and Captain Beech joined him there. The jockeys walked past in their bright silks, swinging their whips and chatting to each other as they made their way to the paddock to mount their horses for the Cyril and George.

'Right on time,' Captain Beech said, looking at his watch. Then he turned aside and took out his handkerchief. 'Damn it all,' he said. 'I told you I'd cry. Sentimental old fool that I am.'

Arthur put the phone down and came forward. 'The old man can't believe it, but he'll fill up the van and send it back.' He turned to Captain Beech, who quickly regained his stiff upper lip. 'My father wants to look at the figures after tomorrow, but we reckon we'd like to sponsor another race here and make the bar a permanent feature, like.'

Captain Beech was all deference to this valuable sponsor, but Arthur was too excited and too unassuming to notice. He propelled Gerry out of the office, talking all the while.

'Honest, Gerry, I don't reckon even Grace had worked out the whole thing. A seafood bar near the coast'ud be expected, normal-like, but one inland proves the whole point about Blue Oceans and the frozen fish, don't it? I mean, these poor buggers have never seen a decent prawn in their lives! . . . No, no, Gerry-lad,' he said, as Gerry began laughing. 'It's *true*! Honest, it's true!'

'Oh, Art, I'm not laughing at you,' Gerry put his arm around his brother's shoulders. 'I'm laughing because I agree with you, and because I'm happy . . . happy and terrified too. Hey, Art, here's Grace. Let's all watch the first race together? How about that?'

They would be able to see all of the six-furlong course with ease from high up in the stands, Gerry knew, but he found himself leading Grace and Arthur down across the members' lawn to the rails opposite Cyril and George's bit of wall.

The horses went down to the start, snatching at their bits as they cantered past the grandstands, and the racecourse announcer gave out the names of the horses and the colours of the jockeys. The bookmakers in the next enclosure were shouting odds and the tic-tac men wearing their white gloves were gesticulating from the lower tiers of the stand ... It was exactly like any other racecourse. Gerry turned and looked back up at the stands. They were packed ... *packed*! He felt dizzy, a kind of upside down vertigo as he saw all the people standing on what, five years ago, had been thin air, empty hillside grazed by sheep.

The racecourse announcer, to fill in time while the runners were having their girths checked at the start, was explaining why the race was named as it was and who Cyril and George Morgan had been. He talked about the wall, and people began walking over to see the relic. It was unusual for an announcer to chat to the crowd like this and the details were in the racecard anyway, but Gerry had thought it was a good idea. It gave Rede Park a proper history and made it less of a jumped-up parvenu.

'They're under starter's orders,' the announcer said. 'And they're off!'

The thud of hooves came roaring down the track, racehorses going at nearly forty miles an hour, and then the straining heads and the coloured silks flashed past the winning post amid cheers from the stands, and the announcer said, 'Winner number four, second number two, third number thirteen.'

Just over a minute, and the Cyril and George Morgan Stakes was run.

Gerry watched Diana present the prize and then, in a daze, went around the racecourse. Everywhere he went the news was the same: no complaints with what there was, but more was needed.

'Squire'll have to move his sheep from yon field if this goes on,' the man in charge of the car parking said. 'The late-comers had a tidy walk from up near the woods.'

'Did they mind?' Gerry asked anxiously.

The man laughed and spat. 'The women complained a bit about their shoes, and their fellows said as how they'd have to come earlier next time.'

'Next time,' Gerry said.

He watched the next two races from the cheaper enclosures, where everyone seemed to be enjoying the racing and the sun, and then made his way back to the members' stand. Elizabeth James, her face flushed, wiped her arm across her forehead and said, 'I need more staff, Gerry. *More!* We're coping but we're run off our feet, and Jennifer has rung up to say that all the other boxes have been booked for tomorrow.'

'Liz – no!'

'Liz – yes!' She leaned forward and kissed him on the cheek. 'It's a success, Gerry. Relax and enjoy it . . . have a glass of champagne with me. We're free of customers, thank God. There's another race on.'

Gerry grabbed the glass and ran to the doors leading to the viewing stands.

'Another race?' he said over his shoulder. 'It's the bloody Blue Oceans Handicap!'

Quorum won to a great cheer that nearly raised the roofs of the grandstands which were already not big enough to accommodate the crowds come to see him. An unconsidered horse called Alchemist came second and the horse Grace had backed with a minimum stake on the Tote came third.

'Well, I had to,' she said, a touch defiantly, because she didn't really approve of betting. 'With a name like Arthur's Best I had to back the horse.'

Gerry felt a surge of affection for his sister-in-law, although he could almost have felt affection for Diana on this day.

The racecourse announcer thanked Blue Oceans for its generous sponsorship and Rebecca Rosenthal graciously posed for the press photographers as she handed the trophy – a good-sized silver cup – to Quorum's owner. After the presentation, Gerry bumped into Bernard, who was with Sir Henry Blower, a steward of the Jockey Club.

'Congratulations, Beviss,' Sir Henry said. 'You couldn't have expected more, could you?'

'Give us a Saturday and then see what we can do,' Gerry replied. In spite of Bernard's best efforts, all their fixtures were set for weekdays.

Sir Henry laughed. 'It's not my department, I'm afraid. And

anyway, by the look of things today you wouldn't have room for a Saturday crowd.'

'We'll make room,' Gerry said eagerly.

Sir Henry turned to Bernard. 'This chap of yours has grabbed the moon and now he's after the sun as well. Be satisfied, young man. The only people not smiling are the bookmakers after Quorum's win.'

Rebecca joined them, saying she felt a complete fraud giving the Blue Oceans trophy away but that she had enjoyed herself no end. She, her husband and Sir Henry drifted away. Gerry was about to follow them when a heavy hand descended upon his shoulder, anchoring him where he stood. It belonged to Mrs Partington who, along with her husband the Admiral, were members of the Club to such a devoted degree that Elizabeth James often said she wondered if they lived there. Like everyone else, Henrietta Partington was having a splendid time but wanted more of what there was.

'Absolutely top-hole, Gerry dear,' she said. 'But there aren't enough ladies' lavatories. Cecil says the men's are ripping, but I had to wait twenty minutes and the paper had run out.'

Gerry, feeling as though the top of his head was coming off, took out his notebook and wrote it down: 'Ladies' lavs and paper.'

After the last race, he went to his box. As he opened the door, someone cried, 'Here he is! The man of the moment!' and they all began singing 'For He's A Jolly Good Fellow'. Gerry stood, embarrassed and foolish, and looked at his friends. Mark was conducting the chorus, waving his right hand and holding a glass in his left. Rosie and Andrew Coleridge were standing on chairs, Charlie Colley-Smythe was stamping in time to the music and Vanessa's hair was bouncing up and down, not in time with anything at all. James's eyes closed and his chin tilted up on the long 'fe-el-low' and Kate was smiling at him as well as trying to sing.

'Speech!' Richard Kellerway called as they finished their song, and David Smedley handed Gerry a glass.

'Speech!'

Thomas Ewhurst seemed inclined to burst into song again and was hastily hushed. Gerry sipped his champagne.

'Look,' he said, 'I don't know what to say and that's my speech. Will it do?'

They all clapped and Charlie launched himself at Gerry.

'I won, I won!'

'Did you, Charlie?' Gerry asked, picking him up. 'Was it a fortune?'

'Yes! Seven and six, but I have to give some to Anne because she's only three and a half and had to stay at home with nanny.'

'What dreadful luck for her.'

'Dreadful for her not to be here.'

Mark came over and took his squealing son from Gerry.

'See these muscles?' he said, feeling Charlie's thin arms. 'He'll be an oarsman for sure.'

'Will you?' Gerry asked Charlie.

Charlie squirmed out of his father's embrace.

'No, no!' he yelled. 'No I won't. From now and for ever I'm going to be a jockey.'

Chapter 19

Gerry was surprised that Suckers opened the door to the house in Clarges Street. She was supposed to have retired and gone to live with her mother and sister in Ealing. They exchanged Christmas cards, him and Suckers, and she always remembered Gerry's birthday, having promoted him, apparently, to the status of former nursling. He gave her a kiss, as he assumed a former nursling would, and stepped into the hallway of the place he had once called home.

'It's lovely to see you,' he said. 'But why are you here?'

'I come to keep house when she wants to use it,' Suckers replied, jerking her grey head in the direction of the stairs and, presumably, Diana. 'It's not often and never for long so it doesn't bother me. How are you?'

'Well.'

'And how is Rio?'

'He's well, too. If he'd known I was going to see you he'd have sent you a purr.'

She had agreed, sadly, that Rio should go with Gerry and had instructed him to butter the cat's paws and keep him inside for three days, telling him that if Rio didn't take to country life they would have him in Ealing. Diana had no interest in him at all. Rio had licked the butter off his paws every time Gerry put it on, had stalked about howling ferociously, and when at last Gerry had let him out he had bounded off into the woods and reappeared an anxious hour later with a half-grown rabbit, which he had presented to Gerry with a contemptuous glance from his blue eyes.

He was altogether a bit exotic for Wiltshire, but had soon taught the local cats that a Siamese was to be respected.

'He's fighting fit,' Gerry said, 'but honestly, Suckers, I'm surprised at you teaching him such bad habits.'

'What bad habits?' she asked indignantly.

'He's a poacher, Suckers, and a thief. I'm forever having to make excuses for him. I blame you, of course. I say he was badly brought up.'

'You're exaggerating, you dreadful boy,' she said, delighted by his teasing.

'Yes, I am,' Gerry admitted. He paused and then said: 'Where's Diana?'

'In the drawing room.'

'I'll go up, then.'

'You know the way,' she said, and turned aside and Gerry thought she added, 'Good luck,' though he couldn't be sure.

He went up the stairs and stood for a moment outside the drawing-room door. Diana must have guessed why he had asked to see her and had said immediately, 'Yes, darling. We've lots to talk about, haven't we?' He had thought the time she had suggested – eleven o'clock in the morning – was vaguely ominous: drinks at twelve, or even lunch, would have been more . . . what? . . . civilised, less business-like, though God knew he wanted to see her for the shortest time possible. The morning suited him anyway, as it meant he would be home early, even after going to see Bernard and looking into Coate's to have a jar with the chaps. He had things to arrange for tomorrow. It was Kate's birthday, and one of his presents to her had to be picked up tonight . . . yet any present he could give her would pale into nothing beside this one, the one that was in Diana's keeping. He took a deep breath, knocked on the door and walked in.

'Darling!' his wife said, and drifted over amid a cloud of smoke to kiss him on both cheeks. 'Open a bottle, will you?' She waved to an ice bucket on the drinks table.

How could he have forgotten that Diana did not consider any time too early for a drink? Captain Beech's hours were strict: the Glenmorangie was allowed out between twelve and one (unless the weather was so cold that Captain Beech regarded it as medicinal or a matter of life and death) and then put away until six o'clock in the evening. Gerry opened the bottle, poured champagne into two glasses and handed one to her.

'Did you and your friends enjoy the race meeting?' he asked.

'Oh, utterly. But giving out prizes isn't half as much fun as I thought it would be. One of the owners I had to give a silly plate to was utterly frightful, too ghastly for words, and all the time one was thinking, All he wants to do is give one a good grope and have a photograph to put on his beastly wall.' She sipped her drink. 'I don't think I'll do it again unless there's a proper prize, a nice cup or something.'

Gerry sat down, trying not to let his irritation show. The only interest Diana had ever had in the racecourse was in giving out the prizes and they had sweated blood to find something for her to give. The real prize was money, and that never changed hands in any form at a racecourse. Captain Beech had said he was damned if they were going to present useless bits of silver the size of an egg cup as though the whole show was a children's gymkhana, and the idea of commemorative pieces of china had been Kate's. Commissioned from Royal Doulton, they were, enough to last the first season at Rede Park, each in a presentation case, and now Diana had decided that it was boring to give the bloody things away.

'Will you come to the meeting next month?' he asked.

'No. I'm going to Cannes and then to Amalfi. We're on a yacht ... we might be anywhere. Blissful, utterly.' She stood, refilled her glass and came and sat on the arm of the chair he was sitting in. She slid her hand down his chest towards his groin. 'Do you want to come upstairs?'

'No, Diana, I don't.' He brushed her hand away and got to his feet.

'Why have you come then?'

She was playing with him, but what the hell was the game?

'You know why.' He refilled his glass and turned back to her. 'I want a divorce, Diana. It's gone on long enough. Too long. Let's just put the whole thing behind us and get on with our lives.'

'I'll give you a divorce,' she said.

A firework exploded in Gerry's head, throughout his body. In that instant, he imagined how Kate's face would look when he told

302

her, how pleased their friends would be the waiting was over, except James, poor James. Beattie would weep tears of joy, so anxious was she about her niece, only wanting her happiness; and his mother would cry too, because she loved Kate, as any sensible person would, and longed for the grandchild Grace was unable – or unwilling? – to produce; and his father loved Kate: he'd given her Sprite to ride – Joe giving something away and expecting nothing back! . . . Oh and great heavens, he and Kate would live in the house in the woods, and perhaps Kate could, at last, be taken on as a general practitioner as she had always wanted to be. She had applied, often, but in the end had always been told that an unmarried woman was too much of a risk in a country practice. She said she didn't mind working in a hospital, she was healing people anyway, but she had sacrificed so much for Gerry and he had given her nothing at all in return.

He felt relief and happiness spread, shooting out of his fingers and toes, so much relief and happiness that he could have hugged Diana, the cause of all the horror . . . her and Patrick, and Gerry himself, too, of course, and the dreadful muddle he had got himself into about who and what he was, a muddle resolved by Bernard Rosenthal – whom he would never have met if he had not known Diana . . . And the firework became a Catherine wheel instead of the rocket he had thought it was, and it whirred around him, sending off confused little gouts of coloured flame, but at the centre of it all, solid, sure, was his own Katherine. Kate.

He thought minutes must have gone by, but no time had passed. He was standing in the drawing room of Diana's house in Mayfair, a full glass of champagne in his hand, and Diana was saying, 'Yes – I'll give you a divorce.'

She went over to where she had left her cigarettes, took one from the packet, fitted it into her holder and lit it.

'On one condition.'

The Catherine wheel faltered, hiccuped and then died.

'What is that?' he asked.

Diana walked to her desk, opened it and brought out a brown envelope. She threw it at Gerry. He caught it in his one free hand and looked at her questioningly.

'Open it,' she said.

He put down his glass and did so. Several black and white photographs spilled out and fell on the carpet at his feet. He looked down and saw his own face staring up at him. And Kate's. He bent down, and then knelt.

'What are these?' he asked.

'My evidence,' Diana said. 'I will divorce you, Gerry, and cite this Dr Katherine Earith as co-respondent.'

No fireworks in Gerry now: a storm-force wind filled his head. He looked up.

'But Kate and I have never . . . These aren't evidence!'

Diana blew smoke at him.

'My lawyers say they are.'

'But how can it be?' Gerry whispered. He looked at one of the photographs. He was holding Kate against his bare chest and her shoulders, arms and back were bare too. They were in focus, the two of them, and everything around them was blurred. Amid his confusion, Gerry actually wondered if he had ever held Kate naked in his arms. Whoever said the camera never lied?

'I'll divorce you,' Diana was saying, 'only if I can cite this Earith person. She runs around with James Flimwell, too, you know.'

Gerry collected the photographs together and put them back in the envelope. Pandora trying to close the box. He stood up.

'Why do this, Diana? *Why?* We can go to an agency and they arrange it all. The chambermaid gives the evidence.'

'But so commonplace,' Diana said, 'don't you agree? Drink your champagne, Gerry. It's getting lonely.'

The thought of the stuff made him feel sick. It was a drink for celebrations and no use now.

'Those photographs are for you,' Diana said. 'I have other copies – and the negatives, of course. . . . What will you do, darling? I only ask because it would be utterly boring to be summoned from Italy or wherever for some hearing. Not that it's likely to happen so soon, of course, but one would like to know where one stands.'

'I don't know what I'll do,' Gerry mumbled. 'I've got to think.'

'All right, darling. But do remember, won't you, that the photographs and Katherine Earith's name will come out in open court in any divorce case between you and me?'

'Why though?' Gerry asked. 'Why do you want to go on being married to me? It's crazy! It's daft.'

'It's simple, darling. I don't want to be married to anyone else and I don't want you to be either. Divorce,' Diana reminded him, 'is against my religion.'

Gerry sat on the patio area outside the French windows. It was the time of day of the time of year he loved the most: a May evening, and the haze of bluebells in the woods marched to the very edge of the garden, the garden he and Kate, leading each other in ignorance, had designed so that it *was* a garden, with a lawn and flower beds, but it melted away into the woods without any clash of soul or spirit.

This had helped the photographer, of course. It had allowed him to creep close with his camera and take his lying pictures. How could Gerry have supposed he should have surrounded himself with a six-foot wall?

He had the photographs – all twenty of them – spread out on the table in front of him. They must have been cropped, enlarged and then photographed again, so that it appeared he and Kate were lying naked in each other's arms when the original photograph would – could – only show Kate in a sundress greeting Gerry when he had been gardening, or doing some other strenuous physical work on a hot day. . . . Could an expert photographer tell? But then, what did it matter anyway? The original and its negative would have been destroyed, these photographs would be produced in court and the damage would be done by the time any expert witness Gerry had found went into the witness box and refuted them. And Diana would undoubtedly pay the photographer well for a bit of minor perjury.

Gerry poured himself another Glenmorangie and tried to look at the photographs objectively. It was incredible: he had to admit that anyone seeing these would give Diana a divorce on account of her husband's adultery with Dr Katherine Earith. Gerry's own efforts at compromising Diana were amateur in comparison, bungled and amateur: anonymous men entering and leaving the house in Mayfair at supremely innocent hours of the day . . . And he had felt ashamed of himself! Ashamed that he had given the detective his key to the house in Clarges Street and instructions to find his way to Diana's bedroom, had felt perversely relieved when told that the locks had been changed. A boy soldier, he had been, against a master strategist. How well Diana had planned all this.

Kate came round the side of the house and into the garden. Gerry stood up, spilling his whisky, and tried frantically to collect the photographs together and hide them from her view.

'Was I expecting you?' he said, hoping his voice sounded normal as he shovelled the photographs back into their envelope.

'No,' she said. 'Mike owed me a duty and gave it to me. It's a lovely evening and I thought we might go for a ride ... Gerry, what's the matter? What's in the envelope?'

'Nothing.'

She bent down and picked up one of the photographs which, in his haste, he had knocked off the table.

She looked at it. 'Dear God,' she said. 'Where did this come from?'

He shook his head helplessly. 'Diana,' he said.

'Are there more?'

He handed her the envelope. She sat down and tipped out its contents.

'Shall I get you a drink?' he asked.

'Yes, please.' Her voice was calm but her hands shook a little as she sorted through the photographs.

When Gerry came out with her gin and tonic, she was standing in the middle of the lawn. Rio appeared and ran towards her. Automatically she leaned to scratch his head. Gerry went to her and handed her the glass. She took a gulp.

'What is she going to do with them?'

'Nothing, unless I insist on a divorce.'

Her eyes were shocked blue pools. 'And if you do she'll show them in court? ... Gerry, I'd never work again.'

He didn't dare take her in his arms. The next move had to come from her. She walked away from him and stared down one of the grass pathways that led into the woods.

'Is he there now,' she said, almost to herself, 'taking pictures of us? What a dreadful thing to be spied upon. He must have been sneaking around out there for months.'

She was silent then, for what seemed like hours. At last, she turned to him.

'Gerry, I'd like to go for a ride ... do you mind if I go by myself?'

'No,' he said at once, his heart plummeting. 'I don't mind.'

They went up the track to the Club. Gerry caught Sprite, gave him a quick once-over with a dandy brush and tacked him up while Kate went into the Club, where she kept her riding clothes, and changed. He legged her into the saddle.

'Will you stay for supper?' he asked hesitantly. He'd have to get something from Elizabeth James, as all he had was the ingredients for her birthday dinner tomorrow. Would she be eating that, though? And one of her presents, which he was supposed to collect tonight, depended entirely on them being together in the future. Otherwise it was absurd. Her hand brushed his cheek.

'Yes, my darling. I'll stay to supper if I may.'

'Of course you may.' He tightened Sprite's girths for her and stood by the paddock rails and watched Kate and the little grey horse walk away. Florin nibbled at his shoulder and paced up and down, fussing about his companion's desertion of him.

'It's both of us,' Gerry told him. 'All either of us can do is wait.'

She came back to the house in the woods an hour later, having bathed and changed at the Club, and Gerry cooked supper which they ate on the patio. Gerry could not ask what decision she had come to on her ride and, for once, was grateful to Rio for providing a diversion: however many cuffs and scoldings he received, he could never be persuaded that food eaten outside was not his for the taking.

Dusk and dark and it grew chilly, but Kate would not go inside. Gerry brought her one of his sweaters and she put it on.

'Let's walk in the garden,' she said.

Mystified, full of dread, he followed her to the middle of the lawn where she stopped, turned to him and said:

'I'm going to be thirty-one tomorrow.'

'I know you are, my love.'

He waited.

'Gerry, I want to spend tonight with you.'

For the second time today, something inside him exploded: this one a firecracker, all surprises. He had thought she was going to tell him that she would do the sensible thing and marry James.

'Do you want me to?' she asked through the dark that separated them, anxiety in her voice.

He reached for her, held her and kissed her. His cock stirred from its long sleep, could not believe what it had heard and subsided.

'I only want it if you do, truly.'

Her cheek was against his, and the rough wool of the sweater she was wearing — his sweater, her arms in it — was swathed around his neck.

'While you were cooking supper I was looking at the book Bernard gave you. The one about gypsies. How they get married.'

'Yes,' he said.

'There are no priests and no ceremony, but they make a vow to each other in the hearing of their families . . . Gerry, is that how your parents married?'

'I don't know, Kate. I think there are all kinds of gypsy weddings—'

'It said that if they can, they go to a sacred site, though sacred to what I don't know . . . Gerry, this garden is sacred for us, isn't it? How we found it and made it? Even Diana's photographer can't spoil that.'

'I'll make a vow,' he said. 'Even though there is no one else here, I'll make it to you: to love you and only you, for ever.'

'And I to you. And to forsake all others. Say it, Gerry.'

'I forsake all others.'

She kissed him.

'Kate, are you sure?' he asked when his lips were free. 'I – I don't have anything. What if there's a baby?'

'Then I'm ruined anyway and you go to court.'

She was all confidence, he a bundle of nerves. It was Kate who said they should go to the Club, take Gerry's car out of the garage there and put Kate's in it instead and then go, as they often did, to have a nightcap with Elizabeth and Andrew James. Admiral and Mrs Partington were there and when Gerry came back from making his phone call about Kate's birthday present, and was telling Liz what to expect first thing in the morning, he heard his soon-to-be lover having an intense discussion with Henrietta Partington about lavatory paper.

'It's time I went,' Kate said, as she often did, shortly afterwards, and bade good night to the Partingtons and to Andrew and Liz.

They went outside. A half-moon had risen and they walked down a silvered path to the house in the woods.

'Are you sure?' he asked again as they went inside.

'We made our vows to each other. We are as married as your parents are. But I'm a bit . . . frightened,' she said, and then added, as though Gerry did not know: 'It's the first time for me, you see.'

'And for me, Kate, and for me,' he said and folded her in his arms. 'I've never made love before. Only the other. Never love.'

'You're shaking, Gerry.'

'Feel my pulse, take my blood pressure. Anyway, you're shaking too.'

'We both shook the first time we kissed each other under a willow tree on the bank of the Cam.'

'Did we, my Kate?' He supposed he remembered, but what was that compared to now? He was terrified, his cock was as lifeless as a wet weekend in Blackpool and he wondered if he was going to be able to do anything at all.

They went upstairs. She knew the house, of course, and most of the ideas for its conversion from two cottages had been hers: the long, thin bathroom squeezed into the space once occupied by the second staircase; the two small bedrooms – children's bedrooms she had always called them to herself; Gerry's bedroom, twice the size, the dividing wall knocked down so that there were windows on three sides; the double bed bought with the future in mind and also so Gerry could have married friends to stay, as Mark and Vanessa had the previous week, and Gerry and Charlie had slept in the children's bedrooms . . . All so familiar, although tonight it seemed like a foreign land, transformed because of why she had come here.

In spite of their nervousness, there was no awkwardness between them. They had known and loved each other for nearly ten years, no matter that they had spent five of those years apart.

He undressed her carefully, lovingly, and led her to the bed, then removed his own clothes and slid in beside her.

'You won't feel guilty tomorrow?' he asked. 'I couldn't bear it if you wake up tomorrow morning and won't meet my eyes.'

'I won't feel guilty,' she said.

'Say it again, and call me your darling Gerry.'

'My darling Gerry, I won't feel guilty.'

And then his hands and lips were everywhere on her, places she did not think existed screamed pleasure. She was helpless, falling away to his touch as though there were no bones in her flesh. And then, at last, he moved inside her a little way. She closed her eyes, concentrating on that core.

'Look at me, Kate,' he said, and she opened her eyes and looked into his dark brown ones and saw there anxiety, perhaps, and love, and she wanted him. She moved her hips upwards to him. It seemed so right, so natural. He sank into her and gave a gasp and a slight groan.

'Is it all right?' he asked, but she was away and then he was, too.

Gerry awoke. Sunlight poured through the window that faced east and he remembered the photographer and cursed himself for not closing the curtains last night. And then he thought, Diana has the evidence, she doesn't need any more . . . and anyway, was last night real? He turned his head on the pillow and looked at Kate: there she was beside him, beautifully asleep and entirely naked. Would she feel guilty, in spite of what she had said? Or, worse, embarrassed and ashamed? As he looked at her, she stirred and opened her eyes and smiled sleepily at him. She put out her hand – the right one, the one with his ring on it – and ran her fingers through the hair on his chest.

'Happy birthday, my Kate,' he said.

Her hand encountered his cock, which was rigid, straining for her.

'Great heavens,' she murmured. 'What a lesson in anatomy.'

He reached out his own hand and touched her breasts. No barriers between them, none at all. He was overwhelmed with a combination of desire and tenderness.

310

'But you don't need lessons. You're a grown-up doctor,' he said.

'Yes, but there are always surprises.'

He moved closer to her and kissed her. 'If ever you feel the need to test your anatomy, Kate, my body is entirely at your disposal.'

'Why, thank you,' she said, and laughed and wrapped both arms around him.

No guilt or shame, and no embarrassment either. Only love and then – what had so surprised and delighted him last night – intense passion.

He left her cooking breakfast and ran up the track to the Club. Making sure no one was watching, he backed Kate's car out of the garage and parked it innocently next to his Ford, and then went in search of Elizabeth James.

'It's here,' she told him. 'Take it, for God's sake. It's already chewed Andrew's laces and piddled on the carpet . . . Since when is ten-thirty first thing in the morning?'

'Sorry,' Gerry said, but could not help grinning.

Elizabeth James looked at him. He had come back from London yesterday demanding a bottle of Glenmorangie and saying his wife was refusing to give him a divorce, his face so bleak that Liz had thought she would never see that grin again; and last night when he and Kate had come in for a drink he had seemed tense and quite unlike his usual self.

'Has Kate arrived?' she asked.

'Yes,' he said. 'It's her birthday, you know. I must get back.'

She watched him go. She could guess what had happened and was glad of it. Why not? They had held off for four years. She would have to warn Kate, though, about the early morning golfers. It wouldn't do to meet those, the dreadful bunch of gossips that they were.

Kate had burned the toast and the bacon and was staring, fascinated, as the eggs in the frying pan turned brown at the edges. Eventually she worked out that they were burning too, and she turned off the stove and went outside. Her happiness filled her and there was no room for food. The bluebells in the woods were, surely, more beautiful than they had ever been, the columbines in

311

the garden, each one so perfect, the clematis hanging above the door like a shaggy, pink-speckled eyebrow.

She did not feel guilty about what she had done. She could not. All she could think about was last night and this morning, and what it was like to love someone truly, to give him everything you have, to feel him inside you. Did she reject the prudish twenty-two-year-old in her room in Girton, in the hop gardens, the hay fields and the apple orchards of Kent? She did not want to think about it. Her decision then and her decision now were different lives: what was the point of wishing things were otherwise?

But today, *today*! Today she felt full of bubbles like a bottle of champagne, and so taken was she by this idea that she went into the kitchen, took the bottle of champagne from the fridge which was, presumably, meant for later but never mind, and began undoing the foil around the cork. She was struggling with the wire when Gerry walked in and put a tiny black cocker spaniel down on the floor.

'He's for you,' he said.

The puppy's velvet nose quested around and his absurd ears cocked as he heard Kate's cry. She handed the bottle to Gerry and picked the puppy up. He licked her chin and then, tentatively, nibbled her ear. He smelt of milk and comfort.

'For me?' Kate asked. 'As well as the necklace you gave me?'

'I thought he'd live here.' He had thought, before yesterday, that all three of them would – or four, including Rio. 'If Rio doesn't mind, that is. But he's your dog. Do you like him?'

'He's lovely, *lovely*, Gerry. Just like Flash.' Flash who had died earlier this year at the great age of twelve. Kate had been dreadfully upset, which was why Gerry had the idea of this birthday present. She kissed Gerry's cheek. 'Thank you, my darling, thank you.'

'What is this?' he asked, indicating the bottle he was holding.

'Breakfast. I didn't do very well with the rest of it, I'm afraid.'

He went and looked at the frying pan and grill. 'Kate, my love,' he said wonderingly, 'you'd wreck a bloody boiled egg.'

'I'm not that bad usually. I just can't concentrate today.'

He took glasses from a shelf and opened the bottle. 'Why is that, do you suppose? Advancing old age?'

'It must be. I can't think of anything else, can you?'

She followed him outside. He handed her a glass and clinked his own against it.

'To you, Kate, and the next thirty-one years. And may I look as good as you do when I reach your age.'

'Well!' she said, outraged. 'If I hadn't a puppy in one hand and a glass in the other I'd hit you for that.'

'Put the puppy down and do it then,' he said, laughing.

'No.' She bent and let the little dog out of her arms and on to the lawn. 'It might have a terrible effect on him, to hear us quarrelling. Make him feel insecure or something.'

'What will you call him?'

She gazed at the puppy and sipped her champagne.

'Parsnip,' she said at last. 'He looks like one.'

Gerry picked the little black object up and looked at it, its pink tongue and sharp white teeth, its silky body and rounded blotched tummy. 'Parsnip,' he said. 'I see. Your mistress,' he told the puppy, 'is either insane or in love, but she's the boss and that makes you Parsnip.' He found one of Rio's rubber balls (scorned since Rio had discovered live prey) and threw it a few feet out on the lawn. Parsnip let out an excuse of a bark and gave chase.

'Isn't he *gorgeous!*' Kate exclaimed. 'Gerry, thank you again.'

'You're gorgeous, too, Kate . . . no regrets about last night?'

'None. *None!*' she said, clinging to him.

'I must get some . . . you know . . . precautions.'

'French letters?' She looked at his startled face and laughed. 'Gerry my darling, I'm a doctor in an army town. I'm forever telling the prostitutes to use them. We see quite a few of the girls, for one reason or another.'

'All right,' he said hastily. 'Anyway, I'll get some. French letters, I mean.'

She watched Parsnip trying to work out why the ball moved when he put a paw on it.

'I don't know. I rather hope I'll get pregnant. It would sort everything out, wouldn't it? I wouldn't mind those photographs in court if it was because of our child. In fact, I don't mind them so much at all now that it's real, now that it's happened and they could be true. . . . Gerry, perhaps you *should* go to court—'

'No!'

'Gerry—'

'No, I say.'

He turned away from her. Parsnip whined and, absently, she threw the ball for him again.

'Gerry—' she began once more.

'No! And no argument about it.'

She had never seen him angry before. She stretched out her hand and touched him. He took the hand in one of his and squeezed it so hard that it hurt. 'I can't let it happen to you, Kate,' he said, his voice calmer now. 'Your reputation and your career would be slaughtered – assassinated in cold blood in public. You've already given up enough for me. I *won't* let it happen.'

'But if I'm pregnant my career won't matter. By the time I go back to it, I'd be a respectable married woman and everything will be forgotten. Gerry, I want children. Do you?'

He sighed and sat down, pulling her on to his lap.

'I want your children, my Kate,' he said, his voice now back to normal.

Parsnip came up, flopped at Gerry's feet and fell into the abrupt sleep of the very young animal.

Kate wound her arms around Gerry's neck. 'Then no French letters. And if I get pregnant we take the consequences of our actions and go to court.'

He laughed shakily. 'I can't believe we're having this conversation. You're asking me to . . . It's incredible!'

'I suppose it is a bit.' She paused. 'But then I asked you to go to bed with me—'

'And that *was* incredible.'

'I thought I'd have to wait another nine years before you asked *me*, you see.'

'Oh no!' He hugged her tightly. 'You're teasing me, Kate. Tell me you're teasing me.'

'I'm teasing you.' Then, suddenly, she was serious. She sat up in his lap, put her hands on his shoulders and pushed herself away from him.

'Gerry, you meant our vows, didn't you? Every word of them?'

'To love you and only you for ever. And to forsake all others. I meant every word,' he said.

Chapter 20

Paul Marling did not want the money he was owed by Patrick, and he cursed the name of Alchemist and the other horses which had run well, the ghosts of Cyril and George Morgan riding on their tails, urging them on for the sake of their descendant to whom they had bequeathed their gambling blood. The money was an investment, not a loan, and the dividend was due to be paid when Rede Park Racecourse Ltd went public.

Now what was he to do? Patrick's cheque was in his hand and the urge to crumple it up and hurl it to the floor was almost overwhelming.

'Double or quits?' he heard his own voice saying. 'How about it?'

Patrick put his glass down on the bar – they were in the Coach and Horses in Soho; Marling did not care to meet him in City pubs – and stared at him challengingly.

'I'd take it, old boy,' he said, 'but I'm a bit short of the readies at the moment. I couldn't cover another eight thou—'

But he wanted the bet, he wanted it! Christ, but these gamblers were mad! But Paul Marling was mad, too. He could lose sixteen thousand pounds.

He tried to sound casual. 'You wouldn't need to. Tell you what. You win and get this cheque back' – he laid it on the bar next to Patrick's glass – 'and another eight thou. I win and I get the cheque and some of the shares in your racecourse.'

'Some of my shares?' said Patrick, astonished. 'For eight

thousand pounds? My dear chap, the whole lot of them aren't worth that. Anyway I don't think I can get rid of them, not unless it's to a fellow director.'

'You can give me an IOU,' Marling said carefully. 'Old boy.'

'For the money?'

'No, for the shares.'

'But what if I can never let you have them?'

'Well, that's my gamble, isn't it?' He managed a smile. 'But if you don't want to accept, that's fine by me.'

He made to pick up the cheque, but Patrick stopped him and called to the landlord for paper and pen.

Patrick began writing. Paul Marling was trembling and wondered what whirlpool he was getting into. The money he cold lose! Yet consider what he could win.

'Make the whole bet on your shares,' he said.

Patrick put down the pen and stared at him again, this time with concern.

'But it means I can't lose. It's no bet.'

'You can lose. You can lose sixteen thousand one-pound shares – thirty-two thousand ten-shilling ones – when your racecourse goes public.'

'But it will be ages before it does that. So far as I can see the place is up to its eyebrows in debt. I know the first meeting was successful, but it's a puddle in the Atlantic, believe me. You couldn't give the shares away.'

'I want it like this,' Marling said, and there was an edge to his voice and a wild look in his eyes that Patrick recognised as being the gamblers' fever, and who was he – knowing it so well – to argue?

Paul Marling had been amazed at how simple it had been to deceive Patrick, amazed how he'd fallen for that absurd system of betting. Because of some ridiculous code of practice among people who bet on horses, you never said which nag you had backed until it had won or lost, and it had been easy to cheer home the winning horse whenever appropriate or groan when something anonymous was back in the pack. He'd had one or two sticky moments: once, in the early days, instead of clapping Patrick on the back and disappearing in the direction of the bookies to collect his 'winnings', he had offered Patrick a drink and had been unable to say at what odds he had backed the horse; and another time, he found he had supposedly backed a 50–1 winner, not realising that the people behind him (the owners' friends, presumably) and himself were the only people in the crowd yelling for the horse as it took the lead and held on to it. Patrick had demanded he buy champagne in celebration that day, for, as he so tediously continued to point out, Paul had won over two thousand pounds.

Why was he going to these lengths? He had asked himself that question often enough over the past four years, but really the answer was simple: thieving gypsy Beviss junior seemed to be the genius behind Rede Park Racecourse, and what gypsy Beviss had Paul Marling wanted. Ridge Farm was impregnable but twenty per cent of Rede Park Racecourse Ltd was owned by a man who could not resist a bet. The company would go public, Marling knew that; he could wait. Sixteen thousand pounds-worth of shares: what would that represent? He'd have to persuade Patrick to show him the company's annual reports and accounts so he could get an idea of what it was likely to be valued at when it went to the Stock Exchange. ... Sixteen thousand pounds-worth of shares, though, at the flotation price and with no suspicion attached. If he won.

They went to the Derby meeting at Epsom. It was agreed that before each race each would write the name of his fancied horse on a piece of paper and deliver it to a third party, another gambler whom they both knew and who had agreed to act as referee, although he did not know what was at stake. The first to pick a winning horse took the pot.

Paul Marling, for once actually trying to find a winner, simply selected the favourite and in the first race the favourite duly obliged, but Patrick was on it too and the race was declared void by the referee; both their horses were well down the field in the second race, and in the third, the Derby itself, Cyril and George Morgan showed Patrick that they had not followed him to Epsom: having worked out a complicated line of form between Quorum, Alchemist, Crepello and various other horses, Patrick did not believe – as the bookmakers, the housewives and the punters up and down the land did – that Crepello could add the Derby to his Two Thousand Guineas.

No pair of ghosts can stop a good horse from winning.

Gerry and Kate went to the Derby as guests of Sir Henry Blower. The invitations came from Lady Blower on thick cream notepaper and Gerry stared at his for a long time. Bernard's work, of course. Gerry often wondered if the man read his soul.

Kate spun into a female panic which delighted Gerry as it was so unlike her. She and Elizabeth James went on a shopping expedition to Salisbury because Kate declared she hadn't anything to wear. They returned empty-handed saying it was altogether hopeless and made plans to go to London, which involved Kate doing all kinds of duty swaps and Gerry having to stand in as barman at the Club, summoned by Andrew who could normally cope in his wheelchair at quiet lunchtimes by the simple expedient of inviting the Club members to help themselves to drinks. But today was the perfect action of sod's law, he explained, since Maggie, the barmaid, had a cold and everyone had decided to come to the Club. There were more people behind the bloody bar than in front of it, he said, and why did women go away on the very day that they were most wanted?

So Gerry left the office in the grandstand and he and Parsnip ran down the racecourse – until Parsnip tired and had to be carried – and provided an emergency service. Then he and Andrew (and Parsnip) had lunch and Andrew brought out the figures for the catering side of Rede Park's first meeting.

Gerry looked at the neat columns and then back at Andrew.

'Good God,' he said.

Andrew winked at him.

'Shall we poach a bottle of something appropriate from the bar?'

On the first Wednesday in June, along with half a million or so other people, Gerry and Kate converged upon Epsom Downs. It was the sort of day that makes a mockery of summer and Vanessa, with whom Kate – very properly – had spent the previous night, thrust upon Kate the fur jacket Mark had given her. It covered up most of Kate's new and expensive dress, but she was glad of it as they stepped off the train at Tattenham Corner under an unfriendly grey sky.

It was the first time either of them had been to the Derby – Gerry had been to all the other great races but had somehow missed this one, although he had been to lesser meetings at Epsom – and they had decided to come early so they could wander around the Downs among the gypsies and the fun fair and the bustle before joining their august host and hostess.

'You might,' Kate told him, 'meet some of your relations here, mightn't you?'

He tipped back his top hat and grinned at her. 'I might at that,' he said, and he bought a sprig of heather from a woman with a snivelling child clinging to her skirts in case, he said, she was a long-lost cousin.

'For you, my Kate,' he said, presenting the heather to her.

'Thank you, kind sir.'

She put it in the pocket of Vanessa's jacket and they strolled on through the massive good-natured crowd. London had emptied, it seemed, and all because of a horse race which would last under three minutes. Trains were diverted for it; hundreds of open-topped double-decker buses filled with cheerful, noisy people lined the rails opposite the grandstands and more were arriving all the time; offices in the City closed; gypsies made their long, slow way to Surrey and traded horses and talked and fought, no doubt, though were united against the racegoers, inviting them to cross their palms with silver.

And they came here and married, perhaps, in the gypsy way.

Thinking this, Kate's grip on Gerry's arm tightened. He looked down.

'Pleased to be here?'

'Yes! It's our first official engagement together, isn't it?'

'You make us sound like the Royal Family . . . Hey, Kate, have your fortune told by one of these authentic Gypsy Rose Lees.'

'No,' she said. 'She'll tell me about a tall, dark and handsome man, and I've got one of those.'

'A spare might come in handy.'

319

'One keeps me perfectly occupied, thank you.'

'I'm glad to hear it,' he said.

A fun fair brings out the child in the adult at the gloomiest of times and Gerry, who was feeling on top of the world, was longing to try everything and had to be restrained.

'Not the dodgems?' he asked longingly.

'My hat would fall off and my gloves would get dirty and something dreadful would happen to your tails. We wouldn't be allowed into the Prince's Stand, let alone Sir Henry Blower's box.'

She consented, however, to a sedate ride on the merry-go-round, tried the hoopla and held Gerry's coat and hat while he shied for a coconut and, most inconveniently, won one.

'Can't it go into your handbag?'

'No, Gerry, it cannot. Come on, it's time we went.'

Reluctantly Gerry handed his coconut to a small boy who was eating an ice cream, allowed his tie to be straightened and his morning coat inspected for imperfections and then bent his head and stole a kiss.

'I'm henpecked,' he said, 'and I love it.'

Kate looked severely at him and then scrutinised herself in the mirror of her powder compact. Gerry took out the badges he had been sent, put one in the lapel of his coat and tied the other to the strap of Kate's handbag.

'All ready,' he said.

'Put your hat on straight.'

He tilted it further over. 'Why?'

'Because we're supposed to be serious.'

'No we're not. It's Derby Day.'

Derby Day! They left the colourful crowds behind and joined the stream of grey and black tails and top hats, walking past yet more gypsy caravans with women begging them to have their fortunes told, and Gerry was visited by an odd notion: it was not just likely, it was certain that some relatives of his were here. Perhaps he would ask around after racing ... but then perhaps not. What, after all, could he possibly say to a cousin of Joe's, or even an aunt of his own, for Meg had sisters, he remembered. No, there was no point in going in search of them, but enough to know they were there.

He straightened his topper and tucked Kate's hand more firmly into his elbow. A man going to the Derby with his girl on his arm and nothing at all to hide.

He backed Crepello even at the absurd odds of 6–4 because the horse looked unbeatable both on the form and in the flesh, and also out of loyalty to Quorum, beaten half a length by Crepello at Newmarket but, as the papers pointed out, had gone on to win, hard held, the high-class Blue Oceans Handicap at Rede Park.

'How can we not back him?' Gerry asked Bernard.

'We can't,' Bernard replied firmly.

'I'm going to put my shirt on him,' Sir Henry said. 'Dr Earith, would you care to accompany me to the Tote? My wife seems to have vanished and these chaps, I dare say, will be off to the bookmakers.'

'I'd be delighted to,' Kate said, 'but I wish you would call me Kate.'

'Your wish is my command, of course,' Sir Henry said gravely. 'I like being called by my title and assumed you'd like to be called by yours. And, unlike you, I didn't earn mine.'

Crepello won, yet more champagne was called for and drunk. Sir Henry's son, David, who trained horses near Marlborough 'not very successfully', invited Gerry to come and ride out his jumpers when they started work, even said he might put him up in some amateur races if he was any good. His wife, Helen, and Kate hit it off immediately and plans were made for Kate and Gerry to go to dinner at the young Blowers' house.

David Blower, like Gerry, had not been allowed full run at the fun fair before racing and they agreed they'd give it a good workout afterwards. They went on the dodgems (several times), on the big wheel, on the merry-go-round again. Gerry won another coconut, Helen Blower a goldfish in a plastic bag, Kate, with some freakish dart-throwing, a large teddy bear which she could give to Anne Colley-Smythe although that meant she had to win something for Charlie. Helen offered the goldfish but Gerry and David said this was being feeble and spent a fortune before emerging triumphant with a cowboy outfit. By which time they had missed their lifts back to London and so carried their booty to the train and then to a nightclub, where a receptacle for the goldfish was demanded and provided. They had horrible difficulty getting it back into the plastic bag much later, but succeeded with the help of a waiter and a large tip. Kate was put into a taxi together with the teddy bear and the cowboy outfit and sent to Richmond. Helen, David and the goldfish – inevitably called Crepello – took another one to Sir Henry and Lady Blower's London flat and Gerry and his coconut walked to the Oxford and Cambridge Club in Pall Mall in a bubble of alcohol and well being.

He did not believe he had an enemy in the world.

Not an enemy in the world when Kate spent the night with him and awoke when the sun filled their bedroom and she turned and wanted him; or when the windows bulged with grey cloud and rain and she awoke and opened to his touch and wanted him. And after, she would roll from the bed and wander naked to the bathroom and Gerry, unshaven and dressing-gowned, would go downstairs and let Parsnip out to run and greet the dew while Rio, meticulously avoiding the little dog, came in out of it and asked for his breakfast even though he was, surely, full of rabbit or mouse or pheasant poult after his nefarious night in the woods.

No enemy in the world when, after breakfast, Gerry and Parsnip accompanied Kate up the track to the Club where – the only concession – Kate's car was kept in one of the outbuildings. She would kiss Gerry goodbye, pick up Parsnip and kiss him too, promise to see them both that evening and drive away.

No enemy at all when she was on night duty and spent her days dozing in the house in the woods or doing some lazy gardening, Parsnip with her instead of in the office in the grandstand chewing Captain Beech's regimental tie – which he had, regrettably, done.

No enemy whatsoever. Perhaps they were trying to provoke a scandal – Kate certainly was: she was taking terrible risks – which would take the decision out of their hands and push them into the divorce courts. But they were so open about it, so obvious, that no one – *no one* – said a word.

* * *

A board meeting of Rede Park Racecourse Ltd was held in the directors' box in October. Apologies for the absence of Diana Beviss were recorded in the minutes by Jennifer Cody even though none had been received, and Andrew James was invited in to present interim figures for Rede Park's first full season and answer any questions the board might care to put to him about them. After they had done so, Andrew wheeled himself away.

Bernard then made a rapid series of proposals: Elizabeth and Andrew James and Captain Nicholas Beech were to be made directors of the company; Rede Park Country Club and all the catering were to become a separate company, a wholly owned subsidiary of the main one, and Elizabeth and Andrew were to be its joint managing directors. Gerry was to be on that board too. Bernard said he wanted to relinquish his title of managing director of the main board, although he would keep that of chairman, and, with the board's approval, planned to appoint Gerry to the post.

The board approved everything, of course. Bernard's two wise heads, to whom Gerry had not spoken more than twenty words in all the time the company had been in existence, murmured, as they always did when Bernard proposed anything, 'Seconded . . . aye,' and Patrick, appearing somewhat out of his depth, echoed them. Bernard then rattled through the rest of the agenda, cut Patrick short when it seemed he wanted to raise something under 'any other business' and suggested a further meeting in a month's time when the new directors would have had a chance to assimilate the figures and be in a position to contribute fully to the discussion about the racecourse's next step. One of the wise heads brought out a diary and made a note and the other blew his nose.

The two of them then left and, hesitantly, Patrick followed. Gerry felt a little sorry for him, for there was no place for him in the celebrations that would most certainly follow in the Club. His ancestors may have laid the turf for the racecourse, but he had not done anything towards making Rede Park's first season the success it undoubtedly was.

But Bernard was talking to Gerry. He was raising his salary – great heavens! Really by that much? – and discussing the pay rises of the new directors. He went on to say he knew that Gerry had wanted the board's approval today to go ahead with phase two of the grandstands; that although Andrew's figures had showed they were handsomely ahead of even the most optimistic expectations, the company still owed huge amounts of money, and another year's consolidation might be no bad thing.

'It's been phenomenal,' he said, standing up and putting papers into his briefcase, 'but we're still a novelty. We must be sure we're right in the fabric of the racing year, that people will come back and back.'

'They come to see good horses and good horses come for good prizes.'

'The Blue Oceans races certainly proved that,' Bernard said.

'And it's been worth every penny to them. Da's talking of starting up on the east coast. He says there aren't enough shrimps and prawns in the Channel.'

Bernard paused in the act of locking his briefcase.

'Really, Gerry?'

'Well, he's talking. He's having to buy in and he doesn't like that. They sold more than fifteen thousand cartons of potted shrimps and prawns here over the season, just to people who wanted to take them home. They're on sale in Leighminster.'

'Good grief!' Bernard said, stunned.

'It's an advertisement for sponsoring a race at Rede Park, isn't it? That,' Gerry said, 'is what I'm going to spend the winter doing if I can't watch builders at work here: persuade other companies to do the same. And if they won't, I want us – the racecourse – to put more money up for the prizes.'

'I wouldn't object to that.' Bernard put his arm around Gerry's shoulders and guided him out of the door of the directors' box. 'And I'm not saying we shouldn't go ahead with the extensions to the grandstands. Let's all think about it for the next month, and your new directors must have their say too, you know. Speaking of which, shouldn't you inform them of their new status?'

Gerry stared at him. 'No – shouldn't you?' he said.

'Absolutely not. You don't want your authority handed over by me. You must take it as though by right.'

'But you're coming to lunch at the Club, aren't you? You said you would.'

324

'I am indeed, but I have one or two things to do in Leighminster first. I'll be there in an hour or so.'

Gerry watched him drive away. What had he ever done to deserve the confidence, faith and trust of a man like Bernard Rosenthal? . . . And what the hell was Bernard going to do in Leighminster for an hour? Give Gerry time, that was all. Time to take hold of his kingdom. He turned and looked at it: the paddock, the entrance to the Tote hall, the Blue Oceans Bar, the grandstands towering above . . . Not everyone's idea of a kingdom, perhaps, but it would do him.

Chapter 21

Parsnip pricked his ears, ran to the back door and whined. Gerry opened the door and the little dog shot out into the dark. He had heard Kate's car arriving half a mile away – incredible, but true: they had synchronised their watches and timed it – and had gone to meet her. Gerry tasted the boeuf Bourguignone, went into the sitting room and threw another log on the fire, then prepared Kate's gin and tonic and poured himself another Glenmorangie.

Kate came in, Parsnip bounding hysterically around her. Gerry removed various knitted objects from about her person and, on at last encountering naked flesh, kissed it and said,

'Is it really that cold?'

'There's a nasty wind.'

He took off her coat, hung it up and handed her the gin and tonic. She took a sip and looked up at him.

'Gerry, I've been offered a job. In general practice. Completely out of the blue, because I'd stopped applying since . . . well, since we thought we'd have a baby.' Parsnip brought her one of Gerry's socks and invited her to play tug o' war with him. She removed it from his silky jaws and unwrapped the newspaper from the bone she had brought him. 'And today,' she went on, 'this man – Dr Badger – rang up and came and had lunch in the canteen at the hospital. He's from Trowbridge way. There's him and another partner and they want a junior – and, Gerry, they've actually decided they want a woman.'

'But that's wonderful!' he exclaimed.

'Yes . . .' She watched as Parsnip dragged his bone under the table and settled down for a good chew. 'Yes,' she said again, 'but I don't think I can accept it.'

'Kate! Whyever not?'

'Let's go and sit by the fire.'

Gerry checked that dinner was behaving itself and followed her into the sitting room.

'How can I?' she said, taking the guard from the fire and sinking down on to the hearthrug. 'How can I when I intend to have an illegitimate baby? But a general practice at last! And Dr Badger is such a nice man.'

'Perhaps we should start taking precautions,' Gerry suggested.

'But I want the baby! That would resolve everything, wouldn't it?' She gulped at her drink and gazed into the flames of the fire. 'Gerry, are you sure we shouldn't go to court now and get it over and done with?'

'Not until you're pregnant. We agreed. No,' he said as she started to speak. 'We agreed.' He picked up the poker and prodded the fire. 'Kate, I want a divorce, God knows I do. It's bad enough that I'll get it at the expense of your reputation, but then we'll have our child and that will be all right.' He put down the poker, reached out his hand and turned her face towards him. 'Think about it, Kate,' he said gently. 'Think. What if Diana did her worst and the case made the papers? Would the hospital renew your contract? What would you do all day? You aren't at all domesticated, you loathe housework and you can't cook, and I love you for it, but what the hell would you do? All your training gone to waste . . . You'd be bored and frustrated and you'd end up hating me. Now isn't that true?'

She sighed. 'Probably. All but the last bit anyway.'

'There you are then.' He sat back in his chair and picked up his glass. 'We'll go to court when you're pregnant. Yes?'

'All right.' She leaned against his knees. 'I don't understand why I'm not already,' she said. 'After all, we've been trying for – what? – six months.'

'Trying!' he said. 'Oh my Kate, what a word to use! Perhaps we haven't been *trying* hard enough.' He looked at his watch. 'We could *try* again now, except we've got a dinner party and there isn't time.'

'Later, though?'

'Later.'

'Promise?'

'I promise to try *very hard* later, my Kate.' He bent and kissed her. 'What did you tell your Dr Badger?'

'That I'd let him know.'

'I haven't been much help, have I? What will you say?'

'I can't say yes, can I? So I must say no.'

'Oh Kate,' Gerry said, dismayed. 'Must you? Just like that? It's what you've always wanted.'

They were silent for a time. Parsnip, in search of friends, brought his bone in and seemed inclined to bury it under the cushions of the sofa.

'He's so badly disciplined, Gerry,' Kate scolded, hauling the dog down. 'You must be firmer with him. He mustn't climb on the furniture.'

But Gerry wasn't listening. 'Do you think it might be worth telling Dr Badger the truth?' he asked. 'If he's enlightened enough to want a woman partner, he may be prepared to take that risk with everything else.'

She gazed at him. 'It's hardly likely, is it?' she said, but hope was in her eyes.

'It would be better than a straight refusal. It would give you a chance, even if it's only a squeak of one.'

'The merest whimper in the dark,' she said.

Gerry stood up and pulled her to her feet.

'Let's think about it. Maybe Helen and Susan will have something to add.'

David and Helen Blower and their other dinner guests, Michael and Susan Lewis, arrived at the same time, wearing wellington boots and thick winter coats and carrying torches and their evening shoes.

'Christ, Gerry,' David said, struggling out of his coat as Kate took the two women upstairs, 'why can't you live somewhere civilised?'

'He does,' Michael Lewis pointed out, indicating the warm, friendly kitchen, the table at the far end laid for six and sniffing the delicious cooking smells. 'It's only getting here that's the challenge.'

328

David and Helen had become great friends and had introduced Gerry and Kate to several other young couples in the area, including Michael, an army captain, and Susan Lewis. All of them knew about Gerry's situation and Helen was, in fact, distantly acquainted with Diana since they had been débutantes together.

'She was known as a first-class—' Helen had said, and then stopped awkwardly and flushed bright scarlet.

'Bitch. That's right,' Gerry had said cheerfully. 'Only I didn't discover that until it was too late.'

No one had mentioned Diana since, and Gerry and Kate were invited out together and treated as though they were married. Some people knew and others suspected that they slept together, but no one mentioned that either. There were some fractionally raised eyebrows when it was learned that Gerry's family (a gypsy family, some said) owned a frozen fish company, but since he was so open about it – even proud of it, especially of Blue Oceans' successful sponsorship of races at Rede Park – it was difficult for even the most hardened snob to cut him. One man born, another made by Cambridge, the third welded from the first two by Bernard Rosenthal, a Jew . . . a confident man, a complete one. One who, it was to be hoped, would make no more appalling mistakes with his life.

'Stop complaining and have a drink,' he told David now, as Kate brought Helen and Susan, their shoes changed and their hair set to rights after their trek through the woods, back into the kitchen.

'Lovely,' David said, 'but go easy on the Glenmorangie, Gerry. You're racing on Saturday.'

Gerry nearly dropped the sherry bottle he was holding.

'I'm *what*?'

'On Extol. Amateur three-mile chase at Wincanton.'

'Good God!'

'You've been nagging me to get you a ride ever since you got your permit. You might at least thank me.'

Gerry handed Susan and Helen a glass each.

'You might at least have given me more warning.'

'Less time to worry about it. The owner's broken a leg, so if you do well you'll have the ride for the rest of the season.'

329

'But we've got our big board meeting next week—'

David took a glass. 'Extol may not be the fastest thing on four legs, Gerry, but it won't take him that long to go three miles.'

'Is Gerry fit enough, though?' Kate asked.

'He'll be as fit as his rivals, fitter probably,' Helen said. 'It'll be a doddle. Nearly everyone falls off in amateur races anyway, so if he stays on board he's sure to get placed. Extol's a good enough horse, better than his form suggests. His owner insists on riding him and he's not much cop. We call him the Arse-end Charlie because he always tries to come from behind and gives the poor horse too much to do.'

David put an arm around Kate, squeezed her and smiled into her anxious face.

'Gerry will be fine,' he told her. 'Honestly he will. He's got the show jumper's eye and can see a stride into a fence: one, two, three and up. All he has to do is avoid the other runners when they fall over.'

'And presumably he'll have his own personal medical officer in attendance,' Michael Lewis said.

'He certainly will,' Kate said grimly.

Leaving the men to keep Gerry company in the kitchen, Kate, Susan and Helen went and sat by the fire in the sitting room, a reversal of what usually happened in other households which startled the men when they first encountered it and charmed the women.

'Gerry will be thirty next year,' Kate said. 'He's too old to start this sort of caper.'

'Nonsense.' Helen sat on the sofa, grimaced, rummaged under the cushions and removed Parsnip's bone. 'I wish I could do it. It's so unfair that they don't let women race.'

'It's another worry, though,' Kate said, and she told the other two about her unexpected offer of a job and the dilemma it posed.

'Talk to him, as Gerry suggests,' Susan said promptly. 'What is there to lose?'

'I suppose there's a possibility that he would feel obliged to tell my bosses at the hospital. . . . That's how he heard of me, you see. Mr Finch told him. You can't deny it: I'm morally unsound.'

'Well, if he does that Gerry can go to court and get his divorce, can't he?' said Helen, who knew more than anyone else – more, even, than Beattie, before whom Kate had to wear her bravest face – how much Kate wanted to be married to Gerry. 'So why not chuck the whole thing into the melting pot and let fate cook it as it will?'

Kate stood up, took three purposeful steps across the room and then swirled around and looked at her friends.

'Yes,' she said. 'Yes, that's what I'll do. Thank you.'

'Are you quite sure about the baby?' Susan enquired. 'The twins decided that my Christmas pudding lacked something and they tipped a bottle of scent into the mixture. A whole bottle! And it was Chanel Number Five.'

Kate laughed. 'Quite sure,' she said.

She rang Dr Badger the next day and arranged to see him 'patients permitting' that afternoon before evening surgery. Evening surgery! The words chimed at her from her childhood, those and morning surgery. She knew it was absurd, but she could not help hoping Dr Badger's offer of a job would hold. She wondered if she could make any compromises, but there was none that she could see: being married to Gerry and having their baby came first, even if they happened the wrong way round, and these she would not give up for all the general practices in the world.

Amid all these thoughts, she had not considered what she would say to Dr Badger, and she sat tongue-tied in his comfy sitting room until he said, smiling pleasantly as he handed her a cup of tea, 'Well, doctor, what's the verdict?'

Hesitantly, she told him that although she would love to be his and Dr Jones's junior partner, she could not accept the post, and when he asked her why she explained. He was wondrously easy to talk to and his face was thoughtful and grave as he listened to what was, in many ways, a sordid story.

'I see,' he said when she had finished. 'Well, I'm grateful to you for telling me.'

'What will you do?'

Dr Badger laced his fingers together on one knee and contemplated them.

331

'With your permission, I should like to discuss it with Dr Jones – in confidence, of course.'

'Then you're not turning me down flat?' Kate asked in some surprise, her blue eyes eager on his face.

He hated to take the light from her. 'You have done me the courtesy of being honest with me. You could have taken this job which, obviously, you want so much, and presented us with an . . . embarrassment at a later date, and that would have reflected upon the whole practice and not just on you—'

'I know. I couldn't have done that.'

'As I said, I am grateful. And in return I will not turn you down flat, as you put it. I will discuss it with my colleague and see if there is a way around it.'

'But you doubt it.'

'And so do you. Come, doctor, you know full well our profession must be above reproach.'

'Yes,' Kate said, feeling a stab of guilt even though there was no censorious note in Dr Badger's voice. She prepared to leave.

'I'll ring you next week,' he said.

'Thank you,' she said, and drove away, a tiny spark alive in her, the merest whimper in the dark.

Gerry stood on one leg and then the other, and waggled his feet.

'They feel funny,' he complained.

'It's either lightweight boots or a tiny saddle,' David Blower said brutally. 'If you'd bothered to shed a couple of pounds you wouldn't have had to choose. Anyway, stop thinking about your bloody boots and concentrate on the horse . . . Ah, here comes the owner at last,' he added, as a man wearing a trilby hat hobbled on crutches into the paddock accompanied by a woman wearing a well-cut tweed coat and a smart felt hat. 'Mr and Mrs White,' David said.

Gerry stared at them, nerves and the discomfort of his boots forgotten as the man fiddled with his crutches so he could raise his hat to Helen and Kate and explained that they were late because Eileen drove at the pace of a snail and they had taken a wrong turning. Eileen, once McLennan, smiled at Gerry and said:

'Well, Gerald Beviss, still with the horses?' And her husband, Stephen White, once master of the Cambridge University Drag Hounds, took Gerry's hand, shook it firmly and said,

'I thought it had to be you, but I didn't quite believe the coincidence.'

'Extol is yours?' Gerry asked, knowing the question was foolish.

'Didn't David tell you?'

'No . . . No, he—' And Gerry stopped, because David referred to his owners, collectively and individually, by various epithets none of which included their names. 'How long have you and Eileen been married?'

Stephen glanced fondly at his wife, who was greeting Kate with much laughter and cries of astonishment.

'Just over three weeks. I bust the leg on our honeymoon. What a thing to do, eh? How about you and Kate?'

Gerry was saved the explanation as David interrupted them, enquiring sarcastically if Gerry intended to ride in this race or was he planning to stand and gossip in the paddock for ever?

Gerry was legged up on to Extol and David himself led him around the paddock. Gerry was expecting another blistering attack, such as he had endured on David's gallops these past few mornings, but David chattered about nothing consequential, saying how extraordinary it was that he and Stephen White should have known each other all those years ago and then, as he swept the rug from Extol's quarters and let go of the bridle when they went on to the racecourse, merely told him: 'Relax and enjoy yourself, Gerry. And for God's sake, stay out of trouble.'

And Gerry did all those things, and won.

Helen ran out as, with the last of his strength, Gerry pulled Extol down to a trot. The muscles in his shoulders and arms felt like jelly and his calves and thighs were agony. He smiled at Helen and shook his head as she congratulated him, having no breath to speak.

'I must get fitter,' he panted at last, and then, as he realised that the crowd was cheering him, said, 'What's all the fuss?'

Helen laughed up at him. 'You didn't know? We hoped you wouldn't. You were the favourite, Gerry.'

He lurched in the saddle. 'You mean I was expected to win?'

'Oh yes,' she said. 'We backed you three days ago. You've just won us our winter feed bill.'

She gave up her place to Extol's lad and Eileen White gingerly took the other rein of the bridle as she led her husband's horse into the winners' enclosure, where Stephen White slapped Gerry so hard on the back that he nearly fell off his crutches and Gerry, in his weakened state, was practically floored.

A winner is always welcome, even if it is only of an amateur race at a small West Country course. The celebrations began, vaguely punctuated by the running of the other five races on the card, at the track and then, after some discussion, at the Blowers' house. One of David's other horses won the last and the party expanded, but it did not include Kate for she was on duty that evening and begged a lift back to Rede Park with Jennifer Cody and Captain Beech. Many toasts were drunk, omelettes were cooked and eaten and records were put on the gramophone. Gerry – since Stephen was *hors de combat* – danced with Eileen, and they recalled how they had danced together once before.

'An eightsome reel,' Eileen said. 'You managed very well.'

She and Stephen had known each other distantly at Cambridge and had met up again at a wedding last year. And that, said Eileen, had been that. She had given up translating documents for the Board of Trade and was looking forward to settling down to life as a farmer's wife in Somerset.

'Who would have believed it?' Gerry said.

'Who indeed?' she responded.

Love – or time – had softened her hard edges and the same had injected levity into Stephen, who now called for his wife and used her to lean on as he poured Gerry yet more champagne.

'You'll ride Extol for me again?' he asked. 'At least until this damned leg mends.'

'Tell me when and where,' Gerry said, and was dragged off to dance by the owner of David's other winner who was, if it were possible, even more thrilled about her horse's success than Stephen was about his, and who wrapped her arms around Gerry's neck and told him things with her body, though he was too high in the air to interpret what they were.

Later, much later, he found himself sitting in an armchair with the woman on his lap.

'I don't live far away,' she murmured in his ear. 'Why don't you come home for a nightcap?'

She brushed her lips over his cheek, found his mouth. He felt her breasts and his hands ran down over the rest of her. His cock was interested, but something was wrong. He gazed at her blearily.

'Is your name Kate?' he asked.

'You know it isn't,' she said, not at all put out.

'Then I won't go anywhere with you.' He decanted her from his knees and wandered unsteadily into the kitchen, where he found Helen and Eileen drinking coffee.

'Where is everyone?' he demanded.

'David and Stephen are matching brandies in the library, and everyone else has gone home,' Helen replied. 'It's late, Gerry. What have you done with the Strawberry Tart?'

'Who?'

'The woman you've been canoodling with for the past two hours.'

'I haven't been canoodling with anyone,' Gerry said carefully. 'I only canoodle with Kate. You know that.' He sat abruptly on one of the kitchen chairs and smiled dozily. 'I only canoodle with Kate,' he said again. 'Shall we dance?'

Gerry arrived at the Club the next morning feeling dreadful. The woman known as the Strawberry Tart had finally been persuaded to go home and Gerry had finally been persuaded that it was to her home and not his that she was offering to drive him. The rest of them had spent the night, Stephen and Eileen in the library because Stephen had been unable to manage the stairs and Gerry and David – although more than willing to try – had been deemed too drunk to help him.

All this Gerry had learned at a rather subdued breakfast this morning, although David declared defiantly that if a chap wasn't allowed to celebrate his first training double in style then what could he do? And he went on to tell them, as though he hadn't at least twenty times during the previous afternoon and evening, that they had twelve horses in the yard better than Extol and the Strawberry Tart's viley named Sweetiepie, and that this season was going to see David Blower really make it as a trainer.

'Why is she called the Strawberry Tart?' Stephen had asked.

Helen cast a swift glance at Gerry. 'Can't you guess?' she said, and David, with hangovered tactlessness, having shifted Stephen White in some subtle way from Owner (all of whom he professed to despise, although God knew he needed more of them) to Friend, had added:

'All our owners have nicknames.'

Eileen, sharp as a tack, immediately asked what Stephen's nickname was and Gerry, seeing panic in Helen's eyes, created a cowardly diversion by saying he had to go, and did so, having taken possession of Stephen and Eileen's telephone number.

He climbed stiffly out of the car, every muscle squealing with pain, and was assaulted by Parsnip whose delighted barks set bells ringing in his skull. Elizabeth James took one look at him and made him coffee.

'Congratulations,' she said.

'On what?'

'Your win, you fool! Bernard rang last night asking if we were in need of a new managing director and I said, no, we'd heard you were triumphantly in one piece. But now' – she handed him the coffee – 'now I'm not so sure.'

Gerry sipped the coffee and gave her and Andrew a not very coherent account of how he had ridden Extol to victory and how the horse's owner and his wife had turned out to be old friends of his. In the midst of this, Parsnip ran from the room and reappeared a short time later followed by Kate.

'He's all yours,' Liz said. 'Can you manage him?'

Kate's eyes rolled heavenward. 'I've been patching up drunks all night. I suppose I could manage another one.'

'My legs and arms don't work, doctor,' Gerry said. 'And I think I need an operation on my head.'

She surveyed him. 'A couple of aspirins should do the trick,' she said, and offered him a hand to help him out of his chair. Groaning, he stood up.

They thanked Liz and Andrew for looking after their dog and

walked down the track, Parsnip hunting pheasants in the woods around them. Gerry put his arm around Kate's shoulders.

'Shall we go to bed?'

'Are you tired?'

'I thought you might be. Anyway, it's Sunday. You don't need to feel tired to go to bed on Sunday.'

'Don't you?' she said, laughing at him.

He stopped, hugged her to him and kissed her.

'I was offered a nibble of a strawberry tart last night,' he said, pulling away her scarf so he could nuzzle her neck. 'But I refused.'

'Refused even a nibble?'

'Absolutely. But I might – I just *might* – have had a little taste.'

'Without swallowing any.'

'That's right. I can't, you see, perfectly remember.'

She was silent for a while, and they walked on.

'Is this by way of being a confession, Gerry?' she asked eventually.

'Yes – no. It would be if I had anything to confess.'

'But you haven't – apart from a little taste.'

'That's right. I've forsaken all others, you see.'

'Any more of this, Gerry,' Kate said, thoroughly confused, 'and I'll need an aspirin too. My head's in as great a spin as yours.'

'But do you forgive me?'

'What do I have to forgive, for God's sake?'

'Nothing.'

'Then I forgive you.'

They had their board meeting the following Tuesday. Liz wheeled Andrew's chair into the directors' box – Andrew with a mountain of files on his knees – and sat beside him, then Captain Beech came in and, a little self-consciously, took another chair. When Gerry had told him he was to be a director, he had widened his pale blue eyes and said, 'A director? Me? Well, I'll be damned. No one's made me that before,' and then when Gerry told him, slightly awkwardly – the man was, after all, over twice his age – who his new managing director was to be, Captain Beech had brought out his Glenmorangie and congratulated Gerry saying, 'Quite right too. We've got the ship in the water and now we need a strong chap on the bridge. What?' And had pulled out his handkerchief and wiped away an errant tear or two.

Bernard and his wise heads came in and there was a little flurry as they were introduced to the new directors, and as soon as that was over the door opened again and Patrick ushered in Diana.

She hadn't been to a board meeting since they had begun holding them at Rede Park three years or more ago, and had only sporadically attended them before that. Gerry, rising to his feet along with the other men in the room – except for Andrew – was stunned to see her. It was November. She should be soaking up the sun somewhere in the Southern Hemisphere: what the hell was she doing here? Patrick helped her off with her fur coat and pulled out a chair for her. She sat, took out her cigarettes, fitted one into her holder and waited for someone to give her a light, which rather spoiled the effect of her entrance as no one had one until a wise head searched through his pockets and produced a box of matches.

Bernard opened the meeting by welcoming their new directors and saying blandly that it was a pleasure to see Mrs Beviss. Gerry winced at the name, Liz looked sharply at him and Captain Beech coughed. Diana blew out smoke and demanded an ashtray, which was found for her by Jennifer Cody.

She sat quietly, a presence among them, while Bernard signed the minutes of the last meeting, discovered that no one had any matters arising and they all listened to Andrew's financial report.

'Now,' Bernard said. 'We come to the main business of the day.'

Diana stubbed out her cigarette. Bernard glanced at her and continued:

'We had a most successful first season, so much so that the stands were overcrowded and the catering facilities stretched to the limit. We already have the plans for extending the grandstands, and there would be no problem completing the work before our opening meeting next year. Isn't that so, Gerry?'

Gerry unrolled the plans and weighted the corners down with water glasses.

'Phase two is outlined in red,' he explained. 'The plans have been somewhat modified from the originals to account for things

338

we learned during last season. The architects are satisfied with these, and so is Liz.' He looked at her. 'Right?'

'Right,' she said.

'It will be the catering staff who will be most affected, you see,' Gerry said. 'Anyway, we have the planning permission and the builders are standing by. We have their estimates here—' He gestured to Jennifer Cody, who stood up and went around the room placing a sheet of paper in front of each director, all of whom were leaning forward staring at the plans, with the exception of Diana, who was studying her scarlet fingernails.

'The only thing we have to fear,' Gerry added, 'is an extended period of freezing weather, but that would apply whichever winter we chose to build the extensions.'

'What exactly would the extensions give us?' asked a wise head, tapping the plans with his gold pen.

'About a third again of everything,' Gerry replied. 'And a new entrance into the enclosures from the extra car parks over here.' He pointed.

'Why not have the car parks on the other side?' Patrick said, speaking for the first time.

Gerry smiled at him. 'Because people would be able to sit in their cars and watch the racing from there. You can see the whole course.'

'That won't do,' said a wise head in a shocked voice, and everyone laughed.

'It's why we ask your man to put cattle in there,' Gerry said to Patrick. 'To deter picnickers.'

'Oh,' said Patrick, flushing slightly.

Bernard took a sip of water and replaced his glass on the corner of the plans.

'What else is going to help us decide?' he asked.

Andrew opened another of his files and produced for each of them an immaculate graph showing the attendances in each enclosure for the season's racing at Rede Park. The peak of the first two days was only matched by the three-day meeting in August – which Gerry, with monumental cheek, had billed as the Rede Park Festival, and whose highlight had been the Blue Oceans Sprint – but the intervening days showed a steady rise. Gerry pointed out, for the benefit of the two wise heads (and Diana and Patrick, he supposed) because the others knew his views on the subject well enough, that the prizes brought the horses and the crowds and the racecourse executive should be prepared to invest money in them. Here, he said, indicating Andrew's graph, was the proof. He reported that a local brewery was almost committed to supporting a race, but they were envious of the Blue Oceans Bar and wanted something similar.

'We've offered them a tent,' Liz said, 'and I think they'll go for it.'

'But they'll pay us?' the canny wise head asked.

'Oh yes. For the tent and for the site.'

'They want a gold cup,' Gerry added. 'I've told them they can have it any colour they wish.'

The wise head leaned back in his seat. 'I'm satisfied,' he said. 'I propose that we proceed with phase two of the building programme.'

'Seconded,' said his colleague.

Carried, *nem. con.*

Diana lit another cigarette as the discussion began on how to finance the new building. Bernard said he had taken the liberty of chatting to one or two people in the City and that there would be no problem about raising further loans, using the racecourse and existing buildings as surety. Their current loans were considerable, but so had been the first season's profits; and the Club and catering business, he said, bowing to Andrew and Liz courteously, had been turning in good figures for the past three years.

'Or we could go public,' Patrick said, interrupting him, 'and raise the money that way. We're allowed to next year, aren't we?'

'We will be able to satisfy Stock Exchange requirements, yes. I suppose it is an option,' Bernard conceded.

In the brief silence that followed, the chink of Diana's cigarette holder against the ashtray sounded very loud.

'Darling,' she said, addressing Bernard. Everyone turned to look at her, all of them, including Gerry, having forgotten she was there. 'Darling, I've got money in this place, haven't I? And some of this loan you talk about is owed to me, isn't it?'

340

'It's not precisely a loan, but you have money invested in this company, yes.'

'All right, but some of the other loan has my . . . assets – is that the word? – as surety?'

'Yes.'

Diana lit another cigarette. 'I only ask, darling, because I've got a new accountant. He's utterly divine about things like small print, and he's told me how I can get my money out. I don't perfectly understand, but my sweet little man will be writing to you.'

'You want your money back?' Bernard asked, startled.

Diana blew smoke at him and smiled.

'Yes, I do,' she said. 'It's all to do with not having shares any more, you see, and I've decided to sell all my shares to darling Patrick here. Then I can have my money back and buy an utterly divine place on Antigua. Owning a racecourse,' Diana said, 'is boring.'

If she had intended to shock, she certainly succeeded. Bernard for once looked discomposed; the two wise heads conferred in low voices, and Andrew scrabbled through his files to check exactly how much money Diana had in the company. Patrick stared at the table top: what the hell was his game? Gerry wondered frantically. He attended board meetings reasonably regularly and he came racing; apart from that he showed little interest in Rede Park Racecourse Ltd. Captain Beech's hand strayed to the inside pocket of his suit jacket and then, remembering where he was, he withdrew it. Elizabeth James looked at Diana, a hard gleam in her normally friendly eyes.

Diana stubbed out her cigarette.

'I propose – I'm a director, so I'm allowed to propose things, aren't I, darling? – I propose that this company goes public or whatever you call it.'

'Seconded,' muttered Patrick without looking up.

The wise heads glanced at Bernard, who shook his head imperceptibly.

'Diana,' he began, 'this has been something of a . . . surprise. We need time to consider the implications—'

'But my divine little man has done all that,' she said. 'He looked at all those pieces of paper you keep sending me and said that if you go ahead with this phase two of yours and I withdrew my

341

money you would have to go to the stock market. That's what he said. He asked if any of the other directors were millionaires, and I said no.' She smiled at them all. 'Was I right, darlings? Apart from Bernard, of course, but he has money all over the place and it would be very inconvenient to get it out. So my man said.'

'We could postpone phase two for another year – more,' Gerry said, not sure why going public was such a disaster, but if Bernard was against it so was he.

'But you've all just agreed it was essential—'

'Desirable,' Bernard corrected her. 'Not essential.'

'Good for business, then.' No fool, Diana. Gerry had always known that: foolish, his wife, but no fool she. She turned to Andrew and Liz. 'It would be divine for you, you know. You haven't got any shares now – have you? – and this way you could get some. And you, Mr Beech. The same applies to you.'

Captain Beech's back straightened and his fist clenched on Andrew's graph on the table in front of him.

'There is such a thing,' he said with immense dignity, 'as loyalty.'

'What's disloyal about it?' Diana said carelessly.

Patrick raised his eyes and looked at Bernard.

'A motion has been proposed and seconded. It must be voted on.'

'By all means,' Bernard said smoothly, raising his hand to silence Andrew who seemed about to speak.

Defeated, seven to two.

Patrick proposed that the issue be raised again at another board meeting in two weeks' time, and this motion was carried and a date agreed on. Diana stood up, Patrick helped her on with her coat and they had gone before the others in the room had moved. Gerry was about to go after them, but Bernard held him back.

'No heated words,' he said. 'Let's keep calm.'

'But what are they up to? What is Patrick doing?'

'Obviously he's in debt and thinks he can clear it by selling his shares on the open market.'

'Then how can he afford to buy Diana's? Why does he want those?'

'Probably he doesn't. Diana wants him to have them rather than you or any of the rest of us. Come on, let's not waste time on speculation. You, Andrew and I had better bury ourselves in some of those files and see exactly what the position is.'

Captain Beech, Liz James and Jennifer Cody left the room, and the two wise heads got to their feet.

'Let us know,' one of them said. 'We'll do what we can.'

The other, the taller one who had been worried about the brewery paying for the tent, looked around the directors' box and then out of the glass doors to the valley and the racecourse draped in drab November. He sighed.

'I'm all for us going public, but it would be a pity to do it so soon,' he said. He turned to Gerry and gave him a smile, one of totally unexpected youthful exuberance. 'It has been such enormous fun only being answerable to ourselves, hasn't it?' He nodded to Bernard. 'You know that Mrs Beviss got at least one of her facts wrong, don't you?'

'I know,' Bernard replied, smiling.

Chapter 22

Paul Marling was seething. Everything was going so well and then Patrick Morgan and the dirty gypsy's bitch of a wife hatched up this plot. Why would people not obey? Why would they not listen?

When Patrick told him that Diana Beviss was planning to get rid of her shares, Marling's heart had leapt. God was on his side! Buy the bitch's shares, he longed to tell Patrick. I'll give you the money. The more money you owe me the better it will be for me. Sign the piece of paper I put in front of you: a simple IOU to be repaid in due course in shares.

But then Patrick had come on the gentleman, saying that a gambling debt must be paid, that the shares Marling had won must be handed over legally. Thinking Marling would be pleased, thinking he wanted to cash in. Had taken him to meet the gypsy's wife whom he'd had to smile at while listening to the advice her fool of an accountant had given her about divesting herself of her shares (well, that advice Marling could not fault) so she could get her money out of Rede Park Racecourse Ltd because by doing so – and forcing the company to go public – she had some idea that it would harm the gypsy. That Marling could not fault either, but he planned his own vengeance.

He needed time, though. Time to get Patrick into debt to him again, time to raise money to lend him. He could wait: couldn't the idiot Morgan see that? He'd told him often enough. The last thing he wanted was for the company to be floated on the Stock Exchange now. He'd set up his pawns for a long, slow game and they were rushing off to checkmate the king. And Marling had to laugh all the time, be jolly, call Patrick 'dear boy' and 'old sport' and pretend to be indifferent to everything but how some stupid horse raced. And then, worst of all, when Patrick left the restaurant table for a short while, the gypsy's wife had invited him to go home with her. Just like that! He went to prostitutes in Soho occasionally, got himself inside them, paid and left, but he didn't like women's bodies. Not really. They leaked and did horrible things, and anyway he had no desire to handle a body the gypsy had rejected . . . One he did not reject, though? That would be a different matter altogether, one to contemplate with pleasure, perhaps. . . .

But the bitch had her hand on his thigh and was repeating her invitation. Quickly he invented a fiancée, and she withdrew the hand, shrugged and lit another of her interminable cigarettes.

And here was Patrick, come from the board meeting, saying it had all gone to plan, that the next meeting in two weeks' time would see it finalised. Two weeks! How long to float the company after that? A year? How would he get hold of the money to buy enough shares for his purpose in that time?

So many questions to be asked and answered and all of them in this dreadful roundabout jolly way, as though he was Patrick's best friend in all the world and was only helping him out and having a bet as a good gambling man was likely to do. It was easy enough to manipulate Patrick; the man swallowed half-truths like a child taking sweets. Why Paul would not go to Rede Park Racecourse, for instance: Gerald Beviss — or Gerry, as Patrick called him and so Marling had to too — had done the dirty on him when they had both worked at Rosenthal's bank; he didn't want to go into detail, it did not reflect well on . . . Gerry. He, Marling, had been fired as a result. Patrick would understand that he did not wish to come face to face with either Rosenthal or Beviss, and would rather the whole thing was not mentioned.

'Of course!' Patrick had exclaimed, and then added: 'Doesn't sound like old Gerry, though.'

'He's a gypsy,' Marling had reminded him. 'They're all thieves and cheats at heart. Blood will out.'

And Patrick had absently agreed, knowing nothing about gypsies anyway, and concentrated on the horses for the next race,

345

never once connecting this to Marling's scarcely concealed desire for shares in Rede Park Racecourse Ltd.

Time! He needed more of it. And yet, and yet . . . He listened to Patrick's description of today's meeting and wondered if he and the whore bitch had not done the right thing after all. Bernard Rosenthal would hate being forced into a corner by two lightweights like Patrick Morgan and Diana Beviss and he would fight. On principle he would fight and give Marling time.

'I know why you've come,' Diana said. 'And the answer is no.'

Bernard poured himself a cup of tea from the tray Suckers had brought in since his hostess did not seem inclined to, being occupied in mixing herself a drink.

'Why have I come?' he asked.

'To get me to sell my shares to you instead of Patrick. And I won't.'

'All right,' Bernard said and sipped his tea. 'But I do have another request to make of you.'

'What's that?'

She was, Bernard reflected, quite ugly when she was making no effort to attract or please.

'Give Gerry a divorce,' he said.

She eyed him over her glass. Ice tinkled as she drank.

'Gerry knows I'll divorce him.'

'Really?' he said, surprised.

'Hasn't he told you? I thought he told you everything. I thought you were his closest confidant . . . Oh well!' She laughed, the sound matching the ice in her glass, and went to her desk. 'He knows I'll divorce him if these are shown in court.'

She handed him an envelope. He put down his tea cup, opened the envelope and in silence looked through the photographs. In silence he replaced them and stood up.

'I wish your mother had never met your father,' he said. 'My own mother would have hidden her face in shame if she heard me say such a thing, but as God is my witness I wish it with all my heart.'

*   *   *

Gerry told Kate about their dramatic board meeting without noticing how silent and distracted she was. Parsnip, taking his cue from her, lay between the fire and where she was sitting on the hearth rug and allowed his ears to be stroked without turning it into a game. Rio, his prejudice against the dog overcome by winter, lay curled up on the sofa, sure in the knowledge that dogs weren't supposed to go on the furniture while cats could do precisely as they pleased.

'So Patrick and Diana swept out?' Kate asked.

'Just like that,' Gerry said. 'And the wonderful thing about it was that the vote was invalid anyway. Only share-holding directors can vote on an issue which will alter the status of the company, and the votes are on the holding, not on numbers. Andrew knew, and so did Bernard, of course, but he wanted a show of solidarity – and he got it, by God!'

'Did you know?'

'I did, but I forgot in the heat of the moment,' he admitted. 'Some managing director I am, aren't I? . . . Do you want another drink? Supper will be about half an hour.'

She picked up her glass. 'I haven't finished this one.'

Parsnip rolled over on to his back and she tickled his exposed stomach.

'Dr Badger rang me today,' she said.

He slid out of the chair and knelt beside her.

'Kate! Why didn't you say?'

'I couldn't get a word in edgewise,' she said, smiling at him wryly. 'Anyway, he said no. I knew he would. It doesn't matter.'

'But it does!'

'No, it doesn't. We won't talk about it again . . . Oh, for heaven's sake!' This to Parsnip, who was now among them, all wriggling black body and pink tongue. Kate restored order and said, 'Go on about your board meeting. Why is Patrick doing this, do you suppose?'

'It's sure to be a gambling debt. Bernard says he should have made more effort to keep in touch with him and then he would have come to him if he was in trouble, but I don't think Patrick would have. I should have foreseen it, too. I know what Patrick's gambling is like.'

'And Diana?'

'Diana,' Gerry repeated. 'Who knows how her mind works? The whole thing is a great mystery, but we'll sort it out.' He kissed her cheek. 'Kate, I am sorry about your job.'

'He was very kind and said to contact him when I'm married. He said he hoped things work out for me.' She put a log on the fire and watched it burn. 'I shouldn't have hoped, that's all. I didn't really, but I couldn't help it. Just a bit.' She paused. 'At least Dr Badger isn't going to say anything to the bigwigs at the hospital.'

'That's one good thing, then.'

'Yes,' she said. 'That's one good thing.'

Bernard rang Gerry the next day and told him to call the builders in.

'No trouble, then?'

'None at all,' Bernard said, and rang off.

Captain Beech was jubilant when he heard. He was too polite to say so, but he had disliked Diana intensely and had always considered Patrick a wastrel. He and Patrick's farm manager played draughts twice a week and drank Glenmorangie in the Rede Arms most Saturday nights. Two old bachelors infinitely experienced at their jobs but never having made it to the top of the pile, each under the authority of a very much younger man. Captain Beech didn't listen to gossip, but he had no doubt at all about which one of them had the better bargain. And, more to the point, he also knew that they could fill their new stands.

Elizabeth and Andrew James were more cautious. Both were outraged at the idea of being out-manoeuvred by Diana Beviss – whom they had never met before – and Patrick Morgan – whose bill for drinks in the directors' box on Rede Park's opening day was still unpaid – but Andrew's accountant's brain and his middle-class soul rebelled against the company taking on huge new debts as well as repaying Diana the vast amount of money she was demanding.

Gerry took them through it again.

'We get the crowds in,' he said patiently, 'and we know how to do that.'

'By increasing the prize money – more expenditure!' Andrew interjected.

'We've shown it works. Now listen. We have the crowds. They pay – most of them – to park their cars. They pay to come into the stands. Once they're inside they pay to turn around. Racecourses eat money!'

'Bookmakers do.'

'Who pay us to put up their boards. And when people win, they buy drinks. When they lose they buy drinks to drown their sorrows. Here they buy lots of drinks because it is so easy and comfortable to do so. They eat lunch before racing and have tea afterwards, and with the new buffet we'll be able to feed more of them. Your own figures show it, Andrew! The catering takings don't correlate with the number of people. When the place is less crowded, the takings per capita go up because no one has to wait to be served.'

'Couldn't we put up the entrance fees?' Liz asked.

'Not in our second year. We must keep faith with the local people, the ones who will come on a rainy day. We must make sure we're always good value.'

'And Bernard can raise the money?'

'Lord yes! It's his business.'

'So your . . . your wife's chap got it wrong?'

'He underestimated Bernard's standing in the City. They'd lend him the Crown Jewels if he asked for them.'

Andrew wheeled his chair in a tight circle and brought it to a halt again: his equivalent of pacing the carpet.

'Will we go public eventually?'

'I expect so. For phase three of the building, probably. We'll all have our say, Andrew.'

'We'll all do what Bernard wants, though,' Andrew said, but there was no rancour in his voice.

'I will. The rest of you can disagree.'

Andrew took his wife's hand and held it. 'As though we would!' he said. 'This place means everything to us. I mean, who else would have taken on a cripple like me?'

Gerry grinned at him. 'It's your head we're interested in, Andrew, not your legs.'

'That's what I mean! It's why we'll follow you and Bernard to the ends of the earth if you ask us to. And you bloody well know it.'

They all congregated in the directors' box once more. Diana, again accompanied by Patrick, making a slightly late entrance. Bernard signed the minutes and asked if there were any matters arising. The taller wise head, the one with the unexpected smile, raised a finger and Bernard nodded to him.

'I propose that Mrs Beviss, since she has declared her intention of selling her shares and removing her financial support from this company, be invited to resign her directorship forthwith.'

His colleague's 'seconded' did not hide Diana's gasp of surprise.

Bernard called for a vote. For the motion: seven. Against: two, one defiant, one embarrassed.

'Carried,' Bernard said and waited, one eyebrow cocked enquiringly at Diana. 'We thank you for your services to the company in the past and hope you will remain a friend of it in the future,' he said at last, his voice larded with irony. Still Diana did not move, and eventually the tall wise head, with a grunt of exasperation, stood up, took Diana's coat from the back of her chair and held it out for her.

She looked around, her eyes narrowing.

'I have to go now?' she asked.

'You are no longer a director and thus no longer privy to our meeting,' Bernard told her. 'For God's sake, Diana, what did you expect?'

She allowed herself to be helped on with her fur, picked up her handbag and went to the door. She turned and gazed at them once more. How did she think she could do it? Gerry wondered. She and this new accountant of hers. Outwit Bernard Rosenthal? In this she was as amateur as Gerry had been when he'd tried to find grounds for their divorce. Now her eyes came to rest on him. Gerry saw speculation in them, and calculation, and then – and it shook him because in spite of everything he didn't think her emotions ran so deeply – a flash of pure hatred. And she was gone.

In the silence that followed, they could hear her car starting up and roaring away. Patrick fidgeted in his seat and was obviously wishing he, too, could be gone. Bernard spoke to him.

'We could do the same to you,' he said. 'And don't you forget it. Do you now wish to propose to the board the motion that this meeting was called to vote on?'

Patrick shook his head.

'Very well. As agreed at the last meeting, phase two of the building goes ahead.'

Patrick attempted to make a quick escape, but he had neither the advantage of surprise or of Diana's car. Bernard intercepted him and, grabbing the younger man by the elbow, took him outside. The wise heads stood up.

'That young man will soon own thirty-five per cent of this company,' the tall one said. 'I don't like it.'

'He's not wicked,' Gerry said, defending Patrick out of some ancient feeling of loyalty. 'He's just . . . well, rather silly. And he's a gambler.'

'That's what I don't like.'

Gerry had always thought of the two wise heads as just that: two faceless men who supported Bernard when he needed it and who had taken the directorships of Rede Park more or less as a favour. He now realised this was unfair. They were, presumably, busy men but they travelled into Wiltshire uncomplainingly for meetings – though normally these did not take place with anything like the frequency they had been doing of late – because they accepted that it would be difficult for Andrew to get to London. And recent events had shown that they cared about the company and the racecourse, really cared; they minded what happened to it, and Gerry was touched.

'I was wondering,' he heard himself saying, 'if you would like to join us for lunch at the Club.'

The tall wise head consulted his watch and then his colleague, and gave Gerry his wonderful smile.

'We'd like that very much indeed,' he said. 'Thank you.'

'We were expecting a lengthy and bloody battle,' the short one added, 'and therefore made no appointments in Town.'

Andrew stacked files on his knees. 'You had the blood,' he remarked.

351

'So we did,' the tall wise head agreed.

Bernard came back into the room and stood, his arms folded, his head bent. They all watched him until he raised his head and stared out over the racecourse.

'He doesn't particularly want the shares,' he said slowly, 'but she's making him sign something to say he won't sell them to any of us. And he won't tell me why he's so anxious for us to go public. I don't understand it. His thirty-five per cent might raise enough money to pay off a debt that is causing him such worry, but he's got other securities of far more substance than a fledgling racecourse.' He looked at Gerry. 'Can you do some investigating? Find some clues? . . . I don't understand it,' he repeated.

'You can't have the shares,' Patrick told Paul Marling. 'I'll raise the sixteen thousand and pay you.'

Marling gritted his teeth.

'Don't worry about it, old boy,' he said. 'I can wait.'

'A gambling debt must be paid,' Patrick insisted.

'The bet was on the shares, not money.'

'It must be paid.'

'It will be. I'll have the shares.'

Marling wanted to hit him. His fists clenched ready to make contact with Patrick's jaw, and into his mind came a picture of his family home: Ridge Farm in the company of its four oasts asleep in the sun amid its green fields. Despoiled. All of it despoiled by a filthy gypsy family.

'The bet was on the shares,' he said again. 'I told you, I can wait.' I don't want your fucking money!

Had he said it out loud? Patrick was looking at him with a curious expression on his face.

'Well, if you really mean it,' he said at last.

'I mean it,' Marling said. 'Old chap.'

Bernard invited Gerry to lunch at the City Club, the place where, all but seven years ago, Gerry had asked Bernard for a job.

'A lot has happened since then,' he said.

'It has, Gerry. And I might add that giving you the job you so

352

unexpectedly asked for was one of the best things I ever did.'

'Oh, I say!' Gerry exclaimed, feeling his face redden in pleasure and embarrassment, and then, regaining his composure, he said: 'And me having the nerve to ask you was the best thing *I* ever did.'

'Then we're pleased with each other. Cheers,' Bernard said, raising his glass. 'And I haven't congratulated you properly on your win at the races, so here's to that too.'

'I thought we might have a gentlemen riders' flat race at Rede Park,' Gerry said. 'It could be fun. Would it be the done thing for me to ride in it, do you think?'

'I don't see why not. But mind you don't win a race there before I do.'

Bernard had achieved a second and two thirds during Rede Park's first season, and coveted the first-place spot in the winners' enclosure.

'Put me up on one of your horses and perhaps we'll have a dead heat,' Gerry suggested.

'Now that's an idea!' Bernard said, much taken by it. Their plates were cleared, coffee was brought and Bernard got down to business. 'You have no further clues about what Patrick's up to?' he asked.

'None at all. He's not been home since our last board meeting. The farm is doing well, though. That I do know. He has a first-rate chap in charge and he cares about the house and the land.' Gerry ran his hand over his curly head. 'I know he doesn't spend much time there, but he does care. He's not going to let the estate fall back into the mess his father left it in. The gambling is a sort of disease, but he won't take it as far as Cyril and George did.'

'I don't think compulsive gamblers have a choice, Gerry. I've decided,' he said after a short pause, 'with the permission of the board, of course—'

'Of course,' Gerry agreed politely, both of them knowing he would get it.

'I've decided to offer our three new board members a stake in the company. Only a small one, but I think it is important to reward their loyalty and hard work in a more tangible way than a directorship, and it gives Patrick three people he can sell his shares to without contravening his agreement with Diana. I believe that her terms were "any current shareholders".' He stirred his coffee. 'I'm reducing my shareholding still further,' he went on. 'I don't like doing it, but I don't see any alternative. The removal of Diana's capital has stretched us, and I don't want to add to our burden of borrowings. Lionel Moreton is covering it for another five per cent holding, which is extremely generous of him under the circumstances ... Lionel Moreton, Gerry,' he added impatiently, seeing Gerry's puzzled expression, 'the man you persist in calling the tall wise head.'

'Sorry,' Gerry said hastily, and then, having assimilated what he had been told: 'But that means you lose your controlling share. Is that wise?'

'I don't imagine it is dangerous. Patrick is doubtful, perhaps, but everyone else is loyal and we can always hope that he will sell his own shares to us or Diana's to the other three. The only other option – apart from not building the new stands and we've all agreed we need them – is to go public straight away. Diana's accountant was right about that.'

'Diana's out of it now, though,' Gerry said with satisfaction. 'She can't do any more harm.'

Bernard put down his coffee cup and stared at him.

'But she can, Gerry. Surely you realise that? She can harm you and she can harm the company. . . .'

'How?' Gerry asked, bewildered.

'She knows perfectly well that a scandalous divorce case involving the managing director would jeopardise a company when it was attempting a flotation, and could bring about the downfall of a managing director of a public company.'

'But you've always known I want to get a divorce,' Gerry said, some undefinable terror rising in him. 'You made me managing director knowing it!'

'I didn't know Diana was intent upon a nasty public divorce. I hadn't , until recently , realised how vindictive she is and how she could be planning her moment to take you to court and achieve maximum damage. And,' Bernard added gently, 'I hadn't seen the photographs.'

Gerry closed his eyes and saw the grandstands of Rede Park Racecourse dissolve before his gaze. The house in the woods reverted to ruin, its garden given back to the trees. He saw the black-and-white photographs in Diana's envelope with their distorted images and he wanted to cry out that they were lies, lies, but he couldn't because there was a truth in them, and what difference would it make anyway? He opened his eyes and saw Bernard through a haze of disappointment, confusion and pain.

'I'll resign, shall I?'

'You'll do nothing of the sort.' Bernard signalled for brandy. 'I'm sorry, Gerry, really I am. I was sure you had worked it all out.'

'No – no, I hadn't.'

Why hadn't he? Would he ever get things right? He had thought that, at long last, he had stopped blundering through life and had found a straight – if somewhat thorny – path, and now it was twisting before him like a drunken snake, full of poisonous pits and things far worse than thorns.

'I thought of Kate,' he said. 'All the time of her. The photographs weren't true until after we saw them.'

'They'd ruin her.'

'We know that!' And he told Bernard their plan, concluding, 'If it comes to a choice, I'll have Kate and our baby and not the racecourse.'

'You won't have to make a choice,' Bernard said. 'Come now, Gerry, cheer up. So long as we remain a private company, we'll support you and stand by you whatever happens.'

'And if we go public?'

Bernard smiled at him, a smile of enormous affection. 'We'll try not to. We're secure for the next couple of years at least.'

Gerry felt a great weight lift from him, but there remained a shadow on his heart. He picked it up, unravelled it and identified it. It was a secret he would keep from Kate, one he would tuck away somewhere deep inside and try to keep secret from himself as well. Everything will be all right, it whispered, everything will be just perfect: you have Kate and you have the racecourse. Without a baby – the thing Kate wants most in the world next to marrying you – you will never have to choose between them.

He would not repeat his conversation with Bernard to Kate. He told himself it was because of the despair that would flood her beautiful eyes, because of the heartrending bravery she would display as she offered to take precautions in their lovemaking – which would leave him free to be the managing director of the newest and most exciting racecourse in the land while Kate's career and their relationship descended into sterile gloom.

He would not repeat this conversation to Kate, because she would offer and he had a dreadful premonition that he would accept.

Chapter 23

Gerry had Kate and he had the racecourse. He had the new stands which people filled and cheered the horses home that had come to compete for the rich prizes which Gerry wheedled out of his board of directors and, increasingly, out of companies which followed Blue Oceans' lead and saw that sponsoring a race at Rede Park was, for the right product, a reasonably cheap and thoroughly effective form of advertising. Gerry was all for having every race sponsored but agreed to limit it to two a day when Captain Beech pointed out that the hoardings would make the place look like Piccadilly Circus. He continued to search for his dream, though: a huge prize for a mile and a half race at the Festival meeting in August, a race that would bring Derby winners to Rede Park.

He rode Extol for Stephen White, since Stephen's leg continued to give him trouble ('Or, more likely,' Kate said, 'Eileen has put her foot down, and quite right too.'), and was asked to ride in amateur races by other owners. His father sent him a horse 'with a lep as high as a house' which Grace had not managed to persuade to take to show jumping. Under Gerry's and Helen Blower's tuition, it took to steeplechasing and in its first season won a race, Gerry wearing the colours designed for Joe Beviss by Grace. ('Probably pink prawns on a sea-green background,' he said to Kate. 'Nonsense,' she had replied. 'Your sister-in-law is far too clever to do anything so crass.' And Kate, as usual, had been right.)

Gerry still rode Florin, though, around the racecourse in the mornings or, with Kate on Sprite, on summer evenings. Every joint in the old horse's legs creaked, but his eyes were as bright as ever and he often startled Gerry with a youthful buck, once depositing him on the turf in front of the grandstands and galloping back to his stables at the Club with the speed of a two-year-old, leaving Gerry – his breeches ignominiously stained with grass – to follow on foot and to endure the taunts of the Club members who had witnessed Florin's riderless return.

No baby grew in Kate's womb.

Diana continued to refuse to give Gerry a divorce.

Patrick would not sell his shares. No one knew why and after a time it did not seem to matter.

Paul Marling held IOUs for shares he estimated would amount to ten per cent of Rede Park Racecourse Ltd.

There was a party in the Tote hall on the New Year's Eve of 1959. Originally it was to have been for the staff of the racecourse and the catering company, but the guest list, like Topsy, grew and grew. Mark and Vanessa came, and Stephen and Eileen White. Helen and David Blower were there, of course, and James brought the latest in a line of débutantes whom he introduced to every man he knew in the room so he could be free to dance too often with Kate. Rosie and Andrew Coleridge came, Rosie pregnant with their fourth child which made Kate feel horribly jealous . . . over two and a half years, and not even a false alarm.

As midnight struck and 'Auld Lang Syne' was played, Gerry, released from his duty dances with the staff, removed Kate from James's arms almost as he had done twelve years ago, took her under some mistletoe and kissed her and wished her a happy New Year. It was the start of a new decade, but they did not know then the whirlwind changes the 1960s would bring. Something called a pop group would sing 'Let's Spend the Night Together' and many of the young people – and the not so young – would do just that, and openly. By the end of the decade, the idea of divorce being any kind of a stigma would seem as outdated as the Victorian bustle. The photographs which would ruin Kate in 1960 could have been printed in a family newspaper in 1970 with scarcely a hair of a single eyebrow being raised. Some newspapers would certainly reject them for not being explicit enough.

None of this, though, Kate and Gerry knew as they welcomed 1960, a pair of lovers as star-crossed as any Montague or Capulet.

'No, it's lower.'

Kate moved her hands further down her patient's abdomen. She did not feel comfortable with him, this man who had come in complaining of a persistent pain in his stomach. She could feel his eyes upon her, but every time she looked at him he was gazing at the ceiling of the cubicle.

'Lower,' he said again.

He was getting an erection, she noticed, and the young houseman who had been on duty and, perplexed, had summoned her, came forward and pulled up the blanket. His boyish cheeks reddened on her behalf – or perhaps on his own? – but their patient seemed not at all concerned. The erection grew larger and pointed to her from under its covering.

'Does this hurt?' Kate asked.

'Yes.'

Kate went to the basin, washed her hands, dried them and turned back to the couch on which her patient lay. Her hands now in the pockets of her white coat, she said:

'There's nothing wrong that I can find, but since you are in discomfort I think we had better keep you in for observation overnight.'

A flicker of the cold eyes.

'Will you examine me tomorrow?' he asked.

'One of my colleagues will. I am not on duty tomorrow. I'm not officially on duty now.'

The man raised his head from the pillow and looked deliberately down at the blanketed mound at his groin.

'But I like being examined by you,' he said softly.

Kate had had difficult patients before: drunks making suggestive remarks as she stitched up their cuts after pub brawls, ribbings from old men long past doing anything with their shrivelled cocks who half resented, half enjoyed being examined by a woman

359

doctor. But never anything like this man with his intent gaze – only on her, not on the young houseman or the nurse – and his strange pain which could be a duodenal ulcer, cholecystitis or inflammatory bowel disease, considering the way it moved about.

'Is it serious, doctor?' he asked, challenge and not – which was normal among people in pain – fear or pleading anxiety in his eyes.

'No, I don't believe so,' she answered, 'but it is as well to be sure. We'll have you in for the night and see how you are in the morning.'

'Will you examine me, though?' he persisted.

'I told you, I'm not on duty tomorrow. One of my colleagues will look after you.'

She nodded to the houseman and the nurse and they left the cubicle, but the man called her back. Called her by her name.

'Dr Earith!'

She made a face at the houseman and returned to the cubicle.

'Yes?'

'Enjoy your day at the races.'

He must know Gerry then, know Gerry was riding tomorrow. But why hadn't he said? And why that satisfied glance at his erection and now the mocking smile that stretched his lips but in no way reached his cold blue eyes?

There was nothing the matter with him, nothing whatsoever. Kate had known it all along and so had the houseman, but if a patient tells you it hurts what can you do? She rejoined the other doctor and together they made out their notes.

'What shall we do with him?' the young doctor asked.

'All that's uncomfortable,' Kate replied, most improperly.

He grinned at her. 'Let's order a barium meal and follow through,' he said. 'They never like that. And,' he added, relish in his voice, 'we'll do lots of blood tests and only allow him bedpans.'

'Steady on!' Kate said, but she understood his feelings. No doctor likes to be made a fool of, and this man – she looked at his registration form: Paul Dennis Smith – was trying to do just that.

She was not entirely surprised to learn that Mr Smith did a bunk – dressed himself and vanished from the cubicle where they had left him even as they were discussing his case.

The incident irritated rather than disturbed her, and she had forgotten about it the next day when Gerry came second on Fandangle, Joe Beviss's horse, at Plumpton.

Joe Beviss waved his stick in triumph and fury.

'He would'uv won!' he yelled. 'He would'uv if that loose horse ain't a-got in his way. Ain't that so?' He looked at Meg, who had watched the race in an agony of fear, her small hand fiercely gripping Kate's. It was the first time she or Joe had seen Gerry race – or, indeed, been to a racecourse at all – and she had found the whole thing terrifying, but she said 'yes' dutifully and Joe grabbed her and hauled her away to the winners' enclosure saying, 'This does show jumpin', don't it? Does it out of sight!'

Kate, with Charles and Beattie, followed at a more decorous pace.

'*Most* exciting, my darling,' Beattie commented. 'What fun that Gerry could ride here.'

Kate took her aunt's and uncle's arms and walked between them as they came out of the grandstand and reached level ground.

'Gerry wanted his parents to see their horse,' she said. 'It was lovely that you could come too—' She stopped, her attention caught by a man walking across their path.

Trilby-hatted, his head lowered, his coat collar turned up around his neck and ears, she was nonetheless sure she recognised him as he disappeared among the crowd moving towards the bookmakers. It was the patient of yesterday, the man with the mysterious pain. And what was more, Kate had the distinct impression that, in spite of the hat and the upturned coat collar, he had intended to make his presence known to her as, in passing, he brushed against Charles's shoulder causing her uncle to let out an involuntary 'Hey there!' as he did so.

She was going to tell Gerry about it, but really what was there to tell? It had all happened too quickly and as the short February afternoon drew to a close she began to think she had imagined it all: a racegoer in a hurry to reach his bookmaker, nothing more.

Paul Marling waited in the woods. It was bitterly cold and already frost glinted on the branches of the trees among which he hid. But it was not the cold that was causing Paul Marling to shiver. He felt quite warm, in fact; anticipation and excitement enveloped him like an additional overcoat.

He had heard the woman doctor's car arrive – he knew it was hers because he knew which garage she parked it in – and soon she would come down this path on her way to the gypsy. He had watched her from the Club's outbuildings several times. He wasn't sure what he was going to do to her once he had her, but he knew he had to do something. He was tired of hearing how successfully the thieving gypsy's son was running Rede Park, tired of reading that he was the leading amateur jockey this season, tired, above all, of playing Patrick, a whale on a line meant to land a three-pound trout. It was time for action.

Footsteps in the woods coming this way. A wavering beam of torchlight.

Marling stiffened. He had been wrong about the cold. His fingers were numb. He flexed them in his gloves. He had to get his hand over her mouth. He mustn't let her scream.

He stepped forward.

All kinds of thoughts went through Kate's head, and even as she struggled against the dark figure who seemed to be trying to drag her away through the woods towards the racetrack she was aware that some of them were foolish. Her torch lay on the ground and she had an idea that she must get to it and switch it off because the batteries would be running down . . . and she mustn't fall, because this was a new coat and she didn't want it covered in mud and leaf mould . . . and thank God for Beattie and her great long knitted scarves because her assailant could not get through the wool to her neck. Her neck! And now she was frightened. For a moment the gloved hand slipped from her mouth, but she had forgotten how to scream. She kicked out and her wellington boot thudded into shinbone. The man grunted and held on, and again he attempted to pull her away from the path and through the trees.

And then Parsnip arrived. Hurtling out of the dark, he launched himself at his mistress and then, when this did not produce the usual response, he circled the pair of grappling figures and barked loudly.

Paul Marling had not known about a dog. Because the leafless trees afforded no cover, he had not been close to the house in the

362

woods and had done all his spying from the Club after dark. He did not know that the animal barking madly was a cocker spaniel who had never bitten a person in his life: it was making enough noise to account for three Alsations, each of them full of teeth.

He let go of Kate and ran.

The policeman was unimaginative and firm: it was a tramp. They'd search the woods tomorrow and they'd find him holed up in some hut or barn, or they'd find the remains of his fire because likely as not he'd be on the road again by now. It was no good Kate saying she was sure the man who attacked her had been clean-shaven, that he hadn't smelt unwashed, that when her cheek was pressed against his coat she had vaguely registered that it was of good quality. Certainly it was not of rough tweed, she said.

A tramp, the policeman told Gerry. The coat was no doubt given to him by some well-meaning person. Why, the vicar's wife keeps a store of old clothing collected from the parish for the gentlemen of the road. The young lady is a bit hysterical, he said. And it was no good, either, Gerry saying that Kate was the least hysterical person on earth, calm even now after her ordeal although very much shaken.

When the policeman had gone, Kate told Gerry about the houseman's strange patient and how she thought she had seen the same man at Plumpton races.

'You think it might have been him who attacked you?' Gerry asked.

'I've no idea, but it was more like that sort of man than a tramp.'

When they found no sign of anyone living a vagrant life in the area, the CID in Leighminster took an interest. Had Kate made any enemies? Had she perhaps . . . erred in her duties?

'I understand what you're saying,' Kate told them, 'and, no, I haven't killed any patients recently.'

They traced several Mr Paul Dennis Smiths but all were innocent. The name meant nothing to anyone. Why should it? Gerry had not thought of Paul Marling for years, had entirely forgotten that Dennis Marling had once owned Ridge Farm. The Leighminster CID could do nothing more. Kate was to report anything suspicious and was to take special care about where she walked alone after dark.

Gerry had already taken frantic care. He and George rigged up wiring and lights down the half-mile track from the Club to the house in the woods. He had bought himself a stout walking stick and a new torch with a beam like a young lighthouse. He was going to buy a shotgun, but Andrew dissuaded him: a stick would be more use if the man attacked again and Gerry, he pointed out, was not a good shot. To his relief Gerry agreed, for in truth Andrew was worried that in his present mood he would shoot at anything that moved in the woods.

He could find no fault with Gerry's other arrangements, though: Kate was to drive up to the main doors of the Club, leave her car there for Gerry to park and wait inside for him and Parsnip. She didn't even need to telephone because the dog would tell him when she arrived, but she must phone Gerry before she left the hospital and get an escort from the hospital entrance to the car park. She must spend her evenings and nights on call in the hospital rather than in her flat as she was not to risk running the hundred or so yards at all hours.

Kate complied with all these conditions, for she was devastated by what had happened. Like the police, she supposed her attacker had been a disgruntled patient – or the relative of a dead one – but she could not think of a likely candidate. And she could not forget the cold, challenging gaze of the man with the pain.

'I do feel a bit like a parcel, though,' she said. 'Forever being passed from one pair of hands to the next.'

'Never mind that,' Liz told her. 'You mustn't take any risks. Look,' she added as Parsnip came into the room, his claws skidding on the polished wooden floor, 'here's the advance guard of your escort.'

Kate hugged the dog.

'He saved me,' she said. 'He might not have meant to, but I don't know what would have happened if he hadn't turned up.'

Gerry arrived to collect her. They went outside and George proudly turned on the lights.

'Why, they're beautiful!' Kate exclaimed. 'I thought it would look all suburban – you know, like street lamps.'

They were high up, lighting the woods for yards around. There was no chance of anyone cutting the wire without first having to climb the trees and that would make a noise and give Gerry plenty of warning.

'You can turn them on and off at either end,' George said. 'Clever, ain't we?'

'Aren't we just?' Gerry gripped his stick and they set off down the sparkling frosty path.

None of their precautions was necessary. Paul Marling realised he had made a mistake even as he let the gypsy's woman go and fled from the barking dog. What on earth did he think he was up to? If he had got the woman away, what would he have done with her? He didn't want the police after him for kidnapping, rape, or worse.

Paul Marling sometimes wondered if he was mad.

Mrs Ian Stewart – otherwise known as the Strawberry Tart – gave a party on the eve of the May meeting at Rede Park to celebrate her and her husband's fifteenth wedding anniversary.

'Why celebrate being married to that, though?' Helen Blower whispered to Kate as they passed through the receiving line and took some champagne from a tray proffered by a waiter – one of Elizabeth James's, for she was doing the catering for the party.

'Desperation, I should think,' Kate said. Ian Stewart was a dour, dry man who spent most of his time turning money over in the financial capitals of the world. He was a complete contrast to his vivacious, bouncy wife and the fact that he was so often from home gave her plenty of opportunity to live up to the nickname bestowed upon her by Helen and David.

'He must love her, though,' Helen commented. 'He's buying her another racehorse.'

'Good for business, then. Don't complain.'

'Oh I'm not, I'm not . . . Good Lord, Kate, look: the old stick is chatting to Gerry. He seems almost animated. What on earth can they have to talk about?'

Kate looked. Ian Stewart had left his wife to receive their guests alone and had taken Gerry aside. He was now introducing him to another man and the three of them stood and talked importantly, Gerry paying the kind of attention he usually reserved for Bernard alone. Kate adored that serious, concentrated expression and stood there and gazed idiotically at her best friend, her lover, her husband in all but name until Helen, murmuring in her ear, recalled her.

'Who is that beautiful woman?'

She was standing unselfconsciously alone a few feet away from the little group of men, obviously not listening to what they were saying. Kate did not know a great deal about clothes and high fashion, but this woman's dress screamed money. Shining blonde hair coiled expensively under an elegant hat and jewellery flashed from her ears, her hands, her wrist. She was beautiful all right, but yet ... Kate looked again. She was beautiful but she was not happy. Kate glanced at the man Ian Stewart had introduced to Gerry: the woman's husband, she assumed. He was bald, red-faced, pot-bellied and at least thirty years older than her. Presumably the money, the clothes and the jewels were worth it.

As Kate was thinking this, the woman's green eyes caught and held Kate's for an instant. Kate smiled uncertainly at her, half wondering if, in spite of her air of aloof composure, the woman would like to come and talk to her and Helen as it was evident that she knew no one at the party. But the beautiful face remained a blank mask and the eyes travelled on to survey other guests.

Beautiful, beautiful but bored as sin. For no reason that she could determine – she had never even met Diana – Kate thought of Gerry's wife.

The three men parted. The bald one went up to the blonde woman and led her away, Ian Stewart returned to stand by his wife and Gerry, now wearing his biggest grin, came over to Helen and Kate. Putting an arm around each of them, he swept them out of the pink silk-swathed open-sided marquee and into the garden, gathering up David Blower on his way.

'It's it, it is *it*,' he crowed, nearly dancing in his excitement. 'Oh I could kiss the Strawberry Tart and her oh so handsome husband—' In his urgent desire to kiss something he kissed Helen and Kate and then took the lapel of David's suit jacket in his hand. 'Listen to this, you dreadful old article,' he said. 'That fat man is president of some huge American corporation. They're launching a new range of cosmetics in Britain next year – move aside Helena Rubinstein and all that – and he *just loves* the idea of sponsoring a horse race to help their powders and paints on the way . . . Christ, the money he's talking!' Gerry let go of David's lapel, grabbed Kate's glass and drank from it. 'He wanted Royal Ascot because of the association with fashion, but Ian Stewart told him there wouldn't be a race sponsored there in a million years. He and his wife are coming to Rede Park tomorrow. The Strawberry Tart is entertaining them in her box and Ian is coming too . . . Oh Kate, my one and only Kate, my precious Kate, pray for fine weather so the women dress up and Carling C. Thompson decides to give us his gorgeous dollars!'

Kate laughed at her lovely man and pushed him away, since his ardour was threatening to make a spectacle of them both.

'I'll pray, Gerry, and Helen and I promise to look our very smartest, don't we?'

'We'll do our best,' Helen said, 'but we won't be able to outshine Mrs Carling C. Whatever her name is.'

The sun shone for Gerry, the racecourse looked its perfect best, the crowds came and Carling C. Thompson seemed impressed by them and Gerry's file of newspaper clippings which showed the space given to the sponsored races. He examined the morning papers with their headlines speculating about which horse would win the Blue Oceans Handicap.

'And all these are national newspapers,' Carling C. Thompson said. 'We don't have those back home.'

And he was impressed, too, by the fact that Gerry had on his desk the contract for the televising of the principal meetings at Rede Park. Starting next year, the coverage was guaranteed for five years.

'And it's national television, too?'

'This is a small country, Mr Thompson,' Gerry said. 'There's only one time zone.'

'Small, maybe, but it's an important market,' Carling C. Thompson stated firmly.

'Oh indeed, sir,' Gerry agreed.

Carling C. Thompson was impressed, no doubt about it, but he said he and his wife wanted to go to other racecourses; one nearer London would, perhaps, suit their purposes better.

'Kempton, maybe, or Sandwich.'

'Sandown,' Gerry corrected, gritting his teeth at the prospect of Carling C. Thompson and his thousands of dollars going east.

'Ask his wife to present the Blue Oceans Cup,' Rebecca Rosenthal suggested when Gerry took his frustration to the directors' box.

'But you always do that!'

'Always! Always and it's the fourth year only. Ask her – ask him to ask her. She has her fat old husband by the balls, anyone can see that. If she likes giving cups away at Rede Park you'll have a chance.'

'I'll have to consult my brother,' Gerry said, somewhat taken aback by Rebecca's earthy language but appreciating that the ploy might work. 'It's his cup.'

Grace had seen Mrs Carling C. Thompson and promptly informed Gerry that she and Arthur did not mind at all that such a beautiful and glamorous woman should give away their trophy.

'We might get photos in the papers,' she said. 'We haven't had any since the first year. Is she famous as well as beautiful, do you think?'

Gerry had no idea. He had hardly noticed Mrs Carling C. Thompson as he had shown her and her husband around the racecourse, so intent had he been upon Carling C. and his money.

But Brigitte Louisa Thompson had noticed Gerry. She was not used to being ignored by men, for she held her own beauty in very high esteem. It had taken her from the wrong side of the tracks in Chicago, through the smart hotels in the Windy City and from thence, under the protection of a series of old but always rich men, to Hollywood, a few bit parts in movies and the odd modelling assignment to, finally, marriage to a millionaire.

Kate had been right. She was bored: of her besotted husband and his blubbery body, of his business friends and associates always so much older than herself, of this trip to Europe . . . And Kate had also been right when she had looked at Brigitte Louisa

Thompson (born Patsy-Su Bartelski, but that had stayed the wrong side of the tracks) and thought of Gerry's wife. The two women had a lot in common: not the most obvious thing, perhaps, but certainly in the relentless pursuit of self.

Mrs Carling C. Thompson greeted the news that she was to present the prize for the feature race of the day at Rede Park Racecourse with a cool smile. Carl was thrilled and kept telling her what an honour it was, but Brigitte – or Patsy-Su – knew better. She often wondered how Carl had made all his money for there were times when he was extraordinarily naïve.

She made no objections, though. The fact that the managing director (whatever that was) of this outfit had recognised that she just could be the path to Carl's money was interesting. Still the handsome, dark, curly-headed man had paid her no attention, merely smiling at her politely and asking what the announcer should say about her when the presentation was made. Did he think this little gesture was enough to secure Carl's sponsorship of his horse race? The cosmetic line was hers. It was called Brigitte-Louisa (they had wanted to call it simply 'Brigitte' but there was another woman of that name, a rather more famous one who had threatened litigation) and Brigitte Louisa Thompson would have a considerable say in how the line was launched in Britain.

If she wanted it.

And, suddenly, she did.

Chapter 24

Kate stared dubiously at the presentation pack of Brigitte-Louisa products.

'Do I have to wear some of his beastly make-up?' she asked. 'I could manage the eye shadow, I suppose. And one of the lipsticks, but only if you insist.'

Gerry peered at the box.

'Is it really that awful? Perhaps we shouldn't be bothering at all. It's just that we could have *such* a race—'

'I'm sure it's not awful,' Kate said bravely, picking up a tube of lipstick. 'It's just that I'm not sure the colours suit me.'

'That one looks lovely.'

'Even so, let's give the rest to Charlie and Anne to play Indians with.'

They were both staying with the Colley-Smythes for this night out in London with Mr and Mrs Carling C. Thompson and Bernard and Rebecca Rosenthal. It had been Vanessa and Mark who said it was silly for Gerry to be at the Oxford and Cambridge Club and Kate out at Richmond. The feeling was absurd, but Kate could not prevent it: discussing make-up with Gerry in a strange bedroom (it was not the one she usually occupied) seemed so married and adult – and she having just celebrated her thirty-fourth birthday.

'We liked the other places,' Carling C. Thompson said as he sipped his brandy. 'The guys in charge were friendly and they seemed to want my money, but' – he smiled at his wife through the smoke of

370

his cigar – 'no one asked Brigitte to present any prizes. She just loved doing that at Rede Park.'

'So you'll come to us?' Gerry said, trying to keep the excitement out of his voice.

'We don't know if we'll go for this race sponsorship at all. We haven't finally decided, have we, honey? It's really Brigitte's decision,' he added with another fond glance in her direction. 'The cosmetic line is hers.'

Gerry looked at Brigitte Thompson, who was sitting on his right. She stared back at him, her green eyes revealing nothing at all.

'I've said what we'll give you – if Brigitte agrees, of course,' Carling C. continued. 'And I've seen your files, which are most interesting, but you have yet to tell us both exactly what it is you are offering us.'

Gerry leaned forward, pushing aside glasses so he could get closer to Carling C. Thompson, as though that might convince him.

'A race over a mile and a half, open to colts and fillies of three and over – not a handicap: just weight for age and sex – at our Festival meeting in August. It's the classic distance. We could attract horses from Ireland and France to run in it, considering the prize you are speaking of, as well as from Britain.' He sat back. 'It could be the middle-distance championship of Europe.'

'You mean you don't already have one of those?' Carling C. Thompson asked, his American soul jibbing at anything less than constant cutthroat competition.

'Only the King George VI and Queen Elizabeth Stakes at Ascot,' Gerry said dismissively, consigning that great race to the status of also-ran and ignoring the Prix de l'Arc de Triomphe. 'But there's plenty of time between that race and ours. Horses could run in both. Derby winners at Rede Park for the Brigitte-Louisa . . . think of it, Mr Thompson!'

Rebecca Rosenthal, who was sitting on his other side, tapped Gerry's knee and he realised he was sounding too desperate.

'I'll get the sponsorship from somewhere,' he concluded, hoping his voice was confident and convincing. 'Especially since we are being televised next year.'

371

Carling C. Thompson stubbed out his cigar.

'Brigitte wants to talk to our PR men here,' he said. 'Discuss the whole launch with them. Isn't that so, honey?'

Gerry turned to her again. Again her green eyes were on him.

'That's right, Carl,' she said, without turning her head.

'How do you think it went?' Gerry asked Kate as they sat in the taxi on their way back to Richmond.

Kate yawned. 'Hard to tell. They're both inscrutable in their different ways.'

'The Brigitte-Louisa, though,' Gerry said. 'What a name for a horse race!'

'I wonder what the trophy will be,' Kate murmured sleepily. 'How about a giant gold-plated powder compact?'

'Yeah – and one of those presentation packs of make-up for the winning trainer and jockey. Never mind. It's the prize money that counts.'

'I tell you something, though,' Kate said, laying her cheek against his shoulder. 'Brigitte Thompson wasn't wearing her own brand of lipstick.'

'Wasn't she?'

'She was not. You have a look at it next time you see her.'

'I probably won't ever again,' he said gloomily. 'Probably they'll decide not to sponsor us at all.'

But Mrs Carling C. Thompson rang Gerry two days later and asked him to come to a meeting in her suite at the Connaught Hotel the following day.

It was excruciating. Carling C. Thompson's PR men knew nothing at all about racing and, in their desire to impress their employer's wife, made the most absurd and inappropriate suggestions. Gerry had to struggle to keep a straight face when they indeed came up with the idea of giving the winning trainer and jockey special packs of Brigitte-Louisa products, and they greeted the news that these two individuals would inevitably be male with utter disbelief. They cheered up, however, when Gerry produced racecards from past meetings at Rede Park, the front covers of them advertising the day's principal sponsor in a way that would touch the heart of any self-respecting public relations man.

372

'You can have the back cover as well,' Gerry told them, 'inside and out.' They could have the whole bloody thing if Gerry got his hands on Carling C. Thompson's forty thousand pounds.

They took the racecards away, pleased to have something they understood and Gerry, too, prepared to depart.

'Won't you have a drink before you go, Mr Beviss?' Mrs Thompson said. 'Or may I call you Gerry? It's a cute name.'

'Yes, to both questions,' Gerry replied, re-seating himself and hoping for good news.

'And you call me Brigitte – okay?' She handed him a whisky into which she had put about half a bucket of ice. Americans liked their drinks deep frozen, he remembered.

She sat beside him on the sofa, rather closer than was strictly necessary, and crossed her legs. Yet again she subjected him to scrutiny from the cool green eyes. Boldly he met her gaze. He refused to give in and ask if this meeting meant a final decision on the sponsorship had been made: he had been over-eager the other night and must now be offhand and pretend it didn't matter; pretend he had lots of companies lined up ready to give him forty thousand pounds, even though none had come within twenty-five lengths of it.

'Why are you looking at me?' Brigitte Louisa Thompson asked softly.

Was that her game? Gerry could play it, even though he was slightly out of practice.

'Because you are looking at me, and because—' Well, why not? 'Because I'm interested to note that you are not wearing your own brand of lipstick.'

She gave a low, throaty chuckle.

'How smart of you to notice,' she said. 'It isn't in the range, that's true, but it *is* my own. My very own. It is made specially for me, you see.'

Christ! Gerry had thought he knew everything about rich people, but even Diana hadn't come up with this idea.

'Is the Brigitte-Louisa line successful in the States?' he asked, anxious to make the conversation more businesslike, less intimate.

'Oh sure,' she said casually, 'and it will succeed here. Carl's

British company will see to that.' She smiled at him, the green eyes mocking. 'It'll succeed,' she repeated, 'with or without your horse race, Gerry Beviss.'

She stood up, went to the door of the suite and opened it.

'Goodbye,' she said.

Annoyed by the way he had been so summarily dismissed – he hadn't even finished his drink – Gerry went to the Rosenthals' flat in Eaton Square. Bernard was not home, but Rebecca listened to what Gerry said about his inconclusive meeting with Brigitte Thompson.

She patted the top of his curly head.

'You watch out,' she said. 'That woman is after you. It's so blatant it's almost subtle.'

'I'm blatantly after her husband's money.'

'Just you be careful of her,' Rebecca warned. 'Ask yourself if this race of yours is worth it.'

He was summoned to another meeting. This time there were no PR men in the sitting room of the Thompsons' suite at the Connaught. Brigitte was alone.

Is this it, then? Gerry wondered. Was Rebecca right? It would be exceedingly awkward if Brigitte Louisa Thompson threw her expensive clothes to the floor and herself into his arms. She wouldn't take kindly to a rejection under those circumstances and that would be an end to any chance of her sponsoring his race . . . for he *would* refuse her. He had to. He had forsaken all others.

He listened with half an ear while she talked about who would design the trophy – *if*, she constantly implied, they went ahead with the Brigitte-Louisa Stakes at Rede Park – and amused himself by imagining how she would go about seducing him . . . Appear at the door of the bedroom wearing the titillating underwear that got her fat old husband going, perhaps? And then she'd unpin the luxurious coils of rich blond hair . . . how long was it? He could see that no back-combing had been needed to give it its bulk. She certainly was a very beautiful woman. How could she get into bed with Carling C. Thompson every night?

She had talked herself into deciding to go to Cartier for

inspiration when they reached Paris, where they were going in a few days' time.

'We'll be back here in three weeks,' she said. 'You have another of your race meetings around then, don't you? We'd like to come to that – you know, see the place in action one more time.' She smiled lazily at him. 'And then I guess I can promise I'll have a final answer for you.' She laid a hand on his knee and looked at him, the green eyes earnest, pleading. 'You won't make a deal with anyone else before then, now will you, please?'

Before he could reply, she uncrossed her long legs and got to her feet.

'And now I must ask you to go,' she said. 'Carl is taking me to the theatre tonight and I want to take a nap . . . my beauty sleep, you know.'

Once more he had been peremptorily dismissed. He drove the long miles back to Wiltshire wondering what on earth was going on. This latest 'meeting' hadn't been necessary at all: Rebecca must be right and Mrs Carling C. Thompson was after him – but, if so, why hadn't she made a move? . . . Not that he wanted her to, of course. He had no desire at all to be seduced by the bored wife of a very rich man.

Had she noticed the erection his own imaginings had produced? Those green eyes missed very little.

Cartier for a horse race! *Cartier!*

No, he had no desire at all to be seduced by Mrs Carling C. Thompson. But he was rather piqued that she hadn't even tried.

The gap came and Gerry, having had a double handful of racehorse under him and nowhere to go, launched Calipers through it. Within a few seconds he was clear of his field, could hear the roar of the crowd and saw the winning post flashing by. He pulled Calipers up, wheeled him around and trotted back towards the grandstands. The lad came to the horse's head, swiped the sweaty neck affectionately and led him towards the winners' enclosure until Bernard, smiling broadly, took the rein.

'Oh Gerry! Well ridden indeed!' he said.

Gerry grinned down at him.

'We got our dead heat then.'

375

'The result of the Rede Park Gentlemen Riders' Handicap,' the racecourse announcer said over the loudspeakers. 'First, number twelve, Calipers, owned by Mr Bernard Rosenthal, the chairman of Rede Park Racecourse, trained by Peter Thornton and ridden by the managing director of Rede Park, Mr Gerald Beviss . . . our own Gerry, ladies and gentlemen!'

Someone cheerfully shouted 'Fix!' but a great roar greeted the announcement. Gerry could almost feel the affection for him and Bernard as he rode through the crowd, his hand to his cap brim as he acknowledged the congratulations and cries of 'Well done, our Gerry!' It might have been because Rede Park was becoming an important employer in the area – albeit seasonal and casual – or because Calipers had been second favourite and his win had put money into people's pockets: no matter, it was there and almost tangible.

Cameras clicked as Bernard led his horse into the winners' enclosure, and Gerry posed for the photographers before taking his feet from the stirrups, jumping off and removing the saddle.

'How does it feel, our Gerry?' a reporter called.

Gerry paused, the saddle over his arm. He shook his head.

'Like nothing else,' he said. 'It's the biggest thrill of my life.'

He went to weigh in and the reporters converged on Bernard.

'Yes, my first winner here,' he replied to every question, 'and my twenty-third runner . . . how splendid that Gerry was riding. He's broken my jinx. You know that all this – the racecourse, everything – is due to him . . . ?'

It wasn't entirely true, but it was a nice story and they would print it.

Gerry showered and changed and went to the directors' box, prepared for a celebration to end all celebrations. Rebecca Rosenthal flung her arms around him.

'Oh, *well done*, Gerry . . . my Bernard had tears running down his face. He won't admit it, but it's true.'

David Blower handed him a glass of champagne. 'Weren't you worried about that gap?' he asked. 'It looked pretty tight to me.'

'I was a bit,' Gerry admitted. 'But it's all so much easier when you don't have bloody fences to think about as well as everything else . . . Where's Kate?'

'Here.'

She was beside him, holding a plate of sandwiches.

'Eat, Gerry, before you start drinking. You've been starving yourself for a week.'

'Nag, nag, nag.' Gerry wound his arm around her neck, picked up a sandwich and took a bite out of it, his cheek against hers. 'It was worth losing the weight to win the race, though, for Bernard . . . Isn't this fun? Isn't everything wonderful?'

'Wonderful,' she said, twisting her head and kissing his cheek. She offered the plate. 'Have another.'

He took a second sandwich and looked around the room. For the first time he noticed Brigitte Thompson and her husband, standing on the far side of the directors' box near the plate-glass doors that led out to the balcony. He had entirely forgotten they were coming.

He swallowed the remainder of his sandwich, unwound his arm from Kate's neck and went towards them. Carling C. Thompson extended a pudgy hand.

'Congratulations,' he said. 'The reception you were given was real nice. Kind of moving, too.' He turned his heavy head to his wife. 'You thought so too, didn't you, honey?'

Brigitte did not speak and Gerry, to fill the space, said, 'It isn't an important race, but for me to ride Bernard's first winner at our racecourse . . . well—'

'A great moment. I understand that,' Carling C. Thompson said, and then added as more people piled into the box and called for Gerry, 'I guess you'd better go join your friends.'

Gerry, well aware that this kind of riotous party was not giving a good impression but unable to stop it, said, 'They won't come back after the next race. We can talk then. . . .'

'Don't you worry about us,' Carling C. Thompson said. 'We'll go to Mr and Mrs Stewart's box until it's calmed down some here. Okay, honey?'

Brigitte Thompson moved off on her husband's arm, giving Gerry a cool smile as she passed him. He watched them go, thinking it was goodbye to the Brigitte-Louisa and forty thousand pounds.

It did not, of course, occur to him that the sight of him being cheered past the winning post, the racecourse announcer's 'our own Gerry, ladies and gentlemen', the lionising he was receiving now, and even him eating his sandwich with his arm around his girlfriend – she acted like a wife but she wore no wedding band; obviously she was very close to him – all this made Gerry Beviss irresistible to Brigitte Louisa Thompson.

Another meeting at the Connaught, the PR men there. Endless discussion about when and how the announcement of the Brigitte-Louisa sponsorship should be made; another ice-filled whisky.

'You said you'd have an answer when you got back from Paris,' Gerry said, hearing the petulant tone in his voice too late to correct it.

She laid her hand on his thigh. 'Be patient a little longer. The race is more than a year away.'

Yes, but he wanted to know now! He finished his drink and said, 'I must go.'

'Must you?'

'It's a long drive.'

'Okay.'

She took her hand away, stood up and Gerry left, conscious of a perverse feeling of disappointment that had nothing to do with a horse race.

Another summons three days later: lunch in the suite at the Connaught. Carl would be there as he wanted to clear up a few minor details.

Carl was not there. He had been 'called away'.

A typical English midsummer lunch: asparagus, salmon with new potatoes and peas, strawberries and cream. A bottle of cold, crisp Muscadet and, with the strawberries, Dom Perignon champagne.

'Is this because we're celebrating?' Gerry asked as she handed him the bottle to open.

'We might be,' she said.

After the plates had been cleared away, she picked up the half empty bottle of champagne.

'Come along,' she said, and walked towards the bedroom door.

He followed. Truly he could see no alternative. Was the race worth it?

At that moment he thought that it was.

Kate was waiting for him in the Club. He still wouldn't allow her to walk through the woods alone, even though the evenings were light; and, in any case, she knew Gerry was not at home because Parsnip was with Andrew.

They had agreed to go for a ride, Gerry remembered. Only this morning. It seemed a lifetime away. He was desperate to have a bath and rid himself of Brigitte Louisa's scents. Golden pubic hairs could be mixed up with his black ones, blond hairs perhaps on his chest. Her hair was twenty-three inches long, she had told him; heavy, silken, golden, she had spread it over him . . . and he smelt of sex. He had to! Three times she had made him come and after the third time she had handed him a sheet of paper: a letter confirming that Brigitte-Louisa Cosmetics would sponsor the race at Rede Park for one year and, if both parties were satisfied, for three years after that. There was the amount of money in both US dollars and pounds sterling, the rows of satisfying noughts. The letter was dated five days earlier, the day after he had won the race on Calipers, and signed in solid ink by Carling Conrad Thompson.

He should have showered at the Connaught but had dressed, forced himself to kiss the woman lying in the huge bed, her hair hiding her breasts, her green eyes sated, had taken the letter and run. It was in his pocket. He had to celebrate, but how could he?

He smiled at his lovely Kate.

'We've got the race,' he said, and then she wanted to hug him. He held her away. 'I stink of London. You get the horses ready and I'll go and change.'

'They are ready. I didn't think you'd be so late.'

Take the initiative. Grapple with it.

'Jealous, my Kate?' he said. 'I don't get jealous when you go to London to see James.'

Though he did, wildly.

She stared at him.

'I go to see all my friends,' she said. 'I don't want to lose touch and it's difficult for them to come down here.'

It was the nearest she had ever come to reproaching him for their complicated circumstances. Seven years since she said she would marry him, three since they had started sleeping together; only the slightest clouding of her glorious eyes when Gerry's annual application to Diana's lawyers for a divorce came back refused, and the monthly disappointment of not being pregnant was entirely concealed ... All this, to say nothing of what had happened to her career as a doctor because of him. And of course she could not invite her friends to stay in the utilitarian one-bedroom flat near the hospital.

'Jealousy is a green-eyed monster, Gerry,' she said. What had possessed him to bring up that dreadful word?

He had, then, to risk taking her in his arms, sure that the guilt weighing on him was as evident as the smells of scent and sex.

Chapter 25

Guilty, guilty, but undiscovered. Brigitte Thompson and her husband returned to America, she apparently as reluctant as Gerry to repeat their experiences. Gerry, relieved, assumed that she did not want to threaten her marriage, did not want to be parted from Carling C. Thompson and his millions, but the truth was very different. Brigitte Thompson did not need good sex all that often. If she had, she would not have married Carl in spite of all his money. She could be satisfied for months after the kind of session she had enjoyed with Gerry in her bedroom at the Connaught Hotel. The hunting of Gerry Beviss had been just as pleasurable as . . . the kill. And the fact that he was not eager to get back into her bed again made the prospect of her trip to England next year to see the inaugural running of the Brigitte-Louisa very interesting indeed.

The announcement of the sponsorship was greeted with headlines PR men dream about. There was concern that the stake money – the entry fees – would make the prize richer than the Derby and Gerry thoroughly enjoyed fielding questions from the press. The controversy even crept out of the racing pages and into the main part of the newspapers; the story ran for days.

Sir Henry Blower rang Gerry up.

'I can't do anything about it,' Gerry said. 'The Derby was fifty-three thousand pounds last year and we won't come anywhere near that, what with the place money and everything. If they are worried about it at Epsom, tell them to find a sponsor.'

'The Epsom Derby sponsored?' said Sir Henry, shocked. 'I'll shoot myself the day it happens.'

Luckily, perhaps, he died peacefully in his sleep seven years later.

Gerry spent that winter fighting sponsors off, although he agreed to another Blue Oceans race because Blue Oceans was so much a part of Rede Park, because it was family and because at last he had been granted racing on Saturdays. Two of them, one in July and the other in August. Their Festival meeting was now four days, and the Brigitte-Louisa would be run on the Saturday.

'It's going to be too crowded,' he groaned to Kate. 'We should be building phase three now.'

'You must see how it goes,' she said. 'The race is only effectively guaranteed for one year.'

The name Brigitte-Louisa was often on their lips but it never meant the woman with the twenty-three-inch-long golden hair. It must be even longer now. Gerry hadn't heard a word from her and was glad, although memories of that afternoon in the Connaught would come upon him: of her taking him in her mouth, her hair falling over his thighs, her green eyes very wide as he entered her. . . .

A television crew came to Rede Park to decide on the sites for the cameras and Gerry had a television installed in the directors' box; everyone cheered as John Rickman raised his famous hat and said, 'Good afternoon, everyone, and welcome to Rede Park.' The Brigitte-Louisa range was advertised during the commercial breaks, so the PR men weren't such fools after all.

Mr and Mrs Carling C. Thompson arrived in England in August, a week before their race was to be run. Gerry sent flowers to the Connaught 'from the directors of Rede Park Racecourse' – Liz James's idea – and the book of newspaper cuttings. He was anxious that they should be able to announce the next three years' sponsorship and persuaded Bernard to join him in taking the Thompsons out to lunch, as he feared Carling C. would be inexplicably called away again if he went on his own.

'Always so impatient, Gerry,' Bernard murmured.

'The momentum is important, though.'

But it was last year all over again. Carling C. Thompson puffed

382

at his cigar and insisted it was his wife's decision. He admitted they were pleased with the launch of the Brigitte-Louisa range but seemed to think it had nothing to do with the bulky file of newspaper clippings. Brigitte Thompson kept her green eyes on her husband or on her plate and said not a word.

Gerry was furious. The race was everything he had said it would be. They had last year's Derby winner, St Paddy, coming – running in the same colours as Crepello – and Right Royal V, his French conqueror in the King George at Ascot. This year's Derby winner, Psidium, was also in the line-up and Die Hard was travelling over from Ireland: even now, perhaps, being settled in the racecourse stables. The antepost betting had been reported almost daily, as had been Captain Beech's assessment of the going for the great day as it was considered to be the soft ground that had beaten St Paddy at Ascot.

What more did she want, for heaven's sake? He didn't expect to be congratulated, but neither did he expect to be ignored.

He took his temper home to Kate, and she rejoiced in it. She had her suspicions about that day last June but had preferred not to put them under too close a scrutiny. They had renewed their vows to each other three months ago – as they did every year on the eve of her birthday – and she had detected nothing but love in him. He took the vows seriously, if only because she did: they were all she had.

So she listened to his rantings about Brigitte Louisa Thompson convinced that, had he indeed been guilty, he would not force the woman's name upon her now. And she was, in a sense, right for at that moment he had entirely forgotten that afternoon in the Connaught, and this was in no way the railing against a woman who had bedded him and then ignored him.

'You've been turning down other sponsors,' Kate said. 'You don't have to rely on Brigitte Louisa.'

'But they have the option, and no one else has come anywhere near the money.'

'Then, my darling, you just have to wait. It's only a few more days. Are you too overwrought to cook supper or shall I?'

That got him out of it. He laughed, finished his Glenmorangie, stood up and put his arms around her.

'Oh my Kate, no!' he wailed. 'Haven't I been punished enough today?'

There was a huge crowd on the first day of the Rede Park Festival. Gerry always hired a box for this meeting and he was on his way back there when he heard his name being called. He turned and found Nick O'Rourke smiling at him: Nick O'Rourke who hadn't spoken to him since – when? – 1952 when he had discovered Gerry was a gypsy.

'This is all splendid, Gerry,' Nick said, as though his fury then and the intervening nine years hadn't existed. 'Congratulations.'

'Well, thank you,' Gerry said and then, since Nick seemed to expect something more and it was impossible to converse in the crowd, 'Come to my box and have a drink.'

'Love to,' Nick said quickly. 'The wife's just collecting her winnings, but we'll be along shortly.'

Gerry gave him the box number and directions and went on his way. Should he have given Nick a dose of his own medicine and cut him dead? Perhaps he should, but who cared? Nick was going bald, he had noticed. Serve him right. Then he met Bill Staple and his wife, the cockney millionaire he had done business with during his brief career as a merchant banker, and he invited them for a drink too. If Nick O'Rourke was still a raging snob, let him despise Bill's loud check suit and his wife's dress decorated around the collar with grotesque fake pearls – except, good grief, they were probably real.

Arthur and Grace were hovering, as usual, around the Blue Oceans Bar, people standing six deep waiting to get their stomachs around Joe Beviss's seafood, and Gerry tried to persuade them to come for a drink too.

'No, lad,' Arthur said. 'We like to stay here and keep an eye on things.'

'We'll have to rebuild this bar. We need more room, Gerry,' Grace said.

And then Gerry's wife appeared.

'Darling!' she screeched, as oblivious as Nick to what had happened between them in the past – or, in her case, was still happening since she continued to refuse him a divorce. 'They're all calling it the August Ascot. Isn't it utterly wonderful?'

She did not wait for introductions and for that Gerry was thankful, since the prospect of introducing her to her own brother-in-law after all this time seemed overwhelming. He had the feeling that fate was closing in on him. Out of this vast crowd here today he had met, one after the other, a representative of each element of his disparate past. It was like lightning flickering in the distance wondering where to strike.

He reached his box. The waiter told him that Mrs Carling C. Thompson wanted to see him, and the feeling grew.

Brigitte Thompson could wait. Gerry went over to Kate and kissed her.

'Great heavens, Gerry,' she said, blushing slightly for there were lots of people in the box. 'What was that for?'

'For being my undisparate present,' he told her, and felt the sky clear.

'I've never seen such crowds. Any idea how many people are here?' James asked. Since the very first day's racing at Rede Park it had become a tradition that he should escort Kate, and he never brought one of his débutantes here.

'Over thirty thousand,' Gerry replied. 'Fantastic, isn't it? Hello, rascal. Got any tips for me?'

Charlie Colley-Smythe took his racing very seriously. His masters at his prep school had been most impressed by his interest in newspapers until they discovered that he only read the racing pages.

'Accredit will win the Blue Oceans Sprint, I think,' Charlie said, a frown on his white freckled brow.

'I'm going to put my money on it,' his sister put in loyally.

Two red heads converged over the racecard.

'It's an interest, not a compulsion,' Vanessa said, knowing what Gerry was thinking. 'Truly it is ... Gerry, you should see their Post Office savings books! Mark and I are wondering if we should apply for a loan, but Charlie is so careful with his money I doubt he'd give us one. And Anne does whatever he does.'

Gerry was sure she was right, but he could not help being a little disturbed. Rede Park Racecourse would have celebrated its

385

centenary by now if it had not been for a compulsion to bet. But Charlie did not seem to display, even in embryonic form, any of Patrick's alarming symptoms – and, unlike Patrick's, Charlie's tips often won.

After the next race, Gerry went to the Stewarts' box where he assumed he would find Mrs Carling C. Thompson. He had not realised that she was coming here today. He hoped she would have good news for him, and he cursed himself for accepting that letter as a contract. It gave all the power to the Carling C. Thompsons and none at all to him, and there was not even a time limit on when they had to take up the option. Except it was difficult to argue over minor details when someone was offering you forty thousand pounds.

(And when you were given that letter as you lay on top of the wife of the man who had signed it, your waning cock inside her.)

Would she demand the same price for the next three years as she had done for this one? All defences up, he entered the box.

Brigitte Thompson was there, talking to the Strawberry Tart.

'Gerry!' she said, and came over to him holding out both hands. 'Thank you for coming to find me.' She drew him out on to the balcony where they could talk in private. 'I'm sorry for being such a crosspatch the other day at lunch. I wasn't feeling so well. The flight over had been bad and I was kind of jet lagged, I guess. I never even thanked you for the flowers . . . Now, say you forgive me.'

'Of course I do,' Gerry stuttered, this being the last welcome he expected.

'And our race is wonderful! The press coverage all the way through has been just terrific. Carl says you have done a swell job.'

'Does he?' Gerry managed.

'Truly. And today – the crowds!' She gestured vaguely out at the racecourse, but her green eyes remained on him, full of warm friendliness.

He would not ask her about the option, he would *not*. He kept his mouth firmly closed unless the words came out of their own accord.

'We're staying at the Benton Grange Hotel,' Brigitte continued.

'We were lucky to get a room, apparently, and Yvonne' – Who the hell was that? Oh, the Strawberry Tart, of course – 'Yvonne always has a houseful for your Festival meeting she says, and this year, because of the Brigitte-Louisa, she has people staying in the attics almost.'

'Really?' What had got into the woman? She was chattering like a magpie.

She laid a hand on his shoulder. He stiffened.

'Do you know the Benton Grange, Gerry?'

'Yes, I do. We – my party and I – always go there after the Festival meeting. We'll be there on Saturday night.'

'To celebrate?' she asked.

'Yes. I suppose so.'

'Well, maybe we can all celebrate there on Saturday night. Toast the first winner of the Brigitte-Louisa and – who knows? – future ones as well.'

'We'll do that then,' he said.

Disappointment: she would not tell him that the future of the race was secure until after it had been run for the first time.

Relief: he was not being summoned to any 'meetings' at her hotel. She would not see him until Saturday and they would be surrounded by people all the time they were together.

. . . Disappointment?

She led him off the balcony and back into the interior of the box.

'Business is over!' she announced gaily. 'Now let's be serious about the Blue Oceans Sprint.'

'Any ideas, Gerry?' asked the Strawberry Tart.

'I'm told Accredit will win,' he said.

And it did, at a juicy 11–1.

If the truth of Gerry's dictum that good prizes brought good horses and good horses brought the crowds needed any further proving, the day of the Brigitte-Louisa was it. By one o'clock the car parks were a glittering mass of metal and glass and Patrick's cattle had to be moved from the fields overlooking the racecourse to provide more space.

'How the blazes did you get them out?' Gerry asked, when

George found him and told him the news. Visions of racegoers faced with a herd of fat beef cattle went through his mind, smart shoes sinking into fresh cowpats.

'We cut through the wire of five fences, took 'em right round the back,' George said. 'The Captain sorted it all.'

Gerry pushed his way to Captain Beech's office, where he found Jennifer Cody ruefully surveying her laddered stockings.

'Well, someone had to move the bloody things,' she said in answer to his query. 'Captain Beech worked out the route but couldn't leave his post, and there wasn't time to call the farm workers. Admiral and Mrs Partington helped and Lionel Moreton is up there now redirecting the traffic.'

'Good God!'

'He's enjoying himself. He's making sure no one skulks in their car and watches the racing free. I offered to take over and George positively begged to, but he wasn't having it. We couldn't find you.'

'I was with the brewery people.' They had wanted their race moved to the Saturday but felt – understandably enough – that it was being overwhelmed by the Brigitte-Louisa. He had to keep them sweet because the future of the Brigitte-Louisa was so uncertain.

Captain Beech handed both Jennifer and Gerry a glass, a generous finger of pale gold Glenmorangie in it.

'Here's to our race,' he said, 'and to the most successful racecourse in Britain.'

Gerry drank, feeling elation fizz in him, fill him, and love – yes *love* – for the people who had made this day of days possible, had moved cattle and cut fences and directed traffic and cared . . . And then Andrew James phoned from the main gate to say that the number of people known to have entered Rede Park today was fifty thousand. Fifty thousand people come to the August Ascot to see the re-match between St Paddy and Right Royal V!

Then a man arrived in the office and asked if Mr Beviss cared to go on television. Mr Rickman would like to interview him during the build-up to the big race . . . would he? Jumping out of his skin, Gerry agreed.

He was about to go back to his box, have some lunch and tell everyone the good news when the phone rang again. Captain Beech grunted into it, said 'yes' and replaced the receiver.

'Kate's wanted at the hospital,' he told Gerry.

'She can't be,' Gerry said. 'She's on holiday.'

'Perhaps there's been a bad accident and they're calling in all doctors,' Jennifer said. 'Oh Lord, I hope not.'

'She doesn't do that kind of thing any more. She's an obstetrician now.' Kate loved the work, didn't mind the broken nights or the fact that she helped women have the babies she seemed unable to conceive. 'I'd better tell her then,' Gerry said, and made for the door.

The message was greeted with consternation by everyone but Kate, who calmly prepared to leave.

'I know what it is,' she said. 'It's a very young and very nervous first-time mother whose own doctor is away. She's been in several times with false alarms and I – well – I promised I'd be with her when it really happened. She's probably hysterical. I must go.'

'Is your car at the Club?' James asked. 'I'll take you to it. Can we go down the racecourse, Gerry?'

'Yes, do. It's by far the quickest way.' He turned to Kate. 'At least you'll be going against the traffic, but drive carefully.'

'I will, but really, Gerry, it's not an emergency.'

'Will you come to Benton Grange this evening?'

'If I can.'

It was the last conversation they would have for a very long time.

Little Janet Woods gave birth to her baby – a healthy seven-pound girl – at eleven o'clock that night. Kate pulled down her mask and went to tell the young father of his daughter's arrival. The boy rushed to his wife's side and gazed at the baby at her breast. Kate followed him. He looked up at her.

'What's your name?' he asked in rich Wiltshire.

'It's Katherine,' she replied in some surprise.

'We already decided if 'twere a girl we'd call her for you,' the boy said. 'So this liddel maid is Katherine . . . that's so, Janet, ain't it?'

389

Janet nodded and smiled wearily at Kate. Her husband went on: 'We're mighty grateful to you, doctor. My Janet was greatly afraid, and she with no mother to tell her how to go on.' He held out a large, work-roughened hand and Kate, moved, took it. 'Thank ye,' he said, 'thank ye from all three of us.'

'You mind you'en back on the harvest tomorrow, Jack,' Janet muttered. 'We need the overtime now we've got the young 'un.'

'Harvest!' he said, contempt in his voice. 'What's that compared to this?' The hand now touched the newborn cheek. 'Our liddel Katherine.'

'I'm called Kate usually,' Kate said.

'Kate,' he said wonderingly, watching as his daughter's tiny fingers gripped his brown thumb. 'You don't mind us callin' her for you?'

'I don't mind,' Kate said.

They looked in some way holy, the three of them, the mother, father and child, and Kate forgot that bold Jack had had his way with Janet some time last November – in a hay barn, perhaps, perhaps when motherless Janet was on her way home from school, that they had been married for only five months. Their combined ages amounted to two years less than Kate's own.

Still, the boy had done the right thing by his girl and, great heavens! – who was Kate to talk?

The birth had left her full of energy, of life. She looked at her watch. She could finish here, change and be at the Benton Grange Hotel by midnight. A horse race had been run, she remembered, and she wondered who had won.

She knew something was wrong the moment she located their table and sat down. There was no sign of Gerry. She assumed he was on the crowded dance floor, but something was wrong in the over-hearty way she was greeted by James and by Andrew Coleridge, the way they made a great performance of ordering sandwiches for her (it was too late for anything else and she discovered she was starving), the way Rosie Coleridge stared at the tablecloth and Vanessa looked at her in panic, her hair frizzing even more wildly than usual.

Kate did not, of course, know that Carling C. Thompson had

left the hotel at ten o'clock and returned to London in order to be there, well-rested, for a breakfast meeting the next day with a man who was flying in from New York to Heathrow on his way to Zurich. Sundays did not come between Carling C. Thompson and making money.

Or that at ten past ten Gerry had been summoned across the room by a pair of cool green eyes and that he was, even now, discovering exactly how much Brigitte Louisa Thompson's hair had grown in the fourteen months since he had last encountered it.

But after twenty minutes and no curly dark head and wicked grin could be seen either among the dinner-jacketed dancers or at the tables surrounding the dance floor, Kate guessed.

'Where is Gerry?' she asked at last, and the silence that greeted her commonplace question told her for sure.

She stood up.

'Kate, no,' Helen Blower said.

Calmly Kate shook off Helen's anxious, restraining hand. She went to the reception desk and asked the sleepy clerk the number of Carling C. Thompson's room, walked up two flights of stairs, found the number twenty-two on the door. Knocked. Dimly she realised that if whoever was in there was doing . . . what they were doing then they were hardly likely to respond. But she did not know either – how could she? – that Brigitte Louisa Thompson had ordered a bottle of champagne and was expecting just such a knock upon her door. And over her shoulder, past the cascade of blond hair tumbling down the negligée which so casually hid her nakedness, Kate saw Gerry in her bed.

Recognition, shock in his face, she saw him start out of the bed before she closed the door, turned, went back down the corridor and the two flights of stairs.

James was waiting in the lobby.

'Now,' he said. 'Now will you marry me?'

She walked past him and out of the doors of the hotel. Found the car park. By a miracle found her car.

'I'm coming with you.'

'No,' she said.

She got into her car. He tried to hold the door open.

'No, James.'

He felt her desperation and let the door go. She started the engine and drove away.

How sad, she thought. How very sad. I won't ever see Parsnip again.

PART FOUR

Chapter 26

Parsnip whined and Gerry looked at him hopefully, but the dog merely stirred in his basket and went back to sleep. He often whined these days, but it was never to be let out of the door to go up the track to the Club because he had heard Kate's car. Gerry could not stop himself watching the dog, though. Just in case.

He still could not believe the blackness that surrounded him, the pit he had fallen into – though not fallen, he reminded himself, jabbing at the wound: stepped. Stepped deliberately into when Brigitte Louisa Thompson had fixed her green eyes on him and said, as she had done before, 'Come along,' and, as before, he had followed her.

He had not seen or heard of Kate since that dreadful night. No one had except, perhaps, Beattie. Six weeks after Kate had disappeared she had arrived in Leighminster to clear out Kate's flat and to collect the various belongings of Kate's that had accumulated in the house in the woods. He had not wanted her to take them but had cringed before the contempt in her eyes, the steel he would never have thought existed in her comfortably well-padded body. She had gone around the house, opening all the cupboards and drawers, and had taken everything apart from a picture which hung on the sitting room wall, some records and Parsnip.

She would not speak to him, refused to answer his questions concerning Kate's whereabouts until he had asked – surely her grim face could only mean this? – 'She's not dead, is she?' And Beattie had folded Kate's dressing gown into one of the suitcases she had brought and said, 'No. She's not dead.'

She had not even let Gerry carry the suitcases down the track, as though he might contaminate them. It had turned out that all the time Charles had been waiting outside.

At least they had left him Parsnip.

And it wasn't just that Kate had gone: the fabric of his life had gone. Everyone knew what he had done, those not actually present hearing about it soon enough, and they all blamed him. They spoke to him, they had to; but he had lost them a presence, a loved friend, and he had a feeling they would avoid him if they could, that he was a leper among them ringing his bell . . . unclean, unclean. To comfort both of them, he let Parsnip upstairs one night to sleep on Kate's side of the bed, but the dog would not settle and kept Gerry awake scratching at the door, demanding to be allowed back to his basket in the kitchen. That more than anything made Gerry feel utterly rejected. Even Rio's blue eyes seemed to contain accusation.

Liz James took pity on him and they sat up late, drinking at the Club. He tried to tell her how it had happened, how Brigitte Thompson had made it inevitable. It meant nothing, he told her. It made no difference to what he felt for Kate. It was . . . he searched for the words . . . a business arrangement. That's all.

'For heaven's sake, Gerry,' Liz said with some asperity, 'surely you knew Kate would never see it in that light.'

Of course he had known.

'And if you had to do it, why do it so publicly?'

He put his glass down and hid his face in his hands.

'She made me!'

It was, more or less, what Adam had said to God.

But one thing Liz said gave him hope: the fact that Kate had vanished so comprehensively meant that she was fearful of meeting him face to face, of giving in to him and forgiving him if he was sufficiently penitent. And he certainly was that, so all he had to do was find her.

He put advertisements in the personal columns of the *The Times* and he rang up every major hospital, first in London and then in the rest of the country, to enquire after Dr Katherine Earith, but without luck. He then embarked on the smaller local hospitals, and the private ones, but the number daunted him. And what if – because of her changed circumstances – she had at last landed a job as a general practitioner? Thousands and thousands of phone calls! There was a directory of doctors, but not enough time had passed for Kate's new position to be in it. He was driving the local librarians to distraction with his demands and questions but he didn't care.

Phase three of the grandstands was under way and Rede Park Racecourse Ltd was preparing to go public. The need for the new grandstands was so obvious after the phenomenal crowds at the Festival meeting – and there was yet another steady rise in attendances at the other meetings – that Gerry had the builders in within a week of their last season ending. There would, after all, be at least three more runnings of the Brigitte-Louisa even though Gerry never wanted to hear that name again.

At their board meeting in October he had voted for the flotation along with all the other directors and accepted the necessity for it. They were too successful and had grown so quickly they hadn't had a chance to consolidate. The loan for phase two hadn't yet been paid off, and Lionel Moreton and Bernard, who had large amounts of money invested in the company, naturally wanted the opportunity to reap their profits. No, they had to raise the money to build phase three by going public, but if Diana chose to take him to court now he would end up with nothing . . . *nothing*!

He went to see Rebecca Rosenthal.

'Why should Diana divorce you suddenly, after all this time?' she asked, laying out food for him, worried about the amount of weight he had lost.

'To get at me. I'd have to resign if there was a scandal.'

'I doubt if the press would make much fuss about it even if Diana did take you to court,' she said.

Gerry put down his knife and fork and pushed his plate away.

'Because Kate has gone? Is that what you mean?'

'Newspapers like to watch their victims suffer, Gerry.'

'But she might come back.'

'Oh Gerry,' Rebecca said, sighing, 'how can she possibly come back?'

All right. *All right.* It just meant he had to redouble his efforts to find her. He spent a day in London in December touring the minor hospitals; the weather was holding up the building work at Rede Park and he had to do something to make the days pass even if it was only hearing in person, instead of over the telephone, that no Dr Earith worked here.

On an impulse, he made a detour to Richmond on the way home. He could tell Mark and Vanessa were not pleased to see him but they had to let him in, and Charlie – home from school for the Christmas holidays – let slip that he had received a birthday card from his godmother the previous month.

'What did it say?' Gerry asked him.

' "Happy birthday, love Kate," ' Charlie replied with exquisite ten-year-old logic. 'There was a postal order in it. And she's sent us Christmas presents, too.'

'Can I see them?'

Gerry, ignoring the look that passed between Vanessa and Mark, followed Charlie into the sitting room, where Kate's parcels to the two children were under the tree. Kate's handwriting, the return address care of Poutney at Sissinghurst. Was she there then? She had not been all along. It had been the first place he had looked – there and the flat in First Street, innocently occupied by tenants, and he had even been to her parents' old village, knowing Kate had sold the site of her childhood home long ago. He had put a private detective on guard outside the Poutneys' house and the man had reported nothing. After Beattie's appearance in the house in the woods there seemed no reason for the detective to continue at his post, so Gerry had paid him and told him to go.

'It's sad she's gone away, isn't it?' Charlie said, giving the parcels an artful feel as he replaced them under the tree.

'Yes,' Gerry said. 'It's sad.'

Would she go home for Christmas? Where had she been all the time?

'Gerry, I promise you I have no idea,' Vanessa said when he went back into the kitchen. 'I only wish I had. She's my best friend.' She slammed the oven door, straightened up and looked at him. Despite her fury with him, her heart softened at the sight of his all-enveloping misery. 'Oh come on, Gerry,' she said wearily. 'Have supper with us and stay the night.'

'May I? May I really?' Gerry asked, the leper surprised by an invitation to return, however briefly, to the bosom of humanity.

He went home to his parents for Christmas and spent Christmas morning slinking up and down the lane outside Beattie and Charles's house. They appeared and went off to church, but there was no sign of their niece. He would have sensed her presence had she been there in the way he could sense the pull of the tides on the beach.

To fill the dark evenings, and because he did not want to be seen constantly propping up the bar in the Club by people who knew exactly why he was so suddenly at a loose end, Gerry began going to the local pub. He had been to the Rede Arms a few times with Captain Beech but he and Kate had never been there, pubs being the breeding ground for village gossip. But a pub was the one place where a man was expected to be alone, and was made welcome.

The second time he went there he found Patrick regaling the company with an account of how he had backed a winner at 25–1 that afternoon at Newbury.

'Gerry, what a surprise!' he exclaimed, breaking off his story. 'Jim, a pint of – what'll you have, Gerry?'

'Bitter, please.'

'A pint of best, then, Jim. And who is this?' Patrick asked, extending his hand for Parsnip to sniff and then stroking the dog's ears.

'Parsnip,' Gerry replied, knowing the name was foolish but ready to punch the man who dared say so.

'He's a fine-looking fellow,' Patrick said as the landlord pushed Gerry's pint towards him. 'Do you take him shooting?'

'No.' Hadn't Patrick remembered that Gerry didn't shoot? How the years had passed!

But there were no questions as to the whereabouts of Kate, no look of condemnation, accusation or – which was the worst of all – pity in Patrick's eyes as he introduced Gerry to the other men in the bar, all of them farmers or connected with agriculture in some way. Parsnip yawned, sank down at Gerry's feet and went to sleep and Gerry, too, felt himself relaxing for the first time in six months. The Wiltshire burr was nothing like the Sussex accent and farmers weren't fishermen, but the atmosphere was the same: he could have been back in the Anchor.

Or in the Pitt Club in Cambridge, for Patrick had changed not one bit.

'They came to the last together,' he said, his hands, one holding his jug of beer, describing it. 'And mine pinged it and sprinted away – positively *sprinted*, the jockey standing in the stirrups to stop him winning by too far . . . I had a feeling, see, the horse had been set up for this race.'

'And no one else worked it out?' one of the farmers asked.

'Can't have, can they, at those odds.'

No indeed. And at those odds the win must have surprised the stable as well, and Gerry knew it to be a betting one. Patrick was still gambling huge amounts of money on 'a feeling'. Little Charlie Colley-Smythe could have given him lessons on how to follow form.

But Gerry enjoyed his evenings at the Rede Arms. He learned that he was known as the 'second squire', the title traditionally given to Great-great-uncle Cyril's line, for it was generally thought that it was he who owned Cyril's house and the land surrounding it. Everyone took – had always taken, they told him – a powerful strong interest in second squire's race-riding, 'though we bain't be bettin' men,' the landlord, Jim Thorpe, told him. 'Not like first squire and his father before him.'

And when Gerry had his next win – on Fandangle at the Cheltenham Festival, no less – he found in himself a longing to be back at the Rede Arms with a good, honest pint in his hand instead of drinking champagne at the racecourse with Helen and David Blower, before whom Kate's absence seemed more dreadful and painful than ever . . . No lovely woman with a plate of sandwiches telling him to eat because he had been starving himself to make the weight for a race. Not that he had to do that these days, anyway, in spite of the beer he was drinking. And, too, he could never resist asking Helen if she had heard from Kate for he thought that, however justifiably he had been deserted, Kate would not desert her friends.

But unless they were all lying Kate had done just that. The women might be deceiving him but the men were not, for some of them – not in front of their wives, of course – agreed that Brigitte Louisa Thompson would be hard to resist. And James most certainly wasn't deceiving him. He asked Gerry for lunch in London, travelling down from Leicestershire to meet him, and told him what he had said to Kate as she had come down the stairs at the Benton Grange Hotel.

'I'm so frightfully worried that might have pushed her over the top, you see. I think I'm as much to blame as you are.'

'Rubbish,' Gerry said. Which it was, and Gerry did not want to share his guilt with anyone.

James came to stay with him for the opening meeting of Rede Park's next season a new fixture in April, and they drank Glenmorangie until the early hours of the morning, making each other thoroughly and drunkenly miserable.

'She should have married you,' Gerry said.

James sloshed more whisky into his glass.

'No, she loved you,' he said. 'Always did.'

'But where is she?' Gerry asked for the thousandth time. He had done all the phoning he could and was now beginning to think that Kate had gone abroad – to Australia or New Zealand, or maybe Canada or the United States. His head reeled at how big the world was.

'There must be directories of doctors there, though,' he said and James, who had no idea what he was talking about, grunted fuddled agreement. Curiously, Kate's disappearance had made the two men closer friends than they had been for years – since they had shared the same staircase landing at Trinity, perhaps – but even so Gerry liked the impersonal intimacy (a contradiction, but an accurate description nonetheless) of the Rede Arms where Jim said, ' 'Llo squire zir, 'llo 'Snip', and had placed Gerry's beer on the bar before he had even ordered it.

May came. The woods were full of bluebells and the world seemed more full of colour and life each time Gerry looked out of a window or walked up and down the track to the house, every day a new shoot poked out of the ground and unfurled a thing of glory. The wires of Kate's lights, which George kept in working order although Gerry never used them, were obscured by fresh green leaves.

This used to be his favourite time of year, but now all it heralded was a series of dreadful anniversaries. Two years since he had first set eyes on Brigitte Louisa Thompson; and next Monday was Kate's birthday: five years since she had told him she wanted to spend the night with him and he had given her Parsnip.

So many anniversaries . . . Gerry and Parsnip reached the house in the woods and said hello to Rio, who was waiting for his supper even though there was a half-eaten rabbit on the back doorstep which Parsnip seemed to want to do something revolting with. Gerry sorted that out, fed his animals, made himself a cup of tea and a sandwich and sat down at the kitchen table to read his mail. He had only just picked it up from the Club (that being as far as the postman cared to go) because he had been at the racecourse since early that morning preparing for Blue Oceans Handicap day and – as ever – he had made sure there was no envelope with Kate's handwriting on it before stuffing the four letters into his jacket pocket and walking down the track.

One letter, when he opened it, had him groping for the whisky bottle. He took a gulp of the stuff and picked up the letter again, hoping it would say something else.

Someone in his head was shouting in despair, 'No, not that! It's too unfair!' and then began to cry with harsh, choking sobs, but it wasn't Gerry. His eyes were quite dry, the typewritten letters unblurred:

Our client, Mrs Diana Beviss *née* Dalton, has instructed us to inform you that she is now prepared to grant a divorce and wishes the case to go before the courts with all dispatch. . . .

Gerry put down the piece of paper, closed his eyes and tried to think constructively. He must talk to Bernard. It was too late to stop the flotation of the company, but Bernard would have to do something. He loved Gerry, loved him like a son. He would have

402

to do something now, when Gerry was fighting for what remained of his life.

But the office was closed and there was no reply from the flat in Eaton Square. Gerry sat at the desk in the sitting room, the telephone in his hand, and thought. Then he shrugged and dialled the number of the house in Mayfair. After a long while the phone was answered by a woman: not Diana and not Suckers, for her last Christmas card had informed him that her mother had passed away in the autumn and she and her sister were retiring to Bournemouth. But the fact that the phone was answered at all meant that Diana was in England and he asked the woman if he could speak to her.

'No here,' she said. He wondered if she was drunk, and then realised she was foreign.

'Where is she?' he enunciated carefully.

'No here.'

'But where?'

A hiatus, and then a man came on the line. His English was scarcely better than the woman's but he had a lot more confidence.

'Senhora no here,' he informed Gerry authoritatively.

'Where is senhora,' Gerry tried.

A pause. An incomprehensible word and then the man said, 'I spell.'

Gerry wrote down an approximation of the letters, thanked the man, put down the phone and stared at the pad.

'Mor?a?,' he had written. 'Ridiparc.'

In other circumstances, he might have laughed out loud.

He ran down the track and jumped into his car. It would undoubtedly have been quicker to go across the valley, over the golf course, but he would arrive sweaty and breathless and he needed all the dignity he could muster.

The front door of Patrick's house was open. He walked in, heard Diana's tinkling laugh and followed it to its source.

'Gerry!' his wife exclaimed as she saw him standing in the doorway of the drawing room. 'Oh Gerry, we've just been talking about you – nicely, of course . . . Gerry you *are* going to be an utter sweetie and give me a divorce so I can marry my darling Eduardo, aren't you? . . . This is Eduardo,' she went on as Gerry,

403

bereft of words, stood and stared. She indicated a good-looking, dark-skinned man in his early forties, Gerry judged, who had risen to his feet on Gerry's entrance. 'Eduardo da Silva. He's from Rio and I love him utterly, you see.'

Alice in Wonderland was nothing on this, Gerry thought, as Eduardo da Silva declared himself, in faultless American, delighted to meet Gerry and Patrick handed him a drink, and Eduardo da Silva took Gerry's arm firmly and led him over to one of the windows that looked out over the racecourse and said, in a voice that was obviously not used to being contradicted:

'You're not going to cause Diana any trouble over this now, are you, Gerry? – you don't mind me calling you Gerry? Good. I want everything to go ahead as fast as possible. You see, I can't wait' – he fastened upon Gerry a pair of eyes as dark brown as Gerry's own – 'I can't wait, you see,' he said, 'to make Diana my wife.'

Gerry had an urge to say, 'Why? Are you *that* desperate for money?' but repressed it. His mind was in a turmoil. Relief, *relief* that Diana wasn't taking him to court because she wanted the scandal to force him out of his position as managing director of Rede Park Racecourse, and anger that she should demand so carelessly and abruptly what she had been refusing him all this long time . . . and envy that she had found someone with whom at least she thought she could be happy while he had no one. He and Kate could have been married years ago if Diana had been half as decent as she was expecting Gerry to be now.

(And would that have stopped you getting into bed with Brigitte Louisa Thompson? a voice in his head asked, and his conscience answered No.)

Eduardo da Silva's fingers tightened around his arm.

'You hurt Diana real bad once,' he said softly. 'Now don't do it again. You just let the divorce go through – okay?'

Christ! What story had Diana spun him about their pathetic little marriage? And was the man some kind of a gangster? His accent was almost a pastiche – too like the cinema to be real – and there was definitely a threat in his voice. As though Gerry needed to be threatened to consent to divorcing Diana Beviss *née* Dalton!

'I'll let the divorce go through, Mr da Silva—'

'Eduardo, please.'

'Eduardo. On one condition.'

'And that is?'

'No names are to be cited. The grounds are desertion.'

'Oh I don't know,' said Eduardo da Silva. 'Diana and I thought it would be sort of fun to go down to Brighton for a weekend. We talked it over with a detective and he'll arrange for the photographer.' He smiled, his teeth brilliant white. 'Diana bought some fancy underwear in Paris to wow him with.'

Gerry only hoped that Eduardo da Silva didn't discover Diana's most obvious drawback as a wife before the case came to court. Knowing her, she would do more than wow the photographer while her Latin lover was admiring the view of Brighton pier from the balcony of their hotel room.

'I'll instruct my solicitors to cite you, then.'

'Please do that,' Eduardo da Silva said. 'I shall enjoy being "cited" very much indeed.'

Gerry refused Patrick's invitation to stay to dinner, repulsed Diana's extravagant thanks for his generosity, agreed with Eduardo da Silva that they were sure to meet up on the racetrack tomorrow, escaped and drove away. He parked his car at the Club and walked over to the paddock where Florin and Sprite were gorging themselves on the delectable May grass, but they both came over when he called and put their heads over the fence and nuzzled at him hopefully for carrots or sugar.

'I'm going to be free,' he told them. 'But she's not. She's going to marry a Brazilian macho man who'll shut her up in a hacienda and take lots of mistresses . . . what do you think of *that*?'

Their whiskery noses brushed his neck, his ears, Florin occasionally swinging his head at Sprite to remind him that he was senior horse and Gerry was his man.

'Yes,' Gerry said. 'I'm going to be free.' Florin blew into his face and Gerry blew back and said, 'What would Kate say if she knew, do you suppose?'

Florin gave him a sharp nudge in the chest as if to say, 'Tell her, you fool, and find out,' and in that instant the answer came to him. Why hadn't he thought of it before?

He turned, ran over to the Club and found Liz.

A few months ago she had taken him aside and told him to

405

make an effort at least to appear cheerful as it was demoralising for the staff to see him so depressed all the time. Her words had had an effect and he had been looking less miserable recently, but now he was before her seeming quite his old self.

'Have I got a spare *what*?' she asked.

'Birthday card. You must have one!'

He would send it to Kate at Beattie's house with 'please forward' on the envelope. Liz was to write the address in case Beattie recognised Gerry's writing.

'She has to forward a birthday card. How can she not?' he concluded.

Liz was rummaging in her desk.

'I suppose it's worth a try,' she said, 'but for God's sake, Gerry, don't be too hopeful, or too disappointed.'

'I won't,' he said impatiently as she handed him a card in cellophane wrapping. He tore it open and gave her back the envelope. 'Write the address for me – please.'

She sighed and wrote to his dictation.

'Where will you post it?' she asked. 'A Leighminster postmark would be a bit of a giveaway, wouldn't it?'

He paused, thinking. 'I'll give it to someone to post in London,' he said. He picked up the envelope from her desk. 'Beattie will have to forward it, won't she? It could be from any of Kate's friends in London.'

'Don't rely on it, Gerry, though. Please don't.'

'I won't,' he said again. 'Liz, can I have some flimsy paper? I could put a letter in, couldn't I?'

She contemplated saying something, shook her head at him and found him the paper.

He took his spoils away and settled down at the kitchen table at home, brushing aside the letter from Diana's solicitors – a spent firework, no longer needing to be handled with care or respect – and looked at the card for the first time. It was a reproduction of an old master and showed a solemn family, complete with dog, all in rigid poses staring at the painter. It was hardly appropriate, but at least it was a good size. Gerry worked out how many sheets of paper he could risk putting inside it by careful experiment, and decided he could allow himself two. The memory of Beattie marching through the house sensing out Kate's possessions was so strong that he really could imagine her feeling the envelope before deciding to send it on to Kate. He trimmed the two sheets to exactly the same size as the card and began.

He wrote to her as though he was talking to her, saying all those things he had rehearsed night after sleepless night. He said he loved her, her and only her, and he was sorry. He tried to explain what Brigitte Thompson had done to him. He said it would never happen again. He told her how much he and Parsnip and Rio missed her. He said he was sorry once more for what he had done. He said he loved her. Perhaps he didn't expect her to come back, he said, but could she not say where she was? He told her how he had tried to find her – all the phone calls he had made, the advertisements in *The Times*.

He was nearly at the bottom of the fourth side when he remembered the most important thing: Diana wanted to remarry and they were being divorced at long last. The decree nisi would be granted this year . . . probably, he added, for he didn't know for sure and this letter was the truth from his heart. Would she marry him? he asked. And just managed to fit in 'Please' and 'Love, Gerry' in the last empty quarter-inch.

He did not read the letter over. It was Kate's now, not his. He opened the card and realised that it contained more white space he could fill. But he couldn't write any more except 'To Kate' and 'from Gerry, with all love'. He put the letter inside, closed the card, placed it in the envelope and found a stamp. All he needed now was someone reliable who was going to London after racing tomorrow.

Who turned out to be Rebecca Rosenthal.

'Oh, Gerry,' she said gently when he explained.

'You could send one, too,' he said. 'Why not? You've sent her birthday cards in the past. You could send her one and tell her . . . tell her how sorry I am,' he finished lamely.

Rebecca posted Gerry's card and, having made a note of the address, one of her own too.

'My dear,' she wrote in it, 'he is more sorry than words can say and we all miss you dreadfully. He deserves his punishment, I dare say, but do the rest of us? Kate, can we meet? Somewhere anonymous in London, perhaps – and if you do not wish him to know, I give you my word I will not tell him.'

Beattie forwarded the cards along with several others, some of them redirected from the flat in Leighminster though there were far fewer of those than there had been at Christmas. She didn't feel the envelopes, but she did check for Gerry's handwriting for Kate had said she did not wish to hear from him again.

And Kate, wherever she was, some months later – long after Gerry had given up hope of expecting a reply but was still planning to send a Christmas card by the same route – received the card with the solemn family on it and read Gerry's letter, the truth from his heart.

And tore it up.

And then went somewhere private – hard to find though such a place was, where she was – and cried.

Chapter 27

'A gambling debt must be paid,' Paul Marling told Patrick.

'Yes, of course,' said Patrick, hurt that Paul should think otherwise and offended by the edge in his voice.

He was appalled by the number of IOUs that had accumulated over the past five years, but after Paul had so vehemently refused to accept cash for that first one, Patrick had cheerfully signed more. It had seemed like playing with Monopoly money. Until now.

'I want the share certificates put in these names,' Paul Marling said, pushing a piece of paper towards Patrick, and then added casually, 'There won't be a problem, will there, old boy?'

'Good Lord, no. None at all,' Patrick said, hoping he was right. Weren't the shares his? Couldn't he do what he liked with them? He peered at the paper to give himself time to think. 'Who are these blokes? Friends of yours?'

'Friends of mine,' Marling confirmed. 'Be sure the proportions are exactly as stipulated, won't you?'

'Will do,' Patrick said, putting the paper into his wallet.

He hadn't been paying much attention to the details of Rede Park Racecourse going public, but he'd been sent a form inviting him to apply for shares. He'd have to apply for rather a lot, that was all. Paul must be heavily in debt, too, to these friends. The thought cheered him.

Many of the club members bought shares when Rede Park Racecourse went public in November 1962, and Andrew and Liz

James gave a party for them two weeks before Christmas to thank them for their loyalty and support, and also to show them who was boss for, as Liz told Gerry, they were becoming uppity and seemed to think they owned the place, could have a say in everything that happened.

'But they do own the place, in a sense,' Gerry pointed out.

'Only in a sense,' Liz said firmly. She paused and then added, 'I suppose you had better see this. Others will have had one, I imagine, and I wouldn't like you to think I was holding out on you.'

She handed him a Christmas card, still in its envelope. Kate's handwriting, postmarked Cranbrook. He opened the card: 'To Liz and Andrew, all love, Kate'. He turned the card over. 'Printed in Britain'. She *must* be abroad. He could swear she was not in England, not practising as a doctor, anyway, and what else could she do? Doctors couldn't go under assumed names and Gerry had checked the deed poll records in case she had changed her name legally.

'She's hidden herself from you well and truly,' Liz said, following his train of thought. 'She won't even reveal which continent she is on.'

She was, he knew, about to add that Gerry should forget Kate, find someone else and get on with his life, but evidently decided against it. Perhaps he should try to forget her, but he could not. It had all ended so abruptly between them and the gash of their parting simply would not heal. He had written to her again, enclosing the letter in a Christmas card of his own, trying to explain this. Surely, he had asked her, she felt the same?

Liz took the card back from him.

'Now, you are going to be cheerful at the party tonight, aren't you? No long face, Gerry.'

'I'll be cheerful,' he said.

'You've got two things to celebrate, after all. You are the managing director of a successfully floated company, and you are nearly divorced.'

His decree nisi had come through the previous week and the press had paid no attention at all.

'I'll be the life and soul, Liz,' he said. 'I promise you.'

Admiral and Mrs Partington brought their granddaughter along and all but threw her bodily at Gerry. He liked Hilary Partington, who was pretty and unaffected, and he talked to her, danced with her and took her into supper. He could see Liz, Andrew and the Partingtons exchanging satisfied glances, which Hilary also noticed.

'I'm using you,' she confided. 'Do you mind?'

'And I'm using you, I'm afraid.'

'A girl?'

He smiled at her. 'A woman,' he said.

Hilary told him how she, too, was nursing a broken heart. Her father was a diplomat, serving in the High Commission in New Delhi, and Hilary, in India for a visit, had fallen in love with the country and had found herself a job teaching English. She had also fallen in love with the son of a maharajah, and he with her. Both sets of parents had rivalled each other in horrified outrage on hearing that the young couple intended to marry. Hilary had been sent back to her grandparents and Vishnu had been married to the girl his parents had chosen for him when he was eight years old.

Gerry had considered his own case hopeless, but Hilary's seemed beyond recall. She was devastatingly determined, though, he discovered.

'I shall go back to India,' she said, 'when Vishnu's father dies, or sooner if I can save up enough money for the fare and to keep me for a while. It would be better if the old man pegs out, though. He's horribly overweight so he can't last long.'

'Then what will you do?'

'I shall become Vishnu's number two wife.'

'Good God!' said Gerry, shocked in spite of himself. 'Is . . . is that legal over there?'

'I'm not sure, but it doesn't matter,' she said briskly. 'A marriage doesn't have to be religious or legal. The love you have for each other sanctifies it, don't you think?'

It was exactly what he and Kate had done. Hilary was only nineteen but her confidence inspired Gerry. He decided to confront Beattie and Charles. It had been sixteen months now, and surely they would see that his remorse was unabated and take pity on him. But when, a week later, he arrived full of resolution at the

411

house in Sissinghurst it was locked and silent and the landlord at the Bull told him that the Poutneys were away — on a cruise, he thought. Careless of what the villagers might think, Gerry questioned them to find out where Beattie and Charles were cruising, but no one seemed to know for sure. The Caribbean, someone suggested. Or was it the Nile? Then the postmistress threw everything into the air by announcing firmly that Mr and Mrs Poutney had travelled on an aeroplane.

The fact that Beattie and Charles had been so vague about their destination convinced Gerry that they had gone to spend Christmas with Kate, but he was no nearer discovering where she was. She had, indeed, hidden herself from him well and truly, and her thoroughness — the stringent instructions she must have given her aunt and uncle not to reveal where they were going — was quite unnerving.

Gerry had come home early for Christmas because he was riding Joe Beviss's new horse, Plain Dealings, at Folkestone. It was the horse's first outing and David Blower had chosen Folkestone as it wasn't too far for the owner and his family to travel to watch it run. They wished, most fervently, they had not. Plain Dealings forgot everything he had learned on the Blowers' gallops in the excitement of the moment and at the third hurdle he failed to put down his landing gear and Gerry was fired into the ground at a speed in excess of thirty miles an hour, was rolled upon and then kicked. He cracked three ribs, suffered mild concussion and excessive bruising and was still very stiff and sore when, ten days later, casting aside his mother's anxious protests, he drove himself and Parsnip back to Wiltshire through a country transformed by a deep covering of snow.

He and Hilary Partington met up at the Rede Arms on New Year's Eve prior to going on to a party in Leighminster.

'Granny and Granddad are sending messages of triumph to India,' she told him. 'You feature as a knight in shining armour. I talk about you constantly, you see, and they are quite taken in.'

'Don't they think I'm too old for you?' Gerry asked, putting Hilary's drink in front of her and sitting down painfully. 'I feel about a hundred and am divorced — or will be.'

'They don't seem to mind. They think you are wonderful, and

hope you will keep me in Wiltshire and under their beady eyes.'

'And will I?'

She drummed her fingers on the table top. 'I don't know,' she said. 'I need a job. I could get one in London, but then I'd have to pay for a flat and my keep and saving money in London is difficult. They've stopped my allowance, which doesn't help.'

'What sort of a job?'

'A secretary, I suppose. I did a course.'

'We need a secretary,' Gerry said idly.

'Gerry – *do* you?'

Gerry realised too late that he should not have said it. It was one thing to pretend to be conducting a mild flirtation to deceive Admiral and Mrs Partington but quite another to aid Hilary in her scheme to return to India. He should encourage her to go to London where, surely, she would meet and fall in love with a suitable young man and forget her crazy idea of becoming some maharajah's number two wife. Gerry was fifteen years older than her and should know better, but the words were out now and Hilary had pounced on them. Gerry would have to talk to Jennifer Cody, who was having a baby and whose responsibility it was to appoint her successor – though she said she'd come back after the baby was born – and he would have to talk to Hilary, too, and explain that he could not support her against her grandparents. Either he or she would have to tell them her plans. Why did everything have to be so complicated? he wondered as he finished his drink. Then Jim came over to collect their empty glasses and added a further complication by telling them that a wind was getting up, the snow was on the move and the squire shouldn't think of leaving the village this night as his ribs were in no fit state to go digging cars out of drifts.

So they went to the Club, where the Partingtons were thrilled to discover there was a secretarial job at the racecourse and introduced Hilary to Jennifer Cody who all but employed her on the spot.

It was the worst winter for years. George dug a path from the Club to the house in the woods, but Liz was concerned that Gerry would slip on the ice and damage his ribs further, and insisted he stay with them. Rio, wily twelve-year-old cat that he was, had taken up residence in the Club's kitchen as soon as the snow had begun falling, so the house in the woods was temporarily abandoned.

Hilary Partington began work and was – not to Gerry's surprise – monumentally efficient, and she saved her money with ferocious ruthlessness. She had, she told Gerry, a fifth of her fare already. Gerry had to do something about it, but at the moment he simply didn't have the strength to face hers. His ribs were healing, but his back ached like hell and he had caught a cold which would not go away. And then poor Hilary received a letter from her Vishnu telling her that he was happy with his compliant Hindu wife, and Hilary was not to go on writing to him and making plans to come to India to join him.

'His father made him write it,' Hilary wailed. 'I know he did.'

'Do you really believe that?' Gerry asked.

She dried her tears and he gave her a small dose of Glenmorangie.

'No,' she said at last. 'No. To be absolutely honest, I don't.' She squared her shoulders and faced Gerry. 'I've loved working here, Gerry' – it was just under a month but she made it sound like a lifetime's service – 'but I'm afraid I must give in my notice. I'll go to London and get a job there. Pick up my old life, make new friends . . .'

'I'll give you the best ever references,' Gerry said.

'Did you do something as bad to your girl as Vishnu has done to me?'

'Worse,' he told her. 'Much, much worse.'

'It would have been nice if we had fallen in love with each other, Gerry, wouldn't it?'

'Hilary,' he said, gathering her against his injured ribs, 'it would have been wonderful.'

The freeze continued into February and showed no sign of stopping. Gerry reoccupied his house in the woods but the battle against the cold was depressing, his back hurt and he missed Hilary and her determined optimism. For the first time he regretted the fact that his job – especially in winter – in no way accounted for every hour of the day, and the realisation made him even sadder because it was one of the things that had made it such bliss before. Jennifer said she had never wanted to leave anyway,

414

the baby wasn't due for another five months and she was bored at home, so she came back and everything returned to normal.

Helen Blower arrived in his office one day.

'We're fed up with this and we're going to the West Indies,' she said without preamble. 'Come with us, Gerry. Think of it – sea, sand, sun and rum punches till the cows come home. And no bloody snow.'

Sun! He had forgotten what it looked like. Bernard was in Israel and Gerry rang him to make sure it was all right for both of them to be out of the country. Liz said she was sure she and Andrew could preside over a snow-covered racecourse out of season and they would take care of Parsnip and Rio. A break would do Gerry good, she added. A week later they were on St Lucia in a house owned by a friend of Sir Henry Blower's overlooking Marigot Bay.

'I was born in Ceylon,' Helen said one afternoon, 'and I really believe palm trees are in my soul.' Ice chinked lazily in her glass as she turned to look at Gerry on the sunbed next to hers. David and Sir Henry Blower were out fishing for marlin, Lady Blower was having a siesta and she and Gerry were alone. 'Are you asleep?' she enquired.

'Nearly. We had such an energetic morning, I'm quite worn out.'

It was an exaggeration, but it didn't feel like one. He and Helen had taken a taxi into Castries and gone to the market. They had brought some fruit – melons, papaya and fat, juicy mangoes – had enjoyed the noise and the colour and then had returned, also in a taxi. Gerry hadn't even had to raise his hand to hail the cab, for in Castries the cabbies hailed you, but the sun and the atmosphere had so relaxed him that doing anything at all seemed tiring. He had actually fallen asleep while writing a postcard yesterday. His cold had gone, his back was improving daily and he felt as near to happy as he had done since Kate disappeared. He and Helen had had a long talk about that and he felt she had, at last, forgiven him. She had also agreed that it was not cowardly to announce his retirement from race-riding after his fall. He'd had five good years and bones and skulls were precious things, not to be risked when your heart wasn't convinced you should.

415

He rolled over on the sunbed and lay on his stomach in the shade of the palm trees.

'Oh my God!' he said in a horrified voice.

Helen sat up and stared at him in alarm.

'Whatever is the matter?'

'My glass,' Gerry said, holding it up as evidence. 'It's empty!'

After three hedonistic weeks they flew back to England and Gerry learned the shattering news that Lionel Moreton was dead, killed in a car crash on the day they had taken off for the West Indies . . . Lionel Moreton, the tall wise head with the lovely smile who had liked directing traffic. No one had wanted to spoil Gerry's holiday by cabling him with the news and, since Lionel had been a widower, there was no grieving wife who would have found Gerry's presence at the funeral a comfort. Bernard had flown back for it, though, and then returned to Israel immediately. He was due home for good next week.

Patrick phoned Gerry almost as soon as he arrived in the house in the woods and asked him to come for a drink at Rede Park.

'Why not the pub?' Gerry asked. It was where they usually met.

'No, I must talk to you privately.'

Only last week had Patrick realised what he had done, and he had been awaiting Gerry's return with ever-increasing anxiety. It was not the fact that he had actually had to pay for the shares he had transferred to Paul Marling – that had been a shock, but he, his accountant and his bank manager had managed it somehow. Patrick had marvelled at how well his affairs had been handled over the past ten years, agreed to sell off some cottages, some fields his neighbour to the north wanted a lot more than he did and cheerfully promised to curtail his gambling before he lost any more land. Morgans were used to raising money to pay debts – it was as much in the blood as the gambling was – and somehow they always got by. He *had* been curtailing his gambling, too, but he supposed that was because the weather had stopped racing for so long. He'd tried making money on the dogs, even owned a greyhound once, but it didn't seem right. Horses had always been the Morgans' way.

In any case, it wasn't the gambling as such that was worrying

416

him now, although it was very much an outcome of it, and Patrick feared he had done something as spectacularly foolish as his great-grandfather had done when he had struck the bet with his brother Cyril and lost half his estate. He remembered how Paul had been last week and he shuddered. The things he had called Patrick as he described how he had been stalking him from the time Rede Park Racecourse had been set up, how easy it had been to fool him, the wild laughter when Patrick, attempting to stop the flow, said, realising even as he did so it sounded pathetic, 'But I thought you were a betting man!'

And then, when Patrick had asked why, the vitriol about Gerry that had come from Paul Marling's lips. Even now, Patrick recalled how some distant part of his brain had registered that Paul was foaming at the mouth and had found it interesting. Frothy white spittle dribbling from his mouth and running down his chin . . . And Patrick, who never normally did anything that made him feel uncomfortable, knew he had to warn Gerry that a dangerous man was after him.

Gerry arrived and listened to Patrick's confession.

'The man hates you,' he concluded. 'I'm sure he plans to take over the company.'

Gerry helped himself to another drink and sipped it thoughtfully.

'He's had about twelve per cent from you,' he said. 'It doesn't sound that dangerous. Even if he's managed to buy another ten per cent, he's still got a long way to go. And he'll have to carry the board . . . Paul Marling, though!'

Hunting down Patrick for ten long years to strike, through him, at Gerry.

'What will you do?' Patrick asked.

'I'll ring Bernard tomorrow,' Gerry decided. 'I'll see what he says. What can Marling do with twenty per cent – if that's what he's got? He can be a nuisance, but no real danger.'

'True,' said Patrick, brightening. 'I couldn't do much when I had thirty-five per cent, could I?'

'We didn't let you.'

'Exactly!' Patrick went over to the gramophone and put on a record. 'I say, Gerry, why not stay to supper? Mother and O'Nions are in the flat goggling at the telly and Mrs Anderson left a pie for me. All we have to do is shove it under the grill and boil up a few vegetables. Have another drink and say you'll stay – do!'

Two lonely men, Gerry thought. Two lonely men approaching middle age. The peace and contentment he had found in St Lucia vanished with a terrible, lurching suddenness as he realised that, until he could look into Kate's eyes and know there was no love for him there, he would have no peace: only loneliness like a great, grey rolling sea.

Patrick took his silence as consent, turned up the gramophone and led Gerry to the kitchen. The music followed them, transmitted by loudspeakers. It hurtled around the stone walls and ricocheted off the ceiling. Gerry could almost feel the old house's hair standing out in horror.

'It's dreadful,' he said. The dissonances thumped at his head like the worst sort of hangover, or – Gerry's latest nightmare – being buried by a racehorse. 'What the hell is it?'

Patrick handed him potatoes to peel and did a version of the Twist in time to the music.

'Number one in the hit parade,' he said. 'My dear chap, haven't you heard of them? They're the Beatles . . . "Please please me, oh yeah",' he sang.

'Please do *what*?' Gerry asked, revolted.

He awoke at four in the morning and sat bolt upright in bed.

Paul Marling waiting ten years to strike at Gerry.

. . . He would not have given himself away to Patrick if he had not known he had triumphed. Or was near to it.

Which meant a takeover bid.

. . . Lionel Moreton dead. What investment had he made in the public company? Gerry struggled to remember. He had left all that kind of thing to Andrew and Bernard. Lionel had loved the racecourse, though; he was sure to have had a number of shares.

. . . Andrew James being surprised at the brisk trading in Rede Park shares immediately after the flotation, putting it down to satisfied racegoers. . . .

Paul Marling striking at Gerry through others. The attack on Kate that night in the woods . . . a gentleman, Kate had insisted.

But the money! How could Paul Marling have the money to buy all the shares, even given the number he had won from Patrick?

Patrick and his bloody gambling.

Please please me! Oh yeah?

He rang Bernard. He knew there was nothing to be done before trading began on the Stock Exchange, but he was frightened. Bernard, just waking up in his apartment in Tel Aviv, heard what Gerry had to say, swore fluently, told Gerry to wake Andrew and make sure he was alert and ready to receive instructions in twenty minutes' time. He would, he added, come home today.

Neither Bernard's instructions or, later, his presence, did any good. A few telephone calls established the facts: Lionel Moreton's executors, a firm of City solicitors, had received a handsome offer for the shares in Rede Park Racecourse Ltd and had accepted it. They were offended by the suggestion that they had done something their late client may have disapproved of. Selling the shares privately at a small premium, they pointed out, was much preferable to putting them on the open market . . . there were so many of them that their availability would most certainly have reduced their value and the late Mr Moreton's heir, his daughter Mrs Janet Lawrence of Cape Town, had consented to the sale. They gave the name of the stockbrokers who were handling the deal, the stockbrokers said it had been finalised last week and, no, their client would not sell. His name? A company called Paul Marling Ltd.

'He's got over twenty per cent, then,' Bernard said. 'And no effort at concealment. It's a declaration, isn't it? All he has to do is inform the authorities that the three nominees who hold Patrick's twelve per cent have consented to sell their shares to him and that he is ready to make a takeover bid . . . How much more does he have, do you think? Not that it matters.'

Andrew and Liz James, together with Captain Beech, a bulky Jennifer Cody and a mountain of files, arrived in London. Andrew had compiled a list of companies who held shares in Rede Park Racecourse Ltd and a clerk was sent to Companies House to investigate. The man returned and reported that three of them had, respectively, a Nancy, Dennis and Paul Marling as managing director; a fourth, also holding two and a half per cent, had Julie Wiltshire of California, USA, as managing director.

'His sister is called Julie,' Gerry said, as Bernard handed over the list.

'Over thirty per cent,' Bernard said, smiling wanly. 'All but thirty-five.'

'How do we know that he doesn't own other companies through his nominees, though? Or other individual shareholdings? He could have even more than that.'

Gerry's beautiful racecourse in Paul Marling's hands. It was too awful to contemplate.

'The other companies are known to us, sir,' the clerk said.

'We just have to hope,' Bernard said. 'I wonder how long Paul Marling would have waited . . . poor Lionel's death was a godsend to him.'

'And Patrick's gambling.'

'And that. We have been very unlucky.'

They held an emergency board meeting and appointed two new directors: solid City men, friends of Bernard's. The meeting also established that all decisions made by the board would be voted upon by a show of hands, with the chairman having the casting vote in the event of a tie.

'Is this legal, though?' Gerry asked.

'Yes, it's in the articles. The board has the consent of the shareholders,' Bernard said blandly, 'to run this company in the way that most benefits those shareholders. We have not yet received notification of a takeover bid, after all.'

At this point Patrick, who had been sitting in silent misery throughout the proceedings, abruptly tendered his resignation and no one had the heart or the spirit to encourage him to change his mind.

'I'm sorry,' he said. 'I'm most frightfully sorry.'

Gerry watched him leave. Was it really so much his fault? he wondered. They had all known about his fatal addiction and had ignored the danger. Perhaps Gerry should have realised how much of a danger Paul Marling was, or Bernard should have done. And it was Lionel Moreton's death that had finally let Marling in, and that had nothing to do with Patrick. A godsend, Bernard had called it. Unlucky. Two sides of the same coin.

420

'I propose,' Gerry said, 'that Patrick be offered free membership of the racecourse for life.'

'Seconded,' said Bernard, smiling at Gerry.

Carried, and why not? Even in times of crisis the details had to be considered, and Gerry was sure Paul Marling would not think to reward Patrick.

Bernard's entire secretarial staff was set to typing letters to shareholders telling them of the takeover attempt and urging them not to sell their shares to anyone but the company's board. The takeover bid itself, which came just before five o'clock, almost went unnoticed in the frenetic activity. Hilary Partington arrived with a group of friends and they addressed and filled envelopes early into the morning to the accompaniment of Radio Luxembourg on the transistor radio they had brought with them.

'Please please me', endlessly.

Gerry had disliked the song when he had first heard it. This night would ensure that he loathed it for ever.

Most of the shareholders stood firm and the takeover bid failed, but Paul Marling owned thirty-eight per cent of Rede Park Racecourse Ltd and would not sell any of it.

Bernard took Gerry out to lunch.

'Now listen,' he said, having ordered Gerry a large Glenmorangie, 'and listen well. It's my fault, it's Patrick's fault, it's because of you although it is not your fault. It is my dear friend Lionel's fault for having skidded on an icy road and not leaving his affairs in the order that we might have wished. Had we anticipated how things would turn out we would have taken other courses of action. We did not anticipate and we can't undo what is done. So no looking back and wishing things were otherwise than the way they are. Understood?'

'I'll try,' Gerry mumbled.

'You'll try and you'll succeed. Look, Gerry, you've given up – and it shows.'

It was true. He had given up on the day he learned Paul Marling would make a takeover bid. It was why he had proposed Patrick's life membership. His last magnanimous gesture as boss.

'Where's your fight? You are still managing director, Andrew is

421

your deputy, I'm still chairman. Marling has two seats on the board and that you must accept and put a good face on. You can't do anything else. Don't divide the board, whatever you do. Don't use words like "loyalty", or demand allegiance for old times' sake.' He paused and sipped his drink. 'You are young and could turn your hand to anything – I'd give you a job, but I'm sure you'd be snapped up by an enterprising racecourse – but just consider what Andrew and Liz stand to lose. . . . Gerry, if you show a defeated face they could well decide that appeasing Paul Marling would be the best strategy since you are so obviously on the way out. And could you blame them?'

No, he couldn't. 'Who else would have taken on a cripple like me?' Andrew had once said to him and, unfair though it was, Gerry knew he had been right. Most of the time the staff at Rede Park forgot that Andrew was in a wheelchair, and the difficulty and disruption when he had arrived in Threadneedle Street on the day Marling had made his move had been a shock to Gerry and a dreadful humiliation for Andrew. Four strong young men had been summoned from their work to get Andrew out of the car and carry him and his chair up the stairs. And then he had wanted to go to the lavatory and Gerry had helped Liz take him. Andrew had kept apologising and Gerry, acutely embarrassed for him, kept saying, 'It's all right, old chap.' . . . None of this was ever noticed at Rede Park where there was a lift to take Andrew from the ground floor of the Club to their flat above, the bathroom was designed for his wheelchair and, without any particular thought about it, the plans for phases two and three of the grandstands had been adapted to allow Andrew to get around with the minimum of effort and ramps had been put down in phase one where needed. Andrew's dignity was never compromised in any way. But who would employ a man who was helpless when faced with a single step? If Gerry was in Andrew's place, he would appease the devil to keep his place at Rede Park.

Andrew and Liz James, and Jennifer Cody, working through her pregnancy, old Captain Beech who had introduced Gerry to Glenmorangie and taught him everything about running a racecourse, and Bernard Rosenthal to whom Gerry owed everything that was good in him . . . what could Paul Marling do in the face of these people, in spite of his huge stake in the company?

He felt iron seeping back into him. It actually straightened his spine. Bernard noticed it and laughed.

'Well, what are you going to do?' he asked.

'I'm going to hold a charity day,' Gerry said. 'Perhaps in June. A televised day, anyway, so the point gets across to the maximum number of people.'

'And what point is that?'

'That people in wheelchairs have brains and feelings and rights. I wonder how many of them there are? I'll have to think about how to do it – but it's an idea, isn't it?'

'Gerry,' Bernard said, 'there are times when my Jewish blood takes over, and I fear this is one of them. We are an emotional people, you know.'

And he stood up, leaned over the table, took Gerry's face in his hands and kissed him on either cheek while the other men lunching in the City Club pretended not to notice.

'My Gerry,' Bernard told him. 'You're the best.'

There was a meeting of the new board followed by the annual general meeting, held in the Tote Hall. Bernard took the assembled shareholders through the balance sheet, thanked them for their support without making any direct reference to the takeover bid and said they were looking forward to a successful season's racing. Paul Marling and his cohort avoided everyone's eyes, spoke not at all and left immediately after the meeting was over.

'Thank the Lord for that,' Captain Beech said, but Gerry could see no reason to heave a sigh of relief: Paul Marling had been after Rede Park – after Gerry – for more than ten years and he would act when it suited him. The silence and inaction now were, no doubt, an attempt either to intimidate Gerry or lull him into a false sense of security, for undoubtedly Marling wanted his little gypo under his heel again.

He told Kate all about it in his birthday letter to her. He was going to be nobody's little gypo, he said. He was a different man now. He had been offered the job as managing director of a gratifyingly prestigious racecourse and had turned it down.

423

Bernard had said he shouldn't demand loyalty from the original board and the staff as a matter of right, but he felt it worked the other way: he owed loyalty to Liz and Andrew, Jennifer and Captain Nick and everyone else. What did Kate think? he asked.

He was sure Kate received his letters, even though she never replied to them. This particular letter, though, he had to tear up and start again for he had said, without thinking, that going to another racecourse would be like committing adultery.

He tried to love Rede Park less, but as he rode around on Sprite – he had retired Florin – and spring came at last, and then summer, it seemed more beautiful than ever. The crowds came, the horses thudded round the track, Gerry had his charity day when five hundred wheelchairs whizzed around the concourses and the press paid a great deal of attention, one newspaper even running an enthusiastic if short-lived campaign to make public buildings more accessible to disabled people ... short-lived because a government minister had slept with a girl, and that was of far greater interest to everyone. Lots of people do it, Gerry thought. The trouble comes when you get found out.

The Beatles sang 'I wanna hold your hand' and millions of people listened to them.

Hilary Partington turned up for the August Festival meeting wearing a skirt whose hem was fully four inches above her knees. Renewed concerned letters to India, no doubt.

They had the last running of the Brigitte-Louisa – a year early, by mutual agreement and to Gerry's intense relief – and Brigitte Thompson gazed at Gerry from out of her green eyes and smiled her enigmatic smile and Gerry could not imagine how he had ever been attracted to her. Two years now since Kate had gone, two years since Gerry had slept with a woman – and that woman was, most appallingly, Brigitte Thompson.

Another successful season at Rede Park ended, only spoilt by the retirement of Captain Beech. He was nearly seventy, he said, the age the Jockey Club decreed was too old to be a clerk of the course. He would not get another licence, he could teach Gerry no more and anyway he wanted a rest.

In November, in Dallas, John Kennedy was assassinated and people would remember for the rest of their lives what they were doing when they heard the news. Gerry was having a drink in the Club with his new clerk of the course, a young man called Dick Sandhurst who had been at York racecourse, when Andrew had come swinging through the doorway of the bar, his shirt collar undone, his tie in his hand, and told them all. Eileen and Stephen White, with whom Gerry was having dinner, arrived shortly afterwards and Eileen dropped her handbag, put her hands to her face and cried, 'Shot? But *why*?'

Andrew spun his wheelchair around, ready to go and finish dressing.

'Why?' he asked bitterly. 'Because some bloody fool invented the gun, that's why.'

The year turned. 1964. And still Paul Marling made no move and Gerry, in spite of himself, was lulled.

In February, the phone went as Gerry was leaving the house in the woods to go to the office. He called to Parsnip to wait and ran back inside.

He couldn't recognise the voice. It sounded like Rebecca Rosenthal but not like her at all. Her words were all jumbled up and he could not believe what he was hearing.

Surely not. Not that.

'My Bernard, Gerry . . . Gerry, he's dead.'

Dead of a heart attack as he was shaving. He would have wanted to go quickly, everyone said; he could not have borne being an invalid. Cold comfort, though, for those who had loved him and had not had a chance to say goodbye.

After the funeral, Gerry arrived with the other mourners at the flat in Eaton Square. Rebecca was sitting on a low chair in the sitting room. The great gilt mirror above the fireplace was covered by a sheet and on the mantelpiece there was a little candle burning in a glass. When it was Gerry's turn to greet Rebecca, he crouched beside her and she put her arms around him and they both cried. Still sobbing, she indicated a man sitting on another low chair.

'Our son,' she said. 'Samuel. Love him like a brother for Bernard loved you like a son.'

And Samuel held out his arms and Gerry went to him and embraced him and they both cried together too.

At eight o'clock Samuel stood, as did everyone in the room, and he recited what Gerry was told was the kaddish, the memorial prayer, and afterwards the rabbi spoke of Bernard. Many of the men were wearing skullcaps and everyone was crying openly. It could have made Bernard seem foreign and distant and not the man Gerry had loved at all, except it was good not to be ashamed of tears and to be able to mingle them freely with those of other mourners, to hear fine memories of Bernard and to give his own in return. Gerry went to the flat every day of the week that Rebecca and Samuel sat shiva. He could not stay away.

'He called me his Gerry,' he told Samuel. 'You don't mind, do you?'

Samuel smiled at him, a smile like Bernard's although Bernard's had never been loaded with so much sadness.

'I don't mind,' he replied. 'He wanted a son like you, not one who has hardly left his kibbutz for fifteen years. He had both of us and so he was a happy man.'

When Bernard's will was read, Gerry learned that he had left him all his shares in Rede Park Racecourse Ltd and two racehorses of his choice from his string.

Gerry went to the Poutneys' house in Sissinghurst. Beattie opened the door.

'Gerry!' she exclaimed. 'Whatever's the matter?'

He supposed he must look ghastly. He had hardly slept for a week and he couldn't remember when he had last eaten. He thrust out the envelope he was holding.

'Please forward it,' he said. 'Bernard is dead. Kate will want to know so she can write to Rebecca.'

'Bernard dead! Oh no, how dreadful! What dreadfully sad news.' She hesitated and then said, 'Come in and have a cup of tea.'

She took him into the kitchen and put the kettle on. Nothing had changed here since he had first come to this house all those years ago. He almost expected Beattie to bring out swathes of knitting in hideous electric yellow and red.

'Dreadfully sad news,' she repeated. 'Poor Rebecca. I'll write too, of course, if you'll give me the address.'

He wrote it down for her.

'Will you forward my letter to Kate or will you tell her yourself?' he asked.

She cut him a slice of cake.

'I know you've been writing to her in birthday and Christmas cards and getting other people to write the envelopes. She hasn't asked me to open everything and burn your letters. I'll forward it. . . . Eat, Gerry. You look quite ill. No, on second thoughts—' She removed the cake and made him a sandwich of cold roast beef. 'This will do you more good.'

Kate used to force sandwiches on him. Was it a family trait? he wondered vaguely.

'Where is she, Beattie?'

She sighed. 'I can't tell you. She has promised that if we do we shall never see her again.'

'She's determined, then.'

'Very.'

'But she reads my letters.'

'She seems to.'

'It's not really logical, that, is it?' Beattie did not answer, and he went on: 'Is she well?'

'Yes.'

'Is . . . is she happy?'

Beattie thought before she said, 'She is not unhappy.'

'There is no one else, then?'

Again, she did not reply and he knew that meant there was not. If she could tell him Kate was in love or engaged or married she would most certainly do so.

'There's no one else for me either,' he said. 'I did a terrible thing to her—'

'You did several terrible things,' she said, a flash of that steel in her voice.

Gerry looked at the sandwich on the plate in front of him. The faint pang of hunger he had felt on first seeing it had gone, and the very idea of eating it made him want to retch.

'Yes,' he said. 'I did, didn't I? A whole procession of them . . .

427

How strange that should be when I love her so much.'

' "The coward does it with a kiss, the brave man with a sword," ' she quoted.

'Does what?'

'Kills the thing he loves. Oscar Wilde said that each man does it.'

'But that's horrible!'

'It is, but he was in jail at the time.'

'Feeling a bit depressed?'

She smiled. 'A bit,' she said. She felt sorry for him. She couldn't help it. He looked so wretched she could almost forget that her darling Kate had wasted her whole adult life on him. She touched his hand. 'I'm sorry about Bernard,' she said gently.

'He was everything to me, you know. Everything. More than my own father, which I suppose is an awful thing to say, but it is true.' He stood up. 'I can't eat your sandwich, I'm afraid, but thank you for making it. And for forwarding my letter. I must go.'

She saw him to the door and watched him drive away.

Wouldn't it be better, she thought, for them to be together with occasional unhappinesses than apart with continual ones? She had forgiven him, she realised with a jolt of surprise and not a little alarm. If Kate suspected such a thing, she may make good her threat never to see her uncle and aunt again.

Chapter 28

Amid his grief and shock, Gerry had not considered what effect Bernard's death would have on Rede Park Racecourse Ltd, and he was startled and unprepared when Paul Marling walked into his office two weeks later on the heels of a soft knock. He paced slowly around the room examining the framed photographs on the wall, mostly of Gerry riding in races or being led in afterwards, as Gerry struggled to appear authoritative while chewing the bun Jennifer Cody – now the mother of a baby daughter who slept like an angel in her carrycot in Jennifer's office – had brought in with his mid-morning coffee.

Paul Marling picked up the photograph of Kate that stood on Gerry's desk, looked at it, replaced it and said lightly, 'Well, what are we going to do? We can't have the place in the sole control of a gypsy and a cripple, can we?'

'We're managing very well, thank you,' Gerry said, having at last got rid of the bun.

'We need a proper chairman, though.'

'I'm acting chairman.'

'I know, gypsy Beviss. I said a *proper* chairman. One who would, for example, call a board meeting to resolve this – er – constitutional crisis.'

Gerry should have called one, but he could not yet bear the idea of Bernard not being in attendance. He had completely forgotten that they would need to find a new chairman and his failure to take any action would, he suddenly thought with chilling certainty, cost him dear.

'Have you finalised the details of the new sponsorship for the August race?' Paul Marling asked.

'Yes.' Another American company, found with the help of Jack van Rhoon.

'You seem to be quite good at that sort of thing. Strange, isn't it?'

'I don't think so,' Gerry said doggedly.

'No?' Paul Marling made a pretence of straightening a photograph – one of Gerry on Calipers being led in by Bernard – then turned back to Gerry and smiled at him. 'Well, I'd best be off to the Club. I'm having lunch with our deputy managing director.'

'Andrew?' Gerry asked, unable to keep the shock out of his voice.

'Who else? He may be a cripple, but he seems to understand the company's finances and so on. As a major shareholder, I am naturally interested in those.'

Gerry had kept his word to Bernard and had not attempted to divide the board by telling people the history of himself and Paul Marling and asking them for their personal support against the interloper. They all assumed the takeover bid had been made by someone intent upon owning a successful racecourse, not upon revenge. Paul Marling and his other board member could never have carried a motion Bernard was against, but if Marling offered himself for election as chairman which way would the voting go? Could Gerry, as Bernard's second in command, offer himself? The trouble was he knew he wasn't the right man for the job. He had never bothered much about the financial intricacies as Bernard and Andrew understood them so well. Could he find someone else who would be suitable and acceptable? He would have to do it quickly, if it wasn't already too late.

He sat in his office and thought of Paul Marling having lunch, not half a mile away, with nice, honest open Andrew, appearing all sweet reasonableness, no doubt, and convincing Andrew – and through him Liz – that he was tailor-made to take over as chairman. His contacts in the City, his knowledge of business . . . Good God! He had once been Bernard's right-hand man. . . .

He rang, of all people, his sister-in-law Grace.

She listened to him, thought for a moment and then said,

'Go for the chairmanship. It's your only chance.'

'But the financial side—' he began.

'You've got Andrew James and you can always bring in someone else to advise you. Tell Mr and Mrs James about you and Paul Marling. They'll support you, won't they?'

'Probably.'

'And the two directors you appointed last year? What of them?'

He hadn't even considered them and had to admit it. Grace growled impatiently.

'Get hold of them. Go and see them. Is that all the directors, then?'

'There's the short wise head. David Collins. He's been in from the beginning and may vote for me, I suppose.'

'See him too, then.'

All good advice. He thanked Grace and she said, most gently for her,

'Good luck, Gerry. Ring me again if I can help.'

They were fond of each other, he realised; respected each other. When on earth had that happened?

He told Liz and Andrew about Paul Marling and how he had been pursuing Gerry for years. They listened loyally but sceptically – it was, after all, an extraordinary story – but were finally persuaded by the memory of Kate being attacked in the woods and the police's fruitless search for the strange patient who had called himself Paul Dennis Smith. Andrew remembered that Dennis Marling had been the managing director of one of the companies set up by his son to buy shares in Rede Park.

'Christ, Gerry, it's terrifying!' he said. 'Shouldn't we call the police?'

Gerry smiled wryly. 'We have no witness, do we?' he said.

He made an appointment to see Lawrence Makepeace and Michael Williams, the two solid City men, friends of Bernard's. The three of them had lunch together. Paul Marling had been to see them two weeks ago, they said. No one could replace Bernard, of course. He was missed daily, the City was a poorer place without him, but they thought Paul Marling was the man for the job and had pledged their support. He had a major shareholding, after all.

'You were brought on to the board to counter the seats he would demand because of that shareholding,' Gerry reminded them. 'Bernard never wanted him to be in charge.'

Maybe so, they agreed uneasily, but Bernard wasn't with us any more. How old was Gerry? Not yet thirty-six? Too young! Far too young!

David Collins was much more forthcoming. They had seen each other at Bernard's funeral, when they had both been too overcome to do more than clasp hands and a discussion about the succession at Rede Park had been the last thing on their minds.

'You have my vote, of course,' he said gravely, when Gerry had explained everything to him. He drew a sheet of paper towards him and unscrewed the top of his pen. 'Now, where does that leave us?'

'Tied at four votes each,' Gerry said. He didn't need to write it down to work it out. 'I'm going to vote for myself and assume Marling will do too.'

'What happens then?'

'I've no idea. The chairman has the casting vote, and there isn't one.'

If only Captain Beech had stayed on another year, or Patrick hadn't resigned.

David Collins ran a hand over his bald head.

'I know Makepeace and Williams,' he said. 'I'll talk to them and try and make them see sense.'

'I only want to be chairman because I know it is what Bernard would have wanted.'

'He would,' said David Collins warmly. 'He most certainly would. I'll do my best, I promise.'

Gerry went to see Rebecca before going home. She looked ten years older but she was trying so hard to be brave that Gerry felt tears prick at his eyes.

'Stay for supper,' she said, hugging him. 'Stay the night, too. It's a long drive back.'

'I will. Thank you.'

'You can talk to Sam. He's bored of talking to me.'

'Oh Momma!' Samuel said, embracing Gerry in his turn.

'It's true . . . all this time and only his sad mother for company. Sam, pour Gerry a drink. You two can chat while I cook.'

432

'We'll help you,' Gerry said.

He and Sam sat at the kitchen table and chopped things under Rebecca's direction while she bustled among her pots and pans.

'Have you chosen your horses yet?' she asked.

'No.'

'Why not drop in there tomorrow? It wouldn't be out of your way, would it?'

'No.'

'Go, then.'

'What will you do with the other horses?'

'Peter is arranging to sell them. All but two or three for whom Bernard had a particular affection.'

'Which ones are those?'

She bent and kissed his cheek as she walked behind him on her way to the fridge.

'Oh no,' she said. 'You don't catch me that way. Bernard stipulated you have your choice of all of them. If you take ones Bernard loved I'll be happy, and if you don't I'll be happy too. . . . Go now and ring Peter up. His number's in the book by the phone.'

Gerry rang the trainer and arranged a time to be at his stables the following morning. He then rang David Blower and asked if he had room for two more horses and David, who trained Flat horses these days as well as jumpers, said that, for Gerry, he would find room and asked if Gerry wanted any help in making his selection.

Gerry hesitated. Part of him wanted to choose Bernard's legacy to him on his own but he didn't honestly know enough about it. He didn't think Bernard would have wanted Gerry to be reminded of him by horses running badly, so he accepted David's offer and then rang up the Club to ask Andrew and Liz to keep Parsnip for the night and to report on his meetings.

'What do you think?' he asked Andrew. 'What happens if it's a tie?'

'I suppose you, as acting chairman, have the casting vote but Marling's shareholding might complicate things. It would be best if David Collins can persuade Makepeace and Williams to change their vote. No one could argue about two against six.'

'You are with me, though? You and Liz?'

433

'Gerry,' he said reproachfully. 'How could you doubt it?'

Gerry put the phone down and went back into Rebecca's kitchen. She turned to him, her eyes more animated than at any time since Bernard's death.

'Sam's had a wonderful idea,' she said. 'We'll sponsor it, Sam and I, and we'll put it in our wills so it's sponsored for ever ... Bernard's race, Gerry, at Rede Park.'

He should have thought of it. He would have done eventually. Eventually! How much time was there?

'Gerry? You will let us have Bernard's race, won't you?'

He put his arms around her.

'The Bernard Rosenthal Memorial,' he said. 'It's a promise.'

He had to win. He had to.

'I looked up the form of the older horses, and I reckon there's a shortlist of three,' David said, as the first of Bernard's string was led out of its box and paraded for them. 'The two-year-olds are more difficult. We'll have to go on instinct or watch them work But what do you want, Gerry?'

'Something that will go well and give me good memories of Bernard, I suppose. So maybe horses that will race for a long time to come.'

'You can never guarantee that,' David said, 'horses' legs being what they are. Why not have a filly then? You can breed from her and race her sons and daughters.'

'Crocus!' Gerry exclaimed, remembering a delicate little roan that had been lightly raced last year. Had she won? She had certainly been placed.

'She's on my list,' David said. 'So that's one up.'

Gerry chose another filly, a two-year-old called Clematis. He hadn't seen her work, but she was well bred and he fell for her. The two of them could keep each other company when they finished racing. A little paddock of flowers they would be, in memory of Bernard.

David slapped the other trainer on the back.

'How have we done, Peter my boy?'

Peter smiled. 'No comment.'

'Was Rebecca going to keep either of these?' Gerry asked.

'No comment to that too. She said you'd ask and made me promise not to tell you.'

Gerry's two racehorses were transported to David's yard the following morning and Gerry, having seen them installed in their new stables and given them a welcoming carrot each, drove back to Rede Park. Jennifer Cody was looking out for him and ran over as he stopped the car. There couldn't be more bad news, he told himself as she caught her breath and began to speak. There simply couldn't.

There was. David Collins had been rushed to hospital last night with peritonitis. He was dead.

Three of them in little more than a year. It was unbelievable.

'Don't vote for me,' he told Andrew and Liz. 'You'll pay for it later and lose everything.'

'Perhaps he'd already talked to Makepeace and Williams,' Andrew said desperately.

Gerry shrugged. 'Check if you like. It seems a bit cold-blooded, though.'

Cold-blooded or not, Andrew checked. A tearful secretary told him that her boss had been due to lunch with Mr Makepeace and Mr Williams that very day.

A godsend? Bad luck?

A curious fateful peace settled on Gerry. He felt disembodied, as though he was floating above the surface of the earth. High – that was it. What Patrick said he was when he smoked pot.

He went to the board meeting. He voted for Paul Marling. He smiled and congratulated him and waited to be fired. He wasn't. Paul Marling was saying that he hoped the strong team at Rede Park would continue its excellent work . . . How weird! Weird, but good. He had a promise to keep to Rebecca, and when that was dealt with he would resign. He would resign and retire to the house in the woods that he and Kate had found and made into a home. He had to write to Kate and tell her to join him there. They would live happily ever after with the two horses and Parsnip and Rio . . .

Paul Marling was bringing the meeting to a close. Setting a date for the next one. Inviting everyone for lunch at the Club. They toasted the future of Rede Park, and Marling and his sidekick returned to London.

Weird!

He went to see Patrick that evening to tell him how it felt to be high, but Patrick wasn't, for once, smoking a reefer. He was drinking champagne. It was quite a party, in fact. Mrs Morgan was sitting on a sofa looking more loopy than ever, and there were three girls in skirts that left nothing – but nothing! – to the imagination, two more men in silly frilly shirts like Patrick's whose hair touched their collars and the Beatles were caterwauling in the background.

'Not the Beatles,' Patrick said crossly. 'The *Stones*, Gerry . . . Hey, Gerry, congratulate me. I'm engaged.'

'Engaged? You mean to be married?'

'What else?'

'Who to?'

'Debs, of course. Debs! Say hello to my old friend Gerry.'

'Hi,' the girl said. She couldn't be more than eighteen. Was Patrick mad? Or had Gerry been hallucinating this whole, ghastly day?

'When is the wedding?' he asked the girl.

'Wedding? Oh you mean the event?' she said, tossing hair out of her eyes. 'In July. I'm going to wear a Quant dress,' she added in an awed whisper.

'Oh,' Gerry said. 'Good.'

'Yeah,' she agreed and drifted off.

Gerry's head was attached to his body when he woke the next morning and his feet were back on the ground. He was filled with a sense of purpose. He had to get Bernard's race sorted out before Paul Marling fired him, and he had to ensure its future, too. He was not going to give Marling the satisfaction of seeing him look miserable either. He would, he decided, have a party down for the Blue Oceans Handicap next month. He hadn't seen much of Mark and Vanessa recently, but they would come, surely, and Andrew and Rosie Coleridge, and James and the rest. He would go out in a bright blaze.

He arrived at the office and called Dick Sandhurst in.

'A mile race,' Gerry said, 'framed like the Brigitte-Louisa – the Wallingford, I mean. Three years and above, colts and fillies.'

'How much is the sponsorship?'

'I don't know. I expect they'll want me to advise them.'

'Won't that be tricky?'

'I'm sure Mrs Rosenthal has an idea of how much it will cost. She'll want a major race. It must be, for Bernard.'

'How about the August Festival?' Dick Sandhurst asked. 'The second day could do with a stiffener. Let's upgrade the Rede Park Stakes.'

'Perfect,' Gerry said.

Dick Sandhurst gathered up his things and then hesitated at the door.

'Mr Marling rang me first thing,' he said. 'He's invited me to join the board.'

'Has he now? Well, congratulations.'

Dick shifted from one foot to the other.

'I said yes.'

'I'm sure you did.'

'A chap's got to get on, after all.'

'He has indeed.'

He was about to ring Rebecca when she called him.

She had, she said, been thinking. Sam had no interest in business and a business without its founder, his son or a strong natural successor was doomed. She had spoken to Joseph Waller, an old friend of Bernard's whom Gerry knew well, and had asked him – informally, of course – if he would consider buying Bernard's bank.

'What did he say?' Gerry asked.

'He said yes. And he agreed to my stipulation.'

'What was that?'

'That he sponsors Bernard's race for ever and ensures that the prize money always keeps it top class . . . it's not that I wouldn't do it, Gerry, but there will probably be a Labour government and who can tell what will happen? This way it is safe for as long as – well—'

'As long as horses race each other,' Gerry said, 'if your lawyers

437

make sure the obligation is on all successors and assignees and whatever of Joseph's bank.'

'They'll make sure.'

'It's brilliant, Rebecca. Did you tell him how much the race will cost him?'

'I told him twenty-five thousand pounds.'

Gerry spluttered. This was approaching dollar territory.

'We'll have a race for that, won't we? I tried for forty thousand pounds, like the Brigitte-Louisa, but Joseph said it was too much.'

'We'll have a race,' he said.

He put down the phone and wondered what to do. There was an obligation on Joseph Waller to sponsor the race but none on Rede Park to stage it. What were Paul Marling's plans? To destroy Gerry, presumably, him and all his plans.

He searched through his address book, found Joseph Waller's number and dialled it. He was passed through a succession of secretaries until he was put on to the great man himself and could make his request.

'You want to announce the whole thing now?' Joseph Waller asked. 'It's highly premature. I've only had one chat with Rebecca, and the deal will take months to go through.'

'Not announce,' Gerry said. 'Leak. No names – just that a race named after Bernard Rosenthal is to be run at Rede Park and the prize money is rumoured etc. etc. I know the racing journalist who will do it for me.'

'But why? What's the urgency?'

'Paul Marling was voted chairman yesterday and . . . well, he doesn't like me.'

'Dear me. Do you think he would veto it?'

Gerry paused. 'I think,' he said cautiously, 'he will put obstacles in the way of what I most want done.' He had tried to make Gerry put through a loan to a man who was known to be unsound when they both worked for Bernard, Gerry remembered. To what lengths would he not go? 'It's a long story,' he added.

'Yes,' said Joseph Waller slowly. 'I remember bits of it, now you remind me. And you want this press leak so Marling can't kill the race before it is born?'

'That's it. And when I'm rung up, you see, I'll say the rumours are true and details will be announced later. How could Marling stop it after that?'

'You really think he would try?'

'I don't know. I honestly don't know. It seems ridiculous but so does his . . . pursuit of me. Just look what he's done! But we *must* have Bernard's race.'

'Of course we must,' Joseph Waller said impatiently. Gerry waited while he talked to someone else in the room. 'Right,' he said to Gerry. 'Come and have lunch with me tomorrow. That will give me time to get some preliminary negotiations going with Rebecca's solicitors so your "leak" won't be total fantasy.'

'Thank you, sir,' Gerry said, and then, as Joseph Waller was about to hang up: 'Oh, and Rebecca doesn't know about the new chairman here. I'll tell her when we're halfway secure. She'll be upset, you see.'

'I understand,' Joseph Waller said. 'I understand.'

It was like the announcement of the Brigitte-Louisa all over again, only this time Rede Park was said to be threatening the status of the Two Thousand Guineas, which was arrant nonsense, of course, but exactly what Gerry had planned with the *Graphic* journalist who had broken the story.

'You're not kidding me?' the man had asked. 'There is such a race?'

'There is. Print it.'

'Sure. There's sod all else going on at the moment.'

Paul Marling could not possibly deny the race now. Gerry sat back and waited for him to do something, but he made no move. Gerry decided that he would resign after the Blue Oceans Handicap, seven years to the day that there had been racing at Rede Park. Crocus was running in the Blue Oceans, having been entered by her previous trainer, just for a bit of fun. She was pleasing David and he said the outing would do her no harm.

On the first day of the April meeting, Gerry called for a minute's silence for Bernard. And got it. The racecourse froze. The tic-tac men stilled their white-gloved hands, the bookmakers stopped shouting the odds, the horses parading in the paddock twitched their tails and nudged their lads, wondering what was happening. Glasses in the bars stopped clinking. All chatter ceased.

Most of the crowd was local on this relatively quiet day and Bernard had not been local, but every person there stood and remembered the man who had brought George Morgan's sleeping racecourse to life.

After the next race, Gerry went to the directors' box. He could not go on avoiding Paul Marling for ever, and he wanted to give their main sponsor of the day and his wife a drink.

'Effective, I suppose,' Marling greeted Gerry, 'but rather over-emotional, don't you think?'

'Who says so?' the sponsor growled aggressively. He owned a rapidly expanding chain of DIY shops in the West Country, but he had come from the north and, as he was fond of saying, was not afraid of speaking his mind. 'Us around here liked Bernard Rosenthal and appreciated the chance to pay our respects.'

His wife nodded vigorous agreement and Marling raised a supercilious enquiring eyebrow at Gerry. Gerry, unable to suppress a feeling of satisfaction, murmured introductions.

'Rosenthal's successor!' the sponsor exclaimed, 'Well! Over-emotional, eh? Now look here, young man . . .'

Gerry went off to collect drinks for the man and his wife, the loud Yorkshire voice following him.

There were few things to enjoy these days and, although it was grabbing at straws, this he enjoyed greatly.

Gerry had his party for the Blue Oceans Handicap day. He arranged places for everyone to stay the night before and gave a barbecue in the garden of the house in the woods. To his great delight, James came with someone whom he had, over the telephone, described as his 'surprise' – his fiancée, a lovely girl with a bright, open face. Mary had, she said, been comprehensively ignored by James when she rode little woolly ponies while he hunted on his great sleek horses, but he had been her hero since she was twelve years old. He had finally noticed her at a party last Christmas.

'It's all being announced next week when Mary's father is back

440

from America, but Gerry, you'll be my best man, won't you?' James asked.

'Of course I will. James, I'd be honoured.'

He almost forgot the shadows hanging over him as he moved among his guests, and children – so many children his old friends had now – darted around juggling hot potatoes from the bonfire and offering them and sausages, chops and chicken pieces from the barbecue – presided over by Dick Sandhurst and Jennifer Cody's husband – to the adults far more often than they wished. It was half-term, and Gerry had encouraged everyone to bring their offspring to test his latest innovation – a children's playground at the racecourse presided over by qualified staff. Tomorrow was its first day in operation and Gerry wanted to see how it worked. Tying up the last loose end . . . that or because he could not stop himself caring.

Two children who would rather die than sample the playground's attractions Gerry now saw conversing with David Blower and Eileen and Stephen White. He made his way over to them. Eileen smiled at him.

'Charlie's got the winner of the Blue Oceans,' she said, 'and Anne agrees with him, so we'll all make our fortunes.'

'We think we have,' Charlie said, and Anne shook her red head mournfully.

'These early season handicaps are *very* difficult,' she sighed.

Gerry's thigh was nudged and he looked down. An earnest face, a platter of mixed grill held grimly under its chin, gazed up at him. The Coleridge number four, he decided, very determined but much too young for the job. He took a sausage, thanked the face and wondered if he should take the plate as well before disaster happened, but the Smedley number one was apparently in charge, Fagin-like, of a bevy of number twos to fours and the plate was removed by the older children and taken to some secret place behind the bonfire on the edge of the woods. How lovely, Gerry thought; how lovely in spite of everything this night would be if Kate was here and their children were running around with all the rest.

But the party was fun, and one of the best things about it was that there were no frilly shirts, long hair, short skirts and yowling music. Gerry felt that for one night he was holding everything that was most horrible about the outside world at bay. He had been relieved that Patrick and the impossible Debs had not been able to come because of a rival 'event' at Rede Park, and Hilary Partington had, she informed Gerry, come in her squarest outfit on his instructions.

She had started an employment agency for girls up from the provinces who wanted jobs in Swinging London and, since she'd gone about it with her usual determination and thoroughness, it was a phenomenal success. Admiral and Mrs Partington often brought clippings from magazines into the Club, interviews with Hilary, pictures of her in her ultra-modern office, headlines speculating on her latest young man. Gerry was enormously fond of her and hoped she would pick a nice one. She was the only person present who knew he would be resigning tomorrow, and he joked that he would have to sign up at one of her bureaux.

'It's not as bad as that, for God's sake, is it?'

'Nah,' he said. It wasn't, quite. Joseph Waller had offered him a job, but he didn't want to go to London if he could help it; neither did he want to go to another racecourse – for what could compare with what he, Bernard and the team had done here? – and, anyway, he most certainly didn't want to leave his house. He could come back for weekends, he supposed, if he took up Joseph Waller's offer, but what the hell would he do with Parsnip? Give him to Liz and Andrew?

As though reading his thoughts, Parsnip looked over at him and, wriggling his backside guiltily, his eyes on Gerry, he politely accepted a sausage from – Gerry peered: which was this? – the Kellerway number one before running over to Gerry and wrapping himself around his feet. Gerry bent and tugged at the dog's ears. . . . No, he and Rio and Parsnip would stay together in the house in the woods. He hadn't been spending much money these past three years and could afford time to think and plan his next move. He might take up Samuel's offer and go to Israel for a holiday. There were all sorts of things he could do. Lots of possibilities.

'How is everything?' Mark asked him later.

'Couldn't be worse,' Gerry said so cheerfully that Vanessa,

442

hearing the tone and not the words, said, 'How good to see you back on form at last, Gerry.'

Rebecca had not wanted to give away the Blue Oceans Cup this year but Gerry, backed up by Samuel, had persuaded her. She had been devastated to hear that Paul Marling had been elected chairman of Rede Park; she had flung herself at Gerry and cried, 'So that's why you put all that about Bernard's race in the newspapers . . . to make sure it happens because you think Marling will fire you. Oh *Gerry*! Bernard would have done anything – *anything*,' she sobbed, 'to stop this. He blamed himself. He said he should have realised—'

'I should have realised. Paul Marling has been after my family for years, and I happen to be its most exposed member. It is . . .' he found Bernard's expression for it . . . 'bad luck. And now, will you present the trophy for the last running of the Blue Oceans Handicap at Rede Park, as you did the first?'

'The last?'

'Under the circumstances, it's bound to be.'

Had Marling realised that? he wondered. He'd have to find sponsors for three expensive races, and a new tenant for the popular and profitable seafood bar. Joe, Arthur and Grace were philosophical about it. Joe thought they could do just as well – better even – at one of the racecourses nearer London, and Gerry had the beginnings of an idea forming but he didn't want to take it out and give it a proper examination yet.

'So you will, won't you?' he had asked Rebecca, and she had said, 'For you, Gerry, then. If it will please you.'

And it did, most gloriously.

Charlie and Anne Colley-Smythe had it wrong and Eileen White did not make her fortune, but no one minded – not at all they didn't.

For Crocus won the Blue Oceans. By eight lengths.

Gerry put down his binoculars and watched his little roan filly sprint away from her field at the two-furlong marker, too shocked and overwhelmed even to cheer her on. He turned to David Blower, who was standing beside him.

'Did you think this would happen?' he asked, still not believing it in spite of the people congratulating him, the buffets on the back he was receiving.

'I told you she was pleasing me,' David replied. 'But I'll have that boy's balls for breakfast ... winning a handicap by that distance! Hasn't he got a brain? Come on, let's get down there and lead your winner in.'

Gerry allowed himself to be taken from the owners' and trainers' stand and out through the crowds past where the beaten runners were already being unsaddled.

'I must find Rebecca,' Gerry said at one point, but then Rebecca was there, her hand in his, and Crocus was trotting towards them, her nose with its enchanting crooked white blaze in the air as she fought her young jockey because she wanted to gallop again.

Gerry laid his forehead against her sweating neck.

'Oh you lovely thing,' he told her. 'You lovely, lovely thing.'

He and Rebecca walked on either side of her through the crowd towards the winners' enclosure.

'Honest, guv, I couldn't help it,' the jockey was telling David. 'She ran away with me. I gave her one kick and she was off – honest!'

'It doesn't matter,' Gerry remembered telling the boy. 'She won't run in a handicap again.'

Crocus's win wasn't all that popular for a hot favourite had been beaten, but the racecourse announcer – who had briefed him? Gerry wondered – was now telling everyone who Crocus belonged to and how 'our Gerry' had come to own the horse, and the mood changed. It was like that time Gerry had won on Calipers, when the affection of the crowd had washed over him and Bernard. Congratulations showered now on him, Rebecca and Crocus and when they arrived in the winners' enclosures the press was hunting the story for all it was worth. As Crocus was unsaddled and the jockey went to weigh in, Gerry was surrounded.

'It's Bernard's horse,' he said. 'He never won this race, but he has done today.'

Crocus was led away and the presentation of the trophy was announced. People stayed where they were instead of drifting off to the paddock, and Liz James's waiting staff, disgracefully away from their posts, lined up on the balcony outside the bars and restaurant among the paying customers to witness this emotional event. Dick Sandhurst appeared and, taking Rebecca and Gerry by the elbow, urged them towards the table swathed in dark blue velvet upon which reposed the cup for the winning owner and the prizes for the trainer and jockey. Sharp of Dick, Gerry realised. This was usually Gerry's job. Dick left Gerry on the edge of the crowd, beside David Blower, the boy jockey and Arthur and Grace, and led Rebecca on.

'Oh Art,' Gerry said, 'isn't this the best thing ever?'

'Yes, lad,' his brother replied gently. 'So why are you crying?'

Gerry put a hand to his face and found his cheeks were wet. He pulled out his handkerchief and mopped his eyes. The racecourse announcer called him forward and he stepped into a huge cheer. Rebecca picked up the cup, handed it to him and they posed for the photographers. Dick Sandhurst removed the cup, replaced it on the table and Rebecca put her arms around Gerry and, heedless of the crowds and the clicks of the cameras, they hugged each other.

'Bernard's race is a mile,' she whispered. 'Could Crocus win it?'

'She'll try,' he said. 'She'll bloody well try.'

They parted and David Blower and the jockey came forward to receive their prizes. Gerry stood there, clapping at the appropriate times, and decided that he would not resign today after all. It would not look good on the heels of this and the press would speculate on his reasons and make everything seem tawdry and scandalous. He did not want his racecourse to suffer that. If Paul Marling did not fire him – and how could he now? – he would stay until the end of the season, be in charge for the first running of the Bernard Rosenthal Memorial and then go, with the minimum of fuss and damage.

The brief ceremony was over. David rushed away to saddle another runner and Rebecca and Gerry were submerged by friends. Samuel was crying openly but laughing at the same time, and the tears were running down Gerry's cheeks again. Lots of people were crying, even James's lovely Mary who had never known Bernard.

'Liz is sending crates of bubbles to the box,' Andrew Coleridge said. 'There is some serious celebrating to be done.'

'What about him?' James gestured to the boy jockey, still wearing his racing silks, standing forlornly, wondering, no doubt, when such a moment would come to him again. Tomorrow – tonight, even – he would be just another of David's lads, mucking out and grooming the horses assigned to him. She hadn't needed it, as it turned out, but he had taken seven valuable pounds from Crocus's back.

Gerry laid a hand on his shoulder, and the boy turned and looked up.

'What's the strongest thing you've ever had to drink?' Gerry asked.

The boy thought for a moment. 'Why, sir,' he said, 'ginger beer, I suppose.'

'Come along and have a ginger beer, then.'

'The governor . . .' the boy began uncertainly, and then a mixture of relief and disappointment came over his face as Helen Blower came up and told him to go and get changed.

'No,' Gerry said. 'He's coming with us and I want him to wear my colours.' They were the same combination as Bernard's, but in a different configuration.

Helen looked at Gerry and then down into the boy's pleading eyes and smiled.

'Well, all right,' she said.

In his racing silks he would be a gladiator come home, a hero; in his ordinary clothes an insignificant, uncertain sixteen-year-old. Why not let him prolong his moment of glory?

Charlie – who was about the same size as him – asked for his autograph and Anne Colley-Smythe fell in love with him. He tasted champagne and he had tasted success, and he liked both very much indeed.

446

Chapter 29

Three days later, Gerry was at work in his garden when Paul Marling came creeping down the track and appeared silently at the edge of the lawn. Parsnip, the treacherous fool, bounded over barking greetings . . . but then, Gerry thought as he picked up his shirt and put it on, they had met before. Parsnip would not remember it, but Paul Marling most certainly would.

'The gypsy in the woods,' Paul Marling commented. 'How appropriate. As a child, one was warned not to play with such things.'

'Why have you come?'

Marling peered through the open French windows into the sitting room.

'I thought we should talk.' He turned back to Gerry. 'Perhaps we could do so in a civilised manner, over a drink or something.'

'A drink I have,' said Gerry. 'I don't know about something. What did you have in mind?'

'A whisky and soda, if you please.'

He followed Gerry through to the kitchen, looking at everything, and waited while Gerry poured his drink and took a bottle of beer from the fridge for himself. Rio, reckoning it was suppertime, appeared and wound himself around Gerry's legs, and Gerry made Marling wait while he opened a tin of cat food and spooned some into Rio's bowl before handing Marling his drink, picking up the bottle of beer and a glass and leading the way back out to the patio table.

'What would you like to talk about?' he asked, pouring out the beer. He had given Marling ordinary blended whisky and, although it was tempting, hadn't quite dared help himself to the single malt. Anyway, gardening was thirsty work.

Marling took a sip of his drink.

'You might not believe this,' he said, 'but I don't want you to leave, you know. I have been ... concerned that you might be thinking of doing so.'

Gerry laughed. 'No, I'm sure you don't want me to leave. You want me back under your heel, do you not?'

'I want you to continue as managing director.'

'Why? I'm not going to provide you with any entertainment. You can call me your little gypo any time you want and I won't give a damn. Everyone knows who I am – *I* know who I am and I'm proud of it, and for that I have to thank Bernard.' He paused. 'And thus you, of course. How very odd.'

'So you are going to leave, then?'

'Yes, I am. At the end of the season.'

'I see. Where will you go?'

'I'll stay here. This is my home, after all. As to what I'll do – well, I have a few ideas.'

He would not tell him about Blue Oceans. Let him find out that there had never been a contract. No one had ever mentioned one, perhaps because no one wanted to drag up memories of that other time when Grace had considered such a thing appropriate between members of the family. He stood up.

'Mr Marling,' he said. 'I'd like you to go now. Be content that you've taken control of the company and that I am losing the racecourse I always considered mine. It's a fair exchange for Ridge Farm, don't you think?' He held out his hand and smiled. 'Shall we call it evens?'

Marling finished his drink and unhurriedly rose to his feet. His blue eyes were hooded as he took Gerry's hand.

'If you say so, my little gypo. If you say so.'

He left.

Gerry sat down again as soon as Paul Marling was out of sight. He was shaking. At first he thought it must be reaction to having actually said he was going, had in effect given in his notice, but then he identified exactly what he felt.

It was fear. He had felt violence in Paul Marling's handshake; under the surface, certainly, but unmistakably there. But what more could Marling do to him? What more? . . . He had attacked Kate . . . would he attack Gerry? Urbane, cold, controlled Paul Marling? . . . But he *had* attacked Kate, of that Gerry was certain. And then another revelation hit him, the reason behind the violence Gerry had felt in that handshake. Not reason, the lack of it. What else could account for this single-minded pursuit of Gerry all these years? And what would replace that pursuit in Paul Marling's life now that his quarry was at bay and almost disposed of? He'd had his hands around Kate's neck and only the arrival of Parsnip had saved her. . . .

Gerry went inside and poured himself a Glenmorangie. And then another. He hunted out the stick he had bought after the attack on Kate and then tried turning on the lights through the woods, but it wasn't dark and he couldn't tell if they were all working. He would ask George to check them tomorrow, say that guests had complained that there were patches of darkness when they had left the party the other night. Gerry didn't use them as he liked the dark, but he would from now on. . . . Kate's lights.

What else? His third Glenmorangie gave him the answer. He went to his desk and wrote it all down, the whole history of him and Paul Marling, the attack on Kate which would be in police files. Everything. He put it in an envelope, wrote 'to be opened in the event of my injury or death' and decided to give it to Andrew for safekeeping.

He was beginning on his fourth Glenmorangie when the doorbell rang. He checked that the stick was within reach, grabbed Parsnip – who was barking bravely – and, ready for anything, opened the door.

It was Hilary Partington.

'They sent me down to fetch you as they're all getting blotto on the aperitifs,' she said.

He had forgotten. There was a dinner at the Club tonight to celebrate Crocus's win. The members had arranged it for him, Hilary had agreed to partner him and he hadn't even changed.

'Are you all right?' she asked him. 'You look as though you've seen a dozen grade A ghosts.'

449

He wondered whether to tell her, but there wasn't time. Tomorrow, perhaps, he decided as he shot upstairs, calling to Hilary to make him a strong black coffee.

He awoke the next morning with a hangover, his own generosity and the Club members' having formed a powerful alliance. He staggered downstairs, let Parsnip out and took his cup of tea to the patio. The envelope lay on his desk. 'To be opened in the event of my injury or death'. How melodramatic!

Feeling rather foolish, he put it in a drawer.

He had been right about one thing: Paul Marling had wanted to do violence to him as he had shaken Gerry's strong brown hand. He had wanted to put his own hands around Gerry's neck and squeeze until the gypsy went on his knees and pleaded to have his racecourse back.

What right did the man have to laugh at him, to smile and jokingly say that they should call it evens? Didn't he care that he had lost everything he had spent the last ten years building up? And, if he did care, then why the bloody hell didn't he show it? Look what he, Paul Marling, had done in order to bring all this about! The way fate – God! – had intervened on his side! And all he was left with was a racecourse that he didn't want unless the thieving gypsy wanted it more than life itself.

And there was the other matter which Marling would have to sort out soon, and that was the gypo's fault too. It was all . . . it was all . . . most unsatisfactory.

In his frustration he might well have turned to violence, waited in the woods for the gypsy to come home as he had once waited for his woman, but he found something tucked away in Andrew's files. Something he looked at, checked through records, looked at again and found most amusing.

This. *This*, he told himself, would make the gypsy squeal.

Late in June, Gerry received a letter from Kate.

A Sissinghurst postmark and Kate's handwriting, certainly. He stared, not daring to believe it, then ran out of the Club and back down the track. He had to read this alone, but then, unable to wait any longer, he found a fallen tree trunk, sat on it and tore open the envelope. Three sheets of paper, written on both sides.

She was most desperately sorry to hear about Bernard, she wrote. Gerry looked around wildly. He had written with that news over four months ago! Where the hell was she? The Antarctic? He continued to read.

How Gerry must feel his loss. She had written to Rebecca, of course ... more about Bernard ... the takeover bid for the racecourse must have been ghastly ... he was right not to blame Patrick ...

Gerry read on, amazed. Tears filled his eyes as he realised that she was responding to all his letters, not just the one about Bernard. She was glad he had been generous about giving Diana a divorce, could not have blamed him if he'd been tempted to make her wait. She hoped he had recovered from his horrible fall and was pleased to learn that he had given up race-riding. She missed Parsnip and sent him her love, and to Florin and Sprite and Rio. And to Gerry.

Gerry sat on the tree trunk under a green canopy of leaves and stared at the sheets of paper. Kate had talked to him. After all but three years she had talked to him. He was sure that she had done it almost against her will, for the letter was written hurriedly and contained many crossings-out. Not at all like his fastidious Kate. She had written it and posted it in one emotional surge prompted by the news of Bernard's death, and Gerry would bank on her having written him others and torn them up before her heart could persuade her beautiful dark head to post them. Obviously she hadn't yet received his birthday letter – which he'd sent in April – when she had written this, for she did not know that Paul Marling was now chairman. Would she reply to that?

But she had cracked! After all this time she had cracked! Gerry leapt up and Parsnip, who had been watching him anxiously, wagged his tail enquiringly. Gerry bent down and gave the dog a smacking kiss on his black nose.

'That's because she sent you her love,' he said. 'Come on!'

He ran back to his house and rang Beattie.

'I've had a letter from Kate,' he told her.

'I know. I forwarded it.'

451

'I'm going to reply to it, and you're going to forward that, too, aren't you?'

'Yes, Gerry,' she said.

This was too good to be true. He chanced his luck.

'And you're going to tell me where she is, aren't you?'

'No,' she said, 'I can't do that.'

'Never mind.'

He put the phone down and took pen and paper outside to the table on the patio. He wrote the letter he had thought of writing on the day Paul Marling had been voted chairman, though this was more forceful and determined than that would ever have been. He told her that she was to stop messing around and come back and marry him. England was pretty awful these days, he said; she wouldn't believe it if she could see it. Apparently it *swung*. Everyone had gone quite barmy, but he and Kate needn't worry about that here in the house in the woods . . . or, he added, becoming less positive, if she preferred he would come to wherever she was. He would do that willingly if she would only tell him where that might be.

Crocus had won the Blue Oceans and Clematis had come third in the first race of her life. What did Kate think of that? . . . Oh and James was engaged to a lovely girl called Mary. He had kissed Parsnip for her, and Parsnip sent her a great big lick.

And Kate, wherever she was, read this some time later and held the letter to her. She thought of the house in the woods, of the English garden, of the blue dusk that crept into it on summer evenings and tried to imagine the dire things Gerry talked of that they wouldn't have to worry about down the half-mile track. She thought of what Beattie had been hinting at in her recent letters and, more profoundly, of what Rebecca had said in the letter that had arrived in the same batch of post as Gerry's had. It thanked her for her sympathy and her kind words about her beloved Bernard. She said that loving someone as much as she had loved Bernard had seemed the greatest joy to her, and when he had been so abruptly snatched from her she had resented that love for a while because this thing of joy had become her greatest burden. If she had loved less she would have grieved less. But now she had achieved a certain

452

compromise: Bernard had gone and she could not bring him back, and her happiness now was remembering him with as little sadness as she could and in loving his memory without reservation or resentment.

'It is hard work,' she had written, 'it's hard work indeed, but, God knows, I have to cope with something that is well and truly ended. Can you, my dear, say the same? I think not, you see, because if that were the case you would come back and see your friends who so sorely miss you.'

And Kate, wherever she was, experienced some shame that Rebecca could compare their two cases, and compromise inched its way into her heart and replaced some of the resentment, hurt, anger and pride that had lodged there so stubbornly these three years, vaccinating it against love.

Just the slightest softening. Not much. And certainly not enough.

Gerry went to Patrick's wedding. It was being held here rather than in the bride's own parish because Patrick's house would, Gerry gathered, be a groovy scene for the reception. Gerry stood by Jim, the landlord of the Rede Arms and the only other person in the congregation as far as Gerry could tell – apart from Mrs Morgan and the bride's parents – who was dressed normally and watched, stupefied, as Debs (that's what she was called on the service sheet, and Patrick had become Pat) came down the aisle in a white minidress, patterned stockings and high-heeled shoes to the music of some pop group, to be claimed by her groom who was in traditional pinstripes and tails except that these were, respectively, white and silver and white, and there were sequins on the shoulders of his coat.

'Oh my Lord,' Jim whispered. 'What'll Parson Reeves make of this then?'

Parson Reeves married the couple, although he closed his eyes more often than was usual on these occasions. Either pain or prayer, Gerry decided.

Jim escaped to the sanctuary of his pub after the ceremony, but Gerry felt obliged to go to the reception. The pop group that had played in the church was thumping away in the drawing room and another was screaming on the lawn. Miniskirted waitresses and waiters with ruffled shirts open to their waists proffered food and champagne. A girl attached herself to Gerry and said 'yeah' and 'great' to every comment he made. She offered him biscuits on a plate and he took some and ate them. After a while he began to feel light-headed and was about to go in search of something more substantial to counteract the effects of the alcohol when she offered him the biscuits again.

'Why aren't you eating?' he asked the girl.

She giggled at him. Her mini-clad body was jumping up and down in a most alarming fashion, until Gerry realised that it was his eyeballs that were doing the jumping – and that was even more alarming.

Patrick appeared before him in shimmering white.

'Keep still,' Gerry told him.

'How many have you fed him?' he thought Patrick asked the girl. '*Four?* Christ, he's high as a kite.'

Another girl came jigging up, and a man. Maybe two.

'Get your hair cut,' Gerry said to him. Or them.

Patrick was speaking to him, and in a moment of lucidity he understood and was angry. He tried to leave but they wouldn't let him. They kept mentioning the police and now seemed annoyed with the girl who had done this to him.

'It was only a joke,' she said.

Gerry began laughing and could not stop.

They tried to persuade him to go upstairs and sleep it off, but he felt full of energy.

'Let me go home,' he said. 'I want to dance in the woods.'

Then they were no longer in the drawing room but somewhere else, and Gerry was sitting in an armchair and a dark-faced man was leaning over him urging him to drink a cup of coffee.

'It's got something in it,' Gerry said, trying to push the man's hand away.

'Nothing, I promise.'

'Don't believe you.'

'Do you know who I am?'

'No.'

'I'm Eduardo. Diana's Eduardo. Trust me. Drink.'

454

His voice was the only certain thing in a spinning world and Gerry drank the coffee, spilling some of it over his shirt and waistcoat. He felt a bit better, and when he was handed another cup he drank that too and was relieved to find that everything was immobile.

'Who did you say you are?' he asked the man.

'Eduardo da Silva.'

'Ah yes.' Gerry lay back in his chair. 'Diana's Eduardo. How is Diana?'

'She is well. She is here.'

'Are you married?'

'Yes.'

'Diana da Silva. It sounds right, doesn't it? Everything's moving again,' Gerry remarked. 'It's all swirling around. I thought I'd got it to stay still.'

'You have swallowed a quantity of marijuana. It will take time to work through your system.'

'People do it on purpose, don't they? They pay for it.'

'It's best if you don't fight it, they say.'

'I want to go home.'

'I understand the party here is planned to go on all night. They are worried that you will call the police or someone, seeing you, will. They fear what they call a bust.'

'Good idea,' Gerry mumbled. 'Arrest the lot of them.'

'It would spoil Patrick's wedding reception.'

'Liz,' Gerry said. 'Phone Liz. Three-six-three. Phone Liz.'

He remembered nothing more except, halfway down the track to the house in the woods, he had another few minutes when his brain belonged to him.

'God,' he said. 'I hate the nineteen sixties. Don't you? I really hate them. Loathe them. Damn the whole bloody decade. It's after me, Liz, it hates me. It's tormenting me. *I hate*,' he screamed into the trees, '*the nineteen sixties!*'

Apparently, the girl had eaten two of the biscuits – hash cookies they were called – and thought the sight of Gerry in his normal tail coat and striped trousers so exquisitely funny that she had not been able to resist the temptation to get him stoned. No one would tell Gerry her name, which was perhaps just as well because he was dreaming up dire things for her.

Liz had been persuaded by Eduardo da Silva not to call the police, for, as he pointed out, the scandal would not only involve Patrick but Rede Park as well. Gerry could be arrested, for how could he prove he hadn't taken the stuff deliberately?

'I do hate this decade, though,' he said. 'Everything about it. I can't think of a good thing that's happened in it.'

'So you said,' Liz pointed out. 'Several times.'

'It's true, Liz.'

'Maybe it will get better now,' she said soothingly.

She was wrong.

Gerry had to have Florin put down. He called the vet because the old horse wasn't looking well. He was thin, even in high summer, and Gerry could not tempt him with any food. The vet looked at his teeth and listened to his heart.

'He's old, Gerry,' he said. 'How old now?'

'Twenty-four.'

'It's a fine age.'

'Yes.'

'He's not enjoying life. Gerry – look at him.'

Gerry looked and saw his horse as a stranger might. The head lowered, the eyes dull, his ribs showing. No gleam in the bay coat.

'Is there nothing you can do?'

'I can't cure old age.'

Gerry gazed up at the blue sky, at the high white clouds, and around at the paddock and the rustling trees that shaded it at the far end. A good day for a good horse to die.

'Now?' he asked.

'Best get it over as soon as possible.'

'The Club members mustn't—'

'I'll go and phone the hunt kennels. They'll send the van.'

'Yes. He'd like to go to the hounds.'

'You get the other horse out of the way.'

Gerry fetched a headcollar and went and caught Sprite. He led him over to Florin, but the old horse didn't even raise his head then or when his companion was led out of the field and away to the stables. Gerry went back to Florin.

'Horses have always made strong men weep,' he remembered another vet saying when another horse had waited for a bullet. Castor had been reprieved that day, but there would be no reprieve for Florin now. Gerry hoped the van would be able to come straight away. He didn't want to be told to come back at three o'clock this afternoon.

The vet reappeared, followed by Liz. She handed Gerry a glass.

'Brandy,' she said.

'Thanks.'

She stroked Florin's nose.

'He's gone, hasn't he? He doesn't want to live any more. We just didn't notice.'

'No, we didn't.'

They waited until the van arrived.

'Can we get him in it?' the driver said. 'It'ud be easier—'

'No,' Gerry said. 'He's going here. You can use your bloody winch to get him in.'

He held the headcollar rope and closed his eyes as the vet raised his gun. He heard the report of the gun and the shocking sound of his horse's body falling to the ground, dropped the rope, went into the Club and got drunk in celebration of Florin's long and happy life.

Bernard's legacies to Gerry were doing their best to redeem the decade. Crocus won the Sussex Stakes at Goodwood and Gerry and Rebecca tried not to hope too hard that she would win the Bernard Rosenthal Memorial three weeks later. Clematis had come third again in her second race, and David thought he would give her more time before bringing her out again.

Gerry still hadn't decided what he would do when he stopped work in October and Crocus's winnings were making the decision less than urgent, but he brought out the little idea he had and took it to Joe, Grace and Arthur.

'Lots o' Blue Oceans bars at all manner of racecourses, you mean?' his father asked.

'I don't know about lots, but maybe two or three. Most racecourses have jumping as well as the Flat, and you might think

457

of sponsoring some jumping races. The prize money isn't nearly as high and it wouldn't be that expensive.'

'We'd have the bars open in winter, then?'

'That's right.'

'It's a thought, lad. It's a thought. What d'you reckon, Grace?'

'I like it, but will people want cold food in winter?'

'Give it 'em hot, then.'

'Who's going to get it going – talk to likely racecourses and that?' Arthur asked.

Joe's brown eyes gleamed.

'Why, our Gerry, I reckon,' he said. 'I reckon he's going to come an' work for Blue Oceans after all.'

Gerry laughed. 'No, Da, but I'll fix up your races and see about your bars. Anyway,' he added, 'you don't need a sales and marketing man now, do you? You've got one.'

'We've got three,' Grace said.

Gerry drove away feeling satisfied. It would be a nice challenge, he thought, one that would require him to travel the country to visit other racecourses. He wouldn't be out of things entirely, and neither would he have to watch Rede Park go about its daily business without him. He would have some preliminary talks in September, he decided, as he didn't want any rumours about the Blue Oceans sponsorship to mar his last August Festival meeting and the first running of the Bernard Rosenthal Memorial.

Crocus came second in Bernard's race, but she ran so bravely that no one could be disappointed, except for those loyal members of the crowd who thought Gerry's horse should win, and who had backed her.

The sale of Bernard's bank to Joseph Waller was at last finalised and Gerry signed a contract that tied Rede Park to staging Bernard's race every year, fire, floods, acts of God and acts of war notwithstanding.

He spoke to a few people, in confidence as yet, about staging a Blue Oceans race and there was enthusiastic interest.

He hoped daily for a letter from Kate, but none came.

He went to Leicestershire and stood by James as he was married to Mary. The bride and groom, and most of the guests, wore conventional clothing and there were no doped biscuits in the wedding feast.

The leaves turned and the valley looked most beautiful.

They had their end of season board meeting at which Gerry tendered his resignation. Liz James and Jennifer Cody cried.

Gerry left Parsnip and the care of Rio to Liz and Andrew and flew to Israel with Rebecca. They spent a week sight-seeing and then a month on Samuel's kibbutz. Every day Samuel said a prayer for his father and Gerry listened to him. He could not understand but he felt part of it in some way. He joined Sam and the others in the fields and enjoyed the hard physical work. It seemed a fitting barrier between his past life and his future.

He wrote to Kate and told her that she was part of his future, whether she was with him or not. Didn't she realise that?

He arrived home. Parsnip greeted him ecstatically, but no Rio. George had found him dead in the woods. Fourteen years. A good age.

No Rio and no letter from Kate.

No letter from Kate, but a letter from Paul Marling.

Since he was no longer employed by Rede Park Racecourse Ltd he was ordered to leave the house identified in the title deeds as numbers one and two Gamekeepers' Cottages. He was to vacate the aforesaid premises by the end of the year.

He squealed all right.

He went to Paul Marling. The company had given him the house, he said.

Paul Marling smiled and said there was no record of it.

Gerry had designed – he and Kate had designed – and paid for the conversion. The place had been worthless, practically falling down. It would be a heap of stones by now if it hadn't been for Gerry's money.

Paul Marling smiled and said that, if Gerry could produce the builders' and decorators' bills, he may be able to persuade the board to consider paying him some recompense.

Who would want to live there anyway? Gerry asked. Down half a mile of woodland path?

Paul Marling smiled and said he thought it would rather suit

459

him. He would spend the odd night there, perhaps, during race meetings. That and the odd weekend.

Gerry went to Andrew and together they searched through the files, but found nothing as Gerry knew they would. He couldn't remember how he had come to take possession of the house in the woods in those first heady days when the grandstands were being built and Cyril's derelict house was being transformed into the Club. He would have asked Bernard if he could live there, certainly, and Bernard, certainly, had said yes. No one had ever considered whether Gerry owned the place legally.

He did not. There was no question of it.

Liz, Andrew and a somewhat reluctant Dick Sandhurst went to Makepeace and Williams and persuaded those two worthies that Paul Marling's treatment of Gerry could attract some adverse publicity for Rede Park in the press. The two gentlemen said that they did not think they could go against the chairman's wishes in the matter of selling the property to Mr Beviss but they agreed to a compromise: Gerry was paid the mean average of three local estate agents' assessments of the value of numbers one and two Gamekeepers' Cottages.

Gerry and the Glenmorangie raged through the woods. Money? He did not want money, he screamed. He had enough bloody money, thanks to Bernard and Crocus and little Clematis, who hadn't won a race yet but would do next year. He wanted his and Kate's house in the woods. He'd had a Christmas card from her – addressed to all five of them, for she hadn't known when she'd written it that both Rio and Florin were dead – and she hadn't said so but he knew she would come back. He didn't want any bloody money but he wanted his house.

He paused in his ramblings and saw the lights of Rede Park at the other end of the valley. Patrick had *his* house. Saved against all odds by a complicated set of circumstances that had begun with Gerry marrying Diana Dalton. Waving the bottle of Glenmorangie in one hand, checking with the very drunk's calculation in this matter that there was enough left in it to take him where he wanted to go, he ducked under both sets of running rails bounding the racecourse and, followed by Parsnip, plunged into the misty, dusk-filled golf course.

460

Patrick opened the door after Gerry had been hammering on it for what seemed like an age. Gerry brushed past him, Parsnip a miserable black shadow at his heels, and turned in the panelled hall.

'I've lost everything – *everything* – because of you,' he said, brandishing the whisky bottle. 'Every bloody thing. You have gambled me away. Me and Parsnip here, and Sprite, have nowhere to go. We are—' He raised the bottle and drank from it. 'We are a lost bet.' He stared at Patrick. 'What happens to all the losing betting slips?'

Patrick gestured. 'They get torn up . . . and thrown away.'

'Too right. Too bloody right.'

'Gerry, I'm sorry.'

Tears were running down his cheeks, Gerry realised.

'All right,' he said. 'But there's no need to cry about it. I'm not crying, so why should you? Are you,' he asked, creeping up on the word carefully, '*stoned*?'

'I'm trying to be. It hasn't worked yet . . . Gerry, Debs has left me.'

'Left you? She only just married you. I saw it all. I was there.'

'She's run away with the lead singer of Bobbie and the Bobswingers.'

Gerry thought about this.

'That means she's run off with Bobbie, then,' he decided.

'Yeah.'

'Bobbie and Debbie. Debs and Bobs.'

'Yeah.'

Gerry drank the last of the Glenmorangie and placed the empty bottle carefully on the floor.

'It's a terrible decade, this, Patrick. Terrible,' he said. 'And there's another five years of it to go. Just think of that!'

'Don't want to.'

'Got any whisky?'

'Yeah.'

'*Bobswingers!*'

'To hell with them.'

'Yeah.'

*   *   *

461

Patrick offered him house room, but he didn't think he could bear either the music or to be so close to the house in the woods. He stayed with David and Helen Blower for a few weeks until their neighbours offered him a cottage vacated by a farmworker who was not being replaced. Joseph Waller advised him about investing Crocus's winnings and the money he had received for the house in the woods. He would not buy a place to live in, he said, until he and Kate chose it together, and his friends, hearing this, shook their heads and exchanged anxious glances.

'She'll come back,' he insisted. 'I know she'll come back.'

Either Beattie or Kate would give way soon, he was sure.

In the meantime, he was keeping his promise to Blue Oceans. Two racecourses would stage two Blue Oceans flat races each and two jump races. Both courses were building new grandstands offering more facilities to racegoers and were intrigued by the idea of a Blue Oceans seafood bar (especially after seeing the figures for Rede Park's) but there was a small problem.

'Who will run it, though?' Gerry was asked, and, without thinking, he said that Rede Park Catering would.

'Fair enough,' the man replied, 'but only if it changes its name. We can't have the competition so obviously here.'

The idea was so explosive it knocked Gerry sideways. It could be called Joe Bloggs Catering, but if it had Liz James in charge it would be the best. It would also make Andrew and Liz safe from anything Paul Marling might do to them. They didn't even think they owned the place where they lived; they knew very well that they did not. Perhaps Blue Oceans would put money in, help start the whole thing up . . .

He spoke to his father and Grace and then, on their insistence, to the men in charge of several other racecourses. They confirmed what Gerry had always known: the catering at Rede Park was admired and envied; everyone would be delighted to be able to offer it.

He went to see Andrew and Liz. As he drove up the familiar driveway to the Club, he braked sharply and stared aghast. Trees had been cut down, many of them still lying where they had fallen, and a black tarmac road sliced down to the house in the woods. The place had been raped.

He parked the car and walked into the Club. Liz greeted him warmly, kissing him on both cheeks.

'Oh we miss you,' she said. 'We miss you so much.'

'Liz – the road—'

'I know.' She shrugged. 'But what can we do?'

Nothing, of course. The trees were gone for ever, and nothing would bring them back.

Andrew wheeled himself in and Gerry told them his idea: that they, backed by Blue Oceans, could start up their own company specialising in catering for racecourses. They had the expertise, they had the staff, they knew all the suppliers. Gerry would help get them the contracts. If he concentrated on racecourses within a reasonable distance of here – or wherever they chose to live – the travelling Liz would have to do could be kept under control; she was always concerned that she could not promote her most able deputies or give them more responsibility, and here was her chance to do just that – and, once the systems had been worked out, to work less hard herself.

And, he concluded, their lives – their house and their jobs – would belong to them.

They listened in silence and remained silent for a long time after he had finished speaking until Liz sighed and said,

'Oh Gerry!'

'Don't you like the idea?' he asked anxiously.

'We have been most dreadfully worried,' she said. 'We've even been house-hunting, but we don't think we'd get a mortgage because of Andrew.'

Gerry stood up.

'You'll want to talk it over. Let me know.'

Andrew reached for Liz's hand.

'The answer is yes,' he said. 'On one condition.'

'What is that?'

'You be chairman of our company. Sort us out when Liz and I quarrel over policy.'

Gerry laughed. 'Very well.'

'It's brilliant,' Liz said. 'All we need is a few essential supplies—'

'A van,' Andrew said.

'Yes, a van. Plates and cutlery and glasses . . . a few phone calls and we could start tomorrow.'

'Let me find you the racecourses first.'

'You've found them, from what you say,' Liz said.

She escorted him out to his car. He forced himself to look at the road through the woods.

'I suppose it's sensible, really. More convenient, certainly. I would have liked some curves in it, though. Bends around the trees so it still seemed to go to a secret place.'

He opened the door of his car. Liz flung her arms around his neck.

'Thank you, Gerry,' she said. 'Oh, thank you.'

They wanted to stay in the area. Their friends were there and so were their staff, every one of whom declared that he or she would join the new enterprise of James & Beviss. Andrew and Liz found a house they liked, were able to put down a deposit on it and took a loan from Blue Oceans for the balance since they were considered too great a risk by the mortgage companies. Joe Beviss, ever one for the main chance, made Andrew a financial consultant; Andrew happily took the Blue Oceans files on board and soon discovered that the northern sales director had been cheating the company rotten. Jennifer Cody, together with her daughter Charlotte, joined James & Beviss as general organisers and reported that Rede Park was in chaos. Dick Sandhurst seemed paralysed by the loss of the Blue Oceans races, would have forgotten to apply to the Jockey Club for his own and the racecourse's licences had Jennifer not pointed out that he needed to. Paul Marling was taking little interest in the place, or in the fact that the departure of Liz meant the demise of Rede Park Catering. The couple Liz and Andrew had appointed – in consultation with the Club committee – to run the Club were very nice, but it just wasn't the same.

Gerry confirmed the arrangements with the two courses that were to stage the Blue Oceans races, signed contracts with three more for which the new company would begin doing the catering at the start of the jumping season and then, not quite knowing how he felt about it, he went to Rede Park Racecourse, parked his car, walked around the grandstands and knocked on the door of what had once been his office.

'I thought you should know,' he said gently when Dick Sandhurst had invited him to enter, 'that unless you have made other arrangements you will not have any food in your restaurants or drinks in your bars at your meeting in two weeks' time.'

'Christ!' Dick buried his face in his hands.

'We'll do it for you, shall we?'

Dick looked up at him, his face white.

'Please,' he whispered.

He brought out a bottle of Glenmorangie (Gerry had obviously trained him well) and unloaded his heart. He had told Paul Marling that he wasn't ready for this. He wasn't experienced enough. He had come to Rede Park thinking he would have a couple of years under Gerry before moving on, but he'd only had one season here and a year at York. He should know the business by now, but he couldn't cope. Paul Marling was no help. All he said was that he had more important things on his mind and Dick was to shut up and get on with it.

He was so distraught that Gerry didn't like to tell him that he should not have accepted a seat on the board in the first place, however much he wanted to get on. He spent the next hour taking Dick through the procedures for a racing day at Rede Park. The young man thanked him and then said what Gerry knew was coming.

'I can't,' he said. 'How can I possibly?'

'Just be here in the office so I know you're near by.'

'I can't,' Gerry repeated. 'Jeff knows his job as staff manager and everyone else is experienced. Ring me with any query whenever you like, but I can't be here.'

Gerry saw it on television. It would not be obvious to anyone else but he could tell the place had slipped, that things weren't quite as they ought to be. Then the runners for a seven-furlong race went to the mile and a half start. How the hell had that happened? The jockeys quickly realised what had gone wrong and cantered their horses to the correct place while the television cameras showed the starter pacing up and down, graphically consulting his watch. Poor Dick would be reported to the Jockey Club.

It occurred to Gerry that although he hadn't killed the thing he loved, he had given it a hefty punch in a painful place.

And he did not care.

Chapter 30

What now, for Gerry? Whatever now? The little challenges had been met and disposed of. James & Beviss Catering would be welcomed at any racecourse in the country so far as Gerry could see, and it was up to Liz and Andrew to decide how quickly and by how much they wanted to expand. Gerry had to do something else, but he could not settle to anything until he and Kate had sorted themselves out. He'd had another letter from her, and he was sure that something would happen soon. It had been nearly four years and neither of them had let go. Beattie knew that and he thought she was probably telling Kate so. One or other of them had to give way soon: Kate's damnable pride or Beattie's solemn promise to her niece.

And then, one evening, Gerry saw Kate.

Liz had suggested that Gerry experiment with easy to serve and eat hot fish dishes for the Blue Oceans bars, and he had created a prawn curry that he thought was rather fine. He tasted it in the saucepan, piled some on his plate with rice and took it into the tiny cottage sitting room to eat in front of the television. He turned the set on and watched it absently as he wondered who to invite for a further tasting of the curry and whether British racegoers would consider it a bit exotic.

The television was showing lots of little black children somewhere in Africa lining up to be injected with something and the narrator was saying how European doctors were working on a massive training and vaccinating programme.

And the European doctor doing this lot of vaccinating was Kate. No doubt about it. She was now looking down a child's throat and saying something to the mother, smiling at her and gesturing with her hands.

Kate's smile.

Gerry put his plate down and went closer to the television. Too close and Kate became a swirl of black and white dots. He sat back again. Kate was sending the child away with a loving slap on its bottom.

The phone rang and Gerry answered it, his eyes still glued to the screen. It was Beattie.

'Are you watching?' she asked.

'Yes.'

'You can find out where she is by ringing up the BBC, getting on to the producer of the programme and what not,' she said. 'Can't you?'

'Yes. And I will.'

'So,' Beattie said placidly, 'I may as well save you the trouble and tell you.'

Gerry closed his eyes briefly.

'You'll need a pen and paper.'

'Hold on.'

He found a pad and took out his pen. His hand was shaking and he printed the letters carefully in case he couldn't read his own handwriting afterwards.

'She's in Nigeria at the moment, and she's working for Secours, a French charity—'

'But she can't speak French,' Gerry said, absurdly.

'She can now, Gerry dear. As much as she needs, anyway, which isn't a lot.'

Her address was a post office box at a place called Ilorin, about two hundred miles from the capital, Lagos. She was in a village called Kashi, some seventy miles from there.

'You'll need injections, Gerry,' Beattie said. 'Cholera and yellow fever and God knows what else. Ask your doctor.'

He had found Kate because of injections and needed injections to get to her. A nice circle.

'You *are* going, aren't you?' Beattie was asking.

'Yes. I'm going to have injections, fly to Africa and bring my doctor back.'

She laughed and rang off.

Gerry scrabbled through the boxes he had not yet unpacked searching for his passport. The phone kept ringing: Liz, Rebecca, Eileen White, Vanessa, James from the farmhouse on his family's estate where he lived with his sweet young wife who was already pregnant.

'Are you going?' he was asked.

'Yes, I'm going.'

At least, he would be if people didn't keep phoning and he could find his passport.

'I'm cured, Gerry,' James said. 'Mary's cured me utterly. I'm looking forward to seeing Kate and I'll love her as a friend.'

'Don't let Mary hear you. You promised to love only her.'

'She's here. She knows all about it,' James said, and added with some pride, 'She's enormous, Gerry. The thing inside her kicks like a horse.'

The phone rang again as soon as he put it down. Rosie Coleridge. He was touched that so many people wanted to tell him Kate had been on television – and amazed that so many people had been watching the programme – but he had to get on. After talking to Rosie, he left the receiver off the hook and ran his passport to earth. He would need money. How much? Lots, to be safe. As much as he was allowed to take, at any rate. What else? He made a list.

Air ticket.

Bank.

Injections.

Parsnip to Liz and Andrew.

Special clothes?/Pack.

He stared at it. Only that between him and Kate. Only that.

Well, that and nearly three hundred miles of Nigeria. He got himself to Ilorin in a crowded, smelly, noisy train that was slow, slow, *slow*, and when it wasn't being slow it was stopping – at every collection of mud-walled thatched huts that laid claim to be a village. Four days, it took, to go two hundred miles as the crow flies, although this train had apparently never heard of crows and actually travelled nearly twice the distance, sweltering northwards at the speed of a slug with a stomach ache.

At first they travelled through tropical rain forest, bright impenetrable green studded with dots and splashes and darts of colour. There were luscious flowers, butterflies the size of small birds and weaver birds whose nests encrusted the trees like giant barnacles and, once, there was a family of monkeys huddled on a branch of a tree, miserable in the rain that fell and fell. As the train went by, the biggest monkey's eyes met Gerry's; it was fanciful – it must be, a notion bred from the heat and the strangeness of the whole adventure, but unnerving nonetheless – but Gerry thought he saw in that split second's contact the recognition of another intelligence. Afterwards he came to the conclusion that those monkeys must have been ill, suffering from some disease, for the only other ones he saw were swinging glimpses as they fled into the forest at the approach of the train.

The green startled Gerry, the lushness, the dramatic landscape after the train had crept out of the forest.

'I thought it would be flat,' Gerry said to the other two men sharing his first-class compartment. 'I've seen films on television and it's all flat with giraffes and elephants and herds of zebras.'

'That's East Africa,' they told him kindly.

They were both government advisers, they said, on their way to examine the progress of a dam that was being built on the Niger north of a place called Jebba. One had been here thirty years, the other thirty-four, including, they said, scrupulously, the time taken off to fight the war. Both would be going Home (they pronounced it with a capital 'H') shortly; they were colonialists, experts at it, and there were no more jobs for them. They had devoted their lives to a country that was, basically, longing to see the back of them. They spoke of England in terms of tennis at the vicarage on Saturday afternoons and honey still for tea, the Labour government as a passing fad, an unsuitable boyfriend for a favourite daughter who would certainly see sense in due course. Gerry, feeling generous as each sweating mile brought him closer

470

to Kate, felt sorry for for them – even though they looked at him as though he was insane when they asked him his business in Ilorin and he said he was going to see a friend.

It was raining again when he got to Ilorin, rain that could not be even a distant cousin to anything he had experienced before. It tipped from the sky in a solid silver curtain and then abruptly stopped. The sun came out and everything steamed. Gerry's suitcase was wrestled from him by one man and another held open the back door of a rusty Morris 1000 and said firmly, 'Taxi, sah!' Gerry wildly overtipped the porter, saw his case safely bestowed in the boot and crawled into the car. The driver concertinaed himself behind the wheel, said, 'Government resthouse – yes, sah!' in response to Gerry's request (as the advisers had advised him) and flung the car into a minuscule gap between two terrifyingly overloaded lorries, one of which had 'Why worry? God is in charge?' painted on the front of it. Gerry's driver turned to look at him.

'First time Ilorin?' he asked.

'Yes.'

'How long dis place?'

'Not long.'

'While you dis place I driver belong you?'

'If you like,' Gerry said, wishing the man would pay more attention to the road.

'I like.' He dangled a long black arm out of the window and with the other hand simultaneously operated the horn and steered around a colourful flock of women who had casually stepped into the road to avoid a puddle. 'I called Gabriel.'

'I'm Gerry,' Gerry said, sitting back in his seat and feeling the sweat soak through his shirt.

'You my masta,' Gabriel said. 'Masta Ger-re,' he crooned as he swung the car in and out of the traffic before depositing Gerry at the government resthouse, assuring him he would see him the following morning.

Gerry was tired, hot, thirsty and dirty, but he felt quite proud of himself as he unpacked what he needed, showered in a shower that nearly worked and arranged for his filthy shirts to be washed. The journey so far had required patience and endurance more than

471

ingenuity, but he had managed it and there were only another seventy-odd miles to go. He was sharing the same sky as Kate.

He went to the bar and ordered a beer, which was called Star and tasted like nectar, and got into conversation with a Scotsman named Ian MacKenzie, in Ilorin to tie up some kind of deal. Over an indeterminate supper, which Ian told him to eat, ask no questions and take a squit pill afterwards – all of which Gerry had been doing since he had boarded the train anyway – he said he knew of Kashi, though he had never been there. There was a rreasonable road to it, he thought, and Gerry should put worrd around that he wanted a lift there. He also suggested that Gerry go to the post office and leave a note in the box number he had been given as 'your frriend's' address. It would be a general one, used by all the people in the group she was with; the mail must be picked up rreasonably rregularly and mebbe Gerry would get lucky. Gerry thought how long it seemed to take Kate to receive letters and reconciled himself to a journey on one of those terrifying lorries with God in charge.

'Seventy miles isn't that far, though,' he said. 'Can't I hire a car or a truck or something?'

Ian Mackenzie shook his head doubtfully.

'You can try, laddie. Try by all means. It'll cost you a pretty penny even if you do manage it though.'

Mere money wasn't going to keep him from Kate, not now it wasn't. He thanked Ian for his company and his advice, agreed that they would meet the following evening, and, suddenly exhausted, went to his bedroom, undressed, clambered under the mosquito net and slept, rocked by the motion of a train he was no longer on.

The next morning, armed with instructions about how to get to the post office, he went out of the resthouse to see Gabriel unfolding himself from his Morris and smiling at him. The night had been pleasantly cool and Gerry had thought that a brisk walk would be refreshing after the claustrophobic air journey and the days cooped up in the train, but even after this short time outside his shirt was clamped to his body by a glue of sweat, and Gabriel's smile was so very beguiling.

'Where you go?' he asked.

472

'Kashi,' Gerry tried.

'Where that?'

'Outside Ilorin. Long way.'

Gabriel's smile disappeared into his handsome black face as he placed the palm of his hand protectively on the bonnet of his Morris.

'For bush no good dis car.'

'Post office, then.'

'Yes, sah!'

Gerry left a note, marked in large letters 'To Whoever Collects This Mail', in box sixteen and told the clerk to make sure it was read – by the clerk himself if necessary, for it was possible, Gerry supposed, that the person picking up the mail could not read. He returned to Gabriel and asked if he knew of anyone who had a truck for hire, and Gabriel shook his head and said he knew of no such man.

'You ask for me? Any man have truck going to Kashi.'

'I ax,' Gabriel promised.

It rained again that afternoon. Gerry prowled around his room fighting loneliness. He wrote to Beattie and Charles, telling them of his progress so far; to David Blower, telling him to run Crocus and Clematis at his own discretion; to Andrew and Liz, saying they might have Parsnip for longer than they had anticipated, and they'd better not have any differences of opinion while their chairman was away.

Well, why not? It passed the humid rainy hours before he had the company of Ian MacKenzie for another dubious supper. It was practical. Gerry was near a post office and on the lip of the unknown. Perhaps David Livingstone had done the same thing.

Another day in Ilorin. Gabriel took him to a man who had a truck going 'for bush', but the map Ian MacKenzie had given Gerry revealed Igporin to be in precisely the wrong direction – something that didn't worry the truck owner in any way at all. He smiled and nodded as Gerry pointed out Kashi on the map, gestured confidently at his truck and said 'Yes, sah!' It occurred to Gerry that he could accept a lift and be taken miles in the wrong direction without being aware of it. He tried to explain to Gabriel that he wanted to buy a compass, but their fragile system of communication broke down utterly. Gerry, feeling dispirited, wearily told Gabriel to take him back to the resthouse, paid him, agreed to be picked up the next morning and went into the resthouse thinking only of changing his soaking shirt and drinking a cold Star beer. A freckle-faced young man, looking, if that were possible, even hotter and more uncomfortable than Gerry himself, stepped forward and said,

'Mr Beviss? I got your note. You want to go to Kashi?'

Gerry had got lucky. And, he thought, about time too.

His name was Philip Matson, and he was doing VSO.

'Voluntary Service Overseas,' he explained. 'I'm general dogsbody to the project at Kashi and do some teaching. I've come down to collect some supplies – and the mail, of course.'

Gerry ordered him a drink, told him not to move and rushed away to change.

'Kate Earith?' Philip said when Gerry rejoined him. 'Dr Kate? Of course I know her. Why?'

'I do too, that's all,' Gerry said feebly, hardly daring to believe all this was true. 'I want to see her.'

Philip was nineteen and knew nothing of love. He had a place at Cambridge, at Trinity College, was going there in October, so he and Gerry had lots to talk about when, two days later, they set out on the journey north-west in a truck belonging to 'the project'. They started at dawn but still had to spend a night – at a resthouse far more primitive than the one in Ilorin – on the road, which was a perfectly good road where it existed. It disappeared under water when it rained and reappeared miraculously a short time after the sun came out. In many places the rain had eroded it away entirely and they had to take a detour through the bush (anything that wasn't a town or a village, Gerry learned, was called 'bush'), and the truck regularly got bogged to its axles. It was heaved out by the cheerful crowd of hitchhikers, who attached themselves to the back bumper and somehow managed to stay on as the truck pitched and tossed on the rutted road, and by the occupants of other trucks in similar trouble. Many of them wore variations on the 'God is in charge' theme, and Gerry was beginning to understand why.

'Do all your supplies have to come by road?' he asked Philip as they stood under the meagre shade of a flame of the forest tree while the truck was extricated from its latest fix.

'Most do, but the vaccines and drugs come by plane. We have an airstrip,' Philip said, as though he had invented it himself, 'but we have to be pretty nifty getting the plane in and out in the rainy season.'

'I'm sure you must,' Gerry said.

They had only fifteen miles to go. Soon he would see Kate. He didn't know what he was going to say to her, or do; all he could think of was that he was filthy and he stank . . . Ten miles, five miles. Only two to go. The driver stopped for half an hour to talk to a relation and then discovered the truck to have its fifth puncture of the journey.

'You can stay in the resthouse,' Philip said as they got going again. 'We had some television people here a few months ago, before the rainy season, and they stayed there.'

'I saw the programme.'

'Did you?' Philip asked eagerly. 'Did you see me? . . . Look, here's Kashi. There's the resthouse . . . the hospital and clinic are over there, and those are the huts where we sleep and eat.'

He rambled on, but Gerry wasn't listening as he searched for Kate among the people crowded in the compound. He caught a glimpse of a white woman, fair-haired, not Kate, in a nurse's uniform before the truck drove on, around the back of the hospital, and came to a halt. Philip supervised the unloading of the supplies they had brought while Gerry, feeling useless, stood and waited, watched by a gaggle of solemn nearly naked children.

'She isn't here,' Philip told him, coming up followed by a man carrying Gerry's suitcase. 'She's out in one of the villages, but she'll be back by sundown . . . God willing, as they say here.'

He took Gerry to the resthouse on the far side of the compound. It was devoid of occupants, apart from those which scurried and scuttled into corners as they entered.

'We don't have many visitors,' Philip said, 'but Peter here will look after you – eh, Peter? Sheet, blanket, for this place?'

'Yes, sah!' The man put the suitcase down and disappeared.

Philip pointed out the bath house at the back and said proudly that it had been he who had rigged up the pump so there was running water there.

'Can I use it now?' Gerry asked.

'Of course. Just turn the notice to "occupied". Go easy on the water, though, as the tank takes ages to fill up again, and remember to shake out your clothes and shoes before putting them on again.'

'Yes. You told me before.'

'Sorry. I forgot once, you see, and got bitten by something very nasty.'

He left to go about his other duties. Gerry made use of the bath house, and wondered what it could have been like before Philip had organised the running water.... Kate living in a hut and regarding this trickle of water as some kind of luxury. What had he brought her to?

Still he was clean now, and comfortable. The man called Peter had made up his bed and was offering him a cup of tea. Gerry accepted and sat on the verandah drinking it. He did not think of Kate, could not rehearse in his mind how their reunion might go. He felt detached, in the same way he had done when it became clear that Paul Marling would be the chairman of Rede Park; that same fateful calm surrounded him as he sat waiting for Kate, watching the people disperse from outside the clinic and drift away from the compound. Fires were lit, pie-dogs scavenged and were chased away by the children, and the things on the tree growing in the middle of the compound, which Gerry had taken to be dead leaves or large seed pods, stirred and stretched their wings, revealed themselves to be bats, and settled back to sleep.

A man – a white man – came across the compound and up the steps to the resthouse verandah. He was carrying four bottles of Star, which he placed on the table in front of Gerry.

'I am Dr Jean-Luc Rémy,' he said.

Gerry took the proffered hand and shook it. 'Gerry Beviss,' he said.

'Philippe' – he pronounced it in the French way, although his English was perfect – 'tells me you seek our Dr Kate.'

476

'Yes. We are . . . old friends.'

Jean-Luc poured beer into the glasses Peter had brought, pushed one towards Gerry and drank from the other.

'I knew you must exist, of course,' he said as he put the glass down. 'But I did not know your name. You have come to take her away. Is that so?'

'I hope it is.'

'She is,' Jean-Luc commented, 'a most determined and intransigent woman. I have remarked upon it often.'

'How long have you known her?'

'Three years and a half, I think. Since she first came to Africa.'

'She's been gone nearly four years.'

'She would have spent some time at our headquarters in Nantes, learning the special problems she would encounter here.'

Gerry drank from his glass.

'Does Secours operate just in Nigeria or is it in the rest of Africa as well?' he asked, not wanting to discuss Kate with this smooth Frenchman.

'Mostly in Nigeria. Secours was in a sense begun by my grandfather. He was British and spent many years here. He married a Frenchwoman and settled in France, and when he died he left money to finance six doctors to work in this country to help the people.' Jean-Luc shrugged and poured more beer. 'The money was not enough, so my grandmother raised subscriptions from among her rich friends, and that is how it has been ever since. We are not big – nothing like your Oxfam – and all we do is provide trained doctors and nurses. Here in Nigeria we work for the government. In other West African countries we are at the disposal of whoever needs us.' He paused and then continued. 'Help is needed everywhere in Africa. Those people' – he gestured towards the smoking fires beyond the compound – 'they walk for ten, twenty kilometres to get here and for every one we can examine properly another five arrive. Yet they are lucky. Nigeria is the model African country, and there are clinics for them to walk to. Elsewhere in West Africa they could go a hundred – two hundred – kilometres and find no help.'

'So you are saying,' Gerry said, shocked, 'that those people out there are ill and must live outside while they wait to be treated?'

'Not too ill, I hope. We look at them when they arrive and decide who is fit enough to wait. They build shelters, as you can see.'

Gerry had seen. He had thought vaguely that they must be play houses, built for the amusement of children, the fires bonfires lit for fun. He looked at them with new eyes. Smoke rose from the front of each and unappetising smells drifted on the light breeze. The sun, now sinking in the sky, struck out from between piling clouds and invested the scene with a kind of romanticism ... a woman, pregnant, walking gracefully, her patterned skirt and headdress fluttering, a child running with a stick, an old man limping over to a fire and squatting down beside it.

'We cannot make them too comfortable,' Jean-Luc said. 'I wanted to build huts for them, but the government, rightly, said no. The people would come here and never wish to return to their villages. We would have to make more huts for the others that come and soon we would have a town here and the bush empty, with no one growing food or raising cattle.'

Gerry wrestled with this notion but could only come up with the incontrovertible fact that food came from shops, not land, and he could not rid himself of it even though he was the son of a fisherman and a sheep farmer.

'So there they are, waiting for treatment,' Jean-Luc was saying, 'and some of their lives will be shortened because they have to wait. It sounds harsh, but it is a stark reality. Children die for the want of such simple things – clean water, penicillin, the vaccines that we have available but have not yet been able to take everywhere, the money that buys the things we need.' He paused. 'The good Lord may weep for every sparrow that falls, but no mere human can do so and remain whole.'

'Kate?' Gerry asked, after a while to digest this.

Jean-Luc smiled at him. 'Kate. She has shouldered the burden of Africa as though it is a personal load. It is time she went home.'

'But what will make her leave, if what you say is true?'

'I am sure we can come up with something to persuade her,' Jean-Luc said, sharing out the last of the beer into their two glasses. 'I have tried,' he added, 'I have tried very hard to make her forget you. I was sure she could carry Africa with my help, but you seem to be . . . indelible in her heart.'

'As she is in mine,' Gerry said, falling in with the florid style and not, in the presence of this high-flying Frenchman, feeling a bit foolish about it.

Jean-Luc stood up.

'See now. Here she comes.'

A Land Rover driven by a black man with crinkled white hair came into the compound, its sides caked with mud. Jean-Luc went out to meet it and Gerry stood and watched as Kate climbed out, stretched her arms above her head, then abruptly lowered them as Jean-Luc whispered in her ear and she turned towards the resthouse. Gerry couldn't move. Children materialised around her, chanting 'Dr Kate, Dr Kate', as she started to walk towards him. He could hardly hear the sound of the children above the roaring in his ears, and the sky behind Kate had suddenly cleared and was all the colours of the rainbow. Literally. And the way he had been taught to remember them banged absurdly in his head: Richard of York gained battles in vain. Red, orange, yellow, green, blue, indigo, violet . . . Richard of York . . .

'Dr Kate, Dr Kate,' the children chanted, and she put out her hands and touched their heads and bent to them so they could tell her their secrets.

'Dr Kate, Dr Kate!'

The bats in the trees flapped their wings, unhooked themselves from their moorings and peeled off into the green part of the sky.

The children peeled away from Kate and scattered into the red and orange part of the sky.

Gerry found his legs and walked to the verandah steps and down them. Kate was there, one very little child still clinging to her hand. She seemed older – she *was* older, of course, nearly four years – and she was thin, too thin. The trousers and open-necked shirt she wore were covered in muddy dust. Around her neck was a dull silver chain and on her thin brown wrist was a man's watch which looked too heavy for her. Her dark hair was sticking up in tufts, a combination, Gerry supposed, of amateur barbering and the ride in the Land Rover. There were lines around her eyes, and the colour of her eyes matched the indigo part of the sky.

She looked beautiful.

He excavated his voice.

'Kate,' he said. 'Oh Kate, I'm sorry.' He held out his hand and she untangled her fingers from the child and put her hand in his. 'It wasn't Beattie, you know,' he said. 'She kept her promise to you.'

'It's all right.' She ran her free hand through her hair. 'I must bath and change,' she said vaguely. 'Will you wait?'

He laughed. 'I'm not going anywhere, Kate,' he said, and she smiled a little shyly at him, pulled her hand from his and turned away.

The sky was no longer the colours of the rainbow and the sun was already halfway down the horizon. Gerry went back up the steps to the verandah. Peter brought an oil lamp and placed it on the table. Darkness sprang up beyond the mosquito screens.

'Gin-tonic dis place, sah?' he asked, and then, when Gerry appeared bewildered, explained: 'Dr Kate drink gin-tonic dis time. I bring here?'

'Yes.'

'What ding I bring you?'

'Same, please.'

It was familiar, this: sitting with Kate's gin and tonic while she had her bath – except that it was not at all, with flying things bombarding the screens and, now, soft, rhythmic singing from the encampment in the bush beyond the compound.

Kate walked into the pool of light from the lamp and he went to open the verandah door for her. She sat in the chair on the other side of the table, the one Jean-Luc Rémy had occupied earlier, and picked up her drink. Her hair was wet. She had changed into a yellow cotton dress, but still wore the heavy wristwatch and the silver chain around her neck. He wondered what was on it. A cross, perhaps. God is in charge.

'I'm glad,' he said, for he had to say something, 'that you haven't given up your evening drink.'

'No,' she said, sipping it. 'Jean-Luc insists.'

'Doctor's orders, then, is it?'

'He calls it "preserving the integrity of our culture". We must present ourselves for our evening meal looking respectable, have a drink beforehand if we want one, and we are fined if we discuss our work over dinner without first establishing that it is the will of the group.' She shrugged, exactly as Jean-Luc had done earlier. 'He is French, and to the French meals are sacrosanct.'

'It's probably a good idea, though,' Gerry said. This was not what he had imagined discussing with Kate in their first conversation after all this time, but it was lovely to be able to look at her and hear her voice – which, he noticed, had acquired a lilt not unlike Jean-Luc's. He would have felt ragingly jealous if he had not been reassured that the good French doctor was on his side.

'Yes, it is a good idea,' Kate said, and chuckled deliciously. 'And we bought another generator with the fines . . . Gerry, did you see Beattie and Charles before you came?'

'Yes! And they send you all their love. I have a parcel for you from them. Shall I get it now?'

'Later will do.'

'Everyone sends you love, Kate. James . . . Rebecca, Helen and David, Liz and Andrew. Did I tell you about their new company?'

'You did, but not how it's going. I shall soon find out, though.' She smiled at him and he felt his very bones dissolve. 'I've just received eight letters from you, you see, and I haven't had a chance to read them yet.'

Of course. He and Philip Matson had brought the contents of post office box sixteen from Ilorin today. It seemed like a hundred weeks ago. Eight letters. . . .

'Don't read them, Kate.'

'Why not? What do they say?'

'The usual things, I expect. And I'm here to say them now.'

She reached out her thin brown hand and touched him gently on the cheek.

'Yes,' she said. 'You are, aren't you?'

They went across the compound to a low, thatched hut which, like the resthouse, was built on stilts. At one end of the single room were armchairs, a dartboard and an ancient pinball machine. At the other was a table covered with an immaculate white cloth and laid with cutlery, linen napkins and two kinds of glasses. On the walls of the room were framed prints of French Impressionist

481

paintings. Jean-Luc was there, and Philip Matson and another VSO worker called Simon, a black doctor whose name was Matthew and the white nurse whom Gerry had glimpsed in the compound when he had arrived. Her name was Marie and she was in her mid-forties, Gerry guessed.

'I thought we would have wine with our meal tonight,' Jean-Luc said. He led the way to the table and indicated that everyone should sit. 'I keep a supply of it,' he explained to Gerry, 'though the problems of transporting and storing it are shocking.'

'It hardly goes with the rest of the meal,' Philip Matson said gloomily. 'It's goat stew. Again.'

'Innocent has promised us chickens tomorrow,' Jean-Luc said.

'Yes, but how will he cook them? Last time it was like eating emaciated rook that had been in the sun too long.'

'You exaggerate, I think.'

'Oh, I'm not so sure,' said Matthew. 'Philip's description seemed most apt to me. Not that I have ever eaten rook, emaciated or otherwise.'

'Neither have I, but it's how I imagine it to be,' Philip said.

'All right, I concede the food is not perfectly cooked, but even so we should eat it in the correct spirit.' Jean-Luc picked up his glass and sipped delicately. 'One cannot have everything.'

'Gerry is a good cook,' Kate said. 'Why not put him in charge of the chickens?'

Jean-Luc put down his glass and stared at Gerry.

'You can cook?'

'A bit,' Gerry said, helping himself to some of the despised goat stew as the bowl was passed round.

'More than a bit,' Kate said, 'he's excellent.'

'What could you do with our chickens?'

'I could make a casserole, I suppose,' Gerry said, somewhat taken aback. 'If there's an oven—'

'There is, of sorts.'

'And depending on what other ingredients you have.'

'You may go through my store,' Jean-Luc said, as though conferring some kind of honour, and the two VSO boys said in unison:

'Oh gosh – not Jean-Luc's *store*!'

It was surreal. Not two hundred yards from here, people were sleeping in makeshift shelters waiting for attention from people in this room who were drinking wine and discussing the next day's meal . . . But it was all orchestrated by Jean-Luc Rémy, who knew exactly what he was doing. He was lifting the burden of Africa from them for an evening, as presumably he did every evening. He was, without doubt, an impressive man.

'How is dear old London?' Matthew asked him.

'I go there as little as possible. It's full of loud music and short skirts.'

'That must be most interesting, though I cannot quite envision it.'

'Did you do your medical training there?'

'At St Mary's Hospital in Paddington—'

'Fine!' Philip and Simon cried.

'But I wasn't talking about work,' Matthew protested.

'Yes you were. You mentioned "hospital". Fine!'

Smiling ruefully, Matthew put sixpence into the box Simon chinked under his nose.

'Gerry should be fined, too. He mentioned "medical",' Kate pointed out.

'But he doesn't know the rules.'

'I explained them most carefully to him.'

'Great!' The box was jingled before Gerry. 'Fine,' Simon intoned.

Gerry found sixpence and put it in. His face was aching and he couldn't think why, until he realised that he had been smiling constantly for over two hours and the muscles responsible were objecting to having to work overtime after so long out of action. He must have looked an idiot, but however hard he tried to keep it down the smile kept coming back.

After supper Matthew and Marie – who had hardly spoken a word throughout the meal – went off to the hospital to check on the progress of a patient, and Simon and Philip challenged Gerry to a game of darts. He would have much rather sat and talked to Kate, but it seemed ungracious to refuse and, in any case, after one game (in which Gerry came last by a distance) Matthew returned and the three of them settled down to play the latest round in what was evidently a very long-running game of cards. Marie whispered 'good night' and crept away to bed.

'She wanted to be a nun, you know,' Simon said, expertly shuffling the cards. 'But her parents made her swear she'd never take the vows. Out here is supposed to be the next best thing.'

'Hush,' Jean-Luc said sharply. 'This I will not allow.'

'Sorry,' Simon said, subsiding.

Jean-Luc leaned forward and touched Kate's arm.

'You, too, should go to bed. You are nearly asleep, are you not?'

She was. Gerry had been watching her. She yawned and stood up, and Gerry stood too.

'I'll give you the parcel from Beattie, shall I?'

'Yes, please.'

Jean-Luc lent him a torch and he and Kate walked across the compound to the resthouse. Weak light came from the hospital and from the hut they had just left, but otherwise the darkness was comprehensive, uncompromising. Strange sounds came out of it above the clank and whine of the generators. Kate took the torch as they went into the resthouse and turned on light switches. Feeble, flickering bulbs whimpered at the African night.

Gerry found Kate's parcel and she took it and yawned again. He escorted her back to where she and the others slept in another long, low thatched hut. She stopped at the foot of the verandah steps and turned to him.

'I've got a lot to think about, Gerry. It's – it's not straightforward.'

'I know,' he said gently. 'Can I kiss you good night?'

She did not answer, so he bent his head and kissed her cheek and felt the brush of her lips on his own.

Such happiness. Such happiness.

Peter had turned down the sheets under the mosquito netting on his bed. It looked inviting but, in spite of the fact that it had been a long, long day and Gerry was weary beyond words, he knew that he would not sleep yet. He rummaged in his suitcase and found the bottle of Glenmorangie he had bought at Heathrow airport. He and Ian MacKenzie had done some damage to it on Ian's last night in Ilorin, but there was plenty left.

He carried the glass out to the verandah and sat in the foreign dark. There were anonymous squeaks, clicks and rustlings coming from the blackness; a dog barked and, further away, another bark, a different one . . . a truly wild and alien bark ending in a howl and followed by others.

Then something familiar. The sound of a door opening, a spread of light from where Kate and the others slept, a voice – Kate's voice – saying, 'Not tonight. Let's talk about it in the morning—'

And Jean-Luc's French-accented perfect English murmuring something and then, clearly: 'I will tell him if you will not.'

A door shutting, another opening and closing. Silence, apart from the generators before the distant barking and howling once more broke the night. Some little thing scuffled under the floor of the verandah, and another squeaked and died.

Not tonight . . . I will tell him if you will not . . . Was this the thing that was not straightforward and not, as Gerry had supposed, the thousands of sick people in Africa Kate would have to turn her back on if she came home? . . . Yet Jean-Luc wanted her to leave. He had said so, and he had said that he had tried to make Kate forget Gerry, had implied, at least, that he had not succeeded.

Well, Gerry had taken Kate back from one man who was worthy and who had loved her and he would do it again. He had no scruples about that: he and Kate belonged together, and this time he was going to do everything right. He was, on the whole, more worried about the competition from the children who surged around Kate, chanting her name and trying to hold her hands, for he thought that Kate would hear them calling and feel guilty about them for as long as she lived.

Was she – or had she been – sleeping with the suave and charismatic Jean-Luc Rémy? 'Not tonight' . . . What else could it mean? What else would they talk about in the morning?

Gerry finished his Glenmorangie and took himself to bed. He had no right (he told himself severely) to mind who Kate had slept with and, under the circumstances, 'not tonight' was really rather good news.

Peter brought him a cup of tea in bed the following morning and told him that breakfast awaited him on the verandah. Gerry had just finished eating it when Jean-Luc appeared, wished him a cheery good morning and informed him that today he and Kate were to deliver some supplies to one of the outlying clinics.

'It is a good road, so you should have few problems,' he said. 'The community nurse there is more than competent and, unless there is an emergency, Kate will have no excuse to stay and help. Innocent is preparing a packed lunch. It will be' – he made a complicated Gallic gesture with his hands – 'a holiday. A holiday for Kate, and you will be back in good time to prepare our chickens. . . . Have you finished your meal? Perhaps you would like now to see what you need from my store for your recipe, yes?'

Totally bemused, Gerry followed him to his office at one end of the hospital. It was just past seven o'clock and the compound was already crowded. Jean-Luc pushed his way through the people, seemingly heedless, until he stopped suddenly, grabbed a boy of eight years old, perhaps, and tipped his chin up. Where the boy's right eye should have been was a swollen, hideous red mess, crawling with flies.

'Where you from?' he asked the boy.

The boy waved one hand towards the bush and, with the other, flapped at the flies, which lifted, circled and settled once more.

'Long way, masta,' he whispered.

'How you do dis ding?'

The boy went into an explanation which Gerry could not understand as Jean-Luc took his hand and led him through the crowd. They arrived in Jean-Luc's office and Gerry was invited to go through the store of tinned French eatables while Jean-Luc summoned a nurse and they applied disinfectant to the boy's eye and discussed what was to be done about it. Flies buzzed. Once the boy cried out and the nurse made soothing sounds. Gerry stared at the tins and felt sick.

'What are you going to cook us?' Jean-Luc asked.

'Don't know,' Gerry mumbled.

'Make up your mind quickly, then. We are all looking forward to this meal tonight.'

Gerry took out two tins of *champignons* and three of onion soup.

'I could try a *coq au vin*, if you could spare me some red wine.'

486

'I can.'

'It should really have bacon.'

'There is some *jambon* there. Will that do?'

'It'll have to. What about herbs, though?'

'Innocent has those. All dried, of course.'

'We're all right then.'

'Now, turn around and look at our patient. He is a brave boy. A thorn got in his eye and he has walked, all on his own, twenty-five kilometres to get here.'

Gerry turned. The boy had a gleaming white pad over his eye and a gleaming grin on his face.

'You see good now?' Jean-Luc asked him.

'Yes, masta.'

'You no need two eyes. One for good – eh?'

'Yes, masta.'

'Later we put you sleep and take away no good eye. Take and throw in bush.'

'No want no good eye,' the boy said firmly.

The nurse led him away and Jean-Luc looked at Gerry.

'What are you thinking?'

'I was wishing I was a doctor.'

'But you are not. For today you are our chef, which is just as important, believe me. . . . Come. Now I will take you to the kitchen. It will be a shock, but you can spend your day with Kate contemplating how to cope with it.'

He plucked a straw hat from a hook on one door of the room, plonked it on Gerry's head, saying he did not want his chef's brains addled by the sun, and led him out through another door at the side of the building so they did not need to go through the crowds in the compound again.

'That boy must not depress you, you know,' he said. 'He is a success. He will have only one eye, but he will live. In his village they put a cow dung compress on his eye. He removed it and walked here.'

'Twenty-five kilometres. How far is that?'

'Fifteen, sixteen of your miles.'

'Quite a boy.'

'A truly amazing boy. . . . Listen, Gerry. Money buys the trained doctors and nurses, money buys the drugs and vaccines we need. We need doctors and nurses and drugs and vaccines. We don't need martyrs.'

Gerry stopped and looked at him.

'We raise money for Secours, then? That's the way to get her home?'

'It would not be difficult, would it? Pay for three or four more doctors here to replace the one.'

Easy, easy! Gerry was good at raising money, though for other purposes . . . If he still had Rede Park he could raise enough to finance ten doctors.

Jean-Luc urged him on and Gerry was confronted with the kitchen in which he was supposed to produce a five-star meal. It was a hut, about twelve feet in diameter, behind the communal eating room. The oven was heated by an open fire and Gerry's main ingredients sat, uttering occasional dispirited squawks, in a plaited basket under a rickety table in the middle of the packed earth floor.

'This man go help cook chicken for tonight,' Jean-Luc told Innocent, a vast-bellied man in dazzling white chef's overalls.

'Yes, sah!'

'What do you wish him to do?' Jean-Luc asked, and Gerry, now feeling on top of anything, said Innocent should kill and pluck the chickens and put their gizzards and the other good things inside them into a saucepan with water – he picked out a saucepan and indicated the depth – to here with salt, pepper, some herbs – he laid them out – and two tins of the onion soup from France, and cook it all very slowly for two hours.

Jean-Luc conveyed all this to Innocent in pidgin, concluding with a formidable, 'You no let go dry.'

'No, masta. For sure,' Innocent said, affronted.

'Will the chickens go bad in the heat after they are killed?' Gerry asked.

'He will bring them to me. We have a refrigerator of sorts in the hospital. . . . Now you go and find Kate. She will be at the store-room. Behind the hospital you will see a Land Rover and not far away she will be. I will bring your picnic lunch in a moment.'

The man was extraordinary, Gerry reflected as he left the

kitchen: matchmaking with the tact of a herd of elephants, *coq au vin*, a picnic lunch and a boy's ruined eye all in the space of half an hour, and each given his undivided attention.

He found Kate where the truck from Ilorin had been unloaded the day before. With Philip Matson, she was itemising the supplies they were to take and checking them off a list as they were loaded into a Land Rover. The children were around her again, and she was talking to them in pidgin. She seemed distracted, although she greeted Gerry with another of those slightly shy smiles. She was wearing a floppy white sunhat and it looked enchanting on her.

'It has been decreed,' she said, a slight edge to her voice, 'that we do not take a driver. Can you mend punctures?'

'That road is fine,' Philip said. 'It's the best road in Nigeria. Anyway people will always stop and help you if you get into trouble. You know that.'

Kate looked down at the list and threw the clipboard into the back of the Land Rover.

'Isn't it time you started school? I'll lock up here.'

'Well, all right,' Philip said, looking a little put out. 'Come now,' he called. 'School time. Alphabet – how it go?'

'A,' the children shouted, skipping after him as he walked away, a fair, freckled Pied Piper with a touch of prickly heat. 'B, C, D—'

'Shall you drive, or shall I?' Kate asked Gerry.

'You, so I can look at you.'

She blushed under her tan and then turned away and put on a pair of dark glasses as Jean-Luc appeared, carrying a cool box which he placed in the front of the Land Rover.

'Your lunch,' he said.

'Thank you,' Gerry said, when Kate did not speak. There was silence as the two men who had been loading the Land Rover put a tarpaulin over the supplies until Jean-Luc said, looking up at the bleached blue sky:

'Perhaps there will be no rain today. You may be lucky with the weather for your picnic.'

Kate positively flounced into the storeroom, and they could hear her viciously locking the door and pushing the bolts home.

'I have done something quite dramatic,' Jean-Luc murmured. 'I think perhaps she is a little angry with me.'

489

Kate reappeared from around the other end of the hospital, threw a bunch of keys at Jean-Luc and climbed in behind the wheel of the Land Rover. Jean-Luc shook Gerry's hand.

'Have a good day,' he said, and winked. 'And do not worry about your chicken stock. It will all be done as you instruct.'

Kate started the motor and revved it ferociously. Gerry jumped in before she went without him.

She drove with furious concentration, and Gerry wondered what on earth had happened and how he was to start a conversation with this thin, brown termagant who was hiding herself so efficiently behind her dark glasses. He pulled Jean-Luc's hat down more firmly on his head, took his own sunglasses from his shirt pocket, put them on and waited. They had cleared the little thatched village of Kashi and were bowling along at a brisk, boneshaking fifteen miles an hour. If this, Gerry thought, was the best road in Nigeria then he felt sorry for the rest of the country.

Kate braked, brought the Land Rover to an abrupt halt and turned the engine off.

'I'm sorry,' she said.

'For what?'

She shrugged. 'For being in such a vile temper . . . He thinks he is God. He thinks he can control everyone's life.'

'Jean-Luc?'

'Who else?'

'What has he done?'

'He thinks I should go with you.'

Greatly daring, he reached out, removed her glasses and turned her face towards him.

'I'm afraid I agree with him,' he said.

'He's fired me.'

'Good God!' Gerry let his hand drop. She clasped it in both hers. 'Can he do that?'

'He can – and will – recommend that I be removed. The head of Secours is his mother, so he will have no difficulty in persuading her.'

'Perhaps it is for the best. Don't you think it might be? . . . Kate,' he said, for the third time in his life, 'will you marry me? I'm divorced. I'm free now. I'll make you happy this time, I promise.'

490

Her hands kneaded his one, but she seemed unaware of it. She stared out over the bush. Some black-and-white cattle were grazing in the charge of one small boy. A lorry was coming down the road; it slowed enquiringly; Gerry waved it on and it accelerated away. A trickle of sweat was rolling down from under Kate's sunhat.

'I tell you what I think,' she said at last. 'I think we're stuck with each other—'

'Kate!' he protested, but she continued:

'I can't love anyone else. Not in all this long time. How long, Gerry?'

'Eighteen years, nearly, since we met.'

'Not in all this long time I can't.' She turned to face him. 'What madness is it that it should be so?'

Jean-Luc's lilt was very evident in her voice.

'A nice one, maybe. Why not give in to it? We could both be mad together.'

'Oh, Gerry,' she sighed.

'Will you marry me?' he asked her again.

She smiled at him then: Kate's old smile, no shyness or shadows lurking in it. She tugged at the silver chain around her neck. On it was a little bag made of soft leather.

'Open it,' she said.

His fingers fumbled at the tiny strings, but eventually the bag fell away to reveal, threaded on the chain, the ring he had given her twelve years ago – the bigamous engagement ring, a sapphire to match her eyes.

He stared at it.

'See?' she said. 'We are stuck with each other. I swore – after that night – that I would rid myself of everything . . . anything that reminded me of you. And I did. Everything except the thing that reminded me of you most.'

'When would you have come back?'

'I would not. But soon – soon, I think – I would have asked Beattie to tell you where I was.'

'You didn't,' he said, thinking of it now, 'seem all that surprised to see me.'

She paused and then said, 'No. No, I don't think I was.'

He unhooked the chain, unthreaded the ring and took her left hand.

'It's too big. Kate, you're so thin. Perhaps it had better go back on the chain.'

'It will stay on if I'm careful. You wear the chain. I give it to you as a kind of engagement ring.'

'A badge of ownership?'

'Exactly that.'

'Kate, I'll feel a fool wearing jewellery.'

'Well,' she said, 'you'd better get used to it. You are going to wear a wedding ring, so you will see it and remember what you are doing the next time you think of laying your hands on another woman.'

'Put it on,' he said hastily. 'Put it on.'

She attached the chain around his neck, took his face in her hands and kissed him. Their lips were old friends, and they remembered each other well.

'More,' Gerry murmured as she drew back.

'It's too hot. And too public. We must get on.'

'Just one more. . . .'

It was the best road in Nigeria after all.

Jean-Luc arranged everything, of course. He got on the radio and persuaded the relevant powers in Lagos that he needed supplies of vaccine and a new doctor urgently, and organised a friend to acquire a special licence so Gerry and Kate could be married soon after they arrived in the capital. He would not listen to any idea of Kate's that they should wait until they got back to England, and Gerry said that it was, in any case, a matter of principle with him that he should always be married abroad.

'Kate will stay with my friend and his wife,' Jean-Luc announced, 'and you, Gerry, will stay at Fred's Place.'

'The Federal Palace Hotel,' Kate explained.

'We will miss your cooking,' Jean-Luc went on, 'but perhaps Innocent will remember something of what you are teaching him.'

'I'll send him a cookbook with lots of pictures in it,' Gerry promised.

'Ah,' said Jean-Luc drily, 'then we can all look at the pictures and dream.'

492

Jean-Luc did not just think he controlled people's lives; he did it in fact. A combination of Machiavelli, an old-fashioned match-making French mama and fairy godmother was the amazing Jean-Luc Rémy.

The vaccine and the doctor arrived by plane a week later. The children gathered around it as Gerry and Kate prepared to board and, under Philip Matson's direction, sang a charmingly gobbled version of 'Auld Lang Syne'. Kate, half laughing and half crying, hugged as many of them as she could and kissed all the project workers goodbye. She was in Jean-Luc's arms for a long time before he gently pushed her away.

'Go,' he said. 'Go now and raise us lots of money to train doctors and nurses . . . and, Kate, above all be happy.'

Kate watched as they took off and Kashi disappeared under the plane's wing. Tears were running down her cheeks.

'We'll come back, Gerry, won't we?'

'Of course we will,' he said. He couldn't leave his seat to give her a good cuddle because it would alter the trim of the plane. 'And we'll send lots of doctors. Ten, twenty – who knows? – maybe hundreds over the years.'

'Hundreds,' she said. 'That will do.'

Three days later they were sitting on the terrace of the Federal Palace Hotel, overlooking the harbour at Lagos.

Man and wife, they were. Woman and husband.

Jean-Luc's friends, Robin and Sue Jones, had just left. They had acted as witnesses at the brief registry office ceremony and had come back for a celebratory drink. They had been extraordinarily kind but now Gerry and Kate were glad to be alone at last.

'You can take the chain off now,' Kate said.

'Oh, I don't know.' Gerry stretched out his left hand and admired the glint of gold. 'I think I might get into jewellery after all. You can buy me a bracelet for Christmas.'

'*Get into!*' she said. 'What does that mean?'

'Sixties speak . . . Kate,' he said. 'Wife, wife, wife.' He picked up her hand and clinked their rings together. 'Mine feels a bit odd. Does yours?'

'A bit.'

493

'Nice, though.'

'Married,' she said. 'Married and very nice.'

They ordered another bottle of champagne and sat and watched the swift tropical dark descend over the harbour. A boy brought them some telegrams and Gerry remembered the ones they had been given earlier and took them from his pocket.

'Someone's been burning up the wires,' Kate said, surveying the pile. 'How kind of people to bother.'

They had telegrammed only their families, Andrew and Liz James and Rebecca Rosenthal, having thought it impossible to distinguish which friends to inform after that.

They began to open the telegrams. Love and congratulations washed over them – from Mark and Vanessa (a separate one from Charlie and Anne), from Rosie and Andrew Coleridge; Richard Kellerway and his wife; Stephen and Eileen White; James and Mary Flimwell; from David and Helen Blower, whose message read, 'Crocus won Clematis two stop Congratulations'; Rebecca's said, 'Darlings darlings darlings all love' and added, most mysteriously, 'Don't be guilty Gerry stop It is for the best'; Sam's, from Israel, said, 'Congratulations but is she good enough for a schmuck like you?'

'What's a schmuck?' Kate asked.

'I think it's a compliment under the circumstances. He's my other brother and he's teasing me.'

'Do you really think that?'

'That he's my other brother? Yes, I do. Bernard was my other father and Rebecca, Sam and I have agreed on it. He's my other brother.'

And here was the telegram from Gerry's family, offering their unconditional love, and Charles and Beattie's doing the same, but more eloquently.

Kate opened another envelope. Four sheets were contained in it and two dark heads bent over them, wondering why their marriage could inspire so many expensive words. The telegram was from Andrew James, that much was immediately obvious, but the message had become so garbled on its journey that it took fully fifteen minutes before Gerry and Kate could be sure that their interpretation of it was correct.

494

'Well!' Kate said. 'Well . . . Great heavens! I suppose this was what Rebecca was referring to.'

Gerry shook his head. 'I wondered where he got the money from and, Kate . . . Kate, I can't be sorry that he's dead. He would have gone to prison and blamed that on me too. Where – when? – would it all have ended? I told you I was sure it was he who attacked you that time.'

Andrew's telegram said that Paul Marling had been arrested for embezzling money from the bank he had worked for since leaving Rosenthal's. He had blamed Gerry for all his troubles and, in his absence, the police had obtained a warrant to search Gerry's cottage in the presence of his solicitor. They had been most interested in a letter they had found detailing all Gerry's dealings with Paul Marling over the years, but a day later Marling had taken a lethal dose of sleeping pills. All his nominees, trying to distance themselves from the disgrace, had resigned from the board of Rede Park; only Dick Sandhurst and Williams and Makepeace were left. Andrew had agreed to return, temporarily, to sort things out. Captain Beech had been persuaded out of retirement to run the August Festival as Dick was incapable of doing anything. There was to be an extraordinary general meeting of the shareholders and the skeleton board had agreed unanimously to propose that Gerry be invited back as chairman and managing director on any terms he cared to name. It was considered that the title deeds to the house in the woods would be a reasonable part of those terms. Would Gerry please cable Andrew, and when was he coming back?

Oh, and Liz sent love and congratulations, and so did Andrew and Parsnip.

'What are you going to do?' Kate asked.

'I don't know. I can't be sorry,' Gerry said again.

'My darling, no one would expect you to be.'

He felt disengaged. He was in Lagos, Nigeria, West Africa, and three hours ago he had been married to Kate. She was Kate Beviss now and for ever and he had a certificate in his wallet and a ring on his finger, and on hers, to prove it. He couldn't even work out how long he had been away – less than three weeks, surely? How had all this happened in so short a time?

495

'Kate,' he said at last, 'do you think there's a jinx on Rede Park Racecourse? So many people associated with it have died.'

'Jinx?' she exclaimed. 'What nonsense!'

He smiled at her, feeling his spirits lifting.

'Just bad luck, then?'

'Just that. Did you really write it all down? About you and Paul Marling?'

'The Glenmorangie and I did.'

. . . To be opened in the event of my injury or death . . .

'But it could never have been evidence, could it?'

'Maybe not,' Kate said, 'but it could well have put him into the hands of the head doctors. What are you going to do?' she persisted.

He kissed her. 'Do? I'm going to consult my wife, of course. Kate, would you like to go back to the house in the woods?'

She was silent, remembering the sunny glade they had made into a garden, the little stone house full of light. She had been happy there. All the memories were good. She and Gerry would exorcise any ghosts left by Paul Marling's brief occupation and the road Gerry had mentioned could be dug up – or, better, a few bends made in it as Gerry had suggested. It was sensible to be able to drive up to the house and not to have to tramp through the woods, befitting a legally married couple instead of a pair of clandestine lovers.

'Yes,' she said. 'Let's go back. You run the racecourse and we'll live in our house in the woods. Where else will we live, after all?'

It was a good point, and the first time either of them had considered such a mundane question.

'What will you do, Kate? Will you go into general practice at last?'

'Maybe,' she said. She stretched lazily. 'I don't have to rush into anything, do I? I must set up our charity, of course, but apart from that I'll buy clothes, redecorate the house, see friends . . . I'll spend lots of my husband's money and give him a good nag every Saturday night.'

'*Every* Saturday night? Is that a promise?'

'Absolutely. And now I'm going to invite him to have dinner with me, and then I'm rather hoping we'll both go to bed.'

Full of surprises, was Kate.

'I'm dreadfully out of practice,' he said.

She stared out over the garden to the lights of the ships in the harbour. Had she slept with Jean-Luc Rémy? He was feeling much less magnanimous about it now than he had done that first night in Kashi, when he could have exploded with happiness at the sight of Kate's smile and the fleeting brush of her lips on his cheek.

She knew he had really asked a question. He had no right to an answer, but he hoped for one all the same. And, anyway, what he had said was true. His cock had probably forgotten what to do . . . except suddenly it was reminding him that it remembered very well.

At last Kate spoke.

'We'll paint all the walls white,' she said. She gathered the telegrams into her handbag and stood up.

Bewildered, he stood as well.

'In the house?'

'There, too, perhaps, but I was talking about our marriage. I was, you see, still tempted to punish you . . . For me it's been only you and ever you. I tried once with someone else but I couldn't. I could not. It was rather embarrassing and I didn't try again. All right?'

'Kate, I—'

'So we'll both have a lot of practising to do,' she said.

When he awoke the next morning, Kate was propped on one elbow staring down at him. Her tan ended in a V at her neck and above the elbows where she had rolled up her sleeves. She had been shy about it the previous night, saying she looked like some kind of freak, but he had soon put a stop to that and they had quickly discovered all the talk about needing practice was nonsense.

Not that practising wasn't a great pleasure and joy, and he thought it would be nice to do some more now. His cock agreed with him and, what is more, so did Kate.

She stroked his stubbly jaw as he settled inside her, ready to make the long, slow love they had always made.

'Look at me,' she said, and he raised his head and gazed into her wonderful eyes.

'I *think* I recognise you,' he said, frowning. 'Aren't you the woman I married yesterday? The one who put a silver chain around my neck and a golden ring on my finger? . . . Where's the platinum? That's the question: where's the bloody platinum?'

She laughed and pulled his face down for a kiss.

'It sounds like the right woman.'

'Well, that's a relief.'

'Gerry, I'm pregnant.'

In shock, he half drew out of her but she hugged him back in.

'After last night?' he asked.

'When else?'

A baby, a child! Her own – their own – boy or girl who would call to her as loudly as the children of Africa.

'*Can* you know?'

'No,' she said. 'I can't know. Not possibly. But I do.'

Epilogue
1988

Gerry straightened his white bow tie and stood back and admired himself in the mirror. There was no way the brass buttons of his green tail coat would do up, but he was proud that (with considerable ingenuity on the part of his tailor) he was wearing the same coat to what would be, presumably, his last Trinity May Ball as he had done to his first.

Kate appeared in the mirror beside him.

'A dignified elderly-looking couple,' she said after a pause. 'Wouldn't you agree?'

'Dignified – all right. But I don't feel elderly and you sure as hell don't look it. You look gorgeous.'

Her hair had, quite suddenly, turned white ten years ago. She wore it cut very short and it emphasised her stunning blue eyes. She was wearing a long blue dress with glittering threads in it, and her figure was as slim as it had been when he had first met her. He put an arm around her waist.

'I bet you too could wear what you did forty years ago,' he said.

She laughed. 'Except I wouldn't want to, not even for the sake of vanity. I remember that dress very well. There was clothes rationing and a clever woman in the village made it from some of Beattie's old curtains.'

'Really? You didn't tell me.'

'Well, I wouldn't have, would I? Anyway, I thought it very smart at the time and I'm sure you gave me all the right compliments. . . . Have you got the tickets?'

He felt in his pocket. 'Present and correct. It's nice of Caroline to ask us, isn't it?'

'She's a very nice girl,' Kate said. 'I like her rather a lot.'

'So do I,' Gerry said.

Thus, in perfect agreement about their daughter, they went to join the others: Vanessa, Caroline's godmother, her red hair doused in grey; Mark stout and nearly bald; James – now Lord – Flimwell, Caroline's godfather, whose green tail coat showed no signs of strain; Mary, a plump and lovely matron, the mother of four sons. Kate and Gerry had their quicksilver Caroline, born within two weeks of Kate's fortieth birthday, and no others. Others would have been a joy but to be disappointed not to have them meant, surely, that you were disappointed with the one you had, and that was impossible to contemplate. Apart from loving Caroline for herself, Gerry had thanked God constantly for her presence. A fearful genocidal war had broken out in Nigeria the year after she was born and if it had not been for toddling, demanding, Caroline, Gerry was sure he would have lost Kate back to Africa. . . . The money they raised for Secours going to help Jean-Luc Rémy mend gunshot wounds, ten-year-old children with machine guns . . .

Caroline had always said, when asked as a child, that she was going to be a doctor but nothing ever came of it. Kate didn't mind. She minded much more that her daughter chose to go to her father's old college rather than be the fourth generation of her family at Girton . . . though even that decision she understood when they brought Caroline up for her first term at Trinity. Why be two miles away along a road that goes uphill both ways, or nearer the centre but live in the rather hideous modern Girton building, when you could be in part of the glories of the shining city? They went to Girton once – had the building always, Kate asked wonderingly, been so very red? – and paced about its fearsome corridors, the names on the doors announcing male occupants, the hockey pitch apparently given over to football. It was somehow, Kate thought, much easier to cope with women in Trinity than men in Girton.

Yet Cambridge had scarcely changed, and ghosts stalked its streets in flapping gowns. And tonight – tonight – in spite of all the

500

years they could muster between them, they were going to pretend that nothing whatsoever had changed. They set out from the Garden House Hotel to go to a cocktail party some friends of Caroline's were giving in the fellows' garden of Trinity Hall.

'Will they mind six fossils turning up?' James asked.

'It seems not.'

'Who is escorting Caroline to the ball?'

'The object with the earring who came to stay at Easter, I imagine,' Gerry said. 'The one whose razor doesn't work properly.'

'It's deliberate,' Mary told him. 'It's called designer stubble.'

'Ridiculous!' Gerry snorted. 'And horrible for Caroline to have to dance cheek to cheek with it.'

'My darling,' Kate said. 'Even I know people don't dance cheek to cheek any more.'

'I do.' He grabbed her and danced her away down King's Parade.

'Such energy,' Mark complained. 'And we've got the whole damned night to get through.'

Vanessa stopped and clapped her hand to her brow.

'Mark, I'm sorry!' she exclaimed. 'I forgot to bring your walking frame.'

James solicitously took Mark's right arm and gestured to Mary to take his left.

'Just lean on us,' he said soothingly. 'We'll look after you, old boy.'

Laughing, Mark shook them off. 'We're grandparents, Vanessa and I,' he said. 'It knocks the stuffing out of you being called "grandpa" I promise ... Oh, for heaven's sake, look at those two.'

Kate and Gerry – really rather expertly – were doing a tango and had collected an audience of mystified Japanese tourists, some of whom, believing that a white head and one with more salt than pepper in it shimmying about King's Parade was a rare sight indeed, began clicking cameras. Gerry sent Kate into a final twirl and struck a pose with her and there was a sprinkling of inscrutable oriental applause. Beyond them were King's College Chapel, the Senate House, Gonville and Caius College and the entrance to Trinity Street where, a lifetime ago, five out of the six of them had met.

A June evening in Cambridge, that loveliest of cities.

Gerry removed his daughter from the Object and danced with her in one of the marquees where the music was recognisable to him as music. Caroline appeared a little solemn, and he tweaked her chin.

'What's the matter?'

She looked up at him out of Kate's eyes, her lovely young face surrounded by bubbles of black curls.

'I can't believe it's all over,' she said.

'Cambridge?'

'Yes.'

'I felt the same.'

'Did you? Did Mummy?'

He thought back and remembered how Kate had left Cambridge, slinking away before the start of May Week because of him.

'Perhaps not,' he said. 'She had her medical training to go on to, you see. It wasn't such a full stop for her.'

'I suppose not. I haven't a clue what I'm going to do.'

'Don't think about it now. Enjoy yourself tonight.'

'It's morning.'

'Morning then, clever clogs ... Hadn't we better go and find your young man?'

'He's dancing with Mummy. He thinks she's mega. I'm seriously jealous.'

Gerry's estimation of the Object went up several notches. He danced Caroline over, did an old-fashioned excuse me to regain his wife and noticed for the first time that the Object had what Caroline would call a mega nice smile.

Kate leaned against him. 'He must be nice, mustn't he,' she said, 'if he likes Caroline and she likes him? ... And you,' she added, rubbing her cheek against his, 'have a mega case of incipient designer stubble.'

Dawn then, kicking the stars from the wide skies of Cambridgeshire.

A procession of punts goes up the Cam, under Clare Bridge and King's Bridge and the Mathematical Bridge at Queens'. Under the road at Silver Street and into the millpond, up the ramp into the upper reaches of the river and away to Grantchester through meadows filled with buttercups, where horses graze and cows lazily chew the cud.

He steers towards the bank and plants the pole to trap the punt in place. He wakes his lady love with a kiss, and helps her ashore. She is sleepy and he has to kiss her again before taking her hand and leading her away from the river. The dew soaks the hem of her dress and, absently, she hitches up her skirt.

He spreads out the rug he has had the forethought to bring and invites her to sit. She does so. She knows the river is there, not twenty-five yards away, but the only evidence of it is their punt pole against the sky and the occasional sound of raucous laughter. He sits beside her and kisses her for a third time.

'But what will the others think?' she asks.

'That we had a flat tyre on our punt.'

His hand creeps up her leg. Not as high, not nearly as high, as it has been before but somehow it feels like the first time.

'I tried to seduce you here forty years ago.'

'The day I told you I loved you.'

'That day.'

His hand goes higher. She wraps her arms around his neck.

'Can one seduce one's own wife, though?'

'I've no idea, but one can try.'

'You don't need to try very hard . . . But Gerry,' she says, as his hand is at places it knows so well, 'aren't we too old for this sort of thing?'

'No, Kate,' he says. 'No and no and no.'